THE LAZARUS VECTOR

A NOVEL

ERICA OBEY

Blank Slate Press | St. Louis, MO

Published in the United States by Blank Slate Press

Blank Slate Press is an imprint of Amphorae Publishing Group, LLC.

4168 Hartford Street, Saint Louis, MO 63116
www.blankslatepress.com
www.amphoraepublishing.com

Publisher's Note: This book is a work of the imagination. Names, characters, places and incidents either are products of the author's imagination or are used fictitiously. While some of the characters and incidents portrayed here can be found in historical accounts, they have been altered and rearranged by the author to suit the strict purposes of storytelling. The book should be read solely as a work of fiction.

Cover by Kristina Blank Makansi
Cover art from Shutterstock
The Raising of Lazarus by Caravaggio, Museo Nazionale,
The Yorck Project: 10.000 Meisterwerke der Malerei. DVD-ROM, 2002. ISBN 3936122202. Distributed by DIRECTMEDIA Publishing GmbH. The compilation copyright is held by Zenodot Verlagsgesellschaft mbH and licensed under the GNU Free Documentation License.

Library of Congress Control Number: 2016951405
ISBN: 9781943075225

For George, who helps with the research

THE LAZARUS VECTOR

Chapter One

For the first time ever, Jonas believed there was something his old man couldn't fix. It was one hell of a game-changer. An epiphany, he thought they called it. Too bad it looked like it was going to be the last epiphany—hell, the last goddamned *thought*—Jonas was ever going to have.

How was he supposed to have known the kid ran with a gang? Short and skinny, his beltline and boxers both hanging low enough his hipbones poked out, the kid looked all of twelve years old. How was Jonas to guess the kid would close in fast and hard, the moment Jonas turned out of sight of the cheap storefronts and the cars with their blaring hip-hop? The kid might have been small, but he was mean and fast, in the way of kids who had grown up fighting their entire lives. He'd grabbed Jonas before Jonas even knew he was there, shoving him through the creaking iron gate into the tiny weed-choked graveyard, and sending him sprawling against a tombstone, which slewed suddenly sideways, like one of the priests buried there was about to reach up and grab Jonas with a bony hand.

Instead a balled fist rammed into his stomach and a hard arm slammed into his windpipe, choking off his air. In one swift move, Jonas was pinned between one of the gate's stone pillars and a cheap-ass wooden shrine covered in plastic flowers, with some kind of holy water fount jamming his kidneys, his face scraping hard against the bricks.

"You be stealing, bro. You be stealing from us."

Oh, hell. Oh, shit. This was worse than any ghost-priests that might have haunted this place. Because this was real. And this was real bad.

How could he have been stupid enough not to see it coming? How could he have not guessed that if he could figure out how to steal drugs from the shelter, somebody else was probably doing it already? But he'd been too pissed off at the old man to think straight, which was pretty much the story of his whole sorry life, short as it now seemed likely to be. Just a little Ritalin, a few Ambiens circulated among friends, but his father had reacted as if he had unearthed a Mexican cartel and had cut off all of Jonas's prescriptions and made a point of clearing the medicine cabinet of any drug more marketable than aspirin, as well as emptying the kitchen of what he pretended was cooking wine. So what did the old man expect would happen when Jonas had figured out the combination on the medicine cabinet at the shelter? And had opened it and had tasted what was inside. The shelter might be so stone broke that the nun that ran the place insisted Jonas wash and reuse the plastic sporks the local winos ate their free hot lunch with, but what was in that medical cabinet was fancier—and more powerful—by far than what had gotten Jonas thrown out of what was, by his count, his tenth school in as many grades: this one a fancy boarding school that never ever referred to their students as retards or troublemakers or just plain bad seeds. They just dosed you with enough of everything to get you to shut up, and if you asked real nice maybe a little extra to sell on the side.

Jonas had seen an opportunity and had seized it, just like his guidance counselors were always encouraging him to do. No, Jonas had seen more than an opportunity; he had seen payback. Payback for his old man forcing him to go cold turkey. Payback for his old man forcing him to work at the shelter. Payback for his old man hating him—no, worse. Payback for his father just not caring. He was probably watching right now from some remote camera in his lab, chortling like a mad scientist as Jonas learned "a valuable life lesson."

"Okay, okay," he gasped. "I'm sorry. I didn't know."

"You know now," the kid said, as he punched Jonas square in the nuts.

As Jonas doubled over, retching, heaving, his foot caught on a loose board that had peeled free from the shrine. He stumbled to his knees just as the kid kicked him in the stomach. The breath *whooshed* out of him, and he rolled over, clutched into the fetal position, as somewhere above his head, the foot pulled back to strike again. Scuttling away, Jonas grabbed the board, reared straight, and slammed it across the kid's knees.

The kid staggered backward, fumbling at his belt.

Jonas swung again.

Which was when he saw the gun in the kid's hand and knew he had fucked up for real.

And Jonas just barely had time to ask himself whether his father would care enough even to be relieved his fuck-up of a son had finally fucked up bad enough to be out of his hair for good, before the end of his life unfolded with the jerky logic of a movie spinning off the reel.

He lunged for the kid, and they both reeled into the cheap-ass shrine, knocking it over so the statue toppled out: some ugly saint on crutches with dogs sniffing around his feet whose eyes seemed to look at Jonas with infinite pity as his head slammed into the iron gate and the world exploded into light and sound.

And then … nothing. Nothing but a shadow that leaned over him, reaching for him. Not the kid. Another face. An old, wizened face, floating above a white collar.

Aw, *shit*. No way. The last thing he was gonna see on earth was a priest? Jonas tried to scramble backward, but he couldn't move. Couldn't even tell the guy that he didn't believe in fucking God, before the old pervert gathered Jonas into his arms and began to kiss him.

Chapter Two

It didn't take Clare long to come to the conclusion that Sister St. John of the Cross had chosen her name with cruel irony. How else could you explain why an athletic-looking woman with close-cropped salt and pepper hair, the modest cross around her neck the only sign of her vocation, would have chosen to take the name of the greatest mystic of the middle ages? She glared at Clare as she scrubbed down the long folding tables that were ranked across the Church's undercroft—which Clare was certain the no-nonsense nun would insist on calling a basement.

"A Finder's Guide?" the nun repeated.

"For the Archive of the Church of St. Lazarus," Clare said.

"And what, exactly, is this guide supposed to help you find?"

Oh, to start with, a tenure-track position. As if there was any guide for that in this industry any more—especially for a medievalist, a specialty as divorced from reality as a unicorn. About the only road map to success for someone with Clare's credentials would be strewn with the warnings you saw on old maps: "Beyond here lie dragons." Or as the *Wizard of Oz* put it a lot more simply, "I'd go back if I were you."

But even the yellow brick road had presumably been laid one brick at a time, and right now Clare's task was to find one more brick for the edifice now known as *The Lazarites: Nineteenth-Century Appropriations of the Crusader Tradition*. Not a brick, precisely, or even a building block, corner, or capstone. More like a touchstone, a magic talisman that would transform her newly-minted doctoral dissertation into a book that someone would actually want to read.

"I did my thesis on the Lazarites," Clare said.

"Why?" the nun asked, in about the same tone she might have used to ask why Thomas Aquinas was nattering on about God as the prime mover when there were dishes to be scrubbed and floors to be mopped.

Well, frankly, because no one would let Clare write on the Knights Templar. The very suggestion had been dismissed with the academic equivalent of papal anathema including ironic comments about Dan Brown and *Ivanhoe*, and disquisitions on the difference between nuanced historical thinking and cosplay. Obviously Clare's advisors had never once taken a good, hard look at their own fashion sense. It took a lot of nerve to dismiss someone for donning the occasional jerkin and hose at a Renaissance Faire when you trotted out any excuse possible to wear your own chasubles and hoods.

But if Clare had been forced to choke back a rebellious urge to point out that *Holy Blood, Holy Grail* had outsold the Medieval Studies department's entire publication list, she had not been brave enough to simply run off and join the circus—as her parents, who shared her advisors' taste for ironic reproach, liked to term Clare's membership in the Society for Creative Anachronism. Instead, she had played the academic game and now had the dubious distinction of being the world's leading expert on a forgotten order of Crusader priests who differed mainly from the Templars in that they wore a green cross on their tunics instead of a red one. Oh, and instead of mapping the Templars' legendary New World Voyages or the secret meridians that connected Oak Island, Rosslyn Chapel, and Rennes-le-Chateau, Clare's research had painstakingly traced the paths along which an obscure Crusader order—or was it orders?—had splintered, disappeared, and reincarnated across history.

"Currently, the Lazarites are largely a European ceremonial order," Clare plowed ahead, "a poor man's Knights of Malta, if you will, just as they began in the Crusades as—shall we say?—the poor man's Knight Hospitaller?"

Sister St. John glared at her. "Do you have something against poor people?"

How would that be possible, when, if Clare weren't careful, she'd be fated to eke out the rest of her life on an adjunct's pay?

"I'm on a post-doc over at All Saints College, looking for American incarnations of the order," she said. "Being that we are less than a mile away, this was the logical first place to look."

"In an Outreach Center?"

"In the Church of St. Lazarus." Clare drew a deep breath. "I'm sure I don't need to lecture you on the Church's unique history. It was built by a robber baron named Erastus Grinnell, who believed the prayers of the Lazarites had spared his family—as well as most of the local community—from the Spanish Influenza outbreak in 1918."

Or he had built it as a last ditch attempt to save his immortal soul from the infernal bargain his fortune depended on—a bargain some whispered had been brokered by the Lazarites themselves. But Clare was willing to venture that Sister St. John would have as much tolerance for rumors of Satanic cults and pacts with the devil as she had for microbial infections or rich people.

"I was told the Church has an archive. And it's stored in the Outreach Center."

"The Church does have a sacristy," the nun allowed. "It's full of disused altar services and vestments which cannot be thrown out because they are consecrated; typewritten minutes of the Altar Guild and various sodalities, boxes upon boxes of mass cards, as well as shelves of broken missals, Bibles, and catechisms. We use it as storeroom because it has the only reliable lock in this entire building. Holy Mother Church is extremely protective of her relics."

"But not to the point of having a Finder's Guide for them," Clare hazarded, with a wistful look at the battered computer that served as the Outreach Center's office. It looked like it hadn't even been turned on in years.

"No Finder's Guide," the nun confirmed. "And it's nearly five. The Outreach Center is about to close for the day."

"Could I possibly take just a quick look in the storeroom?" Clare pleaded. "While you're finishing up here?"

"It's not down here," the nun said. "You have to go outside. Through the graveyard and behind the sanctuary. You need a key." She pointed to a hook on the wall, and then frowned. "That's funny," she said. "The key's gone. Someone must be in there right now."

∞

As with the great Cathedrals of Europe, the Church of St. Lazarus had been oriented toward the east when it had been built on a prominence just across the river from Manhattan. The rest of the neighborhood had been laid out on the Bronx's typical rectangular grid, so the church and its outbuildings seemed to have tumbled out of the sky and another century in order to land in a catty-corner jumble across a busy intersection that pulsed with car horns, music, and shouting hustlers at any time of the day. But when Clare emerged from the undercroft, the noise suddenly seemed to still, and all she heard was the sweet song of a violin. A shabby fiddler in a threadbare coat had set up shop near the Church's front steps, a battered case littered with a few coins open at his feet. Clare shook her head as she glanced at him. Why was he playing here and not down in some subway station in midtown? The people here were as poor as he was, and unlikely to even hear him, given the noise on the street.

Well, whatever his reasons, he played beautifully, and Clare strolled over to drop a few coins into his case when he finished.

"It's lovely," she said. "What is it?"

"It's called 'Niel Gow's Lament for his Second Wife.'"

"Second?" she said. "What about the first?"

"I guess she was less … lamentable," the busker said. Slipping a neatly pressed handkerchief from one pocket, he began to wipe the chin rest with quick, practiced gestures.

"And who are you lamenting?" She nodded toward the graveyard that lay around the corner from the church steps. "The dearly departed Lazarite fathers? Or are you waking a lost love buried there?"

God in heaven, where had that come from? Why didn't she just go ahead and invite him out for a drink? Or back home to bed for that matter. But the busker just grinned.

"Still too early in the day to wake anyone. I have a strict rule. No whiskey before sundown. And it's scarcely a proper wake without it," he pointed out. "Assuming, of course, that is what you meant, rather than me fighting my way through a hedge of roses and kissing a woman out of an enchanted sleep."

Clare was appalled to feel herself blushing. "I meant the former," she said stiffly.

His grin only deepened. "Smart choice," he said. "I've been told I play much better than I kiss."

Somehow, she doubted it. But that was not a place any wise woman in New York wanted to go with a street musician. Still there was something that appealed to her about the busker, something that set him a cut above any ordinary street performer. Shaggy-haired, half-shaved and with a pair of dark sunglasses obscuring his face, he still, had the bruised, blond perfection of a fallen angel.

In other words, another out-of-work musician. After all, this was New York, where poets and philosophy professors drove cabs. And out-of-work medievalists, if Clare wasn't careful. But still there was something about the man that nagged at her. Almost as if …

"Do you know if we've ever met?" she heard herself ask.

"I'm guessing we don't much move in the same circles," he laughed.

Of course. What had she been thinking? "Well, at least we share the same taste in music," she said, as she turned toward the church.

"And a man can always dream," the busker called after her, as Clare set off toward the graveyard and the Church's side entrance, where the vestry should be. He began to play once more, and Clare found herself blushing as she recognized the tune as "Beautiful Dreamer." She slowed down, fighting the temptation to turn back and talk to him once more.

Only to hear the melody break off in a single, discordant note.

"Don't!" the busker shouted, and dropping his fiddle, he threw himself at her.

He hit her full force, knocking her sideways, Clare fell hard, the force of the impact shattering into a dozen different stabs of pain.

"What the hell…?" she cried, as the world exploded into a single plastic lily arcing across the sky. And then the busker spread his threadbare coat and fell on her …

The flower clattered back to the ground, and the world shuddered with the dying echo of what she instinctively knew must have been a gunshot. Startled shouts erupted, and footsteps began to pound from every direction. Clare tried to get up, but the busker pushed her back to the ground.

"Stay down," he said. "I'll see what's going on."

Scrambling to his feet, he dashed around the corner toward the graveyard. Pushing herself to her hands and knees, Clare hesitated as she thought about following. The fiddler was right, of course. She was in the South Bronx, not the gated safety of the All Saints campus. The bullets that flew around here were real.

But what about the street fiddler, who might have just saved her life?

Chapter Three

Words floated around Jonas, like the remnants of his life.

"What the hell happened?"

"What the fuck you do?"

"Man, we gave you a job. You were just supposed to hurt him, not kill him."

"You were supposed to prove yourself. You were supposed to show you were a true Lazarito."

"Instead you bring a gun? Who tole you to bring a gun?"

"Christ, Rafe, look at the blood. We thought you was dead."

"What the fuck just happened? What the fuck you do?"

Jonas struggled to move, to sit up, to see who the bastard was who had just shot him, but his limbs weren't listening and his vision was fading into a whirling mass of blobs and stars, and maybe it was good idea just to lie there and play possum anyway.

"Shit," the one called Rafe said. The kid. The one that had killed him. "It was an accident. Gun just went off."

"The Man ain't going to care. DA neither. Not when it's some rich, white kid."

"Not while he's lying outside a church."

"You were supposed to handle this quiet. This … this ain't quiet."

"Come on. We need to go. While we can."

His friends hauled Rafe to his feet and their footsteps hurried away. And still Jonas couldn't move. Couldn't so much as twist his neck or even move his eyes to take a look at the bastards who had just killed him.

But some sensations were returning. He was lying flat on his back, out in the street, all the way out in the gutter like some wino or bag man, with the sharp edges of cans and bottles jabbing into his shoulder. And hell everything stank. Beer. Sewage. Piss. He was wet: Dark, cold liquid was running everywhere. Gutter crap? Dog shit? His own blood?

Jonas jerked a hand off the pavement, and nearly wept when he found it could move. He reached down to run it warily across his belly, and froze when he felt wetness. Staining the front of his pants. As if—

Angry tears welling, he managed to look down. And saw he had wet himself like some fucking ten-year-old brat.

No blood. No guts. Jonas had just pissed himself. Right there in the middle of the street. With what felt like a thousand people converging on him from every direction.

"*Santa Maria, Madre de Dios.*"

"Oh, my Lord Jesus!"

"*Gloria al Padre*!"

Footsteps pounded from every direct, and faces began to crowd above him. Touching his forehead. Reaching for his pulse. Praying. Crying. Shrieking and wailing and shouting orders in half-a-dozen languages and snapping pictures with their cell phones. Pictures of Jonas peeing himself like a goddamned baby. *Christ.* How much more fucked-up could one person's life get?

"What happened?"

"*Milagro*!"

Miracle.

The woman's voice was old and quavering, but the word sliced through the noise, quelling everyone else. Even the traffic seemed to stop.

"It was the priest," the old woman went on, bad accent and all, just like some ancient crone making some Satanic prophecy in some lame horror movie. "I saw him myself. Father Enoch come back. Come back to save him. Bent right down and kissed him, and he arose, picked up his bed and walked. I saw it. I saw it with my very own eyes."

∞

Noise erupted from nowhere, as Clare stood. Sneakers raced toward her, and she scuttled backwards as a couple of street toughs in baggy pants and baseball caps ran past, dragging a blood-soaked, skinny kid between them. Shaking, she stayed where she was for another moment, trying to catch her breath before she ventured around the corner, only to reel away, her hand pressed to her mouth as she fought not to retch.

There was blood everywhere. Smeared along the sidewalk, pooling in the gutter, and soaking a frail figure that lay on the ground motionless except for one hand that clenched and unclenched spasmodically. But what was truly frightening was the way the busker had made no move to help the boy; he simply stood there, staring down at the carnage, seemingly oblivious to the blood that threatened to stain his shoes.

At last, with a slow shake of his head, he knelt. Clare assumed he was going to reach for that clutching hand. Instead, the busker dipped his own hand into the gore, as if he were testing its temperature, and recoiled as if he had been scalded. "No," he muttered. "Oh, no, please. Please not this. Not this all over again."

"Is he…?" Clare ventured.

The busker snapped out of his trance. "Go get help," he told Clare. "Now!"

With a lingering look at that twitching hand, Clare nodded and dashed back toward the Outreach Center, fumbling for her cell phone. But the sidewalk was suddenly an obstacle course of running people. A janitor in coveralls ran by, brandishing a broom, as if he intended to mop up the mess on the sidewalk. A couple of anonymous-looking men who might have been part of a recovery group blinked suspiciously at the daylight. Elderly women clutching rosaries moaned and wailed as they milled everywhere.

"I need to report an emergency." Clare raised her voice to shout into the phone. "Someone's been shot."

The dispatcher's answer was indecipherable through the static, and Clare moved back toward the church, trying to find a better connection, nearly colliding with the fiddler, who was suddenly rushing in the opposite direction from everyone else.

"Wait!" Clare called, but the dispatcher interrupted her, asking her to repeat the nature of her emergency.

When she looked up again, the busker had scooped up his fiddle and hurriedly packed it back into his case.

"What's wrong?" Clare cried, as she hurried over to stop him. "I haven't even had a chance to say thank you."

"Best way you could do that is by forgetting you ever saw me," the busker told her. He slammed his case shut so carelessly that several coins and a battered matchbook rained out as he hurried off, leaving Clare to wonder dizzily whether he had somehow simply transformed himself into that shabby pile of flotsam in order to disappear, like some genie in a fairy tale, as she stooped to scoop up the change. And speaking of transformations, what had transformed his lazy, laughing flirtation into this headlong flight?

Straightening up, Clare craned her neck, trying to see where he had gone, but sneakers squeaked to stop her once again. This time they were Sister St. John's sensible running shoes, not some punk's elaborately-laced Air Jordans. "I need you to call Dr. Lukas Croswell," she said, her drawn face suddenly decades older. "Now."

"No point," someone said behind her. "Dr. Croswell's over at the college today. He'll never get here before the ambulances do."

"You don't understand," Sister St. John snapped. Clare was startled to see that the nun looked perilously close to tears. "That's Dr. Croswell's son lying back there. And I think … I think he may be badly injured—or even dying. In fact, I can only pray that he's not already dead.

∞

Clutching his fiddle case to his chest, the busker crouched in the shadows of the trash-strewn alley, asking himself how stupid he really could have been. What if someone had seen him? Recognized him? Even worse, what if someone had seen him touching that kid? Had he really forgotten the circus that had ensued last time? Did he really want to go through all that again?

"Christ," he sighed. "Why did I come here?"

"I think you know the answer to that already," a shadowy presence answered him, as it emerged from behind a dumpster, casually wiping away a drop of blood that trickled from its nose.

Oh, hell. Not this on top of everything else. "Go away," the busker sighed. "You're dead. You're not real."

"Not necessarily the same thing," the old man pointed out.

The busker opened his mouth, only to shut it angrily. God, what was he thinking? Was he seriously going to engage in metaphysical speculation with a ghost at a time like this? Did he really have time for a brief philosophical debate over the possibility that he—or rather his blood—was capable of *awakening* ... well, not the dead; he would go to his own death refusing to dignify that by believing in it. He just awakened ... shit. All he had to do was touch the boy's blood to know that the whole pile of shit he'd hidden from for so many years was going to start hitting the fan in a big way. And common sense told him he needed to run away right now. Before someone saw him. Before someone recognized him. Before he could be blamed for—

For what? Wanting to flirt with a woman just because he liked the way her long, red hair bounced in the late afternoon sun?

For bearing witness to a miracle?

And even though he refused to talk to the *hallucination*, refused to believe that it was anything other than the product of his own screwed-up mind, he heard himself ask, "What the hell just happened?"

"To put it in terms you'd understand, the endgame has begun."

"Do endgames really begin? Sounds like an oxymoron to me."

"You're the expert," the other conceded. He hesitated, then added, "I've missed you."

"You're the one that's dead," the fiddler said. "Innit supposed to be me that misses you?"

"Do you?" the ghost said, and as a sign of how stupid this entire conversation was, the busker would have sworn he sounded hopeful.

"TV talk shows keep saying I need to put you behind me. Seek closure and all that. My barkeep says the same, without the fancy words. And he pours with a freer hand."

A trace of a smile might have been visible on the ghost's bloodied lips. "Unfortunately, I seem to be a little harder to get rid of than you might have hoped."

"Unfortunately."

"*Vocatus atque non vocatus deus aderit*," the old man said. "Summoned or not, God is present."

"Which if you ask me, just makes him one interfering son of a bitch," the fiddler retorted. And, snatching up his fiddle case, he dashed out of the alley before the footsteps that rattled past on the street beyond could turn the corner and find him.

Chapter Four

The old man's silences were even more spectacular than his tongue-lashings. And this particular silence promised to be a regular sonic boom. Jonas could feel it coming even before the minivan squealed to a halt at the curb and his father let himself out.

"Where?" He snapped the single syllable at the nun who was usually busy ordering Jonas to hand out soap and razors—"Items of Dignity" she liked to call them—to a bunch of bums who needed a steam cleaner, not a couple of deodorant wipes, to get rid of their smell.

Right now, though, she wasn't doing a lot of talking. No one seemed to be. Everyone was just standing there staring at him—keeping their distance, like they were afraid to touch him. Probably because right now Jonas smelled as bad as the bums—hell, Jonas was standing inside a cloud that was a thousand times worse than an entire Items of Dignity line. Even the EMTs didn't look like they really wanted to touch him.

Only his father didn't seem to see him. The old man's eyes were fixed on the blood that seemed to be splattered everywhere. "Where is he?" Lukas repeated. "What have you done with my son?"

And then the silence broke—from every side and all at once.

"Oh, Lukas, I'm so sorry," the nun began to babble. "So sorry to have frightened you unnecessarily. We tried to call you back, but your phone was off."

"He's okay," a janitor said. "Banged up, but fine."

"Thank God."

"A miracle."

"He's right there."

With each word, Lukas's silence grew louder and louder, until he turned in the direction everyone was pointing. And a single muscle began to tic in Lukas's cheek as he contemplated the stinking mess that was his son.

Another man might have retched. A real father might have cried. A true believer might have fallen to his knees in prayer. Anyone whose veins ran with something beside ice water would have thrown his arms around his son.

Lukas Croswell frowned, then asked, "Could you please remove your shirt?"

That was the old man for you. All pro, all doctor, as he leaned forward to touch Jonas's skinny, shaking belly. Jonas supposed he should consider it a regular father/son bonding moment when the old man didn't snap on Latex gloves beforehand.

Still, it was a relief to finally be able to look. Jonas hadn't realized how afraid he'd been to do that until now. Afraid that he'd see some gaping wound with his ribs still exposed—proof positive that he really had come back as some kind of zombie walking around the Bronx that everyone was pretending not to see. Same old sucky life as always, in other words. But one thing you could say about the old man, was that he made that kind of fear fly straight out the window—even if he usually did it with a sighed request that Jonas actually use his genius-level IQ for once in his life.

Jonas drew a deep breath as he forced himself to watch his father's swift exam. His belly was beginning to bruise: an angry, pale swelling split by an ugly red weal beaded with drops of blood. It looked almost as bad as it hurt. But no exposed ribs. No gore. All Jonas could guess was that he had somehow just gotten grazed by the bullet, or that the gun hadn't really gone off. Whatever it was, it sure as hell wasn't some fucking angel who threw him back because he wasn't good enough for heaven. He supposed he owed the old man a thank you for that much, at least.

When he had finished probing the wound, Lukas leaned back, frowning. "Could you please remove your pants as well?" he asked.

Angry tears sprang to Jonas's eyes. His father's touch had been professionally gentle, professionally soothing. As close to a hug from the old man as he had ever experienced in his life. Should've known it couldn't last.

"No," he said.

His father raised an eyebrow. "Is there some kind of problem?"

"Yeah, there's a problem. I stink. Surprised you haven't noticed."

And the asshole laughed. Laughed out loud, before he dug into his shirt pocket, and tossed Jonas a plastic tube.

"Vicks Vapo-Rub?" Jonas read the label.

"Masks any smell out there," the old man told him. "Used by everyone from forensics interns to horse trainers with stallions that are being distracted by the smell of mares in season. Dab it under your nostrils. Then, if you will, your pants..."

So that was it? This was the secret of how the old man survived the free clinics he held biweekly, lancing abscesses and prescribing skin ointments and probing anal fissures as coolly as if he had been working on a table full of lab samples instead of a bunch of bag men? And now the secret to how he intended to survive his son?

"Fuck the smell. I crapped myself. Pissed myself, too, if it matters to you," Jonas choked. He waved a hand at the people he could barely see through his angry tears. "So thank you for letting the world know. But do they really have to see it, too? Can't we at least go inside the ambulance and shut the doors?"

The old man shot Jonas a sharp, puzzled glance—like one of his lab specimens had suddenly sat up and grabbed the dissecting knife out of his hand. Then his gaze shifted to the ambulance's open back end and he shook his head. "That could prove more than a little tricky," he pointed out.

And then and there Jonas's world shifted off its axis. For he had just experienced a major violation of House Rule #1. The old man never, ever admitted he couldn't do something. Never told anyone that he needed help. Not to bed at night. Not when he dropped something. Not with cooking. Not with cleaning. Not with climbing into an ambulance. Not with anything that might serve to remind anyone that he hadn't been able to walk in nearly twenty years.

Then, even more incredibly, Lukas spun his chair and wheeled toward the two EMTs who were watching them. "I apologize for barging in and trying to take over," Lukas said. "I would appreciate it, if you would chalk it up to my being understandably distraught. However, my son has made a legitimate point. It might be best if you took him to the ER."

"Fuck the ER," Jonas protested. "I don't need it."

The old man cast him a long look. "That is, in fact, my fervent hope," he said. "However, if it's at all possible—indeed, particularly if it is possible—

that you have been restored to me by miraculous means, then allowing you to die of a ruptured spleen or undetected internal hemorrhaging could only be described as careless, wouldn't you say?"

∞

One thing you could say about the ER, they weren't careless. All they wanted to do was check things out. Run test after stupid test. Ultrasounds, CT scans, X-rays, nurses, interns, and residents, all of them poking and probing. Even when the humans finally left, the machines were still there, watching while Jonas tossed and turned through restless dreams of running down endless corridors where no one could see him because he was really and truly dead—no one, that is, except the damned machines that were going to keep monitoring him straight through the goddamned afterlife and into eternity.

It was enough to make him actually glad to see the old man when he showed up the next morning to take him home. Didn't matter that home had stepped out of the same evil comic book universe the old man had: a leftover piece of faculty housing that had once upon a time been converted to some kind of doctor's office—and not the kind of doctor you really wanted to know about, to judge from the stray bits of medical equipment Jonas had stumbled across in the attic. Jonas felt like Dorothy returning from Oz.

The two of them shared something that might have optimistically been called living quarters in the front of the first floor, while the doctor's office had been converted to a ground-floor suite to accommodate Lukas Croswell's special needs. Out of necessity, the entire upstairs had been given over to Jonas, and he spent a moment staring at the narrow, twisting staircase, wondering how his father had managed to find the clean clothes he had brought to the hospital. Had he crawled up that staircase one step at a time? Or had he asked a neighbor for help? Either idea was equally impossible to imagine.

"In my study, if you will," Lukas said, as he wheeled over to his work table and laid out Jonas's stained clothing, which had been meticulously wrapped in plastic sheeting. Any illusion of homecoming vanished.

"Great," Jonas sighed. "You don't have enough dried-up shit in this lab without my underwear?"

He wasn't certain, but he thought he might have seen the hint of a startled smile flash across the old man's face. But that was impossible. Another violation of the rules of the universe as Jonas knew them. The old man never smiled. Warped, evil geniuses never did. And with his swept-back dark hair and narrow beard, the old man could have stepped straight out of a mad scientist's lab in any of those comic books Jonas wasn't supposed to read. Well, not exactly stepped—Jonas could hear the old man supply the correction with irritable precision—but give his father an old-fashioned lab coat and a pair of rubber gloves, and there wasn't anyone who wouldn't cast him as Dr. Frankenstein—or maybe Dr. Xavier, wheelchair and all.

The old man took a moment to study his son, an odd look flitting across his face as he finally seemed to notice the jet-black hair color Jonas had been experimenting with lately. But no. That was impossible. Noticing would mean that the old man had to think that anything Jonas did actually mattered.

"We need to talk," Lukas said.

"Yes sir. About what, sir?"

"Ironizing is not going to help you avoid the question."

"No sir. What question, sir?"

Lukas's nostrils flared as he drew a deep breath. "Yesterday, I received a frantic phone call from Sister St. John, telling me you had been killed in some kind of shootout at the Outreach Center. However, when I arrived at the scene, I found you not only alive, but relatively unharmed. And while I am admittedly relieved by that fact, I am also, shall we say, puzzled?"

Relieved. Yeah, bullshit the old man was relieved. Because that was the thing about the old man. He didn't feel a goddamned thing—and Jonas wasn't just thinking about his useless legs. He didn't laugh. He didn't cry. He didn't fart. He didn't rage. He barely seemed to even notice what he ate or drank. All he did was solve scientific problems—with exactly the same detached calm. "And although my colleagues over at All Saints would warn me against questioning miracles too closely, my temperament is unfortunately such that I would very much like a clear explanation of actually happened."

A clear explanation? *He'd* like a clear explanation? What did he want Jonas to say? That he was saved by a fucking angel? That an old priest scooped him into his arms and *kissed* him?

"I don't know," Jonas muttered. "I don't remember."

"I suppose that's possible when you think about it. Maybe even likely. Retrograde amnesia is one of the body's defenses against trauma," Lukas conceded. "Well, why don't we start with what you do remember? What were you doing down at the Outreach Center?"

Jonas shut his eyes. He was certain that Lukas knew the answer to that question already. But the old man was like a cat. He liked to draw things out. Play with his prey, letting them live a little before he dismissed them as frauds. "Dunno, sir. Can't remember, sir."

"Then allow me to make an educated guess. Jonas, are you dealing drugs again?"

If he said yes, what would the penalty be this time? Last time, the old man had put Jonas on lockdown. No phone. No texts. No Facebook. No gaming. Nothing but schoolwork and chores around the house, along with that *frigging* volunteering at the Outreach Center, with no end in sight until his old man finally wearied of supervising a teenager's version of house arrest. Which happened pretty much as soon as he wheeled back to his room after pronouncing sentence, leaving Jonas alone to deal with the bouts of the shakes, surges of nausea, uncontrollable itching, and the goddamned diarrhea—although the last was arguably more the fault of the freezer full of cardboard boxes his father called meals than any withdrawal symptom.

"I never dealt drugs," Jonas said. "I gave them to a friend."

"A friend?"

In any sane person, the blank incomprehension with which the old man repeated the term would have been sarcasm. With Lukas Croswell, it was real.

"She was my friend," Jonas repeated stubbornly. I never took any money from her."

To his humiliation, tears began to well in his eyes. But even worse was the emotion that flashed across his father's face. Jonas wasn't sure, but he thought it could have been pity. "People like you and I have no friends," the old man said. "We have people who need things from us. Your life will be much easier when you accept that fact."

Fuck you. Fuck you very much. Just because you want to spend your life with a bunch of dead people …

"It doesn't matter. It wasn't her that shot me," Jonas snarled. "It was some guys I've never seen before that shot me. Gangsters. Drug dealers. They said I was muscling in on their turf."

Lukas's face hardened. "So you were dealing drugs."

"Stealing, not dealing," Jonas snarled. "If you really want to even call it that. Christ, you're lazy about your passwords. My birthday? I mean, really? On both your laptop and the medicine cabinet at the shelter? As well as all your financial information?"

As if it was Jonas's fault that the old man's approach to security was as lame as he was. It had taken no more than an afternoon's exploration to discover that Lukas used Jonas's birthday as the code for everything—his banking statement, his computer accounts, his cell phone. In some men, it might have been a sentimental gesture. When it came to his father, Jonas figured the old man had probably gotten the sequence from a random number generator and still wondered why it seemed so naggingly familiar.

Once again, he might have believed he saw emotion flicker across the old man's face. But Lukas's voice was carefully level. "Thank you, Jonas, for that valuable life lesson. I will take it to heart. Right now, however, I would appreciate you simply telling me the truth."

Jonas shut his eyes against the tears that rose for real now—along with the remains of the breakfast he had eaten what seemed like a lifetime ago. "You want the truth. I'll give you the truth. I didn't take the drugs to deal them. I took them for myself," he choked. "If I could, I'd steal your pathetic scotch, you hypocritical bastard."

And Jonas felt a mingled surge of guilt and satisfaction at the shame in Lukas's face as he glanced over at the battered recliner in the corner of the room where Jonas wasn't supposed to know he drank himself to sleep nightly.

Then Lukas said quietly, "I suppose I could argue that I self-medicate because I'm in pain. But the fact of the matter is, it is the way of fathers to want something better for their sons than they have. Someday, you'll come to realize that."

"And what about my pain?"

"What pain? I thought the ER checked you out thoroughly," Lukas said. His eyes raked over Jonas in quick, professional appraisal. "Actually, now that I think about it, you don't look so good. What's wrong?"

Now that he thought about it. A once in a lifetime event. "Well, Dad, you're the expert, aren't you? So why don't you go ahead and see for yourself? Cut me up and put me into the centrolabe along with my dirty underwear. It's what you're dying to do, isn't it?"

Lukas went white. "Centrifuge," he spat. "And if you ever say something like that again, I will personally throw you out of this house. Now, I would like to know what's wrong with you."

"What's wrong with me? What's wrong is you dumped all my drugs down the toilet, then just left me to deal with it!" Jonas snarled, the tears spilling over at last. "Even a doctor who only treats dead people and bums ought to know better. My bed feels like it's crawling with maggots. And when I get out of bed, those maggots crawl right on out with me, twitching and biting, so I can't sit still in class. When I can manage to sit still, all I want to do is cry. But I *itch*. I *hurt*. I want to throw up. And now you want to tell me I'm running a fucking drug cartel."

His words trailed off into a choking sob, and for a while, he just stood there, head bent, shoulders heaving. And when those sobs trailed off into silence as well, he looked up to see his father staring at him, looking both appalled and relieved at once. For a moment, Jonas believed the unthinkable would occur and his father would stretch out a hand to touch him. But all he said, when he finally spoke was, "Jelly doughnuts or glazed?"

"What the f ..."

"It's a simple enough question. Do you prefer jelly doughnuts or glazed? Or maybe even powdered sugar?"

"Why the hell do you want to know? You think you're going to make this go away with some kind of lame bonding experience?"

The trace of a smile cracked his father's face. "I only wish I could. And no, it's not going to go away. But you're probably craving sugar as much as anything right now. And there's a doughnut shop just off campus. I thought we might take a trip down there. After all, it's about time we had a lame bonding experience, no?"

Without waiting for an answer, he spun his chair toward the counter to scoop up his keys and wallet, leaving Jonas to wonder what the hell had just happened. Had the bastard seriously just tried to make a joke? What came next? A father/son vacation in the morgue?

Then Lukas turned back, his expression unfathomable. "You were wrong to steal the drugs. And we are going to have to deal with that issue at some point. But right now you are quite correct to be angry with me," he said. "What I did was unconscionable—from a medical perspective, as well as from any other perspective you might choose to view it. My only excuse is that I lost my temper—and that's not an excuse at all."

Jonas shook his head, dizzily wondering whether what he had just heard was the honest-to-God sound of Lukas Croswell apologizing.

"So shall we?" Lukas asked. And Jonas folded his arms across his aching stomach as he followed his father out the door, wondering if maybe he really had died and been resurrected into some alternate timeline where his father was not a complete and utter asshole. Because frankly, Jonas couldn't think of a better explanation.

Chapter Five

"Honestly," Clare said. "I didn't see anything. I think I heard a shot. But when I ran to look, all I saw was the blood."

"Was there a lot of it?"

How was she supposed to answer that? As she remembered it, the blood seemed to be everywhere. But Clare wasn't good with blood. In fact, she pretty much got light-headed at anything worse than a paper cut.

"As I remember it, the place looked like an abattoir," she said. "But it just can't have been as bad as it seemed. The boy was fine. Stunned at first, apparently. Maybe even unconscious. But then he just … stood up."

Actually, the boy had pushed himself to his hands and knees, shaking his head like a boxer shaking off a roundhouse, then clambered to his feet. He spent a moment staring at the bloody mess of his clothes, and then uttered a single syllable.

"Shit!"

And the shocked silence had erupted into gasps and hallelujahs. Even Sister St. John had bowed her head and uttered a rapid prayer.

The story had seemed more unbelievable each time Clare told it—giving her statement to cops, EMTs, and worried bystanders in the noisy aftermath of the shooting. Now, telling it to Father Dominic Gregory, S.J., in the serene safety of All Saints College's gated campus, it was simply surreal. It didn't help that being invited to the college's presidential suite felt like nothing so much as a trip to the principal's office. Reflexive anxiety set in as soon as she touched the polished knobs on the imposing double doors and found herself dusting invisible particles of dust off her pants—an anxiety that only escalated as the president himself escorted her inside. Having spent her childhood helping her father brush the cat hair from his cassock when he absent mindedly left the vestry door ajar, Clare was not easily intimidated by the clergy. But Father Dominic Gregory could have made the pope himself feel inadequate. Tall and dark-haired, with just a sprinkling of grey at his temples, he seemed to have been born with the initials S.J.—Society of Jesus—after his name.

All Saints' presidential suite was every bit as papal as its president. The long mullioned windows were inset with stained glass portraits of past presidents, many of them priests. The paneled walls were inset with bookcases and topped with arched finials. The books on the shelves all had the leather-bound air of Bibles. The chairs were heavy and velvet-covered; the desk could have been an altar. When Father Gregory offered Clare a digestive biscuit and a crystal glass of sherry, he could have been offering her Communion.

She tried to keep her hands from trembling as she glanced around for a place to put her plate. Of course, there wasn't one. Any free surface was of such richly polished oak that even a coaster would have seemed insufficient. Grimly, she balanced her plate on one knee. As a vicar's daughter, she had attended more church garden parties than birthday parties, but she had yet to master the art of actually eating something while fielding a teacup and a fiendish little plate of pastries—all the while knowing that someone would thrust a question at you the moment your mouth was full. It was only the first among many signs that she lacked a vocation.

On the other hand, the ability to juggle finger foods was something else Father Gregory had seemingly been graced with at birth. "So how is your semester going?" he asked, managing to sound as if that was, in fact, the reason Clare had been summoned here.

"Oh, quite well," she said, sipping the sherry that was immediately threatening to spill over the rim of her dainty glass.

What was she supposed to say? That it was already getting toward midterms, the point during the semester when a teacher finally had to concede how genuinely unprepossessing even the most gilded of college youth was. It was also the point during the semester where Clare's students were finally forced to concede that there were never going to be any Barbary pirates ripping the bodices off their enticing captives in a course entitled

Introduction to Romance. That the details of the Arthurian cycle found in *Excalibur* were substantively different from those in Chretien de Troyes and Malory and Marie de France and that those differences were obvious enough that Clare was not disposed to pass quizzes that substituted the former for actually reading the latter.

"Then I can only apologize for reminding you of the recent unpleasantness over at the Church of St. Lazarus." Father Gregory segued smoothly to the real reason he had called her there. "Unfortunately, the campus is swirling with rumors about the incident. Before I respond to them, I would like to talk to someone who can give me a lucid account of what exactly transpired. Fortunately, providence seems to have supplied me with exactly such a person. That is, if I've read your very impressive CV correctly?"

If he had read her CV. Clare was certain he'd committed it to memory before his secretary had phoned to ask if it would be convenient for her to drop by for a chat that very afternoon. The secretary had specified the convenient time before Clare had had a chance to say yes.

But 'providential' wasn't exactly the word Clare would have chosen to describe what had happened to her. It was more like she had been in the wrong place at the wrong time. Still, she launched dutifully into her narration, winding up, "In any case, by all accounts the boy is fine. He was very lucky. A miracle, really."

"Well, now," Father Gregory said, "that's rather the question, isn't it?"

He let the suggestive silence that followed resonate until Clare finally realized that this—not some providential accounting—was the real reason for Father Gregory's summons. Her eyes widened. "People are claiming this was a literal miracle?"

Father Gregory frowned. "Well, I don't know if you can really have such a thing as a literal miracle. Seems somewhat theologically uncertain, if not oxymoronic, wouldn't you say? Nonetheless, that's hardly the question here, now is it?" Setting aside his sherry glass, he leaned closer. "Dr. Malley, I'd like to be straightforward, if I may?"

Straightforward? Wasn't there something in the Jesuit Formation that forbade any such thing?

"Please," Clare said.

"Do you believe you witnessed a miracle?"

Clare shook her head. How was she to know? What was a miracle supposed to look like? It was a question worthy of the undergraduate who had asked insistently where exactly Dante had found the mouth of Hell. Of course, as a medievalist, Clare had plenty of examples of what a miracle should look like. The Virgin being taken to heaven in a great, gilded ball. A heavenly song of praise still emerging from St. Cecilia's torn throat as the executioner held up her severed head. An angel descending on great, parrot-colored wings to protect tiny St. Agnes in the brothel. A sea full of fishes listening attentively to St. Anthony when people would not.

But did Clare really believe that was what a miracle would look like? Did Father Gregory? Did anyone? Wasn't it more likely that the miraculous would be so powerful, so awe-inspiring, so impossible to process that you wouldn't be able to remember what you really had seen? Or maybe you would simply be too blinded by the grim realities of day-to-day life—the stupid, mind-numbing tasks of shopping and cooking and raising kids and getting to work on time—to even notice that a miracle had occurred?

"I've told you exactly what I saw," Clare said. "I don't know what else to say."

Father Gregory nodded. "Then, at the risk of sounding … inquisitorial, for want of a better word …" He flashed a quick smile that signaled even college presidents had their little jokes. "Please allow me to phrase this more specifically. Did you see a mysterious priest lifting the boy into his arms and breathing life back into him?"

"Oh," Clare said. "Really?"

"Indeed," Father said. "Your answer, Dr. Malley?"

"I did not see a priest," Clare said, feeling obscurely like she should renounce the devil and all his works and all his ways for good measure.

"Thank you."

Father Gregory spoke the two words like a benediction, and Clare found herself wondering whether she was allowed to go now. At the very least, could she hand back the treacherous plate and sherry glass? But Father Gregory remained lost in reflection, studying her as if she remained an unanswered question.

Uncomfortable with his scrutiny, she shook her head. "But what's so miraculous about a priest saving someone's life in any case? The whole thing happened outside a church after all."

Snapping out of his study, Father Gregory smiled as if she had asked a particularly apt question. "The Church of St. Lazarus has not had a regular parish priest since 1973. All Saints has been offering its priests to celebrate Mass there since then. And the description I've heard of this mystery priest all but eliminate the possibility of its being one of ours."

"How so?"

"He was described as wearing a soutane. And while I'm sure you're well aware that there is no set habit for a Jesuit, the Rule specifies that our clothing, as much as anything else in our life, should make us *disponible*, or ready to serve. In the case of clothing, I would argue that would roughly translate as unobtrusive. And wearing a soutane, especially in the Bronx, would scarcely qualify as unobtrusive, wouldn't you say?"

"No," Clare agreed. Although in her mind, it scarcely qualified as the fashion faux pas of the decade that Father Gregory made it sound like.

"Then there's the fact that all the witnesses used the word soutane specifically," Father Gregory reflected. "Rather an exotic word for the Bronx, don't you think?"

"French," Clare said.

"Exactly."

He leaned back in his chair, steepling his fingers. "So I think you're beginning to appreciate the extent of the problem here."

Well, no. Honestly, Clare wasn't sure she was. As a matter of fact, she was beginning to think this problem might extend as endlessly as a hall of mirrors, with her rattling down the corridor still looking for a place to set her sherry glass.

"You think a rogue Lazarite has come back to the church to perform miracles?" Clare asked. "From where? France?"

Father Gregory drew a deep breath, and for a moment, Clare thought he was not going to answer the question. "It's not so much a matter of from where, as from when," he finally said.

"When," Clare repeated.

"The last Lazarite who served as the parish's priest did so in 1918, during the height of the Spanish influenza. A miracle-worker, it was rumored, who could heal simply by laying on of hands. Not a Lazarite, many said, but rather St. Lazarus himself. Of course, logically, the credit should go to the unsung devotion of our nursing sisters. But Servant of God Father Enoch is the reason the Church still has a reputation as the Lourdes of the Bronx, at least among the more enthusiastically-minded believers in the neighborhood."

He didn't try to hide his disapproval—as if such things as enthusiasms would never have been allowed, had a Jesuit been in charge in the first place. But Clare wasn't really listening. Three words had caught her attention.

"Servant of God?" she asked. "You mean, he's being considered for sainthood? His cause is actually before the Congregation for the Causes of the Saints?"

"For nearly twenty years."

And now Clare really was beginning to understand the extent of the problem. "And so, if this priest's ghost saved this boy," she worked out the syllogism—lucidly, she hoped, "that would be a miracle toward his canonization?"

"I think 'miraculous apparition' would be a better term than 'ghost.' Ghosts land us squarely in the realm of speculative theology, which means you're really nowhere at all. Speaking speculatively, however, you raise a tricky question." Father Gregory threw himself into the trickiness of the question, clearly preferring it to any notion of miracles taking place on his watch. "As I'm sure you're well aware, miracles leading to canonization must be posthumous. To prove the saint is able to intercede with God. A saint may or may not be a thaumaturge—or miracle worker—in his lifetime. But a wizard can work wonders as well. The point is, there's no way to establish what's behind the mortal miracles: Divine will or demonic interference? A posthumous miracle, on the other hand, can only occur if the saint is sitting at God's right hand.

"Now, if you're introducing a third possibility, the possibility of this being … some kind of unlaid spirit, that would introduce some serious complications indeed. One would be forced to assume he is not yet in heaven. In fact, I think that's rather the definition of an unlaid spirit. And yet, hardly mortal. I think that's pretty much the definition of a ghost. Quite a complex issue when you think about it, isn't it?"

He fell silent, inviting them both to savor the complexity of the issue along with their sherry. But all Clare could think about was that this whole conversation was proof positive of the All Saints undergraduates' assertion that the only way to survive debating theology with a Jesuit was to do it stoned. Drawing a deep breath, she tried to steer the discussion toward less speculative shoals. "But this would only be one miracle," she said. "Don't you need two for canonization?"

Reluctantly, Father Gregory allowed himself to be dragged back from the serene world of tricky questions. "Twenty years ago, there was … another boy," he admitted.

"Did someone shoot him, too?"

"No, by all accounts this boy was severely autistic. A savant. Mathematically and musically gifted. But locked in. Completely uncommunicative."

"And Father Enoch cured him?"

Father Gregory's face darkened. "Some said it was Father Enoch. Others said it was St. Lazarus himself. And still others said they were one and the same."

To judge from his tone, they had arrived at the heart of the matter. But Clare was hard-pressed to understand what exactly that was. "I'm sorry, but I'm not sure I see the problem," she said. "Are people worried about canonizing the wrong saint?"

Jesuitically enough, Father Gregory answered her question with a question. "Given your specialty, I assume you're acquainted with St. Lazarus?"

Clare took a deep breath, suddenly feeling like she was back at her orals. "He's really a conflation of two saints: Lazarus of Bethany, the brother of Mary and Martha, who Jesus brought back from the dead, and Lazarus, the beggar in the story of Lazarus and Dives."

"Indeed," Father Gregory said. "That's rather his hallmark, isn't it? Conflation, I mean. He really is a bit of a … syncretic saint."

And there was no mistaking that, in Father Gregory's world, syncretism ranked right there with enthusiasm and soutanes.

"He has been adopted by other traditions," Clare allowed. "Vodou, some say. Santeria."

"Papa Legba, the Trickster of the Crossroads. And in the Cuban tradition, the *orisha* Babalu. Subject of the eponymous song. Of course, one does one's best to respect others' spiritual traditions …"

His voice trailed off with as much distaste as if Ricky Ricardo had just invited him to join a conga line.

"Are they saying the Lazarites were really practicing Santeria at the Church of St. Lazarus?" Clare did her best to keep the interest out of her voice. She had always envied the Templars the rumors of their blasphemous worship of a goat-headed deity called Baphomet. Needless to say, the Lazarites had boasted no such infernal skeletons in their closet. Their theology, like everything else, was strictly missionary position.

"Oh, nothing quite that dramatic. Thank God." The prayer sounded absolutely sincere coming from Father Gregory's lips. "It was more a rumor that in calling on Father Enoch to aid his son, Ezra Grinnell had unleashed … more than he expected. Nonsense, of course, but you can see how the family might find resurrecting the issue—so to speak—distasteful."

Clare's eyes widened. Oh, yes, she could see. In fact, she could fully appreciate the extent of the problem now. All she had needed to hear was the name Grinnell. As in the Grinnell Science Building on the far side of the All Saints campus. As well as the Grinnell Chair in Biochemistry. And the Grinnell Scholarship Fund. Not to mention half a dozen other galleries and dorms and memorial gardens that all bore the Grinnell name. And suddenly, several more puzzle pieces fell into place. Or, as Father Gregory would be more likely to put it, Clare was beginning to understand the real difficulty here: the difficulty of making sure an inopportune miracle did not offend All Saints' largest donor. And who could blame Father Gregory for that? As a priest, Clare assumed his priorities were mixed, but as college president, they were fairly inarguable.

"You mean this boy was one of the old robber baron's descendents?" Clare asked.

"The family prefers the term 'visionary entrepreneur'," Father Gregory said. "And All Saints is happy to accommodate them. Who are we to name-call, after all? But yes. Michael Grinnell was Erastus Grinnell's great-grandson. Miraculously relieved of his affliction during the Jubilee of the Church's construction."

"Then it was determined to be a miracle?"

"Officially, the matter remains unresolved. The Grinnell fortune was built on pharmaceuticals, after all, and it is beyond dispute that Ezra Grinnell promised a fortune to anyone who could find a cure for his son. So it was impossible to eliminate the possibility that Michael's cure was a product of science, not religion. Especially when Michael himself put an end to the discussion by vanishing when he was still a teenager."

"You mean, he's…?" How to phrase it? Raptured? Ascended? Sitting at the right hand of God?

"No one knows what happened to Michael Grinnell. No one's seen him for nearly twenty years." Father Gregory's face darkened. "Although he was rumored to have been seen graveside when his father, Ezra, was buried last year. And to judge from the family's reaction to those rumors, they would not welcome a Second Coming. So to speak."

"Why?" Clare asked. "Do they think he'll bring the *orisha* with him?"

Father Gregory shot her a sharp glance that warned her that he did not encourage a taste for speculative theology in others, either. "I'm afraid if you want an answer to that question, you'd need to ask Lukas Croswell," he said. "He's the only one I know who had first-hand experience of the boy."

And the last penny dropped—with about as much force as an anvil falling out of the sky to brain Wile E. Coyote. "Lukas Croswell?" Clare said. "You mean, the father of the boy who Father Enoch is supposed to have just miraculously saved?"

"In addition to his invaluable contributions as head of All Saints' Health Services, Lukas has often investigated saints' causes on behalf of the Promoter of the Faith." Father Gregory permitted himself another small smile. "Or, as no priest seems able to resist calling it, the Devil's Advocate."

"So Croswell works on behalf of the canon lawyer charged with eliminating any non-miraculous explanations of a saint's cause," Clare said. And that made it official. A logical Gordian knot that only a Jesuit could have tied. But Clare was getting the uncomfortable feeling that it was not going to be up to a Jesuit to solve it.

"And what does Dr. Croswell say about what happened to his son?"

"That his son is too traumatized to be questioned about the … details of his resurrection." Father Gregory raised a shoulder. "Quite an understandable attitude to take, of course, but it scarcely qualifies Dr. Croswell as the sort of dispassionate observer we need."

Another long pause as he let her fill in the gaps for herself. Or, as Clare was certain he would put it, he relied on her obvious intelligence to perceive the extent of the problem.

"Are you asking me to investigate a possible miracle on behalf of the Promoter of the Faith?"

"Oh, hardly anything that formal. In fact, I think a verbal report might be in all our best interests. Nothing but an informal chat, really. After you've had a chance to examine all the evidence for yourself."

With that, Father Gregory arose and effortlessly relieved her of both her sherry glass and her crumbled digestive biscuit, as clear a signal that they were done as if he had pronounced the Mass was ended and she should go in peace. "I have complete faith in you, Dr. Malley," he said as he turned Clare over to his secretary for further instructions. "And I'm looking forward to receiving a lucid accounting—at your earliest convenience. Shall I ask Sister Anne to find a time on my schedule in the next few days?"

Chapter Six

The Grinnell Science Building was the pride of All Saints College—the physical embodiment of the Jesuits' claim to have married faith and reason. It had begun life as a squat, square structure that could well have been a Victorian gaol, with its inmates sentenced to making sketches of the flora and fauna in the college's collection instead of picking oakum. Those long-gone students still graced the hall of the building, in sepia-toned poster presentations that showed them at tall dissection tables or wearing floppy hats as they ventured out into the field to collect specimens. The least moth-eaten of the taxidermy animals they once hunted were displayed in refurbished glass cabinets next to the posters. The rest of the building, however, had been ruthlessly updated by the descendants of Erastus Grinnell. The architectural bones remained, but the flesh was now a state of the art facility dedicated to the man's memory—as well as, Clare was certain, writing off the research that created the enormous profits for the pharmaceutical giant that still bore the family name.

For obvious reasons, Lukas Croswell's campus office was on the first floor, sharing an access ramp with the Campus Health Services he ran. Unlike the clinic at the Outreach Center, this campus clinic showed every sign of the Grinnell dollars that underwrote it. The waiting room looked more like a lounge, and the whole place was preternaturally clean, with a serenity fountain tumbling along one wall, and a counter full of herbal teas and bottles of spring water readily available to students awaiting medical attention for their hangovers.

Clare had only caught a glimpse of Lukas Croswell in the flurry of activity that had surrounded the resurrection of his son, but she had no difficulty remembering him. It wasn't the fact that the man was confined to a wheelchair. It was that he occupied it like a throne.

"I'm Clare Malley," she said, feeling obscurely like she was describing an embarrassing rash. "I believe Father Gregory's secretary called and set up an appointment?"

"Lukas Croswell," he said, and held out his hand. Clare assumed he meant for her to shake it, but there was something about the gesture that made her wonder whether he expected her to kneel and kiss some kind of ring instead. "Yes, I was expecting you. Unfortunately, Father Gregory's office neglected to specify what exactly this was about. I assume it's not a probe into the wait times at Health Services? Or an emergency appendectomy?"

Oh, Lord. He wasn't about to make this easy, was he? She should have known as much after having watched him take over the chaotic scene at the Outreach Center like Cosimo Medici returning to seize control of Florence from the enemies who had exiled him.

"It's about ..." Clare paused to choose her words. It didn't take a leap of the imagination to guess that actually speaking the word 'miracle' would get her ushered out more quickly than a drunken student cursing out the receptionist.

"What happened at the Outreach Center."

Lukas's gaze never wavered. "And what exactly is Father Gregory's interest in that?"

"There was a shooting."

"I am well aware of that fact."

"I assume you're also aware that some of the people who were there claim to have witnessed..." His green eyes sharpened and she hesitated before measuring her words once more. "...an apparition. A ghostly priest who might have saved ..."

Your son. As Lukas Croswell damned well knew.

He drew a deep breath, his nostrils flaring with distaste. "In other words, the Church is resurrecting that old nonsense about the Cause of Father Enoch again?"

"No one's done anything yet. Father Gregory is still trying to make up his mind. That's why he wanted me to talk to you."

"And what does he think that will accomplish? Does he seriously expect me to investigate my own son as dispassionately as ... the fish bone that St. Blaise miraculously dislodged from the choking boy's throat?"

"Of course not. You're scarcely a disinterested observer. That's why he sent me—" Clare broke off, unable to help herself. "You've seen St. Blaise's miraculous fish bone?"

"I've seen at least seven. And given the liturgical symmetry of the number, I feel comfortable in saying I'd be happy if I never saw another one." Lukas studied her in a way that suggested he felt pretty much the same about her. "Are you a student of miracles, Dr. Malley?"

"It kind of comes with the territory. I'm a medievalist."

Lukas cocked his head, as if deciding whether that might be some obscure symptom of some dreaded disease, possibly the plague. "Then it's a pity we don't have more time. I seem to recall having a finger of St. Jude somewhere. Somewhat tellingly, it seems to have been the middle one—rather appropriate for the patron saint of lost causes. Unfortunately, the foreskin with which Christ solemnized his mystical union with St. Catherine of Siena seems to be a fake. Not a fake foreskin, mind you. But nineteenth-century at best—"

"I'm sorry if I got carried away by professional curiosity," Clare interrupted him hastily. Clearly the man was prepared to go on all night if she let him. "Really, that's not at all why I'm here. Father Gregory just asked me to step in because I was there when it happened."

Lukas's eyes sharpened with as much clinical interest as if Clare herself were laid out beside his collection of nineteenth-century foreskins and miraculous fish bones. "You saw what happened?"

"Not exactly. I heard the shots. And then I saw your son lying on the ground."

She hesitated, wondering whether that was too graphic a description, but Lukas barely seemed to notice. Suddenly, he was all scientist. "And did you see this ghostly priest?"

"No."

"Well, there's something to be said for that, at least," Lukas managed to sound both surprised and approving—as if she had been called to the board to solve some particularly knotty problem and had come up with the correct answer against all odds. "Then, if you'll pardon me asking, what exactly do you hope to accomplish by coming here?"

Feeling vaguely like a bishop at Confirmation, she said, "I suppose I need to ask you formally, whether, in your informed opinion, there's any chance that what happened to your son was a miracle?"

"What happened to my son was not a miracle in anything but the most figurative sense of the word," Lukas said. "Thank God."

"Why thank God?"

"My son has been restored to me and all that," Lukas said. "I believe it's the done thing."

"I meant, do you have something against miracles *per se*?"

Lukas stared at her for so long that she began to wonder whether he was going to answer. "Yes," he said, "I do. Particularly when they pertain to my adolescent son."

"Why?"

"Because, clinically speaking, most of the examples that come to mind bear all the hallmarks of mental illness," he said, the careful disinterest in his voice a clear signal that they had finally reached the crux of the matter. "Granted, I'm only diagnosing at second hand, but if you asked me for my informed opinion, I would say Bernadette of Lourdes exhibited symptoms of acute hypochondriasis. Joan of Arc seemed to be suffering from incipient schizophrenia. Nicholas of Cologne leading an army of children across the Alps to Genoa, where the Lord had promised to part the Mediterranean so that they could pass safely to the Holy Land, I can only describe as deranged—although I have to confess a certain self interest in that case. When slavers seized the children as they held vigil at the water's edge, waiting for the waves to recede, their angry parents hanged Nicholas's father. I would prefer not to see the villagers massing with pitchforks outside my own residence, if you know what I mean."

He paused, drawing a deep breath to fight down the tide of his rising emotion, before he concluded, "In short, although I'm hardly a sentimentalist when it comes to children—in fact, I've been reliably informed that I lack the paternal touch altogether—you will forgive me if that is not an experience I would wish upon my son. Or any other man's son for that matter."

Any other man's son. Would that include a man who, if Father Gregory was to be believed, had been willing to move heaven and hell to cure his son—arguably quite literally?

"And what about the one you did diagnose first hand?" Clare asked.

Lukas's face set. "I'm not sure what you're talking about."

"The first boy. Father Enoch's other miracle."

"There's no question of another miracle, if only for the fact that there has never been a first miracle."

A piece of logic only a Jesuit could follow. "Was that your official determination then or now?" Clare asked.

"I beg your pardon?"

"Was that your official opinion when you first examined Michael Grinnell?" Clare repeated. "Or is that only in light of the current situation?"

"There is no current situation. My son has nothing in common with that"—his lips pursed in distaste—"case."

"Well, yes, he does—if only with Father Enoch. Am I not correct in saying you were asked to examine Michael Grinnell on behalf of the Promoter of the Faith?"

Lukas shut his eyes. "Whatever I did, it's all water under the bridge now."

"Well, no. Unfortunately, it really isn't," Clare said. "If Father Enoch's Cause is resurrected, then people are going to want to re-examine his first miracle, along with any new ones. It takes two miracles for canonization, you know."

"Unless, of course, you die a martyr. Killed in *odium fidei*. Out of hatred for the faith. Then it only takes one; for the grace of martyrdom is considered the first miracle," Lukas said with a tight smile. "I've read the handbook. As a matter of fact, I could probably recite it."

And shoot down every last sentence in it as casually as he dismissed Jesus' disputed foreskin. Clare shook her head. You couldn't teach at a Jesuit school and remain completely unacquainted with terms like 'loss of faith' and 'dark night of the soul', but what must it be like to have been born with them as congenital conditions?

"And what would the handbook tell you about Michael Grinnell?"

"That he was a prime candidate for the *odium*, if nothing else."

"What does that mean?"

Drawing a deep breath, Lukas shook his head. "Nothing but a very feeble attempt at a witticism. I apologize."

Clare bit back a surge of guilt when she saw the weariness that slackened his face. Miracle or no miracle, faith or none, the man had nearly lost his son. Was it fair to expect him to face down the Inquisition as well?

"Look, why not just tell me what you know, and we don't ever have to bring you into this again?" Clare asked. "And just for the record, I understand that even that is a pretty big request. But according to Father Gregory, you're the only one left who had any firsthand experience with the boy."

Lukas's face flattened. "Maybe there's a reason for that."

"What does that mean?" she asked.

For a moment, Lukas just sat there. Then, making up his mind, he wheeled over to a file cabinet and pulled out a thin, battered folder. Folding it open, he studied it for a moment.

"The case of Michael Grinnell began when Michael was attending a Mass in celebration of the Jubilee of the Church of St. Lazarus," he finally began. "When the Host was elevated, Michael collapsed. Afterward, there was no shortage of witnesses willing to swear they had seen the spirit of Father Enoch scooping up Michael in his arms, then releasing him. Scientifically speaking, however, all we know for sure is that he was taken home with a raging fever. Three days later, the fever broke, he got out of bed, walked downstairs, and asked his mother politely for a cup of orange juice for breakfast, because he hated milk and wished she would stop making him drink it.

"Perhaps not miraculous in another child. But given that Michael had been unable to communicate meaningfully with anyone for nearly fifteen years, it might as well have been the Second Coming. Unfortunately, the stunned rapture with which his cure was received was rapidly abated when he next asked his mother to lace the orange juice with vodka as she did her own."

And there was her answer, Clare thought numbly. That was what a miracle looked like. No virgins riding in golden globes, no naked St. Sebastian, pierced with arrows, being rescued by a beautiful noblewoman who admired his ... sanctity. A boy who wanted to sneak his mother's vodka. Another boy staring down at the mess on his shirt and simply sighing "Shit."

On the other hand, it was at least ... personable, unlike most child saints, who seemed to be auditioning for a role as Little Lord Fauntleroy.

"Simply put," Lukas went on, "it rapidly became apparent that Michael's miraculous new ability to communicate came with a taste for communicating ... uncomfortable truths."

"And you were looking for some kind of medical explanation for that?"

"Theoretically speaking, it's hardly impossible."

"But what about practically speaking? How could you do a thing like that?"

An odd expression crossed Lukas's face. "I did nothing. I merely hypothesized how it might be done."

"And how is that?"

Lukas glanced up from the folder, studying her as if she was a particularly doltish student. "Think it through logically," he said. "Michael Grinnell was autistic. If you were trying to cure an autistic child, wouldn't you be trying to ramp up his empathy? His ability to read people? To communicate with them? Arguably to the point where he could see inside their very souls? And manipulate them at will?"

"That's your medical explanation?"

"Maybe it would be more accurate to say that there was only one explanation everyone was capable of agreeing upon. Michael Grinnell was ... unholy."

A scientific term, if ever there was one. "And exactly who is everyone?"

"Priests. Doctors. Scientists. Psychiatrists. Specialists on autism. Literally scores of experts approaching the problem from every conceivable angle. Trust me, when I tell you the case was thoroughly researched. By the best in the land. Ezra Grinnell had the money for that. But despite his money, despite the number of PhD's left laying on the table, only one clear conclusion emerged. Michael Grinnell had managed to terrorize them all."

"A fifteen-year-old boy? How?"

"I'm not sure I know. But what I can tell you is that within a year, at least two thirds of those experts were dead. Arguably the rest might have preferred they were."

"Are you saying he *killed* them?"

"Not so anyone could prove it."

"Then ... what? How?"

"Suicides. Overdoses that were more or less the same thing. Mental illness. Self-destructive behaviors." Lukas clenched his teeth. "The last priest to talk to him retired to a monastery permanently after only one month. And he was the one who lasted the longest."

She shook her head. "You make him sound like some kind of monster."

"More accurately, a high-functioning sociopath. With a mean streak a mile wide. The first part is a medical diagnosis. The second part is just an off-the-cuff opinion."

Clare drew a deep breath as she tried to make sense of the senseless. "And how did you arrive at that diagnosis?" she asked. "What did he say to you?"

Lukas glared at her. "I find that rather an intrusive question."

"Then let me rephrase it. Was your hypothesis correct?"

"I think that's something only Michael can answer." Closing the file, Lukas handed it to her. "Take this if you like. Read it for yourself if you must. But I strongly urge you to burn the damned thing."

"In other words, just run away like you did?"

Something flashed across Lukas's face, and she only had a moment to regret her choice of phrasing before he erupted, his voice low and furious. "I did not run away from Michael Grinnell then. And I have done precious little running since—courtesy of a rather a nasty traffic accident on my way to interview him, when my brakes inexplicably gave out on a particularly treacherous curve between Storm King Mountain and West Point. And when I eventually emerged from a medically-induced coma, I was a little too involved in relearning some basic motor skills like feeding myself to be able to devote a lot of mental energy to the Cause of Father Enoch."

Clare felt the blood drain from her face. For a moment, she just stared at him, stunned. And then she stammered, "I'm so sorry."

"Don't be," he snapped. "I'm sure there are many who'd say it was the least I deserved."

"No," she said. "No one deserves—"

He cut her off. "This is why I prefer to deal with relics rather than people. You find yourself in far fewer awkward conversations. Now, if there's nothing else …"

It was a clear dismissal, as well as a fairly firm indication that she was not likely to get anything further from him ever again—no matter how many times Father Gregory's secretary called. And why should he? Talk about awkward conversations. But that made it all the more urgent that she have an answer to one last question, no matter how awkward it might prove.

"As a doctor, a man of science, do you have any kind of concrete evidence to support your belief that Michael Grinnell was responsible for ... what happened to you?"

Lukas raised an eyebrow. "As to who was responsible, Ms. Malley, I can tell you I've put such thinking behind me. Something about moving forward with one's life. The rehabilitation center was big on such things. But what I will tell you is that the first day I met him, Michael warned me to stop asking questions. Told me I'd be very sorry if I didn't." His eyes grew distant. "A childish threat to say the least. And so, I treated it as such. Now, given the benefit of twenty-twenty hindsight, I can only warn you that he was absolutely right."

Chapter Seven

Being punished by the old man was nothing compared to being coddled by him. Temperature and pulse checks every hour or so. Homework help over take-out ordered from half-a-dozen menus. And doughnuts. Ever since Jonas had come home from the hospital, his life seemed to have been transformed by the doughnut fairy. Boston crèmes for lunch. Glazed buttermilk for dinner. When he dozed off on the living room sofa, he awakened to find a blanket tucked around him and a pillow slipped beneath his head—along with a bag of Bear Claws and cold milk in a vacuum flask that looked suspiciously like it might have once seen service in the old man's lab.

Lukas had just dispensed a pair of crullers like they were aspirin when his phone rang. He listened only briefly before snapping, "Impossible. I'm sorry."

The voice on the other end said something more. "I appreciate both your obligations and your concern," Lukas replied, "however, it is my professional opinion that my son is in no condition to speak to anyone."

Another welter of words, and the old man's face fell. Suddenly he just looked tired.

"Well, in that case, I owe you an apology. As well as a thank you," he said. "Would this afternoon be convenient?"

After he hung up, he lapsed into a silence almost as black as when he had witnessed Jonas's resurrection down at the Outreach Center.

"What is it?" Jonas asked. "What's going on?"

"The local prosecutor would like to have a word with you. I'm afraid I can't convince him otherwise." Another long, silent moment, and then just like that, the old man was back in action, snapping out orders like he was in an operating room. "However, he is willing to do it informally, down at the Outreach Center, rather than subjecting you to an interrogation. I will, of course, insist on being present at the interview. In fact, it would be best if you allowed me to do as much of the talking as possible. You can simply tell him you don't remember anything. I can attest to the fact that it's a common result of trauma."

Jonas stared at him. "But that's … a lie."

"No, it's not. It's a medical fact."

"You know what I mean." Jonas folded his arms. "You could go to jail for that. I don't want you to go to jail because of me."

Well, maybe he should have thought of that before he started stealing drugs. Jonas could hear the old man point out the obvious before he said a word.

But incredibly, Lukas didn't say it. And that was the last straw. Jonas couldn't help himself. The next words tumbled out in a rush of anger and fear. "Go ahead. You're just dying to say it," he snarled. "I really fucked it up this time, didn't I?"

His father's shoulders stiffened, and he took his time studying Jonas over his reading glasses as if he were some kind of unfamiliar specimen. "Do you really think that's the case?" he asked, and he sounded genuinely disturbed. "Do you really think I would find this cause to … gloat?"

"Don't change the subject."

"I'm not," he said. "I would very much like an answer to my question."

Jonas shut his eyes. "Nossir."

"Then can we agree that you will let me handle this, and do what I can to make things right?"

"Why should you?" Jonas demanded. "I'm the one who fucked up."

Another long look, like the old man was having trouble identifying exactly who or what his son was. "Because I'm your father," Lukas said. "And while it's clear I'm not a particularly good specimen, I'm the one you were landed with. And this is what fathers do when someone threatens their son."

∞

Jonas wasn't sure how he'd feel walking back into the Outreach Center. But what was strange about that? Jonas wasn't sure how he felt about anything anymore. He supposed the cliché that was his world had been turned upside down, but didn't it make a lot more sense to think that he was the one who was ass-backwards—tumbling in a long somersault down the fast track to the nuthouse? It didn't help that the old man kept shooting anxious glances Jonas's way whenever he thought Jonas wasn't looking—like he was just dying to pull out a thermometer and check Jonas's temperature one more time.

But Jonas felt nothing as he entered the crowded church basement. Most likely because nothing had changed. The place still looked like some third world Ebola camp, filled with sweaty, pregnant women trying to mop up their kids' vomit with crumpled tissues, and bag men belching and coughing up long strings of … who the hell knew what? And as for the smell—hell, take Jonas at his worst after he'd crapped himself and multiply it by one of those exponents that the old man spent their quality time trying to explain in this weird new Mr. Rogers voice he kept trying to use. Sweat and piss and puke and shit, all of it rising from a bunch of swamp people who were mouth breathers.

The nun who ran the place came hurrying over as soon as she saw them. "Are you sure this is wise, so soon after …" Her eyes went to Jonas as she groped for a word. "… the incident?"

"I don't think it's wise at all," Lukas said. "Unfortunately, I haven't been given much choice in the matter. The police have decided to investigate."

"You're bringing the police here?" The nun's face darkened into a scowl. As if somehow she thought this was all Jonas's fault. And why shouldn't she? This was 100 percent Jonas's bad.

"Fortunately, Trey Carey has stepped in to mediate," Lukas said. "He's offered to have Jonas walk him through what happened informally, in order to spare him from going down to the local police station to make a formal statement."

"But Trey's still a prosecutor."

"He's also the husband of Marie Grinnell. Whose family has supported the Outreach Center since it was founded," Lukas said. "Which is why he's making every effort to handle this as a discreetly as possible. It seems to be in everyone's best interest to cooperate with him."

The nun gestured toward a couple of skinny addicts who were emptying sugar packet after sugar packet into their coffee. Too bad Jonas hadn't thought to bring them a couple of spare doughnuts from home.

"In whose best interest? Theirs? These people need to be protected. They have the right of sanctuary."

Lukas's nostrils flared. "Be that as it may, the fact that the shooters are reputed drug dealers complicates the issue considerably. For, as much as I respect the Church's ancient prerogatives, I need to point out that neither the federal government nor the AMA has much patience with physicians who cannot keep track of the medicine in their dispensary. Licenses are revoked. Jail sentences are handed down. Which means, if you are as committed to providing free medical care as you are to the concept of sanctuary, the center needs to cooperate with the prosecutor's office. Complete transparency. So, if you don't mind, I would like to check the medicine cabinet to see if anything's missing before Trey arrives."

Without another word, he wheeled up the ramp that led out of the shelter and back out onto the street. Doing his best to ignore the nun's furious glare, Jonas crept after him.

It didn't matter that Jonas had two good legs, and even once in a while ran track at school, by the time he'd screwed up the courage to follow his father into the storeroom, Lukas was already peering at the medicine chest through his reading glasses as if it were a suppurating chest wound. With a rapid twist of his wrist, he double-checked the lock, then pulled out one of those latex examining gloves he used in the clinic. And by the time Jonas had figured out what he was doing, or had recognized the dented table knife that his father was holding for what it was, the old man had inserted it between the doors of the cabinet and jimmied them open in one swift move.

Which was in a way pretty cool. Jonas wondered what other tricks his father might teach him. "What the f…? You're faking a break-in."

Lukas raised an eyebrow. "Since you're perspicacious enough to realize that, I assume you're perspicacious enough to realize I would prefer it if you kept your voice down."

"But … why?"

Tossing the knife away, Lukas removed the latex glove and crumpled it into a pocket. "Licenses revoked. Jail sentences. That kind of thing."

Yeah. Jonas knew. It was pretty fucking hard to forget it. "I mean, why are you faking it?"

"Because if the prosecutor's office finds drugs missing from a locked cabinet on our little walkthrough, that points to someone with knowledge of the combination," Lukas said. "Whereas anyone could have simply jimmied that lock. They have better security on the communion wine. Now, shall we take a look and see what's missing?"

"No, Dad, please listen…"

"Dr. Croswell? Are you in there?"

A small, slender woman with long red hair materialized in the doorway in a rattle of footsteps. She was the kind of woman you usually only saw here on Thanksgiving, elbowing the others out of the way for the privilege of serving turkey to the homeless. More often, her kind showed up right on their doorstep, angling for the privilege of serving turkey tetrazzini to Lukas Croswell and his pathetic son.

That was another thing about the old man. He was a regular chick magnet. Women always wanted to take care of him—from the yoga teacher who wanted to teach him to meditate, to the librarian who wanted him to join a book club, to the elderly Jehovah's Witness who wanted to save his immortal soul. Three guesses how any of those had worked out. It had gone easiest for the Witness. On the other hand, at least the food was decent during the brief interval between a woman's deciding to take his father firmly in hand and the moment Lukas concluded his definitive demonstration of why they would have better luck taking a pit viper to their bosom. Casseroles seemed to be the weapon of choice in the crusade to save Lukas Croswell's soul.

But one look at the redhead, and a muscle began to twitch in the old man's cheek. So, no. This had nothing to do with casseroles.

"Dr. Malley," he said. "I suppose it was too much to hope you'd take my advice."

"Actually," she said, "the point is moot. Father Gregory heard that the prosecutor's office wants to settle this matter quietly, and he sent me down here to see if I can facilitate matters on his behalf. To tell the truth, I think that translates into him wanting me to run interference with Sister St. John, but if there's something you need from me ..."

Lukas studied the redhead for another moment, then gestured toward the broken lock on the medicine cabinet. "We seem to have had a break-in," he said, refusing to meet Jonas's eyes. "Perhaps you could check whether any other items have been taken while I check the drugs."

"Did this happen when...?" She glanced at Jonas. "You know."

"I couldn't say," Lukas said. "Maybe you'll find some evidence that will help us pinpoint a time in all that."

He waved toward the shelves that were crammed with cardboard boxes and rotting books. But the redhead just kept staring into the cabinet. "That's an awful lot of drugs," she said.

Lukas forced a smile. "The Grinnell Corporation has always been more than generous in funding our pharmaceuticals," he said. "As I'm sure Father Gregory has already informed you."

"I mean, there are a lot of them in there. Why didn't the thieves take them?"

The smile faded; the muscle twitched harder. "Perhaps they were interrupted."

"By your son? That can't be. The shooting took place outside, remember? They would have already cleaned everything out of the cabinets."

"Then maybe they weren't interrupted by my son," Lukas said. He was starting to look uncomfortable. Didn't take much to figure out why. Christ, wasn't he the one that was always lecturing Jonas on how lying was never the answer. How one lie just fed into another until the whole house of cards came crashing down around your ears?

And you got hauled off to jail just because you were trying to help your fuck-up of a son?

"Maybe they weren't looking for drugs," Jonas said. "Maybe they were looking for ... you know ... like relics? Of the priest who's supposed to haunt this place?"

An odd look flashed across Lukas's face. "Honestly, Jonas. The Congregation for the Causes of the Saints is one thing. *The Da Vinci Code* is an entirely different thing altogether." Part of Jonas would have been ready to swear he'd seen his father bite back a smile. If he had, it was gone before Lukas turned back to the redhead. "Nonetheless, if you could check the shelves to see if any relics are missing, that would be very helpful."

He spun back toward the medicine cabinet and pointedly began to count the drugs, but his chair caught against an edge, rattling the shelves and sending a sheaf of papers sliding to the floor. The old man stared at them with about the same expression as he had when Jonas had spilled a tray of saints' teeth all over the floor of his lab. "Those belong on the other side of the room. Who on earth put them there?"

"I'll get them," the redhead said, scooping up the papers. Major violation of house rules, but Lukas barely seemed to notice. Jonas guessed staging a crime was more distracting than his father had thought.

The redhead frowned as she glanced at the paper. "What's the Lazarus Vector?" she asked.

"I honestly have no idea," Lukas said. "I suppose it would be logical to assume it's somehow connected to this being the Church of St. Lazarus."

"Then what was it doing in the medicine cabinet?"

Lukas drew an irritable breath. "I suppose it could be some kind of bottled miracle cure," he said with a tight smile. "The Lazarites' answer to the water at Lourdes. But it might be simpler to assume that it was misplaced. The filing system here doesn't strike me as exhaustive."

"No Finding Aid," the redhead agreed. But she didn't put down the papers. "Still, I'm the world's foremost expert on the Lazarites—at least until someone else decides to write a dissertation. So if anyone should know what a Lazarus Vector is, it should be me. And I've never heard of it." She flipped through the pages, skimming them as she went on, "The Lazarus Map, yes. It's a strangely oriented Hungarian map in which Northeast is straight up instead of North. One of the more arcane theories is that it is pointing the way to the mythical Northern kingdom of Thule …"

"Then I congratulate you on discovering another Templar meridian," Lukas said. "In the meantime, if we could get to work …"

"Oh, no. The Templar meridians are completely different. I've seen them. I once spent an entire summer—"

The redhead broke off, flushing beneath Lukas's incredulous stare. Under normal circumstances, Jonas would have been pissed. Under normal circumstances, he would have pushed her to go on, maybe even asked her what she thought about the Oak Island Treasure. But these weren't normal circumstances. In fact, Jonas was beginning to doubt there was ever going to be such a thing again. Because Jonas could tell them exactly where that paper had come from. Just like he could have told them that, yes, the Lazarus Vector was a drug. A shit-assed, scary drug that had been sitting in the bottom shelf the last time Jonas had snuck into that medicine cabinet, vials packed in a padded cooler bag like some kind of serum a hero dog would rush to a village suffering a plague. One sniff, one taste was enough to make Jonas give it up as a bad idea. He just wanted a buzz—a little relief from the itching and the jitters. He wasn't so far gone that he wanted to mess around with shit you had to shoot up or shit that had to be kept cold.

"Dad—"

An angry shout cut him off. "You want to talk to Lukas Croswell, you head around outside. But you don't come downstairs. You don't violate sanctuary, do you hear me?"

"And that, I believe, is our cue for a facilitating intervention," Lukas said to the redhead. Slamming the medicine cabinet shut, he spun for the door, barely managing to hide his relief. "Sister St. John may be a woman of great courage and faith, but frankly, she has more of a taste for plastic handcuffs than I think is strictly healthy."

∞

A shadow shifted in the depths of the sacristy as soon as the door closed behind them, and the busker slid out from the alcove where he had been hiding. His mouth twisted in an angry smile as he scooped up the computer printout.

"The Lazarus Vector," he snorted. "Really? What is it with you people and names?"

"You prefer to call it the Path of the Awakener?" the ghost asked, materializing beside him.

"I prefer to call it a pain in the ass." The busker shook his head, shoving his hand back through his hair. "Christ, why would anyone want to resurrect this crap? What the hell are they up to?"

"How should I know?" the ghost said. "I'm just a psychological projection, remember? I can't dematerialize and walk through walls to spy for you."

"And here I'd hoped you might be useful."

"You don't value my spiritual advice?"

"Spirit advice, you mean?"

"Have it your way," the ghost said. "I'm here to help."

"How? By advising me to come back from the dead to save the world?"

"I understand it's the traditional path."

The busker cast the ghost a long look. "And it was my understanding this came from a different place altogether."

"You'd know better than anyone." The ghost shook his head and fresh blood trickled from his nose. "Just as you're the only one who can really understand what's at stake here."

The busker sighed. Sure. He knew exactly what was at stake. The memory of red hair bouncing in the sunlight. And the thought of a kiss that could wake the dead. Not to mention the possibility—no, the sure and certain knowledge—that here was a chance for him to play hero once more. And maybe this time earn a kiss as a reward. Too bad the ghost didn't see things as clearly as he did.

Christ, talk about a pain in the ass. He had done everything he could to hide from what he didn't want to see—spent an entire lifetime in shadows where no pretty girl with red hair would venture, so that he didn't have to see the ugly desires, the half-assed evasions, the petty grudges, and venal cheats that pretty much made up people's souls. The secret, stupid shit that no one really wanted to know about anyone else, and frankly people didn't want to know about themselves. No man could hide from the busker. No man could lie to him. The grim corollary of all that was the busker damned well couldn't lie to himself either.

"I didn't come here for that and you know it," he said. "I'm no hero."

"Labels don't matter," the ghost said. "You know what you need to do."

Yes. He did. He also knew that it wasn't what a hero would do.

Shaking off the ghost, the busker began searching the vestry's shelves, pushing aside frayed and yellowed vestments, mismatched chalices and patens, jugs of port wine and a wax paper sleeve of communion wafers—rifling through sagging shelves of parish records, boxes upon boxes of type-written minutes of the Altar Guild and various sodalities, until he found a bent cardboard box that bore the label, "Cause of Servant of God Father Enoch."

He only glanced inside. A faded photograph, dried flower petals lying among carefully embroidered handkerchiefs, a couple of baptismal spoons, and a snake-like tangle of rosaries were enough to convince him he had found what he needed. Tossing the computer print-out on top of the rest of the mess, he grabbed the cardboard box and got the hell out of there—fleeing back to his world of shadows while he still had a chance.

Chapter Eight

Lukas Croswell could say more with a single look than most men could say with a diatribe. And the look he cast Clare made one point abundantly clear. He was not about to have her hanging around while his son gave his statement to the local prosecutor's office. Or, to put it more accurately, while his son fidgeted mutely with his dyed black hair as Trey Carey assured him that they were going to get the SOBs that did this. And actually, Clare was just fine with that. She didn't like prosecutors. Hadn't since the day another prosecutor had promised Clare the same thing in another vestry, with her mother riding shotgun as ferociously as Lukas was now.

Not that the two vestries had anything in common. Clare's mother would have had little tolerance for the sacristy of the Church of St. Lazarus. The vestry of her father's church had been a paean to the firm hand with which her mother ran the Altar Guild, a triumph of careful organization and good hygiene.

Her mother would have long ago disposed of the boxes of forgotten records—finding an intern to catalogue and digitize them, maybe even making it a Youth Group Service project. No stained water glasses would have stood in the special sink that was only supposed to be used to wash the Eucharistic vessels.

But that prosecutor's eyes had been just the same as Trey Carey's—even if she had been a woman and called herself a Victim's Advocate instead. Her gaze moved everywhere, scanning for the rope to hang someone, not even acknowledging anything that didn't serve that purpose, even if it was Clare protesting, "It's not Satanism. It's Catharism."

"You pray to someone named Lucifer," the Advocate had stated.

"It's not a prayer. It's a myth. It's the story of the True Believer ascending into perfection."

"And you do that by worshipping Satan?"

"Not Satan. Lucifer. And you don't even have to call him that. You can just call him the Awakener instead. Because he blows the breath of the divine back into humankind." Clare shook her head. "Either way it's a just a metaphor."

And she had learned about metaphors two years earlier in eighth grade English. So why were the grown-ups all being so stupid? The Advocate looked like metaphors were sitting right next to Satanic possession on her checklist of criminal behaviors. Clare's mother was inwardly fuming that this was what came of allowing children to roam freely through one's bookshelves, just like she had told her husband all along. Clare's father blinked, longing only to retreat to his study and his compendium of British saints.

Abruptly, the Advocate changed tacks, leaning closer, her voice all honeyed reason. "Okay, let's say that this is just a metaphor. You want to tell me what it really means? How did he want to awaken you?"

"He didn't! Not like that! I told you. Nothing happened."

"Then why the rituals? Why the blasphemy?"

"Heresy," Clare sighed. "It's heresy, not blasphemy."

"There's no difference."

"Yes there is! Blasphemy's about defiling sacred things. Heresy's about history getting written by the winners."

"Listen to her," Clare's mother cut in. "Listen to what he's done to her. She never would have said a thing like that before she met him. I want this predator."

"And we're going to get him for you," the Advocate said. "No matter what it takes."

"Can I help you?" The voice cut through Clare's side trip to the past, and for once, Clare actually welcomed the sight of Sister St. John glaring at her—even if she didn't know what she was supposed to have done wrong this time. Whatever it was, it beat the memories.

"Father Gregory wanted to know if there was anything you needed."

The nun cast a baleful gaze at the prosecutor who was helping Jonas reconstruct the shooting, while Lukas watched like an angry cat.

"How about a lawyer for Rafael?"

"Who?"

The nun's lips twisted. "You know, the other boy," she said. "The one that got away."

"Oh, you mean the one who was here when Jonas Croswell . . ."

Did what exactly? Got shot? Died? Was resurrected?

"Yes. Rafael. That's his name. If anyone bothered to ask."

But of course someone should bother to ask. He had been there, too. Had seen what happened. Why wouldn't you care to ask?

"Hasn't anyone talked to him? Asked him what happened?"

"No. Pace St. Martin de Porres, seems like white skin is an essential qualification for miraculous intervention."

"Does that mean you do think it was a miracle?" Clare asked. She felt stupid even asking the question. She couldn't see the nun falling to her knees in ecstatic witness if Jesus himself had appeared and begun to multiply loaves and fishes on her soup line.

The nun's fierce face slackened. "To judge from the bloodbath that no one seems able to explain, I have to think that if Jonas wasn't injured, Rafael must have been—quite severely from the looks of it. But it is the great consolation of faith that I am at least permitted to hope that somehow he, too, miraculously survived."

"Well, why not check? Call the ER?"

"People around here don't go to the hospitals," the nun said. "Especially not with gunshot wounds."

"Why not?"

"The law mandates that all gunshot wounds be reported. Even Lukas would be legally obligated to comply if Rafael asked him for help."

"But he could die!"

"You seem to be the only person here who's noticed that fact." The nun thought for a moment. "If you really do want to help, maybe you could check with the botanica across the street. Rafael's *abuela* runs it. She's hardly a trauma surgeon, but perhaps her prayers were more efficacious than mine seem to be."

"I really shouldn't—" The words were on Clare's lips before she even thought about it. After the Great Cathar Scandal, she had sullenly conformed to the Zen of Anglican life: the spring fete, the harvest dinner, the Blessing of the Animals, the Service of Lessons and Carols, and renouncing, along with the Devil and all his works and all his ways, such baneful influences as mesmerists, Transcendentalists, spiritualists, Shakers, anarchists, Rosicrucians, hermetic orders, Theosophists, and Bulwer-Lytton. One guess which category a botanica fell into.

But that was when Clare had been a fifteen-year-old Cathar. She was thirty now. And able to hold her own in a discussion of thaumaturges with a Jesuit. "I'd be happy to," she amended herself.

"Rafael and his friends usually hang out in the side alley," the nun told her, then hesitated. "If you find him there—or even if you don't—I would very much appreciate you finding out what did happen to him."

∞

The side alley was a gauntlet of dumpsters between the church and the storefronts on the adjacent avenue. If Clare had ever wondered whether anything could smell worse than a homeless shelter, she now had an answer. In fact, the stench was so bad that it took her a moment to recognize the other smell.

Pot. A lot of it. And not being smoked in the tidy little joints that Clare had once rolled with her friends. This weed was being smoked in a big, fat cigar that belonged in a boardroom, being handed around in a humidor to celebrate some fat cat's deal. And the kid who was lounging on an upturned milk crate, puffing away as he studied a fistful of numbers slips like a hedge fund manager looking at his stock ticker, was twelve going on thirty, with a baseball cap perched at an angle that must have cost him hours in front of the mirror to adjust. It went without saying that his pants were slung somewhere down around his knees, and he wore an enormous gold St. Lazarus medallion around his neck, the saint's eyes picked out in ruby chips.

"I'm looking for a guy named Rafael," Clare said. "You know where I can find him?"

He stubbed the blunt out and tucked it away—not so much to hide it from her, but as a signal that this wasn't a social occasion.

"Why?" he asked. "You want to see my scars?"

Relief washed over Clare, startling her. She hadn't realized how badly she wanted to bring Sister St. John good news. "Are you Rafael, then? Are you ... okay?"

"See for yourself. I'll let you look. But it's going to cost you."

Of course it was, Clare thought, so giddy it was all she could do not to laugh. That was a fine church tradition that went all the way back to Joseph of Arimathea's foresighted decision to catch the blood of Christ in the Holy Grail. No sooner do you have a miracle, than the miracle industry pops up around it. Pilgrim's badges along El Camino de Santiago, plastic bottles of water at Lourdes. She was surprised Sister St. John hadn't pounced on the idea as a fundraiser for the Outreach Center.

Fighting down the impulse to ask him whether he took credit cards, she studied him. "I'd be a lot more interested in hearing what happened to you. Were you shot? Did you see the priest?"

"Show me the money first."

As if Clare was ever going to pull out her wallet in front of a kid like this. But when she looked closer, she saw the kid was almost as skinny as the dogs on the medal around his neck, and his baggy pants were clearly hand-me-downs, his sweat-stained wife-beater, too. The gaudy St. Lazarus medal was the only thing of value he owned—and Clare was willing to bet it was only gold plate.

And probably stolen to boot. But, Christ, he was just a child. And clearly in need of some money. The only thing that held her back was that he'd probably put a knife to her throat and make off with her wallet and cell phone, too. And then accuse her of touching him improperly.

"How much?" she asked.

"A hundred bucks. Firsthand account, man. Eyewitness. I swear it."

The kid emphasized that fact by kissing it up to God.

"Twenty-five," she countered. "And another twenty-five if I believe you."

Touching the saint's medal, he held out a hand. Braced against him pulling a knife or a gun, she opened her bag and counted out the bills—hesitating when she saw she didn't have a five. Christ, what was she going to do? Ask him to make change, like a pizza deliveryman you didn't want to overtip?

"So what happened?" she asked, handing over the extra ten. "You see the priest?"

He glanced around, as if worried about being overheard. And then he leaned close, close enough to make her recoil instinctively. "Wasn't no priest."

Her eyes moved to the medal. "St. Lazarus, then?"

"St. Lazarus is for old ladies," the kid snorted. "This is the real thing. Takwin. You know what Takwin is?"

Well, yes. Yes, Clare did. But at the risk of sounding like an elitist, she was … somewhat surprised this kid did. "Are you referring to the secret of Geber? Or more properly Jabir ibn Hayyan? The great Arab alchemist, who claimed to have discovered how to create life, birthing scorpions and snakes in his experiments?"

It was absurd, of course. Impossible. But exactly what words would you use to describe debating the esoteric secrets of the Crusades with a teenage drug dealer in a back alley?

"You call him whatever you want. Point is, we got it. And if you want it—"

She never heard the stealthy footfall behind her, until something slammed into her hard, and an arm snaked around her neck. "She don't want nothing," someone hissed in her ear. "Christ, man. You don't talk to people about our business. Don't you learn anything?"

Because the first rule of Fight Club was, nobody talks about Fight Club, right? Or something like that. Clare's head was suddenly spinning, and it had nothing to do with the fact that someone was choking her, cutting off all her air. What the hell was happening? Was she about to be martyred in the Cause of Father Enoch? And if she was, would that constitute step one in her own Cause? More to the point, if she didn't die, how would this affect her career path? Because if there was one thing she was certain of, it was that Father Gregory was going to like a martyrdom on his turf even less than he liked a thaumaturge.

But above all, what she was really thinking was how stupid she had been to insist on swordfighting lessons when she was fourteen, instead of the women's self-defense course her mother had recommended. Because the fact of the matter was, Clare could knock just about anyone flat on their butt with everything from a two-handed broadsword to a rapier. Unfortunately, another fact of the matter—which was of paramount importance right now—was that all that was pretty much irrelevant if you weren't on a fencing strip and you didn't have said broadsword or rapier to hand.

"Let go of her. Now."

The voice was calm. Distant, even.

"Stay the fuck out of this."

"Just as soon as you let go of her."

"Miguel. C.J. Show the man he don't want to be here."

Now the alley seemed full of kids, all of them with gold chains and low-slung jeans and elaborately laced sneakers. None of them seemed much older than Rafael, but there was nothing childish about the knives that seemed to sprout out of nowhere. Clare tried to suck in enough air to shout a warning, but the figure in the shabby topcoat who confronted them from the mouth of the alley didn't seem to care.

"You're right. I don't really want to be here," the busker said. "What I really do want is for you to let go of her. Right now."

"And why should I do that?"

"Because I've got the answers you need," the fiddler said. "And I'm not going to give them to you until you do."

"Answers to what?"

"The crap that's going on inside your head," the fiddler said. "I can explain it. Maybe even tell you what to do about it."

"What crap, man? What you know about our business?"

"Made you feel like Superman at first, didn't it?" the fiddler asked. "And why not? Damned near impossible to hurt you. You're faster, stronger, meaner than anyone out there."

"Then maybe you don't want to be taking us on."

The fiddler smiled. It was not a nice smile. "Most people tell me I've got a pretty impressive mean streak myself."

"Then bring it on, bro."

"Supposing instead I just give you some advice for free. Consider it a good faith gesture."

The chokehold tightened. "Keep your advice for those who care about it."

The fiddler shrugged. "Have it your way. I guess sooner or later, you'll figure out how to deal with the whispers. You might even do it before they get to you for good."

"What the fuck you talking about man?"

"Like I said, I can tell you about the crap that's going on inside your head. The stuff you're telling yourself you're not seeing, mostly because you're scared that if you tell anyone—even each other—they'll call you crazy and lock you up. Usually it starts with voices—whispers no one can hear but you. You've been trying to ignore them, but I'm guessing that's getting pretty hard by now. You got all you can to worry about whether you really are seeing shadows out of the corner of your eyes. Well, don't worry about that. The monsters really are right behind you. What you ought to be worrying about is when they won't stay shadows anymore." The fiddler shook his head thoughtfully. "That was really the point of all of this, you know. The voices. The mean streak—that was just a side effect. Or maybe it was just to keep you from killing yourself before you learned to deal with them. I'm still working on figuring that one out."

"You done working now," a kid snarled, lunging.

She should scream, Clare thought. At the very least, she should find enough air to scream. Or step on her captor's instep, then kick back against his other knee, as she had been taught in health class. But as she tried to summon the energy to do something—anything other than just standing here ...

"Maybe," the fiddler said, "you're even seeing the monsters right now."

Abruptly, the chokehold was released, just as the kid that had lunged for the fiddler froze with an agonized shriek. His arms spasmed wide; his hands clenched, then splayed, sending the knife spinning. His back arced with such violence he was drawn to his tiptoes, almost seeming to be floating in midair.

And all around him, the other kids were twisting and screaming—some falling to their knees with their eyes raised toward the heaven, other scrabbling backward, trying to escape from invisible demons.

"What the hell?" Clare breathed.

A hand closed on her arm. "Now would be a very good time to get out of here," the fiddler told her.

She shook her head, trying to stop the world from spinning. Trying to stop the kids from writhing. "Did you do that?"

An odd look crossed the fiddler's face. "Depends on how you look at it, I suppose."

"But … what just happened to them? What's going on? Are they going to be okay?"

His face set. "All things considered, I think you should be a little more concerned about your safety now."

"What about you?"

"No worries about me," the busker said. "I wasn't lying when I said I've got one hell of a mean streak. I can take care of myself."

And urging her out of the alley, he took off down the street, disappearing almost as quickly as he had the first time.

Chapter Nine

"I don't see why you want to protect a bunch of gangbangers and drug dealers," Trey Carey complained. "Most people I know would say they only got what was coming to them. A taste of their own medicine."

It seemed to be the sole point he had made for nearly an hour now, speaking in quick, prosecutorial jabs that immediately pulled Clare back to the Great Cathar Debacle. It wasn't a memory she relished. In fact, even though her bruised neck was beginning to throb in earnest now, the similarity between Trey and her nemesis, the Victims' Advocate, was enough to make Clare sympathize with Sister St. John when she planted herself firmly in front of the entrance of the shelter, swearing she would chain herself there before she would allow the police to canvass inside for Rafael.

For it went without saying that every last member of the gang was gone by the time Clare had brought help rushing back to the alley. Whatever had happened, whatever the fiddler may or may not have done to them, they had vanished as completely as if they had been raptured straight up to heaven. And frankly, an hour spent in a meeting with Trey Carey had convinced Clare that she liked the gang's chances facing the Lord God Almighty on the *Dies Irae*, the Day of Wrath, better than their prospects with Trey Carey. He had been cut from the same mean bolt of cloth as the Victim's Advocate, who hadn't been satisfied with anything short of lynching a man whose only real crime, as far as Clare was concerned, was writing bad poetry. The memory still sickened her, as did that of those street toughs writhing and twisting, all staring in terror at something only they could see.

"Do you really think a drug could do that to people?" she asked.

"Have you ever seen a person on crystal meth?" Trey said. "Or bath salts? Down in Florida, one guy chewed a poor bastard's face off."

As far as Clare was concerned, that was as much a product of it being Florida as any drug, but she admitted prejudice in the matter.

Lukas Croswell spoke up suddenly. "Ergot poisoning." He had said little until now, content to position himself between his son and the threat of another interview by Trey just as Sister St. John had done when she blocked the door to the shelter. "Nothing but fungus-tainted rye, but it was probably responsible for most of the mass religious ecstasies in the Middle Ages. Symptoms included visions and convulsions, often followed by, in the words of the Annales Xantenses for the year 857, 'a Great plague of swollen blisters consumed the people by a loathsome rot, so that their limbs were loosened and fell off before death.'"

"You see any of their arms and legs fall off?" Trey asked Clare.

Well, if she had, wouldn't it be reasonable to assume they'd still be littering the alley? Or was she supposed to assume the drug dealers had been tidy enough to pick up their lost body parts and carry them off when they fled? And when it came down to that, why did the man have to sound so damned eager when it came to chewed faces and severed limbs? It was hard not to read that as a subconscious urge to draw and quarter the world.

"They all seemed to see something," she said. "And then their bodies seemed to go rigid. I think a vision followed by a convulsion would be a reasonable description."

"What about drugs?" Trey asked.

"What about them?"

"You see any?"

"No." No fungus-tainted rye, either, for that matter. But then Clare hesitated. "Although, when I think about it, Rafael did mention something called Takwin."

Lukas glanced up. "As in the Arabic artificial creation of life as described by Geber in his *Book of Stones*?"

"Apparently. But from the way he spoke about it, it could have been some kind of drug."

"Rather a metaphorical name for a drug, don't you think?"

"I don't know," Clare said. "Is it any more esoteric than the Lazarus Vector?"

To judge from the stunned silence that followed, Clare might as well have dropped an F-Bomb at the Thanksgiving dinner table. Then Trey asked, his voice ominously quiet, "Mind telling me what you're talking about?"

"Nothing, really," Clare said. "They were just some old records we found in the medicine cabinet at the Outreach Center."

Moving for the sacristy door, Trey reached for his cell phone as if it were a sidearm. "I need to see those records."

"No," Sister St. John said, stepping into his way. "We agreed Father Gregory would search the Church and Outreach Center for the men who assaulted Dr. Malley. Alone. Beyond that, we have no interest in pursuing any criminal matters."

"It's not up to you to decide whether to press charges."

"It is up to me to report a crime when one has been committed in the Center. And right now, I still have no evidence that has in fact happened."

"The papers were probably just out of place." Lukas seconded Sister St. John. "I hate to admit it, but the Center's record keeping is a shambles. I don't think anyone's signed the medicine log in over a year."

Clare glanced at him sharply. From what she had seen, that wasn't true. The log had been meticulously filled out. But why would Lukas lie about a thing like that?

One guess. Her gaze shifted to the feral teenager slinking in his father's shadow, and, despite the fact her neck still ached abominably, she could suddenly see the world through Sister St. John's eyes. Jonas Croswell was troubled. Disturbed. Traumatized. It didn't matter what word you chose; they all meant he was protected. While Rafael—who apparently didn't even deserve the dignity of a last name—was the subject of a neighborhood dragnet.

"Why is the Church insisting on protecting a bunch of criminals?" Trey demanded.

"If Our Lord weren't concerned with criminals, he would scarcely have given them a patron saint, now would he?" Father Gregory's voice rose as sonorously as a benediction from the sacristy door. In its own way, it was as dramatic an announcement of a verdict as if he had sent up a puff of white or black smoke.

"Do criminals really have a patron saint?" Clare asked, turning toward the priest.

"St. Leonard. A nobleman of Limoges. King Clovis promised that he would release any worthy prisoner converted to Christianity by Leonard, and gave him the right to liberate prisoners on his behalf. Not actually a criminal himself, then. For that you'd have to start by looking at Dismas, the Good Thief, although there are plenty of subsequent examples. St. Callixtus of Rome was an embezzler. St. Moses the Egyptian headed a street gang. St. Camillus de Lellis was a con man and a card shark. And if you insist on examining the distaff side of the issue, why indulge in dated views about the criminality of sexually independent women, when we have the particularly bloodthirsty St. Olga? The lady managed to massacre over 5,000 Drevlians by such unpleasant means as burying them alive, locking them in a bath-house and setting it alight, and loosing pigeons and sparrows with incendiary devices attached to their legs. Granted, the Drevlians had killed her husband, but there are limits to marital devotion."

"Seriously?" Clare asked. "They canonized her?"

"The Emperor Constantine himself pronounced her charming after her conversion to Christianity." Father Gregory shrugged. "And who are we to say otherwise? Even St. Francis was, in his day, a bit of a lad."

"Quit stalling," Trey demanded. "Are they in there?"

Father Gregory pierced him with a look that suggested if the gang had actually been inside the church he had been ordered to search, they were safely on their way out a back door by now. Maybe even down a secret tunnel hollowed out beneath the crypt during one of the Expulsions of the Jesuits.

"No," he said. "And I apologize for the delay. However, I did discover something … that bore further investigation."

"Like what?"

"Apparently, whoever broke in wasn't interested in drugs. He was after something else altogether."

"And that was?" Lukas asked the question calmly enough, but the sudden tension in his voice was as noticeable as the muscle that began to twitch in his cheek.

"The evidence in the Cause of Father Enoch," Father Gregory said. "It's all gone."

There was another one of those stunned Thanksgiving Dinner silences. If

Clare had been given to hyperbole—or maybe it was cliché—she would have said Lukas's jaw dropped. Even Trey didn't seem to know what to say. "They went for a saint's paperwork instead of drugs?" he asked. "Why?"

"Indeed, that is the question." Father Gregory turned on Clare. "Unfortunately, I'm beginning to think the answer to that might lie with your mysterious guardian angel."

"Oh, he was no angel," Clare said.

Father Gregory raised an eyebrow, and Clare found herself flushing. "I meant, he was entirely corporeal," she said. "He wasn't Father Enoch. Wasn't an apparition. I'd be willing to swear to it. When Jonas got shot he ..." Her flush deepened as she groped for words. "... pretty much threw himself on me."

Trey leaned forward, his eyes boring into hers as if they were facing each other across a table in an interrogation room. "He's saved you twice now?"

She shook her head, trying to process any kind of sensible answer. "I'm not sure I can explain exactly what he did."

"I'm not worried about that exactly. I'm worried about the facts. And right now the facts are beginning to sound to me like maybe you've gotten yourself a stalker."

Gotten herself? As if she had somehow gone out looking for him, along with a pair of teenaged shooting victims, one assumed. And a bunch of drug dealers suffering from ergotism while you were at it?

"I don't think it really had anything to do with me," she said.

Father Gregory raised an eyebrow. "Then you prefer to believe it was a complete coincidence?" he asked in the same tone as he might have pointed out to Thomas Aquinas that the premise underlying his Argument from Design—summarized in most editions as "We see that natural bodies work toward some goal, and do not do so by chance"—was flawed at best.

"Twice?" Trey added.

Clare drew a deep breath, fighting down the urge to ask him whether he suggested she cut off her hair and start wearing statement glasses in order to discourage any further such attempts.

"Let's just say that if there is a connection, I don't know what it is. The first time I met him, I heard him playing and tossed some money in his fiddle case. He plays beautifully, by the way. There's no reason for him to be earning his living on the street," she said. "The second time, he barely spoke to me, beyond telling me to get out of there. He was talking to Rafael and the others."

"And what did he have to say to them?" Trey asked.

"He told them that he knew what was wrong with them."

"This before or after they all flipped out?"

Clare took another deep breath. She was beginning to wonder if maybe she ought to call a lawyer. Could you be accused of covering up evidence just because your answers were wrong? Or just plain incoherent?

"Before," she said. "I think. But I could be wrong about that. He ... he said something about them seeing visions. Hearing voices. Then, all of a sudden, they did." She shook her head. "I admit the whole thing didn't really make a lot of sense."

"It would probably make a lot more sense if we could have a chance to talk to him," Father Gregory said. "By any chance, did you happen to get his name?"

"No," Clare said.

But surely Father Gregory's fine Jesuitical mind could read the clues as clearly as she was seeing them now. A musical prodigy. A teenager with unholy visions and scary powers. And a man who could apparently induce those kind of visions in others.

"I suppose it's obvious to wonder whether he's Michael Grinnell," Clare said.

She had only given voice to what everyone else must have been thinking—or maybe what they were willing themselves *not* to think. So why were they all staring at her as if she had suddenly begun to levitate? All of them that is, except Lukas. His attention suddenly seemed a million miles away as his knuckles whitened on the arms of his chair. Too late Clare remembered what his last memory of Michael Grinnell must have been.

An angry flush worked its way up Trey's face faster than the thermometer measured All Saints' annual giving. "That's impossible," he sputtered.

"Quite the contrary," Father Gregory said in a way that suggested that his fine, Jesuitical mind had in fact been running down this path all along. "Who else would be interested in those papers? A rabid opponent of the Cause of Father Enoch? A profiteer speculating in futures on his relics?"

"That's not as far-fetched as you might think," Lukas snorted. "Have you ever visited Lourdes?"

Father Gregory cast a sharp, speculative glance his way. "Have you?"

"All in a day's relic-busting."

"Of course," Father Gregory said, and turned back to Trey. "Dr. Malley's theory does have the virtue of simplicity, if nothing else. Occam's Razor, you know. *Numquam ponenda est pluralitas sine necessitate.* Plurality must never be posited without necessity. As a matter of fact, the principle originally pertained specifically to miracles. First-class mind, William of Ockham. Franciscan, of course, couldn't be helped. Before St. Ignatius' time. Even so, he would have made a fine Jesuit."

Unsurprisingly, Trey didn't look much interested in the distinctions between the Jesuit and Franciscan minds. "Michael Grinnell's been dead to us for twenty years," he said.

"Yet plenty of people claimed they saw him at the cemetery when his father was buried last year. There were even rumors that he was in the back of the church for the funeral Mass itself. Of course, if that were true, it would put to rest the widely-held notion that if and when such an event transpires, the Church would collapse."

"Then he wants something," Trey said.

"Redemption?" Father Gregory suggested. "Reconciliation?"

"The bastard isn't capable of either."

"It's said that a father's death can change a man."

"Nothing can change Michael Grinnell."

"Theologically speaking, it's my job to hope otherwise," Father Gregory said. "But assuming you're correct, isn't the most obvious possibility that he feels he's due some kind of inheritance?"

"In hell!" Trey snarled. "That bastard ruined my wife's family twenty years ago. If he thinks he's getting some kind of handout now—"

"But it goes beyond a handout, does it not? Seeing that Ezra died intestate, I mean." Father Gregory shrugged apologetically. "Of course, this is all far outside my personal area of expertise. My only training is in canon law, and I had no natural aptitude even for that. However, it strikes me that Michael's reappearance could cause considerable difficulties for both the Grinnell family and the Grinnell Corporation."

Well beyond his area of expertise indeed. From the sound of things, Father Gregory could have been a Vatican lawyer doing a guest stint on the US Supreme Court, if that's what he had chosen to do. And, to judge from the annual reports about the state of All Saints' endowment, he was no slouch when it came to having a head for money either.

"There's no way he can take back Grinnell," Trey snapped. "Without a will, the estate gets divided equally between Michael and my wife. And if you split Ezra's holdings like that, the family no longer has a controlling interest in Grinnell. Stalemate."

"One that runs both ways," Father Gregory pointed out. "I believe the term is a Mexican standoff."

Trey's ugly flush mounted. "You really think he's going to tear down a billion-dollar company out of sheer spite?"

"His reputation does precede him. Still, a wiser man would be satisfied for much less. Why go to the trouble of litigation, when you could simply pay him to go away?"

"Blackmail," Trey said flatly.

"Many would call it a mutually beneficial settlement."

"Michael doesn't do anything that's beneficial. Causing trouble is his hobby."

"Maybe. But it was always said that Michael had a genius IQ. And you don't need to be a master strategist at chess—which, I don't need to remind you, Michael is, or at least was—in order to see that neither of you can benefit from this stalemate."

"I don't care. If he shows up on my doorstep, I'll personally kick his ass out."

From the exasperation that fleeted across Father Gregory's face, Trey might as well have screwed up a Latin declension. "That's up to you, of course," he said. "But I would be far more puzzled by the fact he hasn't contacted you. That doesn't much sound like a blackmailer's behavior."

"Then what the hell do you think he's up to?"

Father Gregory shook his head. "I'm afraid when it comes to criminality, St. Olga rather exhausts my imagination. But I would strongly suggest that if he does contact you, you do not kick him anywhere until you find out exactly what he wants."

"But who says he's a criminal?" Clare burst in, overcome by her swelling surge of sympathy for a boy she had never met and a man she barely knew. "Who says he's up to anything at all?"

Father Gregory's startled frown rapidly turned into the same speculative consideration with which he had previously eyed Lukas, but she didn't care.

"From what I see, the only thing he's tried to do is take back his own life." She plowed ahead. "So shouldn't you at least consider the possibility that all he wants is his privacy? That he just doesn't want to be anyone's poster boy—for the Cause of Father Enoch or anything else?"

Chapter Ten

"Doughnut run?" Lukas suggested, as he relocked the medicine cabinet. It was like nothing had happened. The lock had been replaced. The prosecutor was gone, too, sent on his way with no more ado than a crying child being handed a lollipop after his shots. And the inventory records for the medicine were hopelessly scattered, with a solid chunk of them in Lukas's car, on their way home to be shredded. Good thing the old man had decided to make his career on the right side of the law. He would have made one hell of a criminal.

Jonas took a deep breath. "Actually," he said. "I was thinking maybe you'd let me drive us home. I mean, it's only five minutes and all that ..."

He had been plotting this moment for a while, had his reasons already marshaled, and wasn't afraid to play the guilt card if he had to. Might as well turn this newfound interest in bonding to his benefit.

Lukas glanced at him with a startled frown. "Do you have a...?"

Voices erupted outside, cutting off what could have been an awkward question to answer.

"Please put away the cigarette," Sister St. John snapped. "The Outreach Center is a substance-free space."

"What the hell does that mean? You live in a vacuum?"

Moments later, heels *click-clacked* into the storeroom. It was another one of those women you only saw around here on Thanksgiving, but unlike the professor with her petite frame and red hair, this one was tall and blonde. Then again, maybe she wasn't really all that tall; maybe it was just that she was wearing six-inch stilettos. Small wonder she stumbled as she crossed the threshold.

"Dr. Croswell?" she asked, catching herself against a shelf full of missals.

"And you are?" the old man asked.

"You don't know me?" she demanded. "My name's Marie. Carey now, but I'm thinking hard about going back to Grinnell. As in those Grinnells. The ones that pay for this place."

Lukas raised an eyebrow. It was a gesture equivalent to a gasp in less people. "Of course. I apologize," he said. "But it's been some time now."

"Three to five," she said. "Months, not years. A slap on the wrist. Too bad. The point was to get them to throw the book at me."

And Jonas saw another look he had never expected to see on his father's face: blank incomprehension.

"I beg your pardon?"

"Oh, come on, I surely can't be your first NVO? You run an Outreach Center, don't you? I figured the place would be lousy with them."

"My. First. What? If I may be so bold."

"NVO. Non-violent offender."

Lukas cocked his head, studying her. "Then am I to infer that you are here to perform some kind of community service?"

"Hell, no," she said. "Bastard doesn't want that kind of publicity. And, before you ask, sure I was drunk when I totaled his car. You tell me another way to survive a fund-raising dinner. But what was I supposed to do, just sit there with a smile pasted on my face, while the asshole was groping her in front of everyone?" She shook her head. "I was hoping they'd haul me off in handcuffs. I would have alerted the press myself. But a felony conviction isn't the ideal accessory in a political wife. So the bastard pulled some strings, got the judge to sentence me to rehab. Again."

"Then why, exactly, are you here instead of there?" the old man asked.

"I'm on the lam, so to speak. Walked right out; the hell with the court order. I mean, what's he going to do to reinforce it? Send the US Marshals in to take me out of here in handcuffs?"

"If I understand the nature of court orders correctly, that would be a distinct possibility," Lukas said. "And not one that Sister St. John would welcome."

"Sister St. John doesn't welcome much."

"Stipulated. However, is there a reason you've chosen to put a project your family has long supported at risk?"

"Have you ever been to rehab?" she demanded. "Found yourself locked in some spa in a desert? Have you ever tried to eat from an all-vegan menu? Have you ever tried to doze through a yoga class with some woman who will not stop smiling at you? Have you ever seen the way those women smile? Never stop trying to share their bliss with you no matter how bad you want them to keep it to themselves. Their smug, self-satisfied bliss …"

An inscrutable expression flashed across the old man's face. "I have encountered the type," he allowed.

"About the only thing that can be said for it is I don't have to face my asshole of a husband over the breakfast table each morning. Talk about a life sentence."

Lukas raised an eyebrow. "This is beginning to sound like you're mistaking an Outreach Center for a counseling center."

"Screw counseling. I'm taking the bastard down. But before I go ahead and just slice his balls off, I want a tour of this place. I want to see where my money is going." She took a lurching step forward. "So bring it on. Show me your Cabinet, Dr. Moreau."

"Cabinet of Dr. Caligari. Island of Dr. Moreau. Although my son prefers to go with Dr. Frankenstein." Jonas's ears went hot, as Lukas studied the woman with clinical detachment. "Mrs. Carey, are you quite all right?"

Clearly she wasn't. That much would have been obvious, even if she hadn't tossed her head and said, "Frankly, I'm doped to the gills. Haven't had a drink in over a month, you know. So first thing I did when I landed, I started going through the bottles in the bastard's wine cellar. Tossing off a glass from one bottle before I moved on to the next. Figure I did a couple thousand dollars damage this afternoon. Can't wait to see his face when he gets home tonight."

"That sounds extremely constructive," Lukas said.

It was one of his favorite lines for dressing down his son. Marie seemed to like it about as much as Jonas did. "I'm not constructive," she snorted. "I've only got one talent. Making a scene."

"So it would seem. But could you do me the courtesy of explaining why you feel impelled to make one here?"

The woman was drunk. And arguably crazy. But Jonas had to admire the way she was standing up to his father. Most people were beyond breathing by now. Marie Carey was just warming up. "Worst thing about rehab is there's shit-all to do," she said. "They call it reflection and self-examination. I call it sitting around with your thumb up your ass. And what there is to do, I don't like. I don't like yoga. I don't like art classes. Or creative movement. Or journaling. I especially don't like group therapy. And I'll be damned if I'm going to talk to a shrink. Does someone want to explain to me why in hell you pay $250 an hour for someone to answer a question with a question? What do you think? Why don't you ask yourself that question? And the granddaddy of them all, 'It's your dream. What do you think it means?'"

"As I said, the Outreach Center is not a counseling center. And I'm not a counselor. So I'm afraid I'm in no position to offer a professional opinion …"

"So what I did," the woman plowed over him, "was to begin reading my financial statements. Try to keep track of all these things I'm supposed to own. The shrinks called it avoidance. I called it trying to get a handle on what's going on behind my back. The shrinks call that paranoid. But I don't care. Because you know what I found?"

"Obviously not. Or shall I assume that question was rhetorical?"

"I found a whole lot of records that make no sense. And you know what most of them pertain to? That is not a rhetorical question by the way. I want to know how much you know."

"About what?"

"About the finances here at the Outreach Center. Have you seen the money that comes into this place?"

"Actually, no. I have nothing to do with budgets."

"Well, take it from me, this place is like a Japanese beetle trap. Grinnell's pouring money into it and none comes out. A million dollars is just the baseline budget. There must have been dozens of special earmarks after that." She waved a hand, nearly sending herself lurching off her shoes. "You tell me if you see a million dollars around this place."

"I'm not sure I'd know what such a thing looks like."

"Well I do. And trust me when I say I'm not seeing it here. I know there's something going on. Now, I want to know what it is."

"And why exactly do you think I can tell you?"

"If you don't mind, I'm the one who's asking questions."

"Perhaps. But I'm the one who's going to decide whether I'm going to answer them. So would you please explain to me, in words of one syllable if need be, what exactly you're looking for here?"

"We could begin with bondage. Pedophilia. Cross-dressing. Threesomes. Human trafficking," she said. "But I'll settle for a girlfriend."

Lukas raised an eyebrow. "Despite the somewhat ambivalent grammar and usage, I assume that was somehow meant to refer to your husband?"

"Who else? You and the nun don't strike me as the type."

"Then I shall do my best to take that as a compliment." Lukas's nostrils flared, a sure warning that he was preparing to ream her out with the kind of gleeful precision he usually reserved for his son. Jonas bit back a grin despite himself. Actually, when you weren't on the receiving end of it, it was kind of fun to watch Lukas Croswell in action. "Unfortunately, my relationship with Sister St. John is such that I've never been comfortable asking her whether her penchant for flagellation is only metaphorical or she has an actual taste for hair shirts and cilices—which as I'm sure you're well aware are actually the same thing, pace Dan Brown."

And that was enough to pull the woman up short. She stared at the old man. "I was not aware," she said.

"Well, I'm delighted to have been able to enlighten you. It's been years since I've held an actual professorship, but there's part of me that remains a teacher at heart."

He swiveled away to open the door for her, a clear dismissal. But the woman didn't move. "So what is it?" she asked. "Just straight, garden variety money laundering?"

Lukas's eyes flared briefly with fury, and for a moment, Jonas braced against seeing the woman vivisected right then and there. "I am trying to make allowances for your being, as you so quaintly put it, 'doped to the gills,'" the old man enunciated, "but I have to admit I'm beginning to find this inquisition downright insulting."

"I don't give a damn. I broke out of rehab to come here. You think I'm afraid to step on a few toes in order to find out what is going on?"

"I think right now you're stepping on the wrong toes." Lukas shook his head. "If these are real allegations and not some drunken fantasy, you need to take them up with whoever is in charge of the finances of this place ..."

"Which would be my beloved husband, of course," she snorted. Holding up one red, lacquered fingernail at a time, she began to enumerate her points. "The way I see it, he's up to one of three things. He's funneling money to a mistress. He's hiding money in advance of a divorce settlement. Or he's being blackmailed."

Lukas raised an eyebrow, the muscle twitching in his cheek the only sign of his mounting anger. "Is that an accusation?"

"Actually," Marie said, changing tacks as only a drunk could, "I was thinking more in terms of my dear brother."

The silence with which Lukas greeted that statement was as deafening as the one when he had come to find Jonas's dead body.

"Michael," he said flatly.

"I've heard the rumors," Marie said. "What I need to know is, are they true? Have people seen him? Has he really been hanging around here?"

Lukas shook his head. "I'm afraid you'd have to ask Clare Malley that."

"Who's she?"

"She's investigating the Cause of Father Enoch for Father Gregory. And, if you believe her story, your brother seems to have appointed himself her guardian angel. It appears he's saved her life not once, but twice."

"My God, why?" Marie's eyes widened.

"I have no idea. As I said, I haven't seen him myself."

"You think he's become infatuated? Thinks he's in love?"

"It is a distinct possibility. I am given to understand that 'love' is the customary motivation for a man's taking up knight-errantry."

"That poor woman," Marie said, and suddenly she seemed extremely sober. "That poor, poor woman."

"What makes you say that?"

"You of all people should know. Hell, you examined him, didn't you? Your first case of miracle-busting, wasn't it?"

"The results were inconclusive."

"The results were he was a monster. Sociopath, was the word I wasn't supposed to hear when I was eavesdropping. Completely incapable of caring about anyone other than himself."

"I was only there to evaluate him from a medical point of view," Lukas said. "I can only repeat that I have no qualifications as a psychologist."

"You didn't need to be a shrink to see that Michael was a ruthless bastard that makes Trey look like Mr. Rogers," Marie said. "So the only thing I can think of that would be scarier than having Michael out to get you, is Michael believing he cares about you."

Jonas wasn't sure he understood the look that flashed across the old man's face. Was pretty damned sure that he didn't want to. "Be that as it may," Lukas said, "I have no real information to give you. In fact, I've recused myself from the case."

"Why?"

"I can hardly be said to be a disinterested party."

Lukas did his best not to look at Jonas as he spoke, but Marie was too quick for him. "You mean the shooting?" she asked, whirling on Jonas. "You're the one? You're the miracle kid? Did you see Michael? Was he the one who saved you?"

And suddenly Jonas found himself tongue-tied, consumed by the notion that if the crazy lady didn't like the answers he gave her, she'd pull off one of those vicious-looking stiletto heels and start pounding him over the head with it.

"Enough!" Lukas snapped. "I don't know what kind of childish bid for attention this is, but I draw the line at having my son dragged into it . . ."

"Then tell me the goddamned truth."

"About what?"

"About why no one seems to have intended to tell me my brother is back, despite the fact I have what can only be described as a vested interest in the matter?"

Lukas drew a long breath, nostrils flaring. "And what, if I may ask, is your vested interest?"

"He's my brother, remember?"

"Of course. But I was under the impression you two were something less than close."

"Of course we aren't close. We hate each other. Unfortunately, I need him."

"Why?"

"Money, of course," Marie snorted. "It's the only thing that would bring him back, and the only reason I'd want him back. True Grinnell family feeling. About the only other Grinnell family truth was that my father loved Michael and never loved me—"

"At the risk of repeating myself, I am not a counselor. Nor do I have the slightest interest in family therapy for myself or anyone else—"

"Don't you see?" Marie cut in over him. "That's why my father would never have Michael declared dead, despite pleas from everyone from the family lawyer to the Board of Directors of the Grinnell Corporation and the SEC. I assume that's also why he didn't leave a will when he died."

Lukas's brows drew together, and Jonas sucked down a breath because, dammit, all of a sudden the cold-blooded bastard looked interested. Interested, and more than a little scared.

"In other words, you believe your father wanted to force your brother to come forward. Why?"

"Figured he could smell the money from the other side of the globe." Marie shook her head. "Unfortunately, that's where the other ruthless bastard comes in. As in, the one I'm married to."

"He wants Grinnell." It was a statement, not a question.

"Trey put the company into court-appointed conservatorship even before I'd finished the thank you notes for the funeral flowers."

"'The funeral baked meats did coldly furnish forth the marriage tables.'"

"What?"

"Shakespeare," Lukas said. His eyes were far away. "And in the meantime, Trey runs everything?"

"He even gives me an allowance—out of my own goddamned money." Marie shook her head as tears welled to threaten her careful makeup. Drunk's tears, but, unbelievable as it seemed, Jonas saw pity flash across the old man's face.

"Please," Marie choked, "tell me how I can find my brother."

Abruptly, Lukas's face slackened, and he shook his head. "Even if I could help you, I'm not sure I would. For, at the risk of trespassing any further into the personal than this conversation unfortunately has, please allow me to offer you some advice. Go back to rehab, Mrs. Carey. Go back to rehab and stay there. Hire a lawyer. Hire an entire legal team, if you want. Seek counseling, marital or otherwise. Seek spiritual enlightenment. Seek a divorce, if need be. But whatever you do, do not seek out your brother. And, for your sake, I only hope he will choose to do the same."

Chapter Eleven

Clare stared at herself in her dresser mirror, tracing the livid bruise on her neck as she asked herself what other evidence she really needed that Michael Grinnell was none of her concern. This had nothing to do with a saint's cause; it was a dangerous criminal investigation. And it didn't take a degree in psychology to realize that whatever anger she felt at the unfair treatment of Michael Grinnell was actually anger at how unfairly she herself had once been treated. The maligned boy she had so vehemently defended was nothing but a figment of her imagination. In reality, she knew nothing about Michael Grinnell. And if she had any common sense, she would keep it that way.

So why were her eyes drawn to the pile of change she had scooped up from the pavement what seemed like a lifetime ago? A motley collection of nickels, dimes, and quarters with a single flash of metallic green winking out from beneath it. Slowly, she reached for it. It was a green foil matchbook for a place called "Danny's Bar and Grill," located right across the borough line in Riverdale. "Live Music Nightly," the matchbook promised, above the sketch of a fiddle. And below that, a street address.

∞

Once upon a time, the stretch from Inwood, where Clare lived, up through Riverdale had been such a thoroughly Irish enclave that it was a St. Patrick's Day tradition to walk the entire length of Broadway in a satellite parade to the big parade downtown. From Manhattan to the Bronx, revelers stopped for a drink in each bar. Very few men made it all the way. Nowadays, that proud, Irish tradition existed only in vestiges: There was still hurling every Sunday in Gaelic Park, a run-down stadium nestled beneath the tracks of the Number 1 train; the Ancient Order of Hibernians still met in unmarked social clubs that opened unexpectedly from beneath parking garages and storefronts; and there were still a fair number of Irish pubs with names like the Liffey and Rosie O'Malley's—most of them with only a slightly less unwelcoming aspect as the AOH storefronts. Danny's was just such an establishment—its grimy window decorated with long-faded shamrocks, its windowless door almost invisible in the shadows cast by the elevated subway line. But as Clare swung open the door, the sound that spilled out left her in no doubt that she had found the busker—even before her eyes adjusted to the gloom, and she saw him up there on the stage, spinning out a melody that meandered through the smoke that swirled everywhere in defiance of every city regulation Clare knew of.

She was certain there were a lot of other regulations that were being ignored in this place as well. But the hard-faced men in worn blazers and tweed caps who sat at the bar made no move to stop her as she asked the bartender for a glass of wine. He lifted an eyebrow as if she had ordered something as exotic as a banana daiquiri, and, not bothering to ask whether she wanted white or red, rummaged beneath the bar to pour a stale-looking rosé into a heavily cut wineglass. Oh well. She wasn't here for the wine list, she told herself, as she settled in to listen.

He played even more beautifully than she remembered, and once again, she found herself wondering why he wasn't out on some concert stage, rather than in this run-down bar. Was it some kind of penance for his past life? If so, what kind of sins could be so unforgivable that he had to cut himself off like this?

When he had spun out the last notes, he looked up, and a trace of concern clouded his face. Setting his instrument carefully in its rack, he stepped down off the stage and moved straight to an empty booth where a pint of lager waited for him.

It wasn't quite an invitation, but it was close enough. She walked over. "May I join you for a moment?"

He cocked his head at her. "Do I know you?"

Seriously? Well, if that's how he wanted to play it.

"I bumped into you while you were playing outside the Church of St.Lazarus," she said, "and then again in an alley where I was being mugged."

"And you were so impressed, you came all the way down here to listen this evening? I'm flattered."

"I came down here because the first time you came to my rescue, you dropped this," she said. She fumbled in her pockets, pulled out the meager pile of change and laid it on the wooden table. "You were in such a hurry to run off that I thought the least I could do was return your takings."

He nodded slowly, making no move to pick up the change. Instead, he muttered something indecipherable about red hair.

"What was that?" she asked.

"I fancy redheads," he said with a sigh. "Always have. It seems to be my curse."

He fell silent, and she wondered if maybe he was about to bolt again. Or maybe even ask the bartender to have her removed, which to judge from the hard faces of the men around her, she had no doubt they'd do in an instant. "Please," she said, setting her glass down on the table, "just one drink."

A quick, nearly indiscernible smile flickered across his face when he saw the wine. "How deep beneath the bar did Martin have to rummage for that?"

"Pretty deep," she admitted. "What would have happened if I had asked for a Cosmopolitan?"

"He would have poured you an Irish whiskey and you would have drunk it like a good girl." He gestured for her to sit. "And probably would have preferred it. You want me to get you one now?"

And use that as an excuse to bolt straight out the back door? No thank you.

"My name's Clare," she said, as she slid onto the hard bench. "Clare Malley."

"Sean," he said. He didn't offer a last name.

She pursed her lips in frustration. But what had she expected, really? Hi, my name's Michael Grinnell, everyone's favorite miraculously-healed psychic monster returned from the dead?

Still, what if she was on the completely wrong track here? What if she had just tracked down some homeless street musician to the bar where he tried to stay warm at night?

Sean took a long draught of beer, and even with the dark glasses obscuring his face, she knew his eyes were glinting with amusement at her predicament. "So how did you find me?" he asked.

"You dropped a matchbook."

"A regular Nancy Drew." He rubbed his chin. "Didn't she have red hair too?"

"What is it with you and my hair?" she asked.

"Couldn't figure out any other reason why Martin would bother to look beneath the bar. Martin fancies redheads almost as much as I do. Reminds him of the auld sod. And it's the only way that he'd put up with any sort of nonsense about ordering wine."

He could go on like this all night, she realized, spinning out banter as easily as he spun music from his fiddle. And he would, unless she did something to stop it.

"Look, I apologize for bothering you," she said. "But, honestly, I need some answers."

"To any questions in particular?"

Yes. Are you Michael Grinnell? Do you actually have psychic powers? Are you really the monster everyone says you are? What do you know about that shooting at the Outreach Center?"

"Absolutely nothing."

"Then why were you there?"

He shrugged. "I heard their food was good. Wednesdays are spaghetti."

"You were playing your fiddle, not eating."

"Singing for my supper. So to speak. Seems only polite to drop a little in the poor box in return for my meal."

"Oh, come on. Do you seriously expect me to believe that?"

"I always tell the truth. It's said to be my stock in trade."

"Then why did you run away like that?"

"I try to keep moving. Couple of debt collectors on my case, that kind of thing."

Debt collectors? She glanced at his shirt—impeccably clean, carefully pressed, but worn through in several places—and she stopped, suddenly appalled. Even if he really was Michael Grinnell, he clearly wasn't worth a billion dollars. She had travelled all this way to return less than a dollar's worth of change. God, why hadn't she thought to bring some real money with her? Rafael was thirty dollars the richer, just for talking to her. How much should saving her life be worth?

Sean's expression softened. "Completely unnecessary," he said.

She shivered against the sensation that somehow he had read her mind. "What is?" she asked.

"Thanks," he said with a shrug. "A hero's welcome. A tickertape parade. Any of it. But it was good of you to make the effort."

Mind-reading. Talk about an overactive imagination. But with his eyes as inscrutable as a highway patrolman's behind the dark glasses he was wearing even in this smoke-filled bar …

"It's nearly pitch black in here," she asked. "How can you even see wearing those things?"

If he was startled by the question, he didn't show it. Just took another drink of his lager. "Maybe there are things I don't want to see."

"Those same things you were warning the kids about today?"

There it was. Cards well and truly on the table, as surely as if she'd asked to see his driver's license.

His face blossomed into a mischievous grin. "What? The woo woo, bad mojo, the Bogeyman's coming to get you schtick? Ah, come on now. You didn't really fall for that?"

"Those kids sure seemed to."

"Kids will believe anything. Hell, when I was their age, I still thought pro wrestling was on the up and up."

"Believing is one thing. Going into convulsions is another."

"Not really. Just depends on how believable you are. And I'm more believable than most. Martin would call it the gift of the Blarney."

And that was certainly the truth. Too bad he was clearly determined to deploy it full throttle against her. "Unfortunately, the local prosecutor is taking the whole thing a little more seriously than that. And if I were you, I'd steer clear of him. I'm guessing he sounds like Jack Webb, even in bed."

Sean laughed. "Why should he want to talk to me? Is he going to accuse me of stealing their lunch money?"

Once again, she sensed the unspoken challenge, daring her to ask the question she really wanted to ask. She plowed ahead. "Did you break into the Outreach Center and steal the files on Father Enoch?"

"Now, why would I do a thing like that?"

"I think that's what Trey Carey wants to ask you."

She thought she saw a flicker of emotion harden his face, but he hid it quickly by taking another drink. "I'm sorry. Who?"

"The local prosecutor. Apparently, he's also married to Marie Grinnell."

"Good for him. I hope they're happy. But I care about that why?"

"She's the sister of the kid those files are about. You know, Michael Grinnell."

She watched his face carefully as she finally threw down the gauntlet, but he didn't betray so much as a glimmer of a reaction.

"Not sure I'm following you anymore," he said, wiping a fleck of foam from his lips. "How exactly does any of this connect back to me?"

"Apparently that scene with the kids in the alley was a lot like some of Michael Grinnell's more well-known episodes."

Abruptly, his lazy humor vanished. "You tell Trey Carey about me and those kids?"

"I told Trey Carey you saved my life."

"Better if you hadn't told him anything at all."

He relaxed marginally, his voice almost reflective now. Evaluating. Considering his options. A chess player trying to consider how to best capitalize on a blunder. Her blunder. As if this were somehow all her fault.

"Maybe it would better if you don't run around saving people's lives, if you don't want to be hailed as a hero," she snapped.

"Trust me, that's my usual philosophy," he said. "You were just an … aberration."

"If you mean a mistake, why not just say so?"

"Because neither of us seems to have learned from it thus far."

Now he was clearly as nettled as she was, and she took obscure satisfaction in having gotten under his skin. For a moment, she just sat there, enjoying their angry silence, before she said coldly, "For what it's worth, I told them I had no idea who you were and where to find you. But I still thought I ought to at least let you know what's going on."

"So you headed straight down here so they could follow you."

He spoke completely without rancor, making the remark all the more cutting.

"Fine," Clare sighed. "Point taken. Case closed. I apologize for bothering you, and I'll get out of here before I can cause any more trouble. But I was just trying to do the right thing."

His expression softened, but only fractionally. "Nasty habit," he said. "You'll find life's a lot easier when you get rid of it."

God, why had she had even bothered? Who cared if he was running from the hounds of hell themselves? There was no reason he had to behave like an outright ass. "All right, I'm done," she said, sliding out of the booth. "Message delivered. Enjoy the rest of your life."

"I was doing just fine up until now," his voice trailed after her across the bar.

And he was welcome to go back to doing it again. Honestly, what was she even doing here? She should have listened to her common sense and stayed away. At the very least, she could take this as an object lesson and hope never to see him again in her life. But as she reached for the door, she saw the police car slide to a halt on the street outside. The cops didn't get out immediately, but it didn't take any great leap of the imagination to know they hadn't picked the spot because it was a good place to eat doughnuts.

"Aw, hell," she sighed.

She was speaking to thin air. The rest of the crowd had already simply faded away—Brigadoon in a speakeasy. But before she could open the door, a shadow rose behind her, and she felt Sean's hand on her arm. "You might want to think about using the back door," he said. "Could be a little awkward trying to explain what you're doing here."

"Why?" she asked. "I haven't done anything wrong."

"Neither have I," he said. "At least nothing that isn't covered by a statute of limitations. But I don't really fancy explaining that to your friend the prosecutor."

Her friend? More like his damned brother-in-law. "Go to hell," she snapped.

"Been there for a long time. Just trying to spare you the same."

"How cliché."

"Doesn't mean it's not true," he said. "Come on. I owe you this much."

And without waiting for her to acquiesce, he steered them both out through the kitchen in the back of the bar, and down an alley, through a warren of dumpsters and basement entrances, moving with such practiced ease that she was certain this wasn't the first time he had been forced to make such an escape. She couldn't have reproduced the crazy, catawampus route in her life, but through some legerdemain, they came full circle and back out, beneath the elevated train tracks, a safe distance from where a pair of cops was staring in bafflement at the shuttered front of Danny's Bar and Grill, its lights darkened, the door firmly locked.

Shaking his head, Sean turned away. "Martin's likely to dine out on this for years. Usually, it's just a pissed-off woman."

"And here I thought it was debt collectors."

"The more the merrier. I like to run."

"From what?" she asked. "And why?"

"From the things I don't want to see, I guess."

"Then it is true. You're—"

"Trouble you could live without." His face grew distant. "You need to go home. And you need to stay out of this. Don't go back to the Outreach Center. No more matchbooks. No more Nancy Drew. Just … forget about all this. Forget you were ever here."

Forget about a miracle cure? Forget about how he had saved her life with seemingly miraculous power? Forget how beautifully he played the fiddle. Or the way his entire face lit up when he really smiled? How exactly was she supposed to forget about any of that?

"Why?" she asked. "How much trouble can you really be?"

He laughed. "Trust me, Clare Malley. You don't want to find out."

He punctuated his words by taking her arm and turning her firmly toward the train stairs. As he did, her breast brushed across his fingers, and they both froze. He was going to kiss her, Clare thought. He was going to kiss her, and she had no idea what she was going to do about it …

"Go," his voice cut harshly into her whirling thoughts. "And just for the record, people who bring the police to the bar are not real welcome at Danny's. Come back again, and Martin's likely to throw you out. Literally. They don't call it hurling for nothing."

Spinning on his heel, he took off down the street, leaving Clare gaping like a lovelorn teenager hoping for her first kiss. Infuriated, she snapped out of it.

"Has anyone ever told you you're the most annoying man alive?" she called after him.

He didn't look back. But even from where she stood, she could hear the laughter in his voice. "Most of the women I meet seem to mention it sooner or later."

Chapter Twelve

Small wonder the old man had a soft spot for St. Anthony of Egypt. His veins clearly pulsed with the water from the country's biggest river: Denial. Not a word about the prosecutor's questions. Not a word about destroying evidence in a criminal investigation. Not a word about a bunch of drug dealers seeing Jesus in a back alley. Not even any lame bonding over doughnuts. Not on the quick drive home, and not when they got to the house. Instead, Lukas went straight to the kitchen, studied the cardboard boxes inside the freezer, and asked Jonas whether he preferred Tuna Noodle Casserole or Chicken a la King. Then he settled himself at the dinner table, folded open up a yellowed phrenological study of saints' heads, and began to read.

It was enough to make Jonas erupt. "You're unbelievable, you know that? Aren't you even going to ask?"

His father glanced at Jonas over the top of his reading glasses. "Ask about what?"

"What I did. What I stole. I mean, you'd think before you went to jail for me, you might want to know what I took."

"Can we stipulate for once and for all that I have no intention of going to jail?" Lukas paused to turn a page, then added, "And the fact of the matter is, I don't want to know."

"Why not?"

"Largely because it allows me to tell the prosecutor's office that I have no idea what might have been stolen from the Outreach Center's medicine supply without committing perjury," Lukas said, and went back to his reading.

Jonas stared his father. More accurately, he stared at the top of his father's head, bent over the pages as a signal the discussion had been ended. Unilaterally. As always.

Well, not this time. Jonas needed answers. Without them, he just might go crazy—more or less literally. "But supposing it's important," he pressed. "Supposing it had something to do with what happened to me?"

The old man never looked up from his article. But he wasn't reading anymore; you could tell that from the way a muscle began to twitch in his cheek.

"Given the fact that I have been mercifully spared the necessity of performing an actual post-mortem on you, I think we should dispense with any figurative ones as well. The case is closed. And I have every intention of leaving it that way."

"But what if it isn't?" Jonas swallowed hard, as he forced himself to give voice to what was really worrying him. What kept him up nights tossing and turning, and then kept following him in his nightmares, until he snapped awake bathed in sweat. "What if I'm turning into some kind of psycho? Just like the other ones."

The old man's face set. "Don't be stupid."

"I thought you said my IQ was 170."

"Don't be ironic either."

"I'm not being ironic! I'm asking a goddamned question. You heard what happened to those guys in the alley. What … he did to them. Did he do it to me, too?"

"What are you suggesting?" the old man snapped, finally goaded into looking up from his paper. "Some kind of … psychotic contagion?"

"I don't know. That's why I'm asking." Jonas bit his lip, then plowed ahead. "Is that why you're so scared of him?"

A long silence—so long that Jonas began to believe his father wasn't going to answer. Then Lukas drew a deep breath. "What happened between me and Michael Grinnell happened a long time ago," he said. "If, in fact, this man is even Michael Grinnell. As for what happened to you, I am operating on the assumption that what you thought you saw was most likely a hallucination, an enabling construct that allowed you to survive what, by all accounts, was a vicious and horrific attack."

And there it was. The moment to spit out the fear—hoping it wouldn't lodge halfway up his throat and choke him. "And supposing it was something else? Something I found—no, why fuck around with words? Something I stole."

His father went rigid. "Then I would very much like to hear what that is."

No turning back now, Jonas thought. "Down in the bottom of the medicine cabinet, there was a cooler. Like the loser vegan kids carry their lunch in. But it was full of vials."

"Vials?" Lukas repeated.

"You know, the kind of shit you can put needles into. The kind of shit that can cause hallucinations. Like heroin. Or acid."

"Heroin, to the best of my knowledge, does not induce hallucinations," the old man corrected him. "And I don't believe people inject LSD."

"Well, you're the expert, not me. All I'm saying is I'm thinking maybe that stuff … caused the … vision."

"A drug-induced hallucination rather than an enabling one?" Lukas raised an eyebrow, his demeanor growing more distant with each word. "And do you have any cause to believe this? For example, did you happen to … sample … any of these vials?"

"Maybe."

His eyebrow crept a fraction higher. "Would you care to be more specific?"

"I might care to be, but I don't know that I can. I sniffed a couple. Maybe tasted one or two. But it didn't seem like a good idea to mess around with shit I didn't know anything about."

Lukas stiffened with each syllable Jonas spoke. Finally, he spoke. "So stipulated. And I hope a valuable life lesson learned. In the meantime, I suggest we should both count ourselves fortunate that nothing more happened, that you were not harmed."

"But what if it's more? What if … I shouldn't have … even touched it? What if, it fucked me up permanently?"

There was a long pause, during which Jonas flinched, sure that his father was going to explode. Yell. Scream. Throw down his fork and reach across the table to grab Jonas by the neck. And Jonas would have welcomed any of that. But when his father spoke, his voice was flat and emotionless. "Have you seen anything since you saw this ... vision?"

"No."

Something seemed to crumble in the old man—something that in someone else might have been relief. "Then I think we should be grateful for the near miss, and do our best to put this episode behind us."

The old man turned back to his reading, peering through his glasses at the dead saints' heads, snorting in disgust as he reread a passage, then double-checked a measurement using his cutlery as calipers, before scribbling a correction in the margin. The discussion was clearly closed, and not even Jonas's pulling out his cell phone and checking his Facebook page—a gesture that usually elicited a furious lecture on table manners and the cost of cell phone usage—could breach the stony silence that followed. In fact, Jonas was certain that they were destined to sit just like that all night—his father deliberately refusing to notice anything, while Jonas aimlessly Liked the pages of *Playboy* models—had not the silence been broken by Lukas's phone ringing.

Lukas stiffened when he saw the caller ID. "Upstairs, to your room," he said to Jonas. "If you would be so good."

And that was scary strange, too. Because, however much the old man tried to hide it, Jonas knew that he hated it when Jonas climbed the stairs up to his room. Hated knowing that there was one place Jonas could go where his father couldn't find him; hated the reminder that there were some things he just couldn't do. Hated having to wonder what Jonas was doing up there. And Jonas had used that knowledge as a weapon every chance he got, turning up the sound of the video games he played when he was supposed to be doing his homework, and working on his computer into all hours of the night, long after the old man had retired to his office to drink himself to sleep.

Now his father was ordering him there? "Why?" Jonas balked. "Who is that?"

"Go!" his father snapped back over his shoulder, as the doorbell rang.

With a snort, Jonas went upstairs. There was an old heating duct between his rooms and his father's lab. Most of the time, there was nothing to hear except the old man's capacity for enduring the world's most excruciating operas. But just then, there was something to hear. And Jonas had every intention of listening.

Lukas greeted his guest with, "No offense, Trey, but it's late. Jonas is already in bed for the night, and I tend to retire early myself."

"I'll make this quick." Trey said. "I just heard about Marie's drunken display at the Outreach Center, and I'd like to apologize on her behalf. She's been under considerable stress as of late ... our marriage isn't all it could be. Still, it's no excuse."

"Well, thank you. I appreciate that. But surely that could have kept until tomorrow."

"I admit there's a little more to it than that. Something I thought we'd be better off discussing privately. I heard Marie made some fairly insulting allegations. Money laundering in the shelter? Blackmail? Payoffs?"

"Allegations I have every intention of overlooking. By her own admission, she was drunk."

"Yes, but even drunks manage to hit the target by accident."

A thunderous silence. And then Lukas said, "If you have an accusation to make, I would prefer you do it publicly. And be prepared to prove it."

"No, no, no. No accusations. At least, not against you. I've asked around. There isn't a person who knows you who wouldn't attest to your stern moral fiber. As a matter of fact, many would say it's your defining characteristic."

"Then who are you accusing? Am I supposed to infer that you believe that Sister St. John is raiding the poor box in order to do what? Buy food for the poor?"

Trey went on as if Lukas hadn't spoken. "I've got to say, though, I was a little surprised at what I discovered when I was reading up on you. "It's quite some bio. Twenty years ago you were All Saints' boy wonder. A regular Doogie Howser. MD/PhD at twenty-five. First Grinnell Science Fellowship All Saints ever offered."

"That was a long time ago," Lukas said.

"Still, it's hard to understand how you wound up like this. Honestly, Lukas. Desiccated fingers? Miraculously reconstituted blood? Is that what you call a career?"

"No," Lukas said. "That's what I do pro bono. Or as other people would put it, for fun."

"Then you consider herding drunken undergraduates and treating bums' skin rashes a career? Personally, I call it a waste of your time and talent." Trey's voice hardened. "Why Lukas? What is this? Some kind of penance?"

"I'm under no obligation to explain my motives to you."

A long pause. And then Trey said, "Well, actually, at times you are. Especially when they come complete with means and opportunity."

"I thought you said you weren't accusing me."

"I'm not. No reason to get defensive."

"I'll try not to. But it would help considerably if you answered the question."

"All right. Cards on the table. I'll be honest with you."

Which Jonas remembered reading somewhere was the surest sign that someone was about to lie to you.

"Look, have you ever had plumbing work done?" Trey asked. "You know how a plumber traces leaks?"

"On some theoretical level, I suppose, yes, I do, although I admit being hard-pressed to recall the specifics."

"They put dye in the water. A different dye in each pipeline. That way you can see which line the leak is coming from."

"And this is important exactly why? Do we have plumbing problems in the Outreach Center?"

"After a fashion."

"Money laundering?" The old man's voice was as indifferent as if he were discussing a clogged drain.

"Drugs," Trey said.

"You mean, the break-in? I've already told you, I can't tell what's missing."

"I mean, the Lazarus Vector," Trey said. "Those records you stumbled across."

Jonas felt his father's thunderous silence racing straight up the heating duct, louder than even the awful opera. "You're saying they're evidence of some kind of drug ring?" he finally said.

"I'm saying they're evidence in a special operation conducted by my office."

Another long pause. "And by 'special' I suppose I should read 'covert'."

"I assure you, we're not doing anything illegal. Hell, I'm a prosecutor. You can take my word on it."

"Unethical, then?" Lukas inquired. "Immoral?"

"Relax Lukas, we're on the same side here. It's the Lazaritos we're after, not you. You know, the punks who shot your son?"

"My son has nothing to do with this."

"If you say so. The point is, those punks have been running drugs through the shelter for years. Couldn't stop them, so we figured we might as well use them. Put markers on different drugs, so we can trace their distribution networks. Map the pathways—"

"You mean, the vectors," Lukas said. "As in Lazarus Vector. Hence, the catchy name."

"We're compiling a case that will take down drug dealing in the Bronx as we know it."

"You're using the Outreach Center to entrap them."

"'Entrap' is a strong word," Trey said. "I prefer map. Tracing the pathways, that's all we're doing."

"And am I to believe that Sister St. John has been apprised of this … plumbing project?"

Yeah. Sure. If the old nun had heard a thing about it, she'd be chained to the church steeple singing "We Shall Overcome."

"Wonderful woman, Sister St. John. A true vocation. Salt of the earth."

In other words, no.

"But not exactly a woman of the world, if you know what I mean. An idealist."

"You say that as if it's a bad word."

"I'm a practical man, Lukas. I admit that. Which is why I'm not ashamed to admit that right now, I think we would all benefit if this program were quickly and quietly shut down for the time being."

"In other words, you want me to cover this up for you?"

"There's no question of a cover-up, because there's no question of any wrongdoing. But, given the recent episode with those gang members in the alley, perhaps emotions are running too high for its worth to be genuinely appreciated."

"Or, to put it a little differently, you're worried about the effect the story getting out could have on your congressional campaign. Well, I'm sorry, Trey, but I'm just not interested."

"Maybe not. But I can't possibly believe that you wouldn't be interested in knowing the exact extent to which your son has involved himself in this … unfortunate incident."

The words hit Jonas like a gut punch. What the fuck was the asshole saying?

"Come on, Lukas. You know and I know, we're on the same side here. Problem is, plumber's dye doesn't know sides. Plumber's dye just marks trails. Leaves traces of whoever's been stealing from the Outreach Center. It doesn't care who left them."

"In other words, you're offering me a quid pro quo," Lukas said, very, very quietly. "You'll hide my son's involvement in exchange for me covering this up."

So it had all been for nothing. The staged break-in. The carefully scattered documents. They had had Jonas all along. And now they were holding him over his father.

Fuck, no. That was enough. He'd go down there. He'd tell the prick to charge him if he wanted to, but lay off his fucking Dad.

But before he could even scramble to his feet, Lukas's voice floated up through the heating duct, about 100 degrees colder than Jonas had ever heard it. "Then it's fortunate for both of us that the question is moot. Whoever broke in left the place a shambles. There's no way anyone could reconstruct anything at this point."

"I knew I could trust you," Trey said. He sounded like he wanted to slap Lukas on the back. Jonas wished he would. He had a feeling the asshole's hand would freeze right off.

"Trust is not the same thing as coercion."

"In my world, it is. Look, all you need to know is that your son is safe. And your hands are clean."

A long pause. "So spoke Pontius Pilate," his father finally said. "And it didn't go so well with him."

"Went worse for a lot of other people in that story," Trey said. "Good night, Lukas. I'll let myself out."

Jonas waited until the door clicked shut. And then he crept downstairs, punching out the combination on the door to his father's lab by sheer muscle memory. "Dad?" he said. "I know you didn't want me to listen …"

But Lukas didn't seem to hear him. As the lab door swung open, Jonas caught sight of the old man spinning his wheelchair before he lunged for the bottle of scotch, only to find himself caught against an imperfectly closed file drawer that forced him to lean awkwardly to shut it with a muffled curse.

The sight made Jonas step back. He had never seen his father physically helpless before; the man was so cat-like, it was hard to even think of him as disabled. And suddenly Jonas found himself wondering what it felt like never to be able to walk again. Whether the great Lukas Croswell ever got tired or sad or just plain frustrated.

Slamming the drawer shut, his father just sat there after he'd freed himself—staring at God alone knew what. And then he picked up the bottle that always sat ready at hand, and simply threw it against the wall, where it shattered, splashing scotch and broken glass everywhere.

Shaking uncontrollably, Jonas turned and slunk upstairs to his room somehow knowing, even then, that when he snuck back down with a broom and a mop in the wee hours of the morning, as if somehow maybe cleaning up the mess his father had made would magically also serve to clean up the even worse mess that lay between them, he wouldn't find the faintest trace of spilled scotch or broken glass anywhere. Everything would have been meticulously tidied, and a new bottle of scotch would sit by the battered recliner, filled, Jonas was certain, to exactly the same level it had been before his father had thrown it.

Chapter Thirteen

Something had changed with the fiddler. He'd always played with the intensity of a man gambling with his own soul, but now he played as a man possessed. And if a couple of the regulars at Danny's could trace the change back to a single conversation with a pretty little redhead, they were wise enough to do nothing but grin knowingly at the real demon that rode the fiddler, and enjoy the wild tide of music that filled the night.

It was nearly midnight when he stepped off the stage, his hair and face damp, his shirt sweat-stained. But as he reached for his lager, a man in black, sitting shadowed in the booth—a priest—raised his own glass. "You're not an easy man to find," the priest said. "But the music was well worth the inconvenience."

The fiddler choked. And then he leaned his head against the wooden back of his seat. "Funny," he said, "I wouldn't have taken your type for a drinking man."

"Our Savior turned water into wine."

"Not in this establishment," Sean snorted.

"Nonetheless, the whiskey is fine." The priest took a long, appreciative draught, then said, suddenly serious, "We need to talk, Mi—"

"Sean," the fiddler cut him off quickly. "I don't answer to anything else anymore."

"Or anyone else either, it would seem. Including your own father …"

Sean lifted a shoulder. "Wouldn't be the first time a son has let his father down."

"And it wouldn't be the first time a son has returned from the mire of a pigsty to accept his father's embrace," the priest said.

Sean's face lit with genuine humor. "Just a friendly word of advice," he said. "I wouldn't say that too loudly around here. These lot are good Catholic lads and all that, but they're not as up on their Bible stories as many. Tend to take a literal view of interpretation, if you know what I mean. They might just hear you compare them to swine and … take umbrage."

"They always said sarcasm was one of your most unpleasant qualities." The priest took a moment to study Sean, then held out his hand. "Father Dominic Gregory."

"Sean," the fiddler said, without shaking hands. "Just Sean. As for the sarcasm, I haven't improved with age. So if this is just a social visit—"

"It's not."

"Official business then? You hoping to cast out a few demons before the lads cast you out of the bar? Or maybe you think you're going to bring me back to the flock? Save my soul after all? Even exorcise me, maybe?"

"That's another department," Father Gregory said. He took another sip and set the glass down. "I suppose if I'm being honest with myself, there's no reason this couldn't have been accomplished with a phone call. So I'm forced to admit to a certain need to see for myself. 'Unless I see the nail marks in his hands and put my finger where the nails were, and put my hand into his side, I will not believe.' I'm afraid a healthy dose of St. Thomas seems to come with the Jesuit formation."

Sean snorted as he reached for his lager. "Sounds to me like you're getting me mixed up with another guy."

"I don't think so," Father Gregory said. "In any case, that's not why I'm here. I need to talk to you about your sister."

The fiddler tensed. "In case she hasn't told you, she and I aren't exactly what you'd call close."

"She's in trouble. Spinning completely out of control."

"It's a phase Grinnells go through."

"I'm afraid I was speaking a little more literally than that. Her BAC was measured at approximately .25 when her car spun out of control after she stormed out of a fund-raiser in a drunken rage. Her husband only just barely managed to convince the judge to send her to rehab instead of jail. Now she's run off with nearly a month of treatment still left."

The fiddler laughed. "She's on the lam? Hell, maybe there's more to her than I thought."

"Be that as it may, she's also played straight into the hands of her husband, who is apparently mentally, if not actually physically, abusive."

"Could have told you that the first time I met the prick," Sean snorted.

"And yet you did nothing to help her?"

Sean's mouth twisted. "People weren't exactly glad to hear my opinions in those days. Probably still aren't. The sarcasm thing and all that."

"He's arranged for your father's estate to be placed into conservatorship, until either all the heirs or your father's missing will can be found. Given your sister's apparent determination to prove she is completely incompetent to manage her own affairs, that conservatorship is very likely to become permanent." Father Gregory took a reflective sip of whiskey. "You could change that."

"You really believe the world would be any better off with me running Grinnell than that asshole?"

"It doesn't matter what I believe. The question is, if you didn't think so, why did you show up at the Church of St. Lazarus after all these years?"

"You don't think I haven't been asking myself the same damned question?" Sean shook his head. "Sheer bloody coincidence, nothing more. But I guess you just can't outrun destiny, no matter how hard you try."

"Augustine, among others, would beg to differ with you."

Sean took an angry swig of beer. "So what do you want me to do? Show up dead on my sister's doorstep with my birth certificate pinned to my shirt?"

"Why are you so bitter?"

Sean froze. And then he shook his head. "I'm not bitter. I just want to be left alone."

"Unfortunately, that's not a possibility right now. You need to exercise your father's will."

"Like I said, you're getting me confused with another guy."

"Once again, I meant it more literally. You need to step forward and claim your inheritance." The priest's eyes darkened. "I don't talk a lot about good and evil. It's out of fashion these days. But I do know a thing or two about the subject—enough to know that I mean it when I say Trey Carey is evil. And, trust me, that is not something one says lightly about one's biggest donor."

"So you've come to make a deal with the devil to stop him."

"I've come to inform you of the situation. Even though I'm fairly certain you have been well aware of what's going on all along."

Sean's face flattened. And then he forced a shrug. "Kind of my stock in trade. Or so they say." He cast a longing look at his empty glass, then shook his head. "So go ahead and have me declared dead. I won't fight it."

"That would be a terrible mistake."

"I don't make mistakes, remember?"

"Then am I to assume you are deliberately turning a blind eye to what will happen if you leave this to your sister? She's … a frail woman."

"You mean she drinks and sleeps around?"

"We all have our weaknesses."

"Tell me about it." Sean spent another moment studying his empty glass. And suddenly his face shadowed. "That why you sent Clare Malley after me, then?"

"I beg your pardon?"

"You figured she's my weakness, so you'd send her down to talk to me into doing what you want?" Sean's voice was carefully casual. "Catch more flies with honey and all that?"

The shadow of a speculative smile crossed Father Gregory's face. "Is that another way of saying that maybe you've found something in life that you're not so sure you want to piss away?"

The change was immediate. The casual tone vanished; Sean's voice grew soft and vicious. "Try to manipulate me with her, and I promise I will destroy you. Not kill you. Destroy you. Make you wish that you were dead. And if you don't believe I can do that, ask someone who knew me when I was a kid—ask Lukas Croswell."

"Oh, I thoroughly believe you can do it. However, I'm afraid I don't scare very easily. You see, I've faced down Sandinistas. If you believe the more hysterically minded of my colleagues, I've faced down a Prince of Hell. More importantly, I've faced down Sister St. John. So believe me when I say that it is common decency, not fear, that impels me to assure you that I sent Clare Malley to investigate a miracle, not to manipulate you. And frankly, I believe if I had asked her to do that, she would have refused outright." Swallowing off the last of his whiskey, the priest stood. "And I think you know that as well as I do. Because that's the attraction, isn't it? No greater aphrodisiac than innocence is there, for those of us who lost it a long time ago?"

"Go to hell."

"I pray none of us do," Father Gregory said. "Still, we're losing track of the point. Your sister's in trouble, and you are the one person who can help her. The choice is up to you."

"No such thing in this world," Sean said. "We're all just pawns in someone else's chess game."

"You're the chess master, not me. But isn't it true that Philidor became the greatest chess master of the nineteenth century—if not the greatest chess master ever—by discovering the importance of pawns?" Not waiting for an answer, Father Gregory turned for the door. "Chess master or pawn, the next move is up to you."

Chapter Fourteen

You didn't have to be Nancy Drew to figure out where those missing files had gone. You didn't even have to have red hair. In the words of another detective, the answer was elementary. Sean was the only one with a reason to take those records; no one was arguing otherwise. But the files were bulky, sheaves of yellowed pages spilling out of a dented cardboard box. You couldn't have helped but notice if someone had been carrying them. And when Sean had confronted those kids in the alley, he had been empty-handed. Clare would be willing to swear to that in court. So logically, he had to have hidden the files somewhere between the sacristy and the alley. And given what Clare was already beginning to understand of Sean's sense of irony, there was only one place he would have left them.

The Outreach Center's recycling had been neatly sorted into green, blue, and clear plastic bags. It came as no surprise that Sean had been equally tidy—to the point of making sure his files were discarded into the green bags with the rest of the paper. Clare found them tossed on top of a mixture of bills, supermarket circulars, catalogues, and used paper plates, with the twist tie that sealed the bag carefully replaced. Only a moment's further searching found the broken box folded and bound with other flattened cardboard.

But as she reached for the crumbling folders, Clare found herself hesitating. Good for you, Nancy, solved that one without Ted or even Georgie. But now what? She supposed she should find a somewhat sturdier box than the one the papers had come in, fold it back into shape, and rescue the papers. They were still salvageable; it looked like they hadn't sustained too much damage from grease or dirt.

But their legibility was one thing; the question of reading them was another. Even if she had a mandate from the Vatican itself, did she really have a right to pry?

But what was the alternative? To leave the papers here, until the garbage trucks finally arrived to take them off for pulping, expunging the Cause of Father Enoch from the human record as completely as scores of other books that had been lost to history? You didn't have to be a medievalist to be acquainted with the grim roster of examples, but it helped. Savonarola and his *Bonfire of the Vanities*. Avicenna burning the Royal Library of the Samanids after he had committed all its contents to memory so that no other man could discover the source of his knowledge. *The Decameron*. *Tyndale's New Testament*. Abelard being forced to burn his own book—arguably a worse injury than the one he suffered at the hands of Heloise's furious kinsmen. The sacred codices of the Mayans, burned on the orders of the priests who professed to have come to civilize them. The Library of Alexandria, which contained such knowledge, that is was said had it survived, man would have been on the moon by the year 1000.

But that kind of thinking belonged to the Cause of Father Enoch. It was another thing altogether if you considered this the Case of Michael Grinnell. Didn't he have the right to his own privacy?

Or had he given up that right when he decided to transform himself from Michael Grinnell into a street musician named Sean?

No, that was casuistry worth of a Jesuit. She had no right to look. She had two choices: Do as Sean wanted and let them be pulped. Or return them to their rightful owner before someone else found them.

But wasn't that just an excuse as well? A reason to go back down to the bar where it had been made clear she was not welcome, in order to badger the most annoying man alive?

"He tell you where to find them?" an all-too-familiar voice cut through her whirling thoughts in quick, prosecutorial stabs. "He ask you to bring them back to him?"

So much for making up her own mind about what to do. It was too late for that now. Tossing the folders she was holding on top of the cardboard box, Clare turned to confront Trey Carey. "I'm beginning to feel like I'd better not answer any questions without a lawyer."

"Clare, please. We're not the enemy here."

She shut her eyes. How many times had the Victim's Advocate uttered that exact phrase? In exactly that same tone of condescending reason?

"And I'm supposed to believe Sean is?"

"Who … oh, is that what he's calling himself these days?" Trey studied her. "Since when are you two on a first name basis?"

She glared at him. "Since I found the bar where he plays at night—and was followed there by the cops. Do you know anything about that?"

If she had hoped to trip him up by being direct, it didn't work. He didn't bother to deny the accusation. He didn't even have the grace to look ashamed. If anything, he looked proud, as he said, "Look, I don't mind admitting we take care of our own. Just like I don't mind admitting, you solved a major problem for us. There was no way we could have tracked him down. But you were venturing into a dangerous situation, a situation that we legally couldn't take on ourselves. And we appreciate that. So I'm not afraid to let you know, we've got your back."

"I'd prefer to have my privacy respected. Along with Sean's. And as long as we're discussing the legality of the situation, since these are clinical evaluations, I assume medical privacy laws would apply." Hastily refolding the box, and tossing the folders into it, she slapped the lid down, feeling absurdly like a wronged wife slamming shut a suitcase before storming out of the house for good. "So I am going to take these papers back to their rightful owner. If you follow me this time, I will file a formal harassment complaint."

Hoisting the box, she turned to go, but Trey stepped in her way.

"Look, I understand he's convinced you that he's some kind of victim here," he said. "And that's not really surprising. By all accounts, Michael can be charming when he wants to. But don't delude yourself. He was … is dangerous."

"You make him sound like some kind of psychopath."

"More accurately, a high-functioning sociopath. According to what's widely regarded as the most definitive diagnosis. Incapable of love or any other human emotion. People are just chess pieces to him. A means to an end."

"And whose diagnosis was that?"

Trey's face hardened. "Lukas Croswell's. Delivered shortly before the car crash that left him in a wheelchair and ruined what promised to be a brilliant medical career."

"And how was Sean supposed to have done that? Telekinesis?"

Trey didn't answer right away, and Clare felt silent. Her mouth was running away from her, just as it always had when she was a kid. But the thing was, she wasn't a kid anymore. And any adult would realize that it was probably less than diplomatic to get shrill with your employer's major donor. Not to mention the local prosecutor.

"Lukas never talks about the incident," Trey said. "But I can assure you that he was a changed man afterward. A changed and very damaged man. Far beyond the physical damage. Gave up on his career, gave up on science. Most count him lucky to have survived. But there are several who would say Lukas survived only because Michael wanted it that way, wanted to keep him alive to play with him, prolong the torture. An extra-special punishment for having spoken the truth about what he was."

No, that was impossible. The stuff out of a horror novel, not real life. Still, Clare couldn't help but remember the concern in Lukas Croswell's voice when he warned her away from Michael. And Lukas had not impressed her as a man who scared easily.

But was that proof that Michael Grinnell was a sadistic monster?

Even if it was, what did it matter? Michael Grinnell was none of her concern. She had never even met Michael Grinnell. The man she had met was a fiddler named Sean, whose only friend seemed to be his music.

"If he's really that dangerous to deal with, why not do what he wants and leave him alone?" she asked.

Trey thought for a moment, his gaze as appraising as if he were about to move a few chess pieces himself. "Because at this point, I don't think he'll go away even if we do," he finally said.

"What do you mean, at this point? What's changed?"

But Clare didn't really need to ask. She already knew the answer to the question. And she already knew it was going to be exactly the same as the last time her life had spun so horribly out of control.

"I'm not sure what brought him crawling out of the woodwork in the first place." The inevitable words fell with the weight of a judge pronouncing sentence. "But I'm beginning to believe that what's keeping him here is you."

So there it was. Just like last time. Not her fault, of course, but her fault entirely. She could feel the resentment begin to swell across more than a decade, and just barely managed to tamp it. "Are you suggesting," she asked, "that I somehow lured him here?"

"Look, no one's blaming you for the situation. You're as much a victim here as anyone. It's just your bad luck that you happened to attract the attention of a sociopath who'll stop at nothing to get what he wants. And what he wants right now is you."

"That's impossible. He didn't even wait for me to finish my drink before he threw me out of the bar pretty much bodily. Told me never to come back."

"He may have meant it at the time," Trey said. "But I'm warning you, he will be back."

Oh, God. This was more than a flash of unwelcome memory. This was it, a replay, all beginning again. The anxious, reassuring words that were really nothing but an accusation: that Clare could have done something differently, that Clare could have prevented this, if only she had stopped to think. That deep down, it was really all Clare's fault.

Her thoughts soured as she thought back to a past she only wanted to forget, and it was a relative relief when Trey's voice jabbed in to stop them. "So maybe," he said, "we should preempt him. Go ahead and find him."

"Well, you apparently now know where to look."

He ignored the obvious bitterness in her voice. "I wasn't thinking me. I was thinking you," he said. "I was thinking that maybe you should go ahead and give him what he wants. Maybe you should head down to that bar and give him back his files."

Clare shook her head slowly, that old feeling of helplessness threatening to overwhelm her. "I should?" was all she could manage to say.

"Don't get me wrong. He's a cold and ruthless bastard. As incapable of feelings for a woman as feelings for anything else. But right now, he wants you. And that's a significant vulnerability. It gives us a chance."

"And you said he was the one who saw people as pawns."

"If you bring him those files," Trey went on as if she hadn't spoken, "you may be able to establish some kind of trust between you ..."

Prosecutor be damned, donor be damned, Clare's temper finally gave out. "And so you want me to use my womanly wiles to find out what he's up to?" she exploded. "Well, not only do I find that morally offensive, I think you are running very close to a sexual discrimination suit to go along with the harassment suit."

Hoisting the box, she turned to go for real this time. And Trey changed tacks, his eyes suddenly snake-cold. Colder than a chess master. Colder than the sociopath he claimed Michael Grinnell was.

"Dr. Malley, romantic as you might find Michael's seeming predicament, I have to warn you that you do not want me as an enemy."

Romantic? What the hell had been romantic about the memories resurfacing in earnest now, memories she thought she had buried long ago? Of the hurt in the eyes of a man being led away in handcuffs, guilty of nothing more heinous than terrible meter and trite metaphors.

"No," she said, "I don't want you as an enemy. But I will not let that stop me from doing the right thing this time around."

"This time?" Trey asked.

Clare's stomach tightened. But what could really happen? The past was behind her. Those records were sealed. "Excuse me," she said. "I'm leaving now."

"Of course." Trey stepped aside with elaborate courtesy. "Just one more thing. Right and wrong, that's Father Gregory's world, not mine. In my world, you are either for me or against me. So I suggest you choose your side carefully."

"Don't worry," Clare said. "I already have."

Chapter Fifteen

The shadow reared out of nowhere, blocking her way into Danny's Bar.

"What part of 'Don't come back or Martin will throw you out bodily' did you see as open to interpretation?" Sean asked.

"How did you know I was coming?"

His mouth twisted into something that might have been a smile. "It was somewhere between predictable and inevitable. Like most things in my world." He waved his hand at the box she was carrying. "But I assume you've gathered all that from your background reading."

She drew a deep breath, reminding herself that she had known this wouldn't be easy. "I've heard some things from Father Gregory and Lukas Croswell, yes," she said. "But I didn't read your files."

"Then why did you take them?"

"Because someone else was bound to find them," she said. "Honestly, if you really wanted to get rid of them, you ought to have done a better job of it."

An odd expression fleeted across his face. "Most people would say I'm not prone to making those kinds of mistakes. Comes along with the evil, prescient genius territory, if you know what I mean."

"So is Trey Carey, right then? Did you really take them just because you wanted me to find them and come after you?"

He flushed. "With all due respect, I'm the mind-reader around here. Not Trey."

"Then you must also already know that he wanted me to come here because he thinks I'll gain your trust and you'll tell me what you're up to."

"I see." The muscles in his jaw twitched. "And how far does he think you're willing to go to get that information?"

The most annoying man alive, remember. And an expert at keeping people from answering questions he didn't want asked. "As far as I was concerned, his even suggesting the idea was going too far. I'm no Femme Nikita."

Sean studied her, eyes inscrutable as always behind the dark glasses. And then he grinned. "A man can always hope."

Hope what? That she was a Femme Nikita? That she would come after him? She tried to marshal her thoughts, reminding herself that keeping her off-stride was just one of the man's impressive arsenal of defenses. "Am I seriously supposed to believe that's why you stole the files?"

"Not files. My life," he said sharply. "And it seems to me like someone stole it from me first."

"So you really took them because you're afraid it's all going to happen again?"

He shook his head. "You have no idea what it was like."

"On the contrary, I think I do."

It was the wrong thing to say. His face hardened. "That's worthy of Oprah's couch," he snorted. "What's next, a group hug? Even if you're no Femme Nikita, I thought you'd be better than that."

"Actually, it's nothing but the truth," Clare said. "But why take my word for it? The way I understand it, you could just go ahead and take a look for yourself."

She felt a small surge of sour satisfaction when she saw him flinch.

"That's not how it works," he said. "It's not a Magic 8 ball, you know."

"Then I guess you'll just have to believe me when I say I understand why you took those files."

"And I guess it really doesn't matter to me whether you do or not," he snapped. "That's why I didn't ask your permission."

She struggled to control her temper. "And I'm not here to give you permission. Just the files." She held out the box, willing herself not to throw them at him and storm off—as he so obviously wanted her to do. "But I'm not going to lie to you and say I don't want to know what's in them."

"Then you should have read them while you had the chance."

"It wouldn't have done any good. I want to hear it from you, not read a bunch of medical records."

He shouldered the box. "And why is that?"

"Because I want to know ... you."

"No, you don't. Ask around. My reputation precedes me."

And right about now, Clare was ready to believe him. She had known he would throw up more defenses than a roadblock at a border crossing, but it still didn't prepare her for how hard it would prove. "I don't care about your reputation. I want to know *you*."

"What do you think you're going to find out that you don't already know?"

"To start with, why did you show up at the church?"

"It was a mistake. There's nothing I want there."

"Two in a row. That must be some kind of record for you." She shook her head. "So what was it you were you hoping to find? What is it you really want?"

"Not a whole hell of a lot." He raised a shoulder. "Music. Decent lager. To kiss a pretty girl now and then."

He broke off, flushing once again, and Clare doubted she would get a better opening.

"Please," she said. "I'm not here to track down miracles. Or your secret, evil master plan, if you have one. And I'm certainly not going to tell Trey Carey anything. But I would ... I mean, if you think you're able ... I'd very much like ... to understand."

He drew a deep breath, clearly at war with himself. And then he checked his watch. "I'll give you half an hour. Then I need to go downstairs and play." A hint of humor flashed across his face. "But if you don't mind, let's take this discussion upstairs. I'm here to entertain the lads with music, nothing more. I don't really fancy branching out."

"What's upstairs?" she asked.

"My place. Martin lets me have it in exchange for the music," he said. The hint of humor broadened into a smile as she tried to hide her surprise. "What did you think? I sleep in train stations?"

Well, yes, she thought as she followed Sean up the cramped, dark staircase. She supposed if she thought about it, that was exactly what she thought. And yet, one look at this apartment, and she could imagine him living no place else. The furnishings were minimal: A threadbare couch and battered recliner with a chess set laid out on a table that stood beside it; a neatly-made bed just visible in the front room; and a small kitchen with a table and two chairs behind her. The only decoration was a spare violin, hanging on the wall above the bed. In other words, it told her absolutely nothing about the man she didn't already know.

"Glass of water? Cup of tea?" Sean offered, moving to the tiny kitchen. "Something stronger? I've got some whiskey up here, and there's what Martin claims to be a fully-stocked bar downstairs."

She winced at the memory of the sticky, sweet wine. "I wouldn't mind some tea."

"With a medicinal splash of whiskey," he decided. "I don't know about you, but I for one could use it."

He turned to the task of making tea with swift, sure movements, situating the kettle on the small stove and flipping on the burner, then pulling down the whiskey bottle from a high shelf, completing his task with such furious concentration that it could have been a Zen ritual.

"So what do you say we get the speed date over with?" he sighed, as he returned to the living room and handed her a mug. "What do you really want to know about me? Sports teams? Drink preferences? Zodiac sign? Whether Father Gregory was right when he said I was an unholy monster?"

Her eyes widened. "How did you know…?"

"Somewhere between predictable and inevitable, and all that," he reminded her with a tired smile. "So go ahead. Fire away. There's no way you're going to shock me, no matter what you ask."

And suddenly she found herself hesitant, blowing on her tea until it was cool enough to sip before she asked, "Are you really a sociopath?"

He snorted. "Nothing like getting straight to the point. Still, I suppose I asked for it." Shaking off her stammered protest, he said, "Yes, that seemed to be the consensus on most of the medical charts I wasn't supposed to be reading upside down."

She nodded slowly, glancing around the Spartan apartment. No, not Spartan. Monastic. Preternaturally clean as well as preternaturally plain. Not just a solitary existence, a hermetical one. The only difference was, a violin hung on the wall in place of a crucifix. "And so… this is all just some kind of penance?"

"Not penance. Peace."

"From?"

"From what I see all around me, unless I'm careful not to look."

"And that's why you wear the dark glasses?" she asked. "To block out the things you don't want to see?"

"Actually they don't do a damned thing except make me trip over curbs if I'm not careful."

"And look cool."

"If you say so."

He flushed again, and she found it absurdly appealing. Some sociopath determined to stop at nothing to get her. When it came to girls, he was as bashful as a ten year old. "What is it you're trying so hard not to see?"

"The ugliest, nastiest part of any person I choose to look at, the part they're too scared to admit even to themselves."

She nodded slowly. It wasn't exactly a surprise, but it still chilled her to hear the words spoken aloud. "And that's why people called you a monster?"

"I was young," he said. "I hadn't learned how to keep my mouth shut."

"Seems to me that's as much their fault as yours. They could always have stopped asking questions."

Even behind the dark glasses, she could feel him shoot a sharp glance in her direction. But he returned to studying his tea with as much intensity as if he were reading the leaves at the bottom. "At first, I tried to scare them just to get them to leave me alone," he said. "Later on, I … I think I liked it."

She swallowed hard, telling herself she was unsurprised at the admission. Father Gregory had said as much, hadn't he? "But you don't like scaring people now," she said.

"Might be more accurate to say, I try to stick around people who can't be scared. Lads like those down at the bar—the kind who've stared their inner demons in the face and come to a gentlemen's arrangement a long time ago. But it's still a hellish thing."

"And what exactly is 'it'?" Clare asked.

Sean shrugged. "Well now," he said, "that really is the question, innit? Unfortunately, I've got no more answers for you than I had for any of those idiots twenty years ago."

And he turned back to his tea with fierce attention, as if willing her to declare the matter closed.

She changed tacks. "Father Gregory said you were born autistic."

He looked up from his whiskey-laced tea. "Regular Rain Man by all accounts," he allowed.

"And then...?"

"I had one hell of a fever for a couple of days. I think everyone thought I was going to die. Instead, I woke up ... me. Plenty of hallelujahs at the time, but it barely took a week's acquaintance with the new me before I think everyone wished I had died instead." He turned his attention back down to the tea. "Sorry. Sounds self-pitying, I know. But it's nothing but the truth."

He waved off her protest and took another long drink, before he went on, "It wasn't so bad, you know. Being autistic, I mean. Yeah, I missed some birthday parties, Cub Scouts. Then again, I got out of Sunday School and family reunions, too."

"Not a bad quid pro quo, if you ask me."

"You have an issue with Sunday School? Or family?"

"Both. Unfortunate side effect of being a preacher's kid."

He laughed out loud, but sobered almost immediately. "Mostly, though, it felt safe. Sort of like an aquarium. You ever been to an aquarium with one of those big tanks where you could walk right up and get face-to-face with things that could ordinarily kill you, like sharks and stingrays, knowing you were perfectly safe behind a pane of glass? That's what it felt like to me. Except I was the one on the inside of the glass and it was the people outside who were dangerous."

He sounded almost wistful. Clare glanced around the room again. Life pared down to its bare essentials. No television. No computer. No photos. No phone that she could see. Looked to her like he was doing what he could to keep that fish tank in place. "Do you wish you could go back?"

"Logically, how could I?" he answered. "I don't much fancy the thought of spending my life drooling in an institution."

Logically, how could he? Emotionally, on the other hand ... but sociopaths weren't supposed to have emotions. Were they?

"And when it happened?" Clare asked.

"It was like the fish tank burst," he said. "Exploded, and all the water came rushing in, knocking you to the floor. Noise—oh God, the noise. Tears. Hallelujahs. Hugs. Kisses. Faces looming everywhere like sea monsters so huge that all I could see was their great, gaping mouths. Everyone wanting me to tell them what had happened, when the day before, I couldn't even tell people when I needed to pee."

Christ in heaven. Seriously? It had taken Clare over a decade to recover from the bruises of similarly ham-handed do-gooders. But even her mother paled in comparison to what had been inflicted on Sean. "All that in the name of a saint's cause?" she asked.

He shook his head. "The Church was only one among many. Suddenly, I was everyone's favorite poster boy. Everybody seemed to have sent in an expert. Autism advocates. Child protective services. Doctors. Psychologists. Geneticists. Grinnell's own scientists. And yeah, more than a few priests. All of them in search of their own kind of miracle. All of them wanting to tell me what had really happened to me," he said. "And just like *Jeopardy!* every last one of them phrasing their answers in the form of a question. Do you think you were abducted by aliens? Was somebody touching you inappropriately? Was it Jesus? Was it Father Enoch? Did they take you to heaven? Did you see any angels?"

"And they blamed you when you couldn't give them the answers they wanted?"

Some sociopath. Some master manipulator.

Sean drew a deep breath. "I think it would be more accurate to say that somewhere along the line, I got tired of the game," he said. "And so, since I couldn't tell them what they wanted to hear, I told them what I did know. And the hell with the inner voice that pointed out I should have noticed that I was scaring them to death. Pretty much literally."

"You were a kid!"

"With the IQ of an adult. Unfortunately, without the moral compass to match. But what's the point in howling at the moon?"

His eerie dispassion never varied. But the way he shifted in his chair and took a long drink of tea, made it clear he was wishing this was over. And how could Clare blame him?

"As for what was actually going on with me, I honestly haven't a clue." He raised his shoulders. "Lukas Croswell thought it was genetics. That somehow someone had managed to unlock some crazy healing power in my DNA. Which I guess makes the most sense to me. My father owned a pharmaceutical company. Word was, he'd promised a million dollar bonus for a cure. But honestly, the cranks were a lot more entertaining—at least in retrospect. Illicit military experimentation. Elixirs of life protected by secret priestly order that dates back to the Crusades ..."

Elixirs of life? Secret priestly orders? Clare's eyes widened as suddenly she found herself contemplating the impossible. That the most boring dissertation ever penned was about to turn into everything she had ever dreamed a PhD could be.

"Takwin," she said. "That's what Rafael called it. The Secret of Life."

And Sean smiled at her. It was not a nice smile. "So that's it?" he asked. "That's the answer you're looking for?"

And too late, Clare realized how neatly she had been trapped. No, manipulated. "Please," she stammered. "Don't do this—"

"Why not?" he said. "You said you wanted to see for yourself. So let's see what I can come up with. A bunch of gangsters have stumbled across a centuries-old conspiracy in a near-abandoned Bronx church? A Persian alchemist's unholy secret, unearthed during the Crusades by the Order of the Lazarites. They brought it back from the Holy Land with them, and handed it down within their ranks across the ages. But they quickly discovered that it's a secret so dangerous that they only dared to use it in the direst of circumstances. Like the Black Death. Or the Spanish influenza ..."

"All right, all right," she snapped. "I get the point. You can be a mean bastard when you want to. And I have an overactive imagination. You're hardly the first person to point it out. Or likely to be the last. But the point remains. Rafael did call it Takwin. And he said the Lazaritos have it."

Sean's face flattened. "The kid has no idea what he's talking about."

"But you do. And so did Lukas..."

All humor vanished from Sean's face, and he stood up. "I warned Lukas," he said, swallowing off the last of his tea. "And he didn't listen. I suggest you don't make the same mistake."

And that wasn't just another defense. It was a clear dismissal. A signal that her time was up, that she needed to leave, so he could get back down to his bar and his carefully pared-down existence, running away to hide behind a near-impenetrable wall of music.

Setting aside her mug, she got to her feet. "All right," she said. "You win.

Thank you for your time. And your first-class demonstration of your evil, monstrous powers. But, you know what? I'm not all that scared. Certainly not scared to death. So do me a favor and answer just one last question. Why is everyone else? What are they all so afraid you're going to do?"

If she hadn't been so angry, the series of emotions that flashed across Sean's face might have been comical. Shock. Annoyance. Embarrassment. Shame.

But in the end, he just looked flummoxed. "Come back from the dead, so to speak," he said.

"And why are they all so scared of that?"

A long pause, before he said with a shrug, "It's complicated. But the simplest way to look at it would be, they've got me confused with another guy."

Chapter Sixteen

Trey and one of his pet shrinks were waiting for Marie at the kitchen table with the paperwork already laid out in front of them. Big surprise there. It was enough to make Marie wonder why they kept calling her the crazy one, when the operating definition of insanity was trying the same thing over and over and expecting a different result. On the other hand, the third person at the table was something new: Lukas Croswell, looking about like he had stepped in a steaming pile of dog shit. Well, arguably he had. How else would you describe a drunken slob who could barely keep her balance even in a $2,500 pair of Christian Louboutin sneakers? But if he didn't want to watch the freaks, what was he doing here at the sideshow?

"We need to talk," the shrink said.

"No, we don't," Marie shot back. "If there's one thing I'm really not in the mood for right now, it's another goddamned intervention."

"Then maybe you should ask yourself why you keep forcing us to stage them."

Christ. Was it any surprise she'd walked out on therapy? Three hundred bucks an hour just to answer rhetorical questions? It made the stupid sneakers look like a sensible purchase.

"I haven't done a damned thing except leave some hellhole of a rehab center that shouldn't even be licensed," Marie said.

"You've run away from a court-ordered program." Just as always, once the niceties had been dispensed with, Trey moved in to start delivering the body blows. "You are currently in contempt of court, if not actually a fugitive from justice. I could call the US Marshals Service right now."

"Then why don't you go ahead and do it? I'll be glad to give them their money's worth when they arrive," Marie said. "Should work wonders for your congressional campaign."

"In other words, all this acting out is nothing but some kind of misplaced desire to punish your husband?" the shrink asked.

"Works for me."

"And what about Dr. Croswell?"

"What about him?" Marie asked. "I'm still trying to figure out what he's doing here."

"According to what I heard, you all but accused him of embezzlement."

And so he'd run to Trey to complain, like most people ran to their parents or the principal's office? Christ, she never would have thought it. Had figured him to be a man with the balls to fight his own fights at the very least. "Is that what you told them?" she demanded, turning on Lukas. "Or have you given up speaking for Lent?"

Lukas drew a deep breath. "You've made some serious allegations about financial misconduct at the Outreach Center," he said. "Obviously, if they are real, they should be investigated. But I would like to be certain they are something more than drunken pot shots before I take action that might irreparably damage a vital community service."

"Drunken pot shots?" Marie snapped. "All I want to know is where a million dollar budget is going each year—"

"Grinnell's grants committee is under no obligation to disclose its deliberations." Trey cut in. "On the other hand, the corporation is very much under an obligation to comply with the Americans with Disabilities Act. And you're skirting dangerously close to involving us in a workplace discrimination suit."

Seriously? Seriously? Marie shook her head at Lukas, wondering how she could ever have been so wrong about a person. "So sue me," she snapped.

Lukas's face stiffened with distaste. "I have no intention of doing so," he said. "And if you all don't mind, I find the suggestion that I would ever resort to such litigation at least as offensive as any allegations of embezzlement. I believe you invited me here to share my considered medical opinion. So shall we stick to the matter at hand?"

"Which is what?" Marie sighed.

"Mrs. Carey. I must be frank. You really don't look too good. Clinically speaking, of course."

"What the hell does that mean? If you've got something to say it, just come out and say it."

"It means, as unfortunate as I find this little psychodrama, I'm forced to agree with your husband that you do belong in rehab," Lukas said.

And speaking of how people looked ... Lukas's skin was pasty; the circles around his eyes darker than her own.

"You look pretty damned hung over yourself,'" she spat.

"I have already warned you about insulting Dr. Croswell," Trey said.

"And I've already said that I would prefer to be the judge of when I've been insulted," Lukas snapped.

"Then why don't you go home? Butt out of this?" Marie asked. "I've got no fight with you. I'll make sure your name stays out of it when I go public with my demand for an audit."

Trey turned on her, the gloves coming off for real. "Look, I don't care whether you're drunk or just stupid, but you will not go public with anything," he snarled. "Or do you seriously want to spend the rest of your life in a Russian airport waiting for the bar to open?"

"What in hell is that supposed to mean?"

"You're a grown woman, Marie," he said. "Certainly you're not completely unaware that a sizeable portion of Grinnell's profits comes from aeronautics and ballistics engineering."

In other words, certainly she was not unaware that whatever part of the family fortune didn't come from pushing pills came from several lucrative contracts with the military—as well her father's close relationships with a score of even more shadowy government agencies. Of course, she was aware—even though she was not supposed to be. All Marie was supposed to know was that she spent her summers riding horses and the rest of the year in finishing school. She was not supposed to know that her father had secrets. Secrets that led him to lock himself behind the door of his study each night, while her mother retreated upstairs right after dinner with handfuls of sleeping pills—a custom-designed fast track to oblivion courtesy of Grinnell chemists. Did it really come as any surprise that Marie found herself careening down that same career path—double-time?

"Certain budget line items are kept confidential by law," Trey went on. "Playing whistle-blower with them would be a one-way ticket to federal prison."

He spoke with insulting slowness, deliberately enunciating each word as if he was dealing with a backward child. Or a suspect he was about to nail on the witness stand. Which could only mean he was right, and he knew it.

"Marie, we all agree you need help." The shrink took over, a smooth good cop to Trey's bad cop. "Please, will you just allow us to do that?"

As she spoke, she pushed a sheaf of papers toward Marie—with the places for her signature efficiently marked by Trey's paralegal with little stick-on plastic arrows. As if perky little Post-its did anything to disguise the fact that the bitch might as well have been hissing "Sign ze papers" in an over-the-top Nazi accent.

And suddenly Marie found herself wondering how far off the mark that really was. Was it possible that this time she had finally gone too far? That Trey was right, and they were now far beyond just an ugly divorce, into the realm of covert military operations, the CIA, Homeland Security? People who would and could make her disappear, as ruthlessly as any activist nun down in El Salvador?

And if she called the shrink on it, what would she say? Probably twist it right back at her with a quick lecture on paranoia and alcoholism. The shrink might even make a note for the case file.

A note? The bitch probably had a voice activated tape recorder running at this moment.

Well, maybe Marie was paranoid. But that didn't mean they weren't out to get her. She pushed the papers away. "Go get yourself a court order," she said. "Because it's going to be an involuntary commitment."

"Come now. It's in everyone's interest to handle this as discreetly as possible," the shrink said.

"No," Marie said. "It's in Trey's interest. Drunk crazy wives don't play well on the campaign trail. Too bad for him that I'd rather see Jerry Springer elected to Congress. As far as I'm concerned, I'm ready to pose for the tabloids in a straitjacket. Right after I telephone Jerry to grant him an exclusive."

"You do not mean that."

"If you think that, you're a lousier shrink than I took you for. I sure as hell do."

Trey studied her, his gaze as cold and clinical as if she were a witness he was deciding how to break. "I can't think of any clearer sign of mental instability than such self-destructive behavior. And I know a half-a-dozen judges who will agree with me. We need you to be a team player, Marie. And if you refuse to buy into that, we will buy into it for you."

"And how do you propose to do that? Pay off another judge? With my money?"

"I believe Dr. Croswell would be best suited to answer that question." Trey got to his feet, jerking his head for the shrink to follow. "We tried to be constructive, Marie, but if you're having nothing of it, we'll play hardball."

A slight numb clenching in her stomach was the only warning she got about what was about to come. "What's that supposed to mean?"

"If in Dr. Croswell's medical opinion, you're in a state that presents a clear and present danger to yourself and to others, he would be ethically obligated to give you a sedative shot to ensure you were brought in for psychiatric evaluation." Opening the door, Trey gestured for the shrink to precede him. "I'll leave that decision up to him. But don't say I didn't warn you. Sign the damned papers, or when you wake up, it will be in a padded cell."

Their footsteps and voices must have died away, the front door must have clicked shut behind him, but Marie neither saw nor heard any of it. All five senses were consumed with one sensation: She was cold—no, she was frozen. Frozen in numb disbelief that this could be happening. That somehow she had found herself trapped in a made-for-TV movie.

So frozen that she couldn't even move when Lukas Croswell drew a deep breath and turned toward her. Couldn't muster any reaction beyond wondering, with a beast's dull acceptance of the inevitable, whether he would plunge the needle into her butt or into her neck.

No! Stop it! Now! Just push him away. The man was a cripple, for God's sake. She didn't even have to push him. All she needed to do was run out into the hall and up the stairs. But the picture of her crashing drunkenly into the furniture, too paralytic to evade even a man who was paralyzed, only rooted her more firmly to the floor.

But rousing herself from this obscene torpor was as impossible as thrashing your way out of a bad dream. And, suddenly, she found herself wondering how it had all gone so wrong. When had she transformed into a pathetic wreck of a woman whose biggest fear was that the airline miniatures would spill out of her purse at a photo-op. It wasn't as if she had spent her childhood mapping out her gradual devolution into everyone's caricature of a neglected wife, complete with a couple of DWIs to go along with the lovers and liposuction and Botox parties. She'd had dreams in her childhood, she was certain of it. Dreams about standing on the Olympic podium in front of a cheering crowd after being the only rider in the world to successfully negotiate what was universally agreed to be the most fiendishly difficult show-jumping course ever constructed. Dreams of quaffing champagne barefoot in a gown with a mysterious stranger who just might be a spy—or just might be the love of her life. When and how had all that been reduced to nothing but the champagne and a string of lovers whose approach in bed was about as imaginative as a stallion's when he humped a sawhorse to produce a flask of semen?

Who cared? Why bother? Despair at last loosened her muscles, and she held out her arm, ashamed to see it shaking. Exhibit A. Goddamned alcoholic tremors. "Go ahead if you have to," she said. "But I'm not signing those goddamned papers."

Lukas's face went as rigid with distaste as if she had offered him a mucus-tainted needle. "I'm afraid you have me confused with the Governor of New Jersey," he said.

Another set of muscles returned uncertainly to life, and she shook her head. "What in hell is that supposed to mean?"

"It means that it's not my practice to force people into treatment, no matter how badly I believe they need it." He nodded toward the sound of Trey's engine in the driveway. "If you don't mind, I'll just wait a few minutes to make sure they're gone, and then I'll show myself out."

And as Marie finally got her head around his meaning—and got her head around the fact he really meant what he was saying—her strength slackened in a single whoosh. Reaching for a chair, she just barely managed to slump into it before she collapsed, furiously fighting off the final humiliation of bursting into tears.

"Shit!" she sighed.

"Language," Lukas said mechanically.

She drew a deep breath, surprised she even remembered how to do so. "I guess what I meant to say is thank you. And I think I owe you an apology as well."

"Shall we just stipulate to both instead?"

"What does that mean?"

"It means please don't confuse my medical ethics with my medical opinion. You belong in rehab. You have a problem and you need to get help. But what your husband wanted me to do is ... unconscionable."

"So why did you come along in the first place?"

"My motives are my own business. It strikes me we might talk about yours instead."

"Must we?"

He ignored the question. "Why do you act out like this? Is it really about your husband?"

"Christ, you've met the asshole. Is it that hard to understand why I'd do anything for a divorce?"

"Not really. But why exactly does he want to stay married?"

"Maybe because I'm one hell of a lay."

Lukas merely raised an eyebrow, and she found herself flushing again. "Well, come on," she protested. "That's not exactly what I'd call a polite question to ask a lady."

"Which is why I would never have asked it, if it didn't strike me as an important one."

"Money. Power. In other words, Grinnell," she said. "His job as a prosecutor was more or less my dowry, and while my father was alive, he was content with that. Had to be. And I was content to let sleeping dogs lie. Once the honeymoon was over—which was more or less when the honeymoon was over—we went our separate ways. Trey played Elliot Ness, and I ..."

"Drank," Lukas supplied.

"I had my horses." And pills. And a succession of younger and cheaper men. But somehow she couldn't take the thought of Lukas Croswell just nodding gravely at the latter, with the same cool, clinical detachment he probed a pus-filled sore.

"But now, Trey senses the big time," she said. "He's got control of

Grinnell—oh, sure, the conservators are a court-appointed panel, but they're all his buddies. Next comes a congressional run. And after that...?"

"So you'll destroy yourself to destroy him?" Lukas shook his head. "If you're in that much of a hurry to launch the Apocalypse, why not do it right and call in Michael? Seems to me the two of you would be a pretty powerful one-two punch."

At just the mention of her brother's name, all warmth leached from the room—along with anything else that was good and pure and right. How to explain it? Michael could just ... get under your skin. There was no other way to put it. Even as a kid, he had had a mean streak that had haunted her entire childhood—a way of getting beneath her skin and ferreting out all her nastiest little secrets from where they were hidden in the deepest crevasses of her soul, and needling them, just so she'd know he could find them. The answers she had peeked at over another student's shoulder. The stupid crush she had had on their parish priest. The even stupider crush she had had on David Hasselhoff. The battered teen romances she wouldn't have admitted to reading. The bingeing and purging she thought no one knew about. Her brother was a sneak that could have given Trey lessons. He spied. He pricked. He goaded—for no other reason than it was fun.

"I'm nothing like my brother," she said.

"Prove it," Lukas said.

"What's that supposed to mean?"

He studied her for a moment. "University Health Services sometimes provides controlled monitoring—very discreet controlled monitoring—for students, as well as for more faculty and staff than I would care to admit. As Director of University Health, I'm in charge of the program. I could backdate a referral—probably all the way back to the original court order. We could argue that your assignment to the other facility was due to a mix-up in the paperwork, and your abrupt departure could be explained by All Saints' efforts to get you into the appropriate program as quickly and quietly as possible."

She stared at him. "Just like that, huh?"

"Being a Grinnell has its privileges," he said with an almost-smile, "especially at All Saints College. I'm sure Father Gregory would be delighted to accommodate you in every possible way."

"And what do you mean, controlled monitoring?"

"Usually, regular blood and urinalysis. Checking in with a monitor several times a day." Lukas raised an eyebrow. "Obviously, I understand if you found such arrangements between us distasteful, and would be happy to stipulate to your participation instead. Although I'm ethically obligated to point out that I still do believe it would be in your best interest to make some kind of systematic attempt at not drinking. And it is widely accepted that such supervision helps."

"In other words, you're not willing to lock me up, but you are willing to lie for me." Marie shook her head. "Why?"

"Because, frankly, it would be in my self-interest as well."

She shook her head. "How does my going to rehab—I'm sorry, controlled monitoring—affect you?"

"Your husband would be getting the result he wanted, if not in the way he anticipated," Lukas said. "I can only hope that the former would move him to overlook my lack of cooperation when it came to the latter. Ends justify the means."

"Trey overlooks nothing," she said. "He's got an enemies list worthy of Joseph McCarthy."

"Maybe. But I can't really see any better way out for either of us." Lukas reached for his cell phone and held it out to her. "So unless you have other pressing plans, would you please help us both out, and call Father Gregory to inform him of your newfound commitment to your spiritual progress?"

Chapter Seventeen

Sean sighed as the ghost castled. "You always castle at this point. How many times do I have to tell you it's the worst possible move you could make?"

"And what would you suggest?" the ghost asked. "A King's Gambit?"

"That's an opening. You gave up that chance with your first move."

"And what about the chance you're giving up?"

"What's that supposed to mean?"

The ghost snorted, sending a fresh trickle of blood down his lip. "It means that I may have a weakness for castling, but you're at least as bad about gambits." he said. "Not that I don't see the appeal. Sacrifice always plays better than prudence. Nobler, and all that. But there's a very fine line between self-sacrifice and self-annihilation. I only hope you see the difference before it's too late."

Sean moved a knight. "Not only don't I see the difference, I don't see any gambits here. All I see is mate in seven moves."

"I'm not talking about the chessboard, and you know it," the ghost said, taking Sean's knight with a bishop. "I'm talking about all that 'stay away from me, I'm a monster' crap. Keep it up, especially with your knack for dramatic demonstrations, and sooner or later, the woman's going to get sick of it and just go ahead and take your advice."

"Then I hope for her sake that it's sooner. And that's a lousy move."

"I'm not here to win a chess game. I'm here to talk to you."

"Kind of late in our relationship for a father-son chat."

"Indulge me," the ghost said. "I never got a chance the first time around."

Sean shrugged. "I suppose it beats watching you making a hash out of this game." He concentrated on a few lightning-quick moves, then asked, "So where do you want to start? When a man loves a woman very much—"

"It's easier to chase her away than admit how scared you are of being hurt," the ghost finished the sentence for him.

Sean snorted and made a final move. "I don't feel things, remember? High-functioning sociopath and, by the way, checkmate."

The ghost just laughed. They could have been just another father and son spending time over a chessboard in a park on a beautiful day—if not for the fact that one of them was a shimmering, translucent figure with a bloody nose. And the other was seemingly talking to himself. Sean glanced over at the knot of lunchtime players who were usually willing to put up ten bucks to play against him. Not one of them would meet his eyes.

"No offense," he said to his father, "but you're not real good for customers. So, now that you've had your chance, would you mind moving along and making room for someone else? I've got a living to earn here."

"Unfortunately," the ghost said, "I'm afraid your regular opponents are going to have to wait a little longer."

"Why is that? You haunt by the hour?"

"There's someone else who wants a word with you."

Something in the ghost's voice made Sean glance up sharply from where he had been setting the chess pieces back into their original ranks. "And who exactly is that?"

"Me."

An old man in a guayabera shirt and a porkpie hat slid into place across the chessboard from Sean. An old man that Sean was fairly sure had died years ago. Once upon a time, he had been a guy that everyone in the neighborhood knew, even though no one knew his name or where he lived. Everyone just called him Papi, and he always seemed to be sitting outside the run-down botanica playing dominos on an upturned crate. Some said he was a shaman, a holy man. Some said he was drug kingpin in hiding. Others said he was an assassin for the cartels. Whoever he was, no one questioned him, even when he had beckoned over a thin boy named Michael Grinnell and set aside his dominoes for a chessboard.

"You have got to be kidding," Sean sighed.

The old man's only answer was to advance his King's pawn.

"This isn't real," Sean said. "None of it."

But his hands moved of their own accord, advancing his pawn in response. Another pawn, then a knight, and already Sean—or maybe he was really the boy Michael now—knew he was destined to lose. For the old man's style was like no one Sean had ever played—cagey, twisty, not a single move really what it seemed. Sean was nothing but a pawn himself, as the old man drove him down a series of fiendish forks that transformed the board into a maze—a tortuous path that took you around a blind corner and straight into defeat when you least expected it. The only reason Sean even managed to hold on for as long as he did was because the old man was letting him. Testing him. Drawing out the match to see every last weapon in Sean's arsenal, before he reached across the board, tipped over Sean's king, and said, "Once upon a time, I found you for your father."

Something cold knotted in the pit of Sean's stomach—something that might have been the whisper of an unwanted memory—and he tried to ignore it by setting up another game. "Found me where?"

But Sean already knew the answer, as surely as if the game they had just played had been a physical thing—a labyrinth of chess positions that all went nowhere except to curve back on themselves, trapping Sean in their center.

"I found you," the old man said, "in between. And I led you out of there. I showed you the way."

The chill in Sean's gut was getting worse, the memory rising. "Truth be told, I don't remember much about that part of my life," Sean lied.

"But you remember me."

No. What Sean remembered was something vast and ominous, his face so terrible it must stay hidden beneath the porkpie hat. Something that made him keep his eyes focused on the chess pieces for fear that if he looked up right now, he would see it sitting across the chessboard from him, meet its eyes and die.

"Maybe."

"Don't trifle with me! You know who I am. I am the stranger you meet at the crossroads. I am the one you ask for directions. I am the one who showed you the way. I am the one who gave you the map."

"What map?" Sean asked, looking up despite himself.

He saw nothing but an old man in a guayabera, who asked, "Do you know the Immortal Game?" His gnarled fingers moved for the pieces once more. "The greatest chess game ever played."

Of course Sean knew the Immortal Game. There wasn't a chess master alive who didn't. Adolf Anderssen and Lionel Kieseritsky on June 21, 1851. But that was adult Sean remembering. The boy Michael remembered the Immortal Game in an entirely different way, as a path that simply appeared one day among the labyrinth of chess games that trapped him, leading him from darkness into light. Leading him home. The boy Michael had followed the shining path—so straight, clear, and pure. No forks, no twists and turns, just the most cunning series of gambits ever played, a seeming fool's errand that suddenly snapped back on the hapless King, who capitulated in an explosion of light and sound.

And Sean was sitting at a chess table in a park, blinking at an old man in a guayabera who couldn't possibly be real.

"So, now the time has come to pay the piper?" Sean asked. "Rumplestiltskin without the cute dwarf?"

"I know no Rumplestiltskin. I know I need your help. Just as I helped you all that time ago."

Sean's mouth twisted. "Let me guess. You want me to lead Jonas Croswell and the rest of the lost boys back from Neverland?"

The old man's face darkened. "The spoiled white boy is not my concern," he said. "It is my sons, my lost boys, you need to save."

And as Sean just stared at him, at a loss for words for arguably the first time since he had been … found, the old man vanished, and it was Sean's father who once again sat opposite him at the chess table. "God in heaven," Sean said. "What in hell have you done?"

"Whatever I had to in order to ransom you. And that is a decision I have never regretted in my life."

"Seriously?" Sean asked. "You expect me to believe you made a bargain for my life and saddled me with some immortal debt to a rogue *orisha* who just happened to have a hunch that he would need me to save his sons, a bunch of hoodlums, sometime in the future when he was presumably dead or called to another dimension or otherwise too disembodied to help them?"

"As one does," the ghost said, "when one loves one's son."

Sean stared at his father for a long time before he shook his head. "This isn't real," he said. "Some kind of post-traumatic stress over your death. A hallucination."

The ghost smiled. "It's possible, of course. But as highly as I have always valued your intelligence, I honestly never would have credited you with that kind of imagination."

∞

Of course it was Sean's imagination. Forget ghosts, forget rogue *orishas*—go ahead and even forget that the encounter had cost Sean pretty much a day's income. The whole fiasco had been nothing but a needlessly showy NOTE TO SELF that there was a folder wedged in the bottom of Sean's fiddle case that urgently needed attention. A bulging folder he had come across as he had paged through his own records late last night, as others might page through an old family photo album—or he supposed, scroll through cell phone photos of their exes—when neither music, nor chess, nor whiskey had been enough to lull him to sleep. As if conjuring the entire Santeria pantheon would have done anything to hide the fact that what was keeping him up at night had nothing to do with any Faustian bargains that his father might have made, or even the enormity of the truth those papers suggested about him. The only truth Sean cared about had long, red hair and a taste for medieval saints' causes. And the only enormity he cared about was what she might feel if she ever found out what those papers implied about him.

He supposed it was some kind of mid-life crisis. He was what? Thirty-six? Thirty nine? He'd given up on counting birthdays a while ago. But even if you counted him an old soul, it still struck him that he was kind of young for all that. Much more likely that this all stemmed from his father's death. Unfinished business, as the ghost himself kept repeating. How much more of a clue did Sean really need?

Well, if that were the case, at least he was handing out pretty specific instructions. So what was Sean waiting for? A chess game he could win? With an angry shake of his head, Sean hurried out of the park, his fiddle case bouncing across his shoulder, as he struck out for Riverdale—All Saints' side of the Bronx—where diplomats lived in gated communities and teams still played cricket in pressed whites in Van Cortlandt Park. Time to test the old saw that you couldn't go home again.

He loped along the shady streets as unerringly as if he had never left them, until he reached the river and a waterfront compound that crouched behind a sign that read "Yacht Club. Private." He ignored the sign, heading straight in through the front gate like he had been a member for years—which, for all he knew, he had been.

Trey was sharing a bottle of wine with an intern on the deck that overlooked the marina, one hand working his way up the girl's thigh beneath the tablecloth. And 'girl' was the only word you could use. Sean wondered if it was a flash of pity he felt for his sister at the sight. Wondered how it could be when he hadn't so much as seen Marie in years. But how else could you explain how hard it was to keep his voice calm and detached as he said, "Afternoon, Trey. Mind of we take this some place private?"

"Now is not the best time," Trey said, ignoring him as if he were nothing more than an annoying waiter. He squeezed the girl's thigh. "If you know what I mean."

"What I know," Sean said, "is that if you think my sister is capable of making a scene over something like this, you haven't met me. So here we go. Hello, Trey, I'm Marie's bro—"

Chairs scraped backward, Trey snarled something, and the girl fled. Moments later, the two of them were striding down to the boat dock, where Trey turned to face him.

"What are you doing here?" Trey asked. "Are you seriously proposing to stake your claim as Mi—"

"Actually, I go by Sean these days," the fiddler told him. "But as for the rest, yes. That's the gist of it. Sorry to miss the wedding. My invitation seems to have been misplaced."

"Sean, then. Makes things easier, I admit. So, Sean, why are you here? Some kind of penance? Making amends?"

"Does this look like a church basement?" Sean snorted. "A twelve-step program? I told you my name was Sean. I didn't ask you for a cup of coffee and a cigarette."

"Money, then?"

"Are you offering?" Sean cocked his head at Trey. "How much? What would you give me to just go away and never come back? Ten million sound like a good place to start?"

"You're selling yourself cheap. Grinnell is worth a hundred times that. Literally."

"Yeah, but at heart I'm a lazy bastard. Hell of a lot of work managing a Fortune 500 company—especially one that's going to be facing a pretty nasty class action suit. Why should I pull your fat out of the fire, when I can make myself comfortable instead? Especially when there might not be any money left for that after you finally crawl out of court."

"In other words, you're threatening to come back and sue for your share of the estate if I don't pay you off now?"

"Aw, hell, no. I told you. I'm a lazy bastard. Certainly far too lazy for that."

Trey shut his eyes in disgust. "Look, I'm a busy man, Sean. Got a lady waiting for me, in case you didn't notice. So what do you say we quit this fencing, and you come out and tell me what you want?"

"I'm here on behalf of a third party."

"Your sister get in touch with you?" Trey asked, frowning.

"Not so much as a Christmas card," Sean said. He paused a moment before dropping his bombshell—nothing but a cheap effect, really, but he was surprised how badly this asshole pissed him off. "I'm here about the gang of drug dealers you've been using the Outreach Center to entrap."

Trey's jaw dropped—literally. As in gaping. It made him look like a carp suffering a thrombosis. And once again Sean felt an unfamiliar surge of pity for his sister. "Why should you care about them?"

"I don't care about anyone. High functioning sociopath and all that, remember?"

"Then why do you think I'm going to give them money?"

"Because if you don't, I'm going to start by suggesting the police check the age of that young lady you were just drinking with," Sean said. "After that, I'll move on to the serious stuff. Like the other records I found hidden with my own files."

Another taste of the hypertensive fish. And then Trey's face settled into lines Sean was much more familiar with: those of a man racing to calculate his options. "You mean the files you stole."

"I'm not going to quibble about semantics. Because even Father Gregory isn't going to care how I got those papers once I tell him what I found in there." Sean shook his head. "Christ, Trey, how stupid can you be? You didn't just leave a smoking gun. You left an entire road map of exactly how you have been entrapping the Lazaritos for nearly a year."

"So this is blackmail."

"I'm not interested in money."

"Then what are you interested in? And please don't try to convince me you're genuinely concerned about those thugs."

Well, maybe Sean wasn't, but someone else on the power grid sure seemed to be. But what did he care about what Trey thought was going on, so long as the asshole did what he wanted.

"Might be more accurate to say I'm concerned about fair play. I'm a chess master, remember? Stickler for the rules. Positively hate it when people cheat. Unfortunately for you, the way I see it, what you're doing to those kids is nothing short of cheating. And, frankly, Trey, that just burns my ass."

Trey just stared at him. "You're not what I expected," he finally said.

"You are exactly what I expected," Sean said. "Which is why I'm fairly certain you're not going to do the smart thing and take my offer, even though it's clearly in your best interest."

"The smart man doesn't give into blackmail."

"But a smart chess player does know when he's being offered a fork. That means a forced choice, if you're not up on your chess terms. It also means that a smart man takes the lesser of two evils when it's clearly presented."

"And what exactly do you think the greater evil is?"

"Well, I'd toyed with the idea of handing those papers over to Sister St. John. But even I'm not that sadistic. Instead, I think I'll give them to those kids. And suggest they find themselves one hell of a good lawyer. When all the dust settles, they should be able to afford it."

A thunderous pause. Trey pushed his jacket back and put his hands on his waist as if ready for a shoot-out at the OK Corral. He looked Sean up and down slowly, clearly not happy with the view. "You'd honestly put the nuclear football in the hands of those lowlifes?"

"Don't see how the world is any better off with you having it," Sean said.

Trey fell silent, nodding slowly. It was hard to read the expression on his face. It might have been appalled. It might have been admiring. It seemed to land somewhere smack between the two. "They always said you were a ruthless bastard."

"I prefer the term 'focused.' I think the religious types call it 'purpose-driven'." Sean said. "Born without a moral compass. Even you would be surprised how liberating it can prove."

He turned to go, but Trey stopped him. "Then why not take the money for yourself? We can come to an arrangement. I'm a reasonable man."

"I told you. I'm not interested in money."

"So it would seem," Trey said with an expressive glance at Sean's threadbare coat. "But you're not going to convince me you give a shit about those punks either. So what is this really about?"

Who in the hell knew? Rogue *orishas*? Red hair bouncing in the sunlight? Or was Sean simply losing his mind?

"Trust me, you wouldn't believe me if told you."

Something in Sean's voice must have given him away, because Trey glanced at him sharply, and then his lip curled in disgust. "Oh, God. It's the woman, isn't it? Clare Malley?"

Sean shrugged. "If that's how you need to think about it, why not?"

"Then why don't you want the money? Hey, I'd be the first to say, ten million looks good on a man."

Sean's hand snaked out and grabbed Trey's wrist so fast he was shocked—no, he was horrified. He hadn't done something like that in years, and the stench of the human cesspool that was Trey Carey was overwhelming. Sins and cheats, both venial and mortal, pressed in from every side, from the laxatives Trey had laced a track rival's water with in seventh grade to an intern that had not only been stupid enough to get herself pregnant, but had been even stupider to believe she could force a rising star in the prosecutor's office to marry her.

"I will cut you slack this time," Sean said, struggling to keep his voice level. Indifferent. Informative. "Because if you really had done your homework about me, you never would have said something as painfully stupid as you just did. But if you ever talk about Clare Malley that way again, I will chew you up and spit you out as fodder for every tabloid out there. Starting with the intern named Daisy—if you even bothered to ask her name."

And then Sean had to let go. Needed to let go, before twenty years of carefully cultivated oblivion was destroyed by a single thoughtless surge of anger.

"You have no idea who you're dealing with here," Trey hissed, massaging his wrist.

"Unfortunately, I have far too good an idea," Sean said, still fighting to keep his voice neutral. Disinterested. In control. "So consider this your fair warning. If you're smart, you'll do what I ask and be my next meal ticket. If you're stupid—which, just for the record, I'm pretty sure you are—you'll be my next meal. So all I can really do is warn you that I've got one hell of a nasty reputation for playing with my food.

Chapter Eighteen

Breaking into his father's emails had been no trouble at all. The stubborn bastard still hadn't bothered to change his password. Breaking into the clinic's records had taken a little more nerve, but once Jonas had decided to do it, it had been easy enough. Their codes were even lamer than his father's. It was always that way. Once you got more than two people sharing a password, they got a case of collective amnesia and couldn't remember anything more complicated than Password01. Unless, of course, there was a major security breach, and then they mixed things up big time by changing it to Password02. The clinic was already up to Password17, and still no one could think of being as creative as using someone's pet's name instead.

"Find something intriguing? A terrorist chatroom on the dark web? Nude pictures of Miley Cyrus? A bonus level of Candy Crush Saga?"

The old man's voice came out of nowhere, causing Jonas to knock the keyboard off the table. Christ, you'd think after all these years, he'd finally be used to the old man sneaking up on him, but the bastard still managed to blindside him with those rubber wheels.

"Checking to see if you'd changed any of your passwords yet," Jonas lied. "You know, it's really going to catch up with you one of these days."

"Jonas, hacking is a serious business."

"Why do you have to assume I'm hacking every time you see me at a computer?"

"Mostly because that's what you're usually doing," the old man sighed. "Most recently into your high school registrar's office to change your grades, if I recall correctly. Honestly, Jonas did it ever occur to you that it would take less effort simply to make honor roll?"

"Yessir," Jonas said. "Guess I just like to give myself a challenge, sir."

Lucas closed his eyes a moment as if to compose himself and then said, "I admit I've had a rather trying day, and my temper is somewhat short," he said. "So I would appreciate it, if we could dispense with the pleasantries and keep this simple. What are you looking for on my computer?"

Jonas decided to dive right in, willing himself to say what he had been working up to all day. "I'm trying to find a way to delete my name from the Lazarus Vector records," he said with a calm he didn't feel.

He had braced himself against his father's rage. Threats. Sarcasm. But Lukas showed no more passion than if he had been asking some bum down at the shelter whether he knew the difference between a deer tick and a head louse. His father said, "And why would you want to do a thing like that?"

This was it. Ground zero. The real reason Jonas was here, to ride to his father's rescue. To his embarrassment, he felt his ears go bright red. "Look, I heard that asshole the other night. I know I wasn't supposed to be listening, but I did. Couldn't help it really. You can hear anything through those heating ducts." Once he got started, the words tumbled out in a rush. "I know he's holding it over your head, even though this is all my fault. My screw-up. And that's not fair. I'm not going to let that happen. I'm just trying to make things right."

"So you decided to handle things by screwing up even more?" Lukas's nostrils flared, the sure sign of a tirade. Then, abruptly, his jaw clamped shut. And, incredibly, impossibly, he said, "I'm sorry. You're trying to do the right thing; it's unconscionable of me to bite your head off. Please chalk it up to the fact I'm under considerable stress at this moment ..."

"Stress I caused." Jonas's ears burned. "No, you were right in the first place. You should just go ahead and say it. I fucked up."

"I have no desire to say any such thing."

"Then why do you look like you're choking on your dinner?"

A moment's thunderous pause. And then unexpected humor flashed across Lukas's face. "Because I'm not sure how to say what I want to say. Expressing my feelings is not exactly my wheelhouse, if you will." He paused, browed furrowed, carefully considering his next words. "So I will just do my best. I am trying to find a way to tell you how touched I am at your trying to protect me. Actually, you will never know how much."

He spoke with no more emotion than if he were deciding which meal to pull out of the freezer for dinner, and it took Jonas a moment to register what the old man was saying. Was his father actually attempting to … share? To bond? The possibility was so seriously awkward that it was a relief when the doorbell rang, the front door crashed open, and heels clacked down the hall.

A moment later, Marie, the crazy lady, was standing on the threshold. And Lukas looked at least as relieved to see her as Jonas was. "Mrs. Carey," he said. "To what do I owe the pleasure?"

She stepped into the lab, and Lukas moved reflexively to protect his equipment, but she seemed to be balancing a little better than usual. She barely swayed as she rummaged in her purse and pulled out a cell phone.

"This," she said, tossing it to him.

Lukas raised an eyebrow as he glanced at it. "And this is?"

"It's Trey's old phone," Marie said. "I stole it months ago, but he never canceled it."

"And why is that?"

"Because he's a lazy bastard."

"I apologize. I wasn't clear. I meant, why did you steal his phone?"

"Why else? I was trying to catch the bastard sexting."

"Sexting?" Lukas rolled the world around in his mouth as if it were a questionable wine.

"The technology changes. Men don't."

"Present company excepted, of course."

Marie's gaze flashed to the wheelchair, and her face fell. "Oh, God! I didn't think …" she stammered. "Oh, Christ, how could I be so stupid … I'm sorry—"

"That was not what I meant," Lukas snapped.

Shit. No. They couldn't be headed there, could they? That was beyond seriously awkward. But Marie's face was flaming as bad as Jonas's ears, and she stared straight down at the floor, refusing to meet the old man's eyes as she muttered, "I was saving it for the divorce. I don't know why. There was nothing on it. Not even internet porn. Big surprise there. The bastard's got about as much sexual imagination as—"

A strangled noise cut her off. "Perhaps you could just tell me what you think you found on this cell phone?" Lukas asked with preternatural politeness.

She finally looked up, her face still red. "Michael threatened Trey somehow," she said. "Made a scene down at the Yacht Club. As soon as he left, the phone started lighting up like a Christmas tree."

"And do you have any idea what that threat was?" Lukas asked, with as much clinical detachment as if he were asking when a patient had first noticed his boils beginning to ooze.

"Not really." She shrugged, and suddenly she looked a lot less steady on her feet than before. "For all I know, it's completely useless. But you said Trey had something over you. I thought … I mean, I hoped that maybe this will give you some leverage back."

"I see." Jonas saw Lukas's nostrils flare—a sure sign his father was savoring the chance to ream her out with the kind of gleeful precision he usually reserved for his son—and bit back a grin despite himself. Actually, when you weren't on the receiving end of it, it was kind of fun to watch Lukas Croswell in action.

But just as he had with Jonas, the old man seemed to change his mind and stop himself. Instead of tearing her a new one, he pocketed the phone and said with careful courtesy, "Thank you, Marie. I appreciate your thoughtfulness."

And as Jonas tried to get his head around the possibility that his father really had been abducted by aliens and replaced with a simulacrum that was more capable of human behavior than Lukas Croswell had ever been, Marie shook her head. "I'm not being thoughtful. You're … decent. You did the decent thing by me. I just wanted to return the favor," she said. She started to leave, then turned back and added with peculiar dignity, "And before you start to wonder, I'm stone sober."

"I never had any doubt," Lukas said.

Her mouth twisted into a smile at the obvious lie. "I owe you," she said. "My father taught me a Grinnell always pays his debts."

"And here I thought that was a Lannister."

Jonas stared at his father incredulously as Marie's footsteps clattered down the hall and the front door closed behind her. He knew his dad didn't spend Sunday evenings watching TV, and he'd never seen a stack of *Game of Thrones* books hanging around. So did Lukas have a serious midnight HBO binge-watching habit? Someday, Jonas would like to know a lot more about that—especially whether he had any theories about who would end up on the Iron Throne. But right now, he had another, slightly more pressing, question.

"So, are we going to look at the phone?" he asked.

"Of course not," the old man said. His eyes didn't move from the doorway where Marie had vanished, as if he were studying a symptom he had never encountered before.

"Why not?"

With a sigh, Lukas turned back to his son. "I won't insult your intelligence by explaining how stupid Marie's suggestion really was. But her heart was in the right place."

Her heart? Would the old man even recognize one of them, if it wasn't dried up and locked in a reliquary?

"Then maybe you ought to respect her efforts by doing something about it."

Lukas made a strangled noise, but Jonas didn't care. The time was now. The die was cast. Or as the old man would insist on correcting him, *alea iacta est*. "Seriously, sir. I know it's my fault that that asshole is pushing you around, but now you've got a chance to stop it. So why not at least look and see what you've got?"

For a moment Lukas stared at his son in shock, as if Jonas had suddenly begun to speak a foreign language. After a moment of absolulte stillness, he spoke. "Maybe, because I already know what's on that phone. I already know exactly what kind of threat Michael is holding over Grinnell's head."

Oh come on. Did he really think he could brush Jonas off like that? "You gonna tell me what that is or am I just supposed to take it on faith?"

Lukas leaned forward. "If I hadn't intended to, I would never have brought it up," he said. "The fact of the matter is, the military got involved in Michael Grinnell's case. They asked one of the doctors who examined him to determine whether a miraculously-cured teenager had any sort of potential as a super-soldier or even a weapon. I trust you can see why they might be reluctant for that to get out. It could prove as big an embarrassment as Psy Ops or the CIA experimenting with LSD."

What the fuck? Did the old man have a stash of Dan Brown novels he sneak-read at night when he got tired of binge-watching *Game of Thrones*? "How can you know that?"

Lukas shook his head in puzzlement. "I thought that much would be self-evident," he said. "Because I'm the one they asked."

Jonas just stared at his father. Talk about speaking foreign languages.

That answer wouldn't have made any more sense if Lukas had lapsed into Greek or Aramaic or any of the languages in the dozen or so dictionaries that were lined up on the shelf above the old man's desk.

"I thought you investigated saints. For the church."

"There's … crossover."

"Seriously, sir? You want me to believe the government's interested in miracle cures?"

"Theoretically, I can think of nothing the government would be more interested in."

"Theoretically?"

"Theoretically—hell, practically, for that matter—the government only ever cares about two things. What kills men. And what makes them tick. Death. And life. And if some autistic teenager who starts miraculously speaking in tongues might provide even the hint of an answer to either of those questions, the government wants to hear it." Suddenly, the old man was off on a roll. "Hell, look at the places we're fighting wars. Crypto-archaeology central. Do you know the secrets that are supposed to be buried there? The lost tribe of haumavarka. An angel's wing. Reptilians beneath the Gates of Ishtar. Noah's Ark—or maybe it's the Ark of the Covenant. I can never keep them straight …"

A question was beginning to formulate in the back of Jonas's mind. A question he wanted to hear the answer to, but actually, honestly, wasn't sure he did. Because the answer would explain everything. But it would also mean…

"So that's it?" he asked. "That's the reason for the lockdown? The secrecy? You were the one who examined Michael Grinnell? You're the one who tried to figure out a way to turn him into a weapon. And now you're afraid that if they find out what happened back there at the shelter, they'd want you to do the same with me?"

The old man flinched. "That's a touch hyperbolic."

"I don't care. In fact, I don't even really know what that means." Once again, Jonas's ears went red. "Why didn't you just tell me?"

"I guess that's one more of the many apologies I seem to owe you," Lukas said. He fell silent, like he was considering saying something more, then shook his head. "In any case, the whole thing was over and done with twenty years ago. It's all water under the bridge now."

"Oh, come on, sir. Even you can't believe that."

The old man favored him with a withering glare. "I beg your pardon?"

"Listen to yourself, sir. Listen to what you just said. Would they honestly get this upset over water under the bridge?"

"You don't understand," Lukas snapped. "The entire project was destroyed. The lab records and samples were quite literally burned. The only way someone could start the whole thing up again would be by capturing Michael Grinnell. And he isn't showing himself to be particularly amenable in that regard."

"Then why are you so afraid to look at those records?"

A long moment passed, while Lukas studied Jonas as if he was trying to figure out how this stranger had appeared in his house. Then he pulled out the phone.

A couple of swift taps, and the cell phone screen was blinking with records. He wheeled himself to his desk and put on his half glasses, and suddenly it was if none of this had happened, and they had gone back to their old life together, when the two of them had shared every evening in silence, each engrossed in his own private world. Then Lukas laid the phone on his desk, and ran his hands back through his hair, rumpling it unmercifully. Which was basically the equivalent of anyone else hurling the phone against the wall.

"The bastard," Lukas said without emphasis.

"What bastard? With respect, sir."

"Ezra Grinnell," Lukas said, his gaze and voice equally distant. "He goddamned well lied to me. He told me he burned all of it. And I was stupid enough to simply take him at his word."

"Why, sir?"

"At the time, it only seemed logical." An odd look crossed the old man's face. "There was a bit of a … hiatus. When I returned to Grinnell, Michael was long since gone, but he did not exactly go gentle into that good night. His farewell tour reportedly included a fist fight in the board room, and a drunken interruption of a shareholders' meeting. He may have even gone so far as to offer interviews to the tabloids. The military couldn't afford that kind of publicity and had no choice but to insist Ezra shut the entire operation down and destroy all evidence as if it had never existed."

Another long moment of silence, then Lukas shook his head. "Of course, Ezra never did it. I should have seen that right from the start."

"Seen what, sir? Not sure I'm following, sir."

"Ezra would never have destroyed my research," Lukas sighed. "Especially after Michael left home. Because destroying my research would be tantamount to giving up on his son. And in his heart, Ezra never gave up the hope that Michael would come back to claim his legacy. How could I, of all people, have been fooled into thinking otherwise?"

"Because you needed to be?"

Lukas shot Jonas a don't-go-there look. "Let's not overindulge in sharing, shall we? I think karma has already made that point quite sufficiently."

"Karma?" Jonas said. What came next? He was going to find out the yoga instructor had had her way with the old man after all, and now he meditated?

"I took Ezra's word the project was shut down." His eyes cut to Jonas. "Arguably yes, because I needed to. Needed to believe something like Michael would never happen again." He shook his head. "But I can't believe they're thinking about resurrecting it. Do you have any idea what kind of scientific mind that would take?"

"One like yours, sir?"

The old man's face set. "I investigated Michael Grinnell," he said. "I did not create him."

"If you say so, sir. In any case, that's not what matters. What matters is what you're going to do about it now."

"About the most sensible thing I can think of doing would be for the two of us to sit down and polish off a bottle of scotch."

"Sorry, sir?"

Lukas's hand ran through his hair again leaving Jonas to wonder if the earth had tilted off its axis. "To rephrase things only slightly, what on earth do you think I can do?"

"Dunno. But I heard the guy, sir. Heard him call you Doogie Howser. Heard him say that you were some kind of fucking genius once upon a time."

"Reports of my genius, like so much else, have been greatly exaggerated."

Yeah, sure. "I don't care. The point is, if anyone can stop them, it's you."

There was a pause. And then Lukas shook his head. "Maybe once upon a time. Now, I'm just ... old. And science is a young man's game."

"Seriously, sir?" Jonas said. "Seriously? Maybe you can believe that kind of crap when you're tanked up with scotch, but when you're sober, seriously?"

Lukas shot him a sharp, startled glance. And then the ghost of something strange—could it have been an unwilling smile?—flickered across his father's face.

"Actually, being sober makes it all the more glaringly obvious. But you're right. I will do what I can. I'll clean out the medicine cabinet at the Outreach Center, and ask Father Gregory to have a quiet word with Trey Carey."

"The hell with a quiet word." Jonas grabbed the old man's arm, which was about as fucking awkward as a group hug, but he didn't care. "Come on, Dad. We've gotta stop this."

Lukas froze. "No," he said very calmly. "I've got to stop this. You are going to go up to your room and forget you ever saw that phone."

Jonas crossed his arms. "Why? You don't think I've earned the right—"

"This has nothing to do with rights. This has everything to do with the fact that you're still sixteen and still my son. And you will do as I say."

Well, so much for the honeymoon. Looked like the lame bonding was right out the window, and his evil bastard of a father was back in town.

"Yessir. Of course, sir. And welcome back, sir. Nice to see that deep down you're still the same old asshole." Jonas snarled. "Christ, are you really that afraid of me being right for a change?"

"I'm not afraid of you!" Lukas exploded. "I'm afraid of them! And of what they can do to you. Do you really want them to cut the brakes on your car to keep you quiet? Or maybe they'll bollix the job as bad as they did with me, and leave you a cr..."

Lukas stopped mid-sentence, but it was too late. Jonas stared at the wheelchair as pain and anger knotted his stomach. A secret military project? Followed by—what had the old man called it?—a hiatus? Those bastards. Those lousy, mean bastards. Was that what had happened to the old man? To *his* old man? To his *father*?

"They did this to you?" he breathed. "Because of Michael Grinnell?"

"It doesn't matter," Lukas said. "It was a long time ago."

Really? Jonas didn't think so. Instead, what he thought was that, for once in his life, the great Lukas Croswell was wrong. It might have been a long time ago, but it sure as hell did matter.

"We'll pay them back, Dad," Jonas said softly. "With interest. We'll take them down. We'll pay them back for what they did to you, I swear it."

His father turned on him, his green eyes distant. "No one is paying anyone back," he enunciated. "Especially me. Doctors don't engage in payback. Doctors heal. It's in the job description. To the point where I would heal that pernicious half-wit who attacked you if the situation arose. Before I made sure he was locked up in jail for good. So I will do what I can to clean this cancer out of the Outreach Center. And you will go to bed or play video games or whatever it is you prefer to do upstairs—I won't insult you by adding the caveat as long as it is legal. And that is not open to discussion. Do I make myself clear?"

Chapter Nineteen

"May I come in?"

Was that anything but a rhetorical question? It didn't matter that Father Gregory had knocked before manifesting and was now waiting on her threshold like a polite Jesuit genie. The college president was the proverbial 800-pound gorilla. The man went wherever he wanted to.

Awkwardly, Clare pushed her guest chair forward. Then she saw Trey Carey hovering in the hallway, and jumped to her feet. "I'm afraid I don't have another chair."

Trey waved for her to sit back down, as if she had been offering him her chair, rather than contemplating fleeing. "Wouldn't have a lady standing. The ghost of my sainted grandmother would flay me alive."

Far more likely that he wanted to loom in the doorway, playing bad cop to Father Gregory, who had clearly been dragooned into the role of peacemaker. Clare's hard, wooden guest chair had been designed not to encourage students to linger, but Father Gregory settled into it as easily as if it had been one of the padded leather ones around his conference table.

"Trey suggested we need to clarify a few issues about you and Michael."

"Sean," Clare corrected.

"I'm sorry?"

"His name is Sean, not Michael."

"Oh, yes. Of course," Father Gregory said. "Well, whatever name he chooses to go by, now that you've dealt with him directly, I think you can understand why, as miracles go, he's always been considered of rather … dubious quality."

As if Sean were some kind of hagiographic remainder. The only thing that kept Clare's temper from flaring was the knowledge that Sean would prefer it that way. "I'm not sure I understand," Clare said. "Do you need me to sign off on something? Prepare a final report?"

"Oh, no, no, no," Father Gregory said. "I think we're all agreed that this matter is best handled informally."

"What matter?"

"Exactly what we talked about last time." Preliminaries dispensed with, Trey stepped in to take charge of what clearly had been his meeting all along. "Michael's infatuation with you. Have you finally come to realize how dangerous that could prove? Have you thought about what it would be like to have him obsessed with you? Stalking you?"

Well, actually, no. Clare had thought about none of that. Clare had simply thought about ... Sean. About a lonely man who flushed like a schoolboy, even though he tried like hell to hide it. A lonely man, who had been a lonely child, first cut off from, and then confronted with, a world he couldn't understand.

"No," she said. "No, I don't see why you think he's infatuated or obsessed with me, and I'm not particularly worried about anyone stalking me."

Trey smiled. It looked like nothing so much as a snake unlocking its jaw to swallow its prey. And Clare barely had time to wonder what was so funny about what she had just said, before he pulled off the gloves, and casually knocked her world for a loop. "That's right," he said. "You're not worried. Because you've been down this road before, haven't you? This is old home week for you."

Still, Clare still had trouble parsing his meaning. Because what he was saying was frankly impossible. How could he know? Those records had been sealed.

As Clare's thought whirled, Father Gregory shot Trey a sharp glance. "There seems to be something here I'm not quite following."

Maybe. But Clare was following just fine. "I have nothing more to say," she hissed. "I want you out of here."

Father Gregory's face darkened with concern. "Perhaps we should all take a moment to recall that we're on the same side here."

"Really?" Clare asked. "And what side is that?"

"Well, the side of the angels, of course."

Father Gregory smiled to signal this was one of his little jokes, meant to defuse the situation, but for Clare, the cord was already sparking. "Look, if you want to call me the Cosplay Lolita why don't you just go ahead and do it?"

She was rewarded by seeing something she never thought she'd see in her life: Father Gregory looking stupefied. "I can honestly say that wasn't my intention."

Jesus! What was she thinking? Her mother had always said she had a self-destructive streak, not a temper, but that little outburst would have exceeded even her mother's expectations.

"I apologize if my words were open to misinterpretation," Father Gregory went on.

"Then why don't you just come out and say what you mean? What do you want from me?" She jerked her head at Trey. "What does he want?"

"I want to help you, Clare. That's all any of us want," Trey said.

"Could you be a little more specific?" Grudgingly, she addressed him directly. Anything else would have been childish. As the Victim's Advocate had explained when Clare had tried the same trick with her. "Tell me exactly what you're planning to do."

"I want you to request an order of protection against Michael. Tell the court he's been stalking you, which is more or less the truth. Then when he comes for you again—which he will—we'll be able to arrest him."

And in that moment, Clare didn't give a damn whether she had a self-destructive streak or not. She pinioned Father Gregory with a glare. "And are you party to this plan?"

Father Gregory didn't answer. It was a silence that was at least as spectacular as one of Lukas Croswell's. In fact, arguably, it was even more so. It was the silence of a Christ being offered all the world's riches if only he would fall down and worship Satan—the silence of a Christ who, even while he was refusing, had to admit the Devil's logic was impeccable.

"I asked you a question," she repeated. "Are you suggesting I gain his trust, then sell him out? Is that somehow okay because I'm doing it *ad majorem dei gloriam* instead of for thirty pieces of silver?"

The words were out of Clare's mouth before she wished them back—before she knew that she wanted to wish them back. God, talk about a self-destructive streak. She might as well begin sending out CV's to other post-doc programs tomorrow.

"It is widely theologically accepted that Judas was a necessary part of God's plan. Some even argue for his salvation on those grounds," Father Gregory pointed out.

"Dante put him between Brutus and Cassius, in Satan's center mouth, being gnawed on for eternity."

"I have always found that man's taste for meting out punishment unsettling."

"But you're willing to let Trey arrest Sean for something he didn't even do? Why? Because as miracles go, he's of 'dubious quality'?"

For a moment, Father Gregory looked genuinely offended. And then he said with forced good humor, "Tempting as it is to take refuge in pointing out that even the Inquisition respected the separation between canon law and civil law, I'll just say no, I am not willing to be a party to that." He turned to Trey. "Honestly, this is going too far—"

"Not half as far as Dr. Malley was willing to go last time."

"How dare you?" Clare was on her feet, her face white with fury.

"I warned you. You do not want me as an enemy." Trey took a step closer, all prosecutor now. "But it's your good luck that I've got larger fish to fry. So I'm giving you one last chance. You can help me bring down Michael Grinnell, or I can take you down—"

"That's enough." Father Gregory sprang between them with the alacrity of a man who had done his time in parochial school playgrounds. "Before we all say things we may regret, may I please speak with Dr. Malley alone? *Now.*"

The last word hung in the air with the force of an exorcism, and Trey cast Father Gregory a long look. Then he shrugged. "I'll leave you to it, Padre."

As Trey's footsteps died off down the hall, Father Gregory closed the door deliberately. Sitting back down, he steepled his fingers and bent his head over them. Clare assumed he was marshalling his thoughts, but, as she slid unwillingly back into her chair, she couldn't help but feel obscurely like she should bow her head, too, and murmur "Amen."

When he looked up, his face was troubled. "First off, I'd like to apologize for involving you in the first place. This was meant to be a simple research project. If I had had any idea that things were destined to get this complicated, I would have handled it myself."

"'Sokay," Clare said, as ungraciously as if she were still a teenager.

Father Gregory frowned. "Unfortunately, I'm not so sure of that. Would I be correct in inferring that Trey Carey feels he has some kind of hold over you?"

"Trey Carey is nothing but a bully."

"That's hardly an answer to my question," Father Gregory pointed out. "Clare, please listen. If you find yourself in some kind of trouble over something I brought you into, I would feel morally obligated to set it right."

"The records are sealed. He has no right ..."

"May I remind you that we in the Church have our seals, too?"

"I'm not Catholic," Clare said, feeling more mulish and adolescent by the minute. "Not even Christian, technically."

Father Gregory raised an eyebrow.

She flushed. "I converted to Catharism a while back."

"As one so often does." Father Gregory ruminated briefly. "Vegetarians, if I'm not mistaken."

"Actually pescetarians," Clare said. "They ate fish."

"Past lives," he went on.

"They believed in reincarnation," Clare confirmed. "In sort of the Buddhist sense. That we are destined to reincarnate endlessly as humans until we can achieve an enlightened state that raises us above the miseries of this world and of the flesh"

And speaking of the flesh…

"Free love."

She winced. "Well, yes, the notion was that if you were not going to strive to become Perfect in this life, it really didn't matter what you did, because you were going to be reincarnated anyway."

"And, if I recall correctly, the Grail," Father Gregory concluded.

"Everyone's favorite New Age heresy," Clare said.

And the sum total of the major rebellion of her teenaged years. The guilty, dirty secret she had been trying to put behind her for over a decade. Out here in the open like this, it merely seemed … quaint. Hardly the scandalous sin that had shattered the rectory's careful calm with talk of cults and defrocking. And ultimately arrests.

"I've more or less lapsed," she said. "I'm beginning to think it was a phase."

"As it so often is. Some of our best people have experimented with dualism, you know. St. Augustine, to name just one." Another moment's rumination, and then he asked, "So is that what's at stake here? Should I be worried about Trey Carey demanding I preach another Albigensian Crusade?"

Clare forced a smile at what she fervently hoped was just another of Father Gregory's witticisms. "With all respect, it's not a joke."

"No," he agreed, abruptly serious. "It's not. Beliefs never are. And while your beliefs are your own, they're not the issue here. This is about my beliefs, not yours. It's about vows I took. Vows I still take very seriously. And those vows mean that if there is one person you could confide in without fear of reprisal, it would be me. I hold the seal of the confessional as a sacred trust."

Clare stared at him, suddenly aware that, despite the clericals, despite the vaguely ritual air he lent to everything he did, it was very easy to forget he was a priest. And then she found herself wondering what it might be like to think of him as one. Wondering, as only someone who had grown up in a rectory could wonder, what it might be like to respect a priest as a man who believed sincerely in his vocation, rather than just seeing a henpecked husband who hid from his family and flock's venial failings behind a wall of books. To trust in his wisdom. Even to confide in him.

But it was too little, too late. That particular spiritual boat had sailed a long time ago. Stifling a vague sense of regret, she shook her head. "Thank you for the offer, but if it's all the same to you, I don't feel the need to confess anything right now."

Father Gregory eyed her another moment, his eyes dark with concern, before he conceded the point. "Nonetheless," he said. "For what it may be worth, *Absolvo te*."

∞

The damned priest was back, sitting in Sean's booth like he was waiting in a confessional—if, that is, priests were wont to sip whiskey while hearing confessions. Which Sean was willing to guess they did. How else could you anesthetize yourself to the endless round of stupid, meaningless, and frankly boring bad choices that most people called their lives?

"Don't you have something else to do?" Sean asked. "Converting the heathen? Saving souls on the Bowery?"

"Just taking a moment to give thanks for the Lord's bounty. Nothing like good whiskey and good music to see His hand in all things."

"Most people say the fiddle is the Devil's instrument."

"Tradition would have it that Lucifer was the leader of the Celestial Choir before his Fall," the priest replied.

With a sigh, Sean set his pint on the table and slid into the booth. "So what is it about this time?"

"Clare Malley," the priest said. "As I assume you've already suspected."

"What about her?" Sean snorted. "That if I come back from the dead, step up and claim what's mine, I'll be a rich man? Rich enough to attract the likes of her? Maybe even enough to make her overlook my—what should we call them, character flaws? It's a lot to overlook, but I'm told a billion dollars sweetens the pot considerably." He shook his head. "You think that's a persuasive argument?"

The priest's smile was almost avuncular. "You clearly do," he said. "I, on the other hand, would be remiss if I did not point out that human love mirrors God's love in all things, but most especially in the fact that neither can be bought or earned, only freely given. In fact, they would never let me teach Faith and Critical Reasoning again if I didn't make that perfectly clear. However, if you were of a mind to step up and claim your share of the Grinnell family fortune, and were looking for guidance in disposing of it ..."

Christ in heaven. Being autistic might have sucked, but at least it had spared Sean Catechism class. He was in no mood to get whatever the Catholic equivalent was of a GED. "I'm not of a mind," Sean said. "You said this was about Clare. What do you want to know? Whether she's the reason I went to see Trey? That I am interested in her? The answer is yes and yes. Apparently, I'm more capable of human emotion than was previously suspected. But I'm also smart enough to know I can't have her. Not even with a billion dollars to sweeten the pot."

"We all make mistakes," Father Gregory said.

"Not me, remember? It's kind of my thing."

"Do you prefer the term 'blind spot'?"

A blind spot? Hadn't Sean spent almost his entire damned life looking for such a thing? Wanting them so bad that on some days—the worst days—he had thought about gouging out his own eyes like Oedipus? Sean took a drink of lager. A long drink. "And what is it you think I'm not seeing?"

Father Gregory's face darkened. "You threatened Trey Carey. Why?"

"To convince him to lay off the drug dealers he's framing. They'll get themselves back in trouble soon enough. Let karma do its work."

"So why the drama? Why confront him publicly in the Yacht Club?"

"People like him are like mules. You've got to bang them over the head to get their attention."

"I'm afraid I'd argue that you banged him over the head, simply because you wanted to bang him over the head." Father Gregory shook his head. "For God's sake, why, when there was a simpler way? Why not just step up and accept what I strongly suspect your father wanted to hand down to you?"

And for a moment, Sean could see the ghost of the old man flickering translucently opposite him, nodding as if the priest had made an important point. "Yeah, well, the whole Father's will thing, that's the other guy, remember."

"Word games be damned! What was that outburst other than the petulant behavior of a spoiled child?"

The will of an *orisha*? Who seemed to own Sean's immortal soul?

No, that way lay madness.

But didn't that pretty much sum up all of Sean's behavior, ever since he had caught that first glimpse of Clare Malley's hair gleaming in the sunlight?

"It was just a threat. A feint, nothing more."

"It was a colossal blunder."

Sean took a drink, startled to realize his fingers were shaking. Which was going to make playing any more tonight impossible. And right now, he wanted—no, needed—to dive back into his music, as badly as an alcoholic needed to dive into his next drink. Another thing to thank this damned interfering priest for. "I thought we'd just agreed I don't make mistakes."

"Not even the pope is infallible. And frankly he was much easier to convince than you are proving to be," Father Gregory said, once again with that damned avuncular smile. But as quickly as it was there, it was gone. "Honestly, Mi … Sean. A chess player of your caliber, and you all but announced to Trey Carey that Clare Malley is special to you? Did you really think you could expose that kind of weakness, and he wouldn't use it against you? Even by your standards, that's quite some blind spot."

The trembling in Sean's fingers redoubled, as his uncertainty became palpable. No. Not his uncertainty. His certainty. His absolute conviction, without any special powers whatsoever, that the impossible had occurred. Sean had made a mistake. Hell, why stop there? Sean had fucked up for real this time.

"What do you think he's going to do to her?" He tried to speak dispassionately, like a chess player considering a particularly complex problem, but the shaking in his hands was uncontrollable now, and the pint glass sloshed mercilessly as he tried to set it back on the wooden table.

"As best I can gather, Trey Carey has some kind of information he thinks he can hold over Dr. Malley's head. Something to do with some sealed juvenile records."

"Clare?" Sean demanded, shock stilling his shaking. "You want me to believe Clare has a juvenile record?"

"Apparently, quite a colorful one."

"What kind of record?"

The priest slanted him a long look. "She didn't see fit to confide in me," he said. "That is, beyond telling me she had converted to Catharism and dropping the somewhat memorable phrase 'Cosplay Lolita.'"

And for someone whose wheelhouse wasn't emotions, Sean was suddenly buried beneath a flood of feelings. Surprise, of course. Confusion, too. But also a sneaking, ugly sense of hope—that if, deep down underneath, Clare Malley wasn't so perfect after all, maybe even a guy like him stood a chance with her.

But since he'd already conceded he didn't have a goddamned chance in hell with her, his chess brain kicked back in, there was only one logical conclusion to be drawn. This was wrong. It couldn't be true. And, blind spot be damned, that was his wheelhouse.

"If it matters, I blame myself as much as I blame you," Father Gregory said.

"Then why don't you go ahead and do something about it?" Sean asked sourly. "Why bother me?"

Father Gregory raised an eyebrow. "Because right now, I haven't the faintest idea what to do," he said. "I'm hoping you do."

"You mean, you want me to … look," Sean swallowed hard, remembering the rush of filth the first time he had touched Trey Carey. He wasn't sure he could do it again. Not even to help Clare.

"Of course not. Even if I'm not entirely certain what exactly 'looking' means," Father Gregory said with a sigh. "All I'm asking you to do is think. You're the master strategist, aren't you? So tell me how Trey Carey would strategize. Size him up like you would an opponent across the chessboard. Tell me about his strengths and weaknesses. Analyze his game."

Sean eyed the priest over the rim of his pint, even though his chess brain was already kicking in, analyzing his opponent's strengths and weaknesses, breaking down his game. Falling into rhythms almost as comforting as playing music.

Not that he really need much concentration to break down Trey Carey's game. His only strength was brute strength; there was nothing elegant about the way he played. Bullying, brutal, and straightforward. Just banging around the field, attacking as many pieces as he could, without any real strategy, just a willingness to keep on punching until something fell down.

And right now he was aiming a roundhouse at Clare.

"If there are drugs involved, even tangentially, it's the most obvious option," Sean said, trying very hard not to think about the words "Cosplay Lolita." And failing miserably. "He'll turn the Lazaritos on her. Tell them, she's trying to muscle in on their territory. They'll go for her, and he'll arrest them. It takes out both of his problems at once."

Father Gregory drew a sharp breath. "Do you really think he would go as far as trying to kill her?"

"He doesn't think that far in advance," Sean said. "He just sees two problems, and is just bright enough to figure that the simplest solution is to turn one on the other. Still, I think he'll step in before Clare gets hurt."

"So he can continue to hold her over your head?"

"Honestly, it's more because the death of a pretty white college professor will garner a lot more attention than a couple of Lazaritos shooting one another. And that's not the kind of attention Trey Carey wants or needs." Draining his glass, Sean got up from the table, doing his best to ignore the shadow in a porkpie hat that suddenly seemed to be swelling in every direction he looked. "So there's my answer. Your mission, if you choose to accept it, is keeping those lowlifes alive and out of trouble, despite their natural inclinations. In the meantime, I'll see what I can manage to do to help Clare. That is, if she's inclined to let me."

Chapter Twenty

Clare had knocked the coffee cup off the table accidentally. She had not thrown it. Honestly. Which was not to say that throwing something wasn't what she wanted to do every time she talked with her mother.

"Your father is upset."

It was her mother's customary salutation—except when she was calling to confirm the command performances scheduled for Thanksgiving, Christmas, and Easter. In that case it shifted to a conditional. Your father would be so upset... Both grammatical moods were frankly nonsense. Clare's father had long ago retreated into his study and the definitive dictionary of British saints that was his life's work, gladly leaving the management of the uncomfortable problems of both his family and his flock in the expert hands of his wife.

"Is something wrong?" Clare asked. Which she knew was about the response most calculated to irritate her mother that she could have come up with. Unfortunately, she really wanted to know the answer.

"What do you think?" her mother sighed. "Honestly, Clare. What do you hope to accomplish with all this? A memoir? Please tell me you're not writing a memoir. You know I loathe memoirs."

Well, actually, Clare did know her mother hated memoirs. But her mother's statement had been strictly hortatory. Not to mention, ominously clairvoyant. Clare eyed the phone, fighting down her rising conviction that, just as her mother had ferreted out the Warden's drinking problem, or the choirmaster's unfortunate taste for under-aged boys, she had found out about the scene with Father Gregory and Trey Carey. But how? Was Clare seriously going to believe that Father Gregory had called her mother to report that she had acted out in class? Or the even more worrisome possibility that Clare was poised to relapse into Catharism?

"I'm sorry. Can you just slow down a little?" Clare said, heading for the kitchen to find some paper towels to mop up the spilled coffee, which she had not meant to throw. Really. "I still don't understand what you're talking about."

Or maybe Clare simply didn't want to understand. Whatever the case, her mother's answer hit her like a body blow.

"Your records, of course. You know that as well as I do."

And there it was—impossible as it had to be. "I don't suppose you're talking about my CDs?" Clare sighed.

"Honestly, Clare. I thought you would have outgrown sarcasm by now."

"I have." It had been more a last ditch hope. A case of denial, if you must. A frantic prayer that this whole thing couldn't be starting again.

But, if it was, at least one thing was going to be different. This time, at least, Clare was going to be in charge of the conversation. "Mother, would you please tell me exactly what's going on?"

Her mother drew an even deeper breath, martyring herself once again to her daughter's petulance. "Someone has applied to have your records unsealed. Your juvenile records. As I'm sure you must be well aware. Because for the life of me, I can't see why anyone else would want to do that but you. Not only that, but, if I understand the law correctly, no one else could have done it but you."

Taking charge was harder than she thought—even if she hadn't been fighting down a lifetime's conditioning. Clare had to keep her voice from shaking, as she said, "Be reasonable. Why do you think I'd want to do something like that?"

"That is what I called to ask you. Honestly, Clare, what on earth possessed you? What can you possibly hope to accomplish by this? Getting back at your father?"

Why would she do that? Clare liked her father, if only in the same, vague disinterested way he seemed to care about her. Now if it had been an issue of getting back at her mother...

"All I can tell you is, it wasn't me. But I promise you, I'll look into it. Okay?" she snapped, switching off her cell phone before she could listen to her mother's spluttered answer. And the hell with the land line that immediately began to ring in protest. And would continue to ring, incessantly, until a worn-out Clare picked up the phone and submitted to her mother's angry bullet points on what she needed to do next. Well, not this time. Things might be spinning out of control, but she could at least control that.

The only question was how? She needed to get out of her apartment, to do something—anything—other than succumbing to the guilty impulse to pick up the ringing phone. But where could she go? Back to All Saints to confess her sins to Father Gregory?

To her surprise, the possibility wasn't as unpalatable as she might have imagined. Advice—spiritual or otherwise—in her family, had been more a matter of a curriculum than conversations. Her spiritual path had been guided by a graded series of readers designed to occupy her quietly during her father's sermons; sex education had been managed by a similar series of books with bracing titles such as *Wonderfully Made*. The one time Clare had ventured to ask her father what a mastectomy was and why it made her next door neighbor cry like that, he had launched an anxious disquisition on St. Gwen the Triple-Breasted being so gifted in order to nurse her sons, the saints Wethnoc, Iacob, and Winwaloe, and the constant danger of confusing her with other Saint Gwens, such as Saint Gwen the Fair-Bearded. It seemed impossible to think of a priest in any other terms—especially in terms of them being a source of Ward Cleaver-worthy wisdom. But that was what they were supposed to do, wasn't it? That was why you called them 'Father,' right?

She considered the possibility as she packed her book bag. It seemed as impossible a fairy tale as St Gwen's (the Triple-Breasted, not the Fair-Bearded) walking back across the English Channel to Brittany when she had been kidnapped by Anglo-Saxon pirates. And yet how was Clare ever to find out if she didn't at least try?

She was still trying to answer that question as she took her usual detour through the park on her way to the train station. Fort Tryon Park was an elegant old aerie, whose steep cliffs overlooked the serene beauty of the Hudson River, a surprisingly suitable setting for the main reason Clare had chosen to live in this neighborhood: the Cloisters, a medieval warren of chapels and walled gardens, that gazed serenely, if unexpectedly, down on the tenements of Washington Heights and Inwood. But today Clare barely noticed the park's spectacular vistas. She was so preoccupied that she barely even noticed when a shadow reared in front of her, blocking her way.

"Excuse me," she murmured automatically, but as she tried to move past, he stepped in front of her, followed by several other shadows that emerged from nowhere to surround her.

"We've been looking for you," one of them said.

Blinking rudely back to reality, Clare stared in bewilderment at the gang of teenagers who had suddenly surrounded her, their hoodies pulled low to hide their faces. Did she know them? She wasn't sure. They were types, not people. Baggy pants, backwards baseball caps, sneers and too many gold chains. Coincidence then? Or Lazaritos? Both possibilities seemed—like so much else today—impossible and a logical inevitability. How could she tell? Was one of them Rafael? She didn't know. Right now, she couldn't even summon a mental picture of the kid.

"Look, if you want my wallet, I'll give it to you. No problem. There's some cash."

The first kid smiled. "We'll take the wallet. After we talk."

God in heaven. This couldn't really be happening. Not on top of everything else. She wondered what would happen is she told them the truth: that she'd already had her fill of lousy conversations today.

"Talk about what? Look, I don't know what you think I know, but—"

Her voice trailed off as one kid flashed a knife, and Clare sighed, once again wishing she'd studied judo or karate or had even taken a single, stinking women's self-defense course. But no, she'd been obsessed with fencing. And archery. And had been at long last able to inveigle her father into allowing one weekend's intensive on jousting. How useful was that? She could all but hear her mother crowing, without a horse or even a lance to hand?

"Look, whatever you think the problem is, this is not going to make matters any better."

Although how could matters get worse than being mugged over a miracle? The thought would be absurd, even on a thirteenth century pilgrimage along the Camino de Santiago.

The kid's mouth twisted, as he flicked the knife from hand to hand. "The Church is our territory. We want you out of there."

"That's fine. You don't have to threaten me."

And truth be told, she'd be happy never to go back there. She could find another article topic. Frankly, the Lazarites had always bored her silly. She was damned if she was going to let them bore her to death—literally.

The kid smiled. It was not a very nice smile. "You right. We don't," he said. "We just do that part for fun."

He flipped the knife again and took a step closer

And Clare didn't think. Didn't reach for her quiver and nock an arrow like Maid Marian. Didn't assume an *en garde* or think about fleches or parries or even couching her lance. She hoisted her bag, heavy with several books and her computer, and swung it at the nearest kid's face.

"Better be careful. I've heard librarians get tetchy when you get blood on their books."

The words whirled, along with Clare's vision, as a lanky figure in a shabby topcoat materialized out of nowhere, a fiddle case slung over one shoulder. Reaching out a hand to steady her almost absently, Sean turned on the kids. "You guys are slow learners, aren't you? You really want a second round with me?"

"Get out of here," one kid snapped. "This got nothing to do with you."

"Well, actually it does. Believe it or not, I've been asked to look out for you."

"For us? By who?"

Whom, Clare thought, fear making her grammatical.

"By someone who apparently cares. But even he could get pretty tired of how dumb you're being."

Sean's voice was lapsing into the same singsong as last time, but this time the kid was ready for it.

"Fuck, no. I'm not listening to you, man. Not going to let you hypnotize me again."

"It's not me doing it," Sean said. "But I could tell you who is. If I thought you had the brains to listen."

"I ain't listening to a fucking thing you have to say."

Sean shook his head. "Predictable," he said. "In fact, downright inevitable. So, I'll do my best to keep things simple. You may be a bunch of assholes, but you're a bunch of assholes that won the lottery, if you're not too stupid to lose your chance. Fate—or maybe something else—has just handed you one giant Get-Out-of-Jail-Free card. Not that I particularly like that fact, especially when you're holding a knife on a friend of mine. But it's your great good luck that I like Trey Carey even less than I like you. So here's some free advice. Find the priest. Trust him. And whatever you do, don't trust a damned thing Trey Carey tells you."

And, pushing aside the knife as casually as if he were waving off a waiter, he took Clare's arm and said, "Let's get out of here."

He started up the path to the museum, moving unhurriedly, seemingly not even noticing when the kids shouted angrily and sneakers squeaked after them.

"They have knives," Clare said.

"Then we'd better not let them get close enough to use them."

She glanced over at the museum's heavy, wooden doors. "We could head inside."

"If we do, they'll follow us, and find themselves arrested," Sean said. "Which is exactly what Trey wants."

"Then what?"

"This way," Sean said, as he led Clare toward the chained-off cobblestone drive that led toward the employee's entrance. His pace never varied, as he went up the cobbled drive, toward a utility path that led around the outside of the walled gardens, skittered down a steep embankment, disturbing a feral cat in the process, then turned to help her hop down onto the path that led past a great lawn overlooking the cliffs that dropped down to the Hudson itself. As you'd expect on a balmy day in May, the grass was crowded with sunbathers and tourists, school groups eating lunches, and a man performing yoga bare-chested, while a mastiff and a miniature schnauzer humped merrily on the grass beside him. It went without saying that the schnauzer was the male.

When they reached the far end of the lawn, Sean paused and turned back, just as the first of the kids raced around the corner, blood in his eye. But Sean barely seemed to care. Instead he focused on a passing woman who was chattering on a cell phone, apparently uninterested in either the baby she pushed in a carriage that looked like it had been designed by NASA or the tiny Yorkie *tip-tapping* along beside her on a retractable leash.

The bare-chested man swung up into a headstand.

At the same moment, the Yorkie caught sight of the schnauzer and mastiff, and lunged to invite a threesome. The woman dropped her cell phone and reached for her baby.

"Let's go," Sean said, just as a thump, a grunt, and an angry curse rang out.

Moments later, a dog growled and a child began to wail.

"Hey!" a woman shouted. "You can't shove a child like that!"

"Shit!" a kid yelled. "Get that fucking wolf away from me!"

"Someone call the police."

Clare cast Sean a covert look, but he never varied his long, loping stride.

"Might as well keep moving," he said. "Just in case."

He said nothing more. Simply strode across the traffic circle at the end of the park, heading unerringly for the shelter of yet another one of the weirdly medieval monuments that popped out of nowhere in this neighborhood. Only when they were safely hidden behind the tall, stone walls, did she find herself able to speak. "So which is it?" she asked. "Do you just see things coming or can you actually cause them to happen?"

"Whichever answer is more likely to make you come along quietly," he said with a quick grin.

"Come along where?"

"Not sure yet," he said. "I suppose back to your apartment, but it doesn't feel quite right."

"What does that mean?"

"That it's not a Magic 8 ball," he said. His face grew distant. "At the very least, you need to make sure you're not just leading that bunch straight there. Although the point may be moot. It seems like someone has already told them where to find you."

"Seriously?"

"Unfortunately, yes," he said.

When it was clear he intended to say nothing more, Clare asked, "At the risk of being pushy, are you going to tell me what's going on here?"

He turned to look at her, his eyes sad, apologetic. "I screwed something up. Badly. I was hoping that wasn't true, but there's no question about it now."

"Screwed what up?"

"It's complicated."

"Oh, come on. We're not quibbling about our relationship here. I'm just looking for an answer."

A startled grin flashed across his face, but he sobered immediately. "Look," he said, "you know I would never invade your privacy, unless it was absolutely necessary …"

Her privacy? Necessary?

"What the hell does that mean?" She shut her eyes as she realized there was only one possible answer to that question. God. Hadn't everyone been trying to warn her? Sean saw things. No, Michael did. Michael saw things and Michael liked to look. Hadn't everyone told her? Just as everyone had also told her that Michael Grinnell liked to play with his food.

"You bastard!" she said, her voice low with fury. "You're the one who had my records unsealed? Why? Because I found yours? Are you giving me a taste of my own medicine? Payback?"

He went pale. "Do you really think I would do a thing like that?"

"Your reputation does precede you."

"So it does." Sean sounded so hurt that Clare wished she could have the hasty words back. Then his face set. "If you thought about my reputation for even one minute, you'd see how genuinely stupid that accusation is," he said without any emotion at all. "If I wanted to know more about you than I already did, I didn't need to unseal any records. I can just go ahead and look. If you don't believe me, want me to demonstrate?"

He reached toward her. And suddenly Clare was as afraid of him as the kids in the park had been. "Go to hell," she choked, snatching away her hand. "Go to hell and just leave me alone."

"Clare, I'm sorry. You know I would never—"

Christ. Clare didn't know what she knew any more, beyond the fact that she had been about to trust a man everyone had warned her was a psychopath. She didn't have to be her mother to see how stupid that was.

"Please, wait! It's not safe."

His voice rang after her as she plunged out through the shrine's heavy iron gate, heading blindly back home, back to the damned telephone that she knew was still ringing, back to the dressing down she knew she didn't deserve. Anything to get away from him.

Her eyes brimmed with a teenager's tears at the unfairness of it all, clouding her eyes as well as her judgment, so that when she finally reached her apartment, she didn't even notice the delivery man with the long, old-fashioned box of roses standing in the lobby, until a hand closed over her arm, and Sean said very quietly, "Please stop now."

"Why should I?"

Sean nodded toward the delivery man. "Him."

Her eyes widened in disbelief as she took in the florist's box. "Peace offering?" she snorted. "That's pretty prescient even by your standards."

"They're not from me," he said. "And I'm willing to wager they're not roses."

Something in his voice made her glance at him sharply. "What then?"

"I'm guessing he's a process server, and there's a subpoena inside that box."

"You're guessing? Or you know?"

He shrugged and glanced at box as if it might explode. "Apologies for being direct, but we're a little short on time, and I'm very short on diplomacy under the best of circumstances. So instead of worrying about exactly how I got to my conclusions, can you just allow me to lay out the situation for you? It stands to reason that Trey Carey would subpoena you."

"Why? What have I done?"

"You don't have to have done anything. You can just be subpoenaed to provide a witness statement or even evidence. But once you're giving a formal statement, it opens you up to obstruction of justice charges if you lie. Or even just contradict yourself. And those kind of threats are a prosecutor's weapon of choice."

And Clare had only to think of the Victim's Advocate and her relentless grilling to know Sean was telling the truth. How many times had Clare changed her story then? Stumbled over a detail? And that was with someone who insisted she was on Clare's side, not someone who'd already warned her she didn't want him as an enemy.

"Still, there's some good news," Sean said. "A subpoena has to be served personally. So if you can just manage to stay out of this guy's way for a couple of days..."

"How can I do that? He's at my house."

"That's why I think we need to get out of here. Go someplace where no one would think to look for you."

He spoke with the casual aplomb of a man for whom this was an everyday occurrence. But what kind of man would that be? What could possibly lead a man to spend his entire life on the run?

The delivery man rang a bell; it might have been hers. Sean cocked his head. "Come with me or deal with Trey," he said, as neutrally as if he were describing a chess opening. "It's your choice."

And he just took off walking toward the train station without a backward glance. She hesitated, glaring after him. What an impossible man! But the memory of Trey's quick prosecutorial questions were worse. "So where are we heading?" she sighed, as she hurried after him.

"I was thinking the Waldorf." The words floated back over his shoulder, stopping her in her tracks.

"You really are insane, aren't you?"

"Not in the least. We'll hole up for tonight, maybe until the weekend—however long it takes for Father Gregory to talk some sense into those kids. Live off room service. Play video games. I can teach you to fiddle, if you'd like. The worst anyone can assume is that it's a passionate tryst. Which may mean people will wonder about your taste in men afterwards, but at least you won't be facing obstruction of justice charges."

And just like anything about Sean, it made complete sense and no sense at all.

"Sounds like a great plan," she sighed. "Except for one small fact: I have approximately forty dollars in my wallet, and as a professor, my credit card is going to be woefully inadequate for a vacation at the Waldorf. I'm guessing you have less. So how exactly are you planning to for our little idyll? Are you going to set up shop on a street corner and fiddle for the rest?"

He turned back to her, and she was startled to see he was smiling for real—eyes twinkling, full lips curved to reveal a row of white teeth, the tiniest dimple in his cheek. The whole shebang. Her heart did a little somersault despite herself.

"Oh, there're a lot easier ways of getting money than that," he said.

Chapter Twenty-one

Bryant Park was more a garden than a park, walled on one side by the beaux-arts rear façade of the New York Public Library, and on the other three sides by skyscrapers. The result was a peculiarly intimate space, a gracious enclosure more closely resembling the cultivated bowers in medieval manuscripts than the wild landscape that was Central Park. The park had seen its ups and downs over the years, but right now it was riding a high, with spectacular flower borders, chattering crowds enjoying outdoor drinks at the two restaurants at the rear of the library, and folding tables and chairs scattered everywhere, in imitation of a Parisian boulevard.

One row of them bore plastic chessboards. And it was there Sean headed.

"You mind giving me that forty dollars?" he asked.

Wordlessly, Clare pulled out the pair of twenties and handed it to him.

Folding them between his fingers, he approached the row of players hunched in furious concentration over the boards. As soon as he did, a bolt of energy seemed to rocket down the line, and a pair of tables cleared, as if by magic. He sat down, placing the twenty between the two boards, and immediately he had two opponents sitting opposite him, each of them throwing down their money for the privilege of playing against him.

It was, Clare discovered as she watched in disbelief, an extremely brief pleasure indeed. He mated one player within ten moves; the other took only a few minutes longer.

"Better than last time," Sean pointed out, as the second player took his leave.

"Been practicing," the kid replied. "One day soon, I might even force you into a stalemate."

"Maybe," Sean allowed, his attention already on the next two players to stake their money.

Those players were followed by another pair in rapid succession, until Clare began to lose count, and her mind drifted—back to what she had once considered the worst mistake she ever made in her life. All she could wonder was whether she was making a far worse one right now.

"You with me?" Sean's voice sent her spluttering back to consciousness. "Something wrong?"

She blinked back to reality to find Sean studying her with obvious concern. "Nothing," she said. "Just woolgathering."

As her mother liked to put it.

"Then it's time to go," he said, hoisting his fiddle over his shoulder. "I've got no more takers here. But this should at least cover dinner."

He handed her a wad of bills. She shook her head in disbelief. There had to be at least a couple of hundred dollars there.

"That's quite some gift you've got."

"Not really," he said with a shake of his head. "Like I told you. I just can calculate possibilities. Very, very quickly. So quickly that I just sort of ... see them."

"Must help when you're playing chess."

"Actually, it kind of takes the fun out of it. But it's a living," he said. "Come on. Let's go."

"Where?"

"Like I said, the Waldorf."

"I think you're going to need to win a few more chess games to do that."

"Oh ye of little faith," he said. And with no further word of warning or explanation, he took off down 42nd Street, straight toward the shortcut through Grand Central Terminal, without so much as a backward glance to see whether she was following.

She caught up with him at the balustrade that overlooked the Main Concourse, where commuters hurried back and forth even at this time of day. And suddenly she found herself wondering what Sean was seeing when he looked down at them. An entire terminal's worth of petty secrets and genuine sins? She shook her head. Was she seriously supposed to believe he had some kind of ability to read people's minds? No, not their minds, their souls? How could she begin to imagine what it might be like? It was hard enough living with your own shortcomings—your own sins—but having the whole world's failings laid bare before you must be nearly impossible to live with.

Her eyes drifted up to the terminal's great painted ceiling, with its golden procession of a water bearer, a fish, a ram, Herakles wielding his club against a bull, a pair of interlaced twins and a crab across a background of twinkling stars. "A God's eye view," she said.

"I'm sorry?" he said.

"The Zodiac up there," she said. "It's backwards. Most people say that was because the artist was an idiot, but there are those who said he painted it from God's point of view, not our own. Which might be fine for a ceiling, but it must be hell to live with."

"When you consider the alternative…," Sean said with a shrug.

She flushed, made even more embarrassed by his matter-of-fact tone. "I'm sorry," she said. "I've no right to intrude like that."

"I don't know. I suppose being on the lam with someone gives you certain rights you might not ordinarily have."

"Is that what we are?" she asked. "On the lam?"

"Well, I'm not spiriting you off to Gretna Green, if that's what you're worried about."

"Would you please be serious?"

"Apologies," he said again. "But a man can always dream."

And shoving his hands into the pockets of his coat, he strolled off, leaving her to follow or not, as she chose.

∞

When Sean strode right past the Waldorf Astoria's main entrance on Park Avenue, which today was flying a British flag next to the American one above the art deco canopy, Clare began to assume with some small measure of relief that he had only been joking. But as soon as he reached the corner, he turned down a side street, to a discreet driveway that cut through the belly of the building for guests who preferred not to advertise their entrance. A security guard with the burly build of an ex-cop scrambled to his feet as soon as they stepped through the sliding glass doors, and Clare shot Sean an apprehensive glare. But the guard's face broke into a smile, and he hurried over to greet them with open arms.

"Sean, my lad," he said. "*Cead mile failte*. Are we to enjoy the pleasure of your company tonight?"

"If you have a room available," Sean replied, "I'd be deeply obliged."

"Sure, and we know who's obliged to whom here," the Irishman said. "And that's a debt that can't be repaid in my lifetime."

"There's no question of debt when it comes to friends helping friends," Sean said. "Still I'd be very grateful if you have a room."

"Of course, of course," the Irishman said. He seemed to notice Clare for the first time, and he took his time appraising her. When he turned back to Sean, there was a hint of mischief in his gaze. "At the risk of being indelicate, do you have any specific preferences in terms of accommodations?"

Sean laughed. "Two beds, please, and nothing delicate about it. This is strictly business."

The Irishman's face fell. "Sure, and that is a pity," he said, with a lingering look at Clare. "Oh well. Just give me a minute, and I'll see what we have."

He hustled off as Clare simply stared at Sean in disbelief. "Do you usually entertain your lady friends like this?"

"I don't have any lady friends," he said. "Most of them write me off as the most annoying man alive, remember? But Bobby never gives up hope. Die-hard romantic, that one, like all Ulstermen."

It took only minutes for the Irishman to return with a pair of card keys. "Two double beds as requested. Still, I'll be saying my prayers that circumstances change."

"Thank you," Sean said gravely, as he took the keys. "For both the room and the prayers."

"Oh, and I'd be very obliged if you ordered whatever you like from room service," the Irishman added, his brogue deepening along with the mischief in his face. "As you can see from the flag flying out front, our distinguished guest today is from England. I've arranged to have whatever you order added to his bill—as a small patriotic gesture. *Tiocfaidh ar la*. Our day will come."

∞

The room was nicer than any hotel Clare had ever stayed in, fitted with deep carpets, warm bedding, luxuriously upholstered furniture, and a dressing room/bathroom area with a raised marble tub and every toiletry you could possible imagine. Clare shook her head as she took it all in. "So how exactly does this work? Do you feed your friend downstairs stock tips in exchange for the occasional room?"

"More a little matter of his son avoiding a very bad choice," Sean said. "I was just pleased to be able to help, but Bobby has an Irishman's reverence for an obligation. Or a feud."

She laughed despite herself. "You know, Father Gregory said that as a specimen, you were of questionable quality. He was talking about miracles, but I still think he has a point."

"Meaning?"

"You make a lousy sociopath."

Sean didn't speak for a moment. "Nicest thing anyone's said to me a long time," he finally said with a reluctant smile.

"As long as we're on the subject, I'm sorry I accused you of spying on my records."

"No need to apologize. Seeing as I'm the one who got you into this mess, you have every right to feel punitive."

"Still, it was a horrible thing to say when you were only trying to help …"

"Hey, still a sociopath, even if I'm a lousy one. No need to overshare," he cut her off. Reaching into his coat pocket, he pulled out a miniature chess set. "As far as I'm concerned, the matter's closed."

She placed her hand on his arm. "No," she said. "We need to talk."

He looked her in the eye. "Usually, it takes some wild sex and a couple of fights before I hear that from a woman."

"Well, what do you say we table the first two for now?" she said. "And let's get this over with."

He studied her. "You sure you wouldn't rather talk to Father Gregory?"

"Why? Are you afraid of what I might have to say?"

"Maybe a little," he said.

"I smoked some pot," she said. "Played some D&D. Learned to joust. Inspired a troubadour. Converted to Catharism. You know, the usual sequence of events. And then things got out of hand."

"As they do," Sean agreed.

The words died off into uncomfortable silence.

"Honestly, I'd like it a lot better if you'd just ... look," Clare said.

"No."

"There's nothing to be afraid of, really. You won't find any horrible secrets if you do." She forced a laugh. "That's what makes the whole thing so damnably embarrassing. I had an upbringing straight out of *Leave it to Beaver*. Well, actually, closer to *Little Women*, complete with playing *Pilgrim's Progress* up and down the stairs on rainy days."

"What kind of game is that?" he asked, sounding genuinely puzzled.

"A smarmily sanctimonious one. Could never understand why my parents loved that book."

"Which one?"

"Either," she said. "Then again, there was a whole lot I didn't understand about my parents. And the feeling was nothing short of mutual."

His fingers clenched awkwardly as he set aside the chessboard, and for a moment, she thought he might reach out and touch her.

"Maybe we should fast forward to the jousting," he said instead.

"It was the high school Medieval Club," she went on. "More or less the Youth Auxiliary of the local SCA chapter."

"SCA?"

"Society for Creative Anachronism. Basically Renaissance Faire geeks. Like to dress up in homemade armor and practice historical swordsmanship."

"Hence, the jousting."

"They hold medieval banquets too. Illuminate manuscripts. Sing madrigals." She could feel her face flame. "Nothing wrong with any of it."

"Not that I can see," Sean agreed, the barest hint of a smile playing at the corner of his mouth.

"Still, it's not the kind of thing that looks good at a tenure review."

"So you managed to convince them to seal your juvenile records over this? I thought it was supposed to be publish or perish."

"Don't be ridicu—" She broke off as she realized he was teasing. A sociopath with a wicked sense of humor? That didn't compute. "The chair of our English department was the club advisor," she said. "Now, he's a registered sex offender."

"Oh," Sean said, sobering. "I see."

"I doubt it. It was a long way from Nabakov—despite the local papers' penchant for referring to me as the Cosplay Lolita."

"It has a certain ring to it."

"Then it's the only thing about the whole stupid episode that did." She shook her head. "He was nothing but a pathetic little dweeb with a wife and two kids. Just wanted someone who'd listen to his poetry, even if he had to get you stoned to do it."

"Did you?" Sean asked.

"Get stoned? Hell, yes."

"I meant, did you listen to his poetry?"

"That too." She flushed at the memory. "You know, that's probably the worst part of it. His poetry was godawful. I could tell that even when I was high."

"Bad enough to throw him in jail?"

"Actually, yes. But technically he was arrested for posting the poems on his blog. I wasn't quite sixteen at the time. Apparently that qualified as distributing child pornography."

"Never knew roundels could be that racy."

"Have you read Bertran de Born?"

"No. Should I?"

"Not really. Arguably his best poem is basically a Frankenstein's monster of his ideal lover, cobbled together from descriptions of women who'd rejected him."

"Kind of like posting a sex video of your ex on the internet?"

"More or less. De Born was a spy, you know. That's why Dante put him in the Eighth Circle of Hell, along with the other Sowers of Discord," she said. "Ezra Pound claimed that the Frankenstein poem was actually a coded spy map, with each woman standing for an enemy stronghold. And the irony of the whole thing is, my advisor would have gotten in less trouble if he'd been doing the same thing, and mapping missile silos for North Korea."

"What did your friend do instead? Tear apart the Cosplay community as we know it?"

"He wrote me a poem. In flawless Occitan. It was supposed to be an homage to de Born. Unfortunately, the red hair didn't get lost in translation.

Along with his claim that he knew it was natural." She glanced away. Even now, the humiliation brought tears to her eyes. "You ever want to know what being someone's muse is like, there you go."

"If nothing else, it's an argument for writing your own poems." Sean's voice was as neutral as if he were asking the time. "Was he right about the red hair?"

"No! I mean, well, technically, yes! But how could you even ask—" She felt the heat rise to her cheeks as Sean struggled to hide a grin. "The point is, he couldn't have known it, not in the way you're thinking. And that's what's so stupid about the whole thing. He plea bargained on the drug charges and was fired from his job, and that should have been the end of it. But it's just like what happened to you. The activists arrived, and all of a sudden I wasn't just a dumb teenager with a crush and a taste for cosplay; I was a statistic in a crusade. One of the 237,868 cases that occur each year. That's the specific number, in case you're interested."

She shook her head. "The worst part of it was, when I tried to tell them that they were wrong, that that was not what happened, they trotted out more statistics about denial and children protecting their abusers. As if I didn't even know my own mind. Do you know how insulting that is?"

"Yes."

There was a world of connection in that single word, and she almost reached out to take his hand. But now that she had started this, she needed to finish once and for all. "All those women, baying for his blood. And my mother was the worst of them. That's what I could never understand. The two of them had been friends. They ran the Tuesday night book club and the Thursday night Bible study together. And here she was, howling for his head. I swear, she wasn't going to be satisfied with anything less than his being chemically castrated and locked up for life. In fact, I'm not so sure she was all that firm on the chemical part of the castration."

"Hell hath no fury."

Her eyes widened as she digested his meaning. *My mother and Mr.—ugh!* "That's disgusting," she said with a shudder.

Sean flushed, and whatever tenuous connection there might have been between them abruptly vanished. "Most of what I see is. Which doesn't make it any less true. But one day, I need to learn how to shut my mouth." He reached for the chessboard and quickly ranked the pieces. "So I'm sorry if I offended you. But, honestly, I still don't see what you're so worried about. You hardly did anything wrong."

"Try explaining that to a tenure committee," she sighed. "They don't have to justify their decisions. They can just decide not to renew your contract."

His fingers hovered over the tiny figures. "I don't think it will come to that. I think Father Gregory will make sure of it."

"Seal of the confessional?"

"In a way, he's as responsible for this happening as I am. And he's not the kind of man that would let you suffer for something he got you into. I don't need to calculate any possibilities to see that."

"And if you're wrong?"

"I'm not," he said. "Father Gregory will handle the Lazaritos and Trey, and this will be over before you know it. Probably even by tonight. You have my word on it."

And if it had been anyone else, Clare would have said he sounded almost sad.

Throwing himself back on the bed, he advanced a pawn apparently at random. "So, as long as we're here, why don't you just go ahead and relax while I think for a bit? Watch TV. Take a nap. Or even a hot bath."

Her mouth opened in protest, but already his fingers were running over the tiny chess pieces, reading them almost as if they were prayer beads. And she was cold and stiff and tired. She glanced at the bathroom, a fantasia out of a bubble bath commercial, the complete opposite of the cramped accommodations of her one bedroom walk-up, and suddenly she had never wanted a long, hot soak so badly in her life.

But was she really going to take her clothes off in front of this man?

Sean laughed out loud at her obvious discomfiture. "Relax," he said. "I'm sure the bathroom door has a lock. And if I haven't convinced you by now that I'm really not one to look, I don't know what else I can say. But, for what it's worth..."

Ostentatiously, he turned his attention back to the tiny chess board, studying it as if it were a scrying ball. It was a clear dismissal. So what else could she do but go into the bathroom and begin running the hot water?

Chapter Twenty-two

And not a moment too damned soon, Sean thought, as he collapsed back against the headboard and gave in to the shadow he had been trying to keep at bay ever since he had spotted it dogging them somewhere about the time he stepped into Grand Central Terminal.

"As tawdry pasts go, you have to admit it's more than a little disappointing," the ghost mused, wiping a drop of blood from his nose as he settled at the foot of the bed. "In fact, it actually borders on charming, if you ask me. But, from your point of view, it can hardly be what you had hoped for. I mean, it's scarcely the kind of thing that's going to make a scarred and damaged woman fling herself into the arms of a creature like you for refuge, now is it?"

"From my point of view, I never once doubted it would be anything else," Sean sighed.

"You mean, you finally gave in and looked?"

"I didn't have to," Sean said, nettled. "Any idiot could see she was nothing like that. Even you."

"I agree. She's a lovely woman. Intelligent; it goes without saying. You could never abide a fool. But more importantly, she's kind. Innocent. Pure, even, some would say. Which is, I'm sure, the main appeal for someone like you." The ghost smiled. "It seems you are not only possessed of a heart, but that it is a decidedly sentimental one."

"Shut up!" Sean hissed. "I'm not at all like that."

"Well, yes, you are. I've known it all along. But you seem to be as willfully blind about that issue as you are about your weakness for gambits."

"This isn't a gambit."

The ghost considered that. "No, you're right. It isn't," he finally agreed. "It's a fork. And I must admit, a damned fine one. A strategy of pure genius, really."

"It's not a strategy! I'd never manipulate Clare..."

"Then what would you call it?" The old man shook his head, and an invisible drop of blood plopped onto the coverlet. "Honestly, Michael. Process servers? Drug dealers out to kill her? It's like the story of Josef Stalin on his deathbed. Do you know that one?"

"I am acquainted with it."

"Well, at the risk of boring you, do allow me to repeat it," the ghost said. "As the story goes, he called in two likely successors in order to test which one was better suited to rule the country. He did so by presenting a bird to each of the two candidates. The first one grabbed the bird so hard that he squeezed it to death. The second held the bird so tenuously that the bird flew away..."

"I know the punch line," Sean sighed. "Do we have to—"

"'Bring me a bird!' Stalin ordered. And when they did, Stalin plucked all the feathers from the bird's body. Then he opened his palm to show the bird laying there naked and shivering. 'You see, it is even thankful for the human warmth coming out of my palm.'"

"And if you think I am capable of doing something like that to Clare ..."

Abruptly, the ghost's face softened. "No," he said, "no, I really don't think you are. But I do think you are desperate to believe you are."

"Why?"

"Because you can't see any other reason why she'd choose a down-and-out street musician of her own free will. And, frankly, neither can I. Now, obviously, there is something you could do about that, but instead of taking the easy way out—"

Sean shut his eyes. "There is no way out, easy or otherwise. As you said, she's smart as hell. She'll never fall for it."

"Who said it was Clare you were trying to deceive?"

There was a moment's silence. Sean balled up a wrinkle in the comforter, then smoothed it flat. "Somewhere along the line, you seem to have missed the point that when no one can lie to you, it's damned well impossible to lie to yourself."

"Then why don't you just go ahead and end this thing?"

"I'm trying—"

"No, you're not. If you honestly wanted to end it, you could just call the family lawyer. You remember Hays Loughlin, don't you? His son has pretty much taken over the practice these days, but Hays is still a partner." The ghost shook his head with a faint smile. "Prosaic, I know, but surely you of all people can see how easy it would be. So the question is, what's stopping you? Is it simply a matter of stubborn pride, or maybe you're just not certain she'd choose you even then, given the circumstances? Purity can be unpredictable, after all."

Sean cut his father off with a glare. "You know, there's a fine line between constructive criticism and Jiminy Cricket."

"I see," the ghost said, beginning to shimmer around the edges. "I suspected as much."

"You don't suspect anything," Sean grabbed for the ghost before he even realized what he was doing. "You don't understand. I can't go back to being that person. Not even for her. It's not me. It's not who I am anymore."

His hand only encountered air as the ghost lingered for one more translucent moment.

"On the contrary, it's all you and always has been," his father said. "It's the sum total of Michael Grinnell and Sean the busker. And it's the sum total of the son I love. And, although I admit I don't have your predictive powers—it isn't one of those gifts that comes from beyond the grave, no matter what they want you to believe—I have a feeling it's the man Clare Malley is coming to love as well. Now the question is, will you let her? Or are you going to screw things up because you want to hurt yourself even more than you want to hurt me?"

∞

Sean's fingers were still working the miniature chess pieces when Clare finally emerged from the bathroom, feeling warm and sleepy and strangely safe for a woman, who, at last count had a process server, a gang of drug dealers, a prosecutor, and the Devil's Advocate all out for her blood. "Were you talking to someone?" she asked, tightening the thick belt on the fluffy white Waldorf robe.

Sean looked up from his chess game, and all thoughts of warmth or safety instantly leached from the room. "Yes," he said flatly. "I was talking with a lawyer. His name is Hays Laughlin, and he'll be meeting with you and Trey Carey tomorrow morning at Father Gregory's office, to finalize the details of your witness statement."

"But why?"

"Because he was absolutely right. I could have ended this with one phone call days ago."

"Because who was absolutely right? Who's he?"

An odd look fleeted across Sean's face. "Doesn't matter. Any idiot could see that this was the only way to handle things." He turned and reached for the phone. "I promise you, this will all be settled by tomorrow. In the meantime, I've been looking at the room service menu. You like club sandwiches?"

Well, yes. Yes she did. But that hardly seemed the issue here. One bubble bath, deliciously warm and soapy as it might have been, and suddenly her world had been turned upside down? "What happened?" she asked. "What's changed?"

"Me, I love club sandwiches," he went on, as if she hadn't spoken. "In fact, it's the one good memory I have of my childhood. My father used to take me out for a club sandwich after every appointment with the shrink. There was a place just around the corner, one of those prefab diners that looks more like a catering hall. You know, mirrors everywhere, and these rotating cases of desserts. Huge strawberry shortcakes with berries that had to have been genetically modified. Pies with meringue crests that looked like you could surf them. Mints with jelly centers in a silver bowl at the cash register." He shook his head. "The shrink had this damned hand puppet he was always trying to get me to use to tell fairy tales, and I couldn't even talk enough to tell him that I had Neverland waiting for me just as soon as I got the hell away from him—"

"Sean, why are we talking about club sandwiches?"

His face and voice stayed distant. "Somewhere along the line, I got it in my head that the club sandwiches were actually castles. Fairy forts. You know those ruffled toothpicks they always use with them? I used them as pennons. The pickle was a siege tower, and that little tub of coleslaw was the boiling oil you poured down on attackers' head. I had to rearrange things a little, of course. The sandwich corners had to point outward, like redoubts ..."

He laughed mirthlessly as she glanced covertly at the minifridge beneath the TV, wondering whether he had been drinking. "Haven't touched a drop," he assured her. "It's just that, whatever else you might want to have said about my father—and, trust me, there's plenty people might have wanted to say about him—he always let me play with my food. Just sat there patiently while I rearranged it. Tipped everyone triple afterwards, including the busboys, to make up for the mess."

Under other circumstances, it would have been the kind of story that she had been longing for him to share. But right now, it was nothing but a distraction, and, she was beginning to think, a carefully calculated one at that.

"I'm sorry, but I don't think club sandwiches are the issue here."

"There is no issue. It's all settled."

"No, it's not. God, I don't even know if I can afford a lawyer."

"You won't have to. Hays is still on retainer with Grinnell. He's going to bill them directly. I've got it all worked out." Sean reached for the room service menu. "So, do you want to order?"

"No."

He glanced up, at last seeming to notice that she was speaking. "Why not? I promise I don't play with my food anymore."

"Because you didn't ask me! You just went out and set all this up behind my back, without even asking me if that's what I wanted."

He looked down at the board, picked up a queen and turned it over in his fingers. "Apologies if I overstepped," he said. "Habits of a solitary existence."

"Well, welcome to the real world. There are two of us in this room."

There was a thunderous silence, then Sean's mouth twisted. "Unfortunately, one of us doesn't seem to be thinking too clearly," he said. "Honestly, how did you think this was going to end? With us catching the next plane to Ireland and lying low in the Gaelteach with the rest of Bobby's friends?"

A sudden vision hit her: a thatched cottage, overlooking the stormy cliffs of the Irish Sea, where pirates had once roved and selkies were still said to swim? "You mean, up in the North, where they only speak Irish?" she asked.

"Wouldn't even be able to order a club sandwich. If they actually had things like bacon and toasters up there."

"I wouldn't be so sure. I'm good with languages, you know," she said. "So far I've only done the Brythonic Celtic languages. I suppose it could be interesting taking on a Goidelic one for a change."

He didn't answer immediately. Instead, his hands moved for the rest of the chess pieces, scooping them up, ranking them carelessly into another game. "No electricity. No internet. Peat stoves. You wake up every morning shivering, and the only warmth you can turn to is my body, nestled beside you—"

He broke off with a wry smile as, despite herself, she took an anxious step away from the bed. "Apologies. Again. As I said, habits of a solitary existence." He shook his head. "Come on, if you look at it logically, you know you've got nothing to worry about from me. If I had any expectations in that department, I could have done something about it a long time ago."

She was oddly touched to watch him flush as he spoke. And even more oddly, touched by his obvious ... chivalry was the only word she came up with. A lifetime spent studying the troubadours—or even a single, misguided affair with one—had not prepared her for how genuinely sexy the real thing turned out to be.

"To be honest, I ... I wouldn't mind that," she heard herself say. "But it might be more sensible to at least try it here first, where we have running water and a bed."

And Clare wasn't sure which of them looked more flabbergasted at the words that had just come out of her mouth.

"What I mean to say is that it would be a pleasure," she pressed, still surprised at herself, but not about to back down now.

He looked at her for a long moment. And then he shook his head. "You're not as hard up as all that, Clare Malley," he said, forcing a smile. "Despite Bobby's wishful thinking, you can do a lot better for yourself than the likes of me. And you will. We'll get this sorted. You won't be stuck with me forever. You can consider that an official prediction."

"I'm not interested in predictions, official or otherwise," she countered. "Or forever, for that matter. All I can see is the here and now. And when I look at that, I see we've already had the talk and the fight. The wild sex is the only thing left on the checklist."

As her words died off into silence, his face twisted with the sudden longing of a child whose closest human connection was a father who allowed him to make fairy forts out of his lunch. Slowly, he set aside the chess set, and Clare wondered if he meant to kiss her.

Then, abruptly, his face set. "For God's sake, why can't you grow up? The Gaelteach instead of Renaissance Faires? A fiddler instead of a troubadour? It's not exactly original, now is it? In fact, I might argue it's downright insulting."

She took a step backward, more hurt than angry. Or maybe it was the other way around. "If you have something you're trying to say, why don't you just come out and say it?"

"To put it somewhat more bluntly, I thought even you might have learned your lesson by now." He shook his head. "God, Clare. Grinnell's not even an Irish name."

Clare stared at him, now adding blank incomprehension to the list of emotions that were roiling her stomach. "I think they'll still let you cross the border. Or are you more worried that the lads at the bar will discover your deadly secret?"

He threw his head back and laughed. "Oh, I believe most of them have far worse things to hide. I have it on good authority one of them is actually French—on his mother's side, of course." He sighed wearily. "The point is, both of us are refusing to face the one fact we both know is true: Michael Grinnell could solve this situation with a single phone call."

She eyed him warily, hating the way those stupid dark glasses made it so hard to read him. "Does that mean you're planning on going back to being him?"

"Does that matter to you?"

"Should it?"

"I dunno," he snorted. "They say a billion dollars looks good on a man. Even one like me."

She stared at him as she fought down the impulse to slap him in the face and lunge out of the room and out his life—mostly because she knew that was exactly what he was trying to make her do. "Easier to be nasty than to simply answer the question?" she asked.

His jaw tightened; she had no idea whether it was in shock or anger. Then, abruptly, his shoulders slackened. "Maybe because it's easier for me to sabotage things up front than enduing the agony of waiting around for the moment you finally wise up and walk away," he said. "Apologies. It's a bitch not to be able to lie to yourself."

"And so you're making up your mind for both of us? You've taken it upon yourself to preempt my right to decide for myself?"

"Habits of a solitary existence and—"

"Need I remind you *again* there are *two* of us in this room?"

"Then consider it a clear taste of what it's really like to deal with me. You want to wake up to that day in and day out?"

"That's not an answer to my question?" she said and waved off his spluttered retort. "Look, all I'm saying is why not do it the simple way? You've already called the lawyer on my behalf. Why not just let him stake your claim while he's at it? Hell, if you don't want the money, give it away. I'm sure Father Gregory would be delighted to help you."

"So he has already intimated."

She sunk down on the bed. "Then why not do it? Honestly, I don't care about the money. And, to be frank, I don't know whether I care about you—although I'm beginning to think I do. So why can't we give it a test run the old fashioned way? Why can't you just call me up and ask me out on a date?"

Again that fleeting look of longing. Then something set in his face. "And which would you prefer? Dinner and a movie? Or a fairy tale straight out of that diner, where I keep riding in on a unicorn to snatch you from Hell's minions?"

Unicorns? Minions? Well, what else could she expect from a man who could only speak of love in terms of a father who allowed him to play with his food?

"Technically, if you were riding a unicorn, you'd be the demon," she informed him. "Amducias rides a unicorn. He's a Duke of Hell. But he's said to provide excellent familiars."

A long moment's silence as he studied her. "I stand corrected," Sean finally said.

And once more Clare was certain he was about to kiss her. Which meant, inevitably, that her phone began to ring. And Sean leapt upon the excuse with every last ounce of his considerable reservoir of emotional cowardice.

"You'd better see who that is."

Clare cleared her throat and fished her phone out of her bag. She looked up when she saw the caller ID. "It's Lukas Croswell."

His face slackened with weary humor. And maybe more than a little relief. "Now, that certainly seems destined to simplify matters, doesn't it?"

Chapter Twenty-three

Rafael's *abuela* would kill him if she ever found out. Would turn all his pictures to the wall and turn her back on him as she pronounced him dead just like she had with Rafael's mother. She loved that fucking Church more than her family, and it didn't matter that the Church had done as much for her as the string of men she'd taken to her bed had ever done for her daughter. Rafael would be dead to her if she found out. And honestly Rafael didn't feel too good about what he was doing anyway.

But what choice did he have? He was lucky enough the Lazaritos were giving him a second chance. There wouldn't be a third. Just as there wasn't any way for him to be able to say that he'd changed his mind, didn't want to join the gang at all. You didn't leave the Lazaritos any more than you left the Crips or the Bloods. Or Holy Mother fucking Church.

So too bad for his *abuela* and her Lord Jesus Cristo. Rafael had a job to do. And fuck the way his fingers were shaking as he unscrewed the cap on the gasoline. Miguel said no one was going to get hurt this time.

Unless, that is, Rafael fucked things up like last time.

He hurried down the steps of the Outreach Center, sloshing the gas in every direction. Was already fumbling with the matches when he saw the pile of rags at his feet.

"*Madre de dios*!" Rafael hissed.

And the pile of rags shifted and sat up.

Shit! And not just Rafael's regular shit-assed bad luck. The guy actually smelled like shit—no, smelled like rotting garbage—like all you'd need to do was light a match and the guy would burst into flame and take the Outreach Center with him.

Yeah. Sure. No one was going to get hurt.

Unless Rafael fucked things up again.

"Go on, man," he said. "Get out of here."

The bum shook his head. "I'm lost."

"Well, get lost somewhere else."

"I can't," the bum said. "Help me find the way."

"Look man. You've got to go. Now!" Rafael sloshed some gasoline at the guy so he'd get the point.

The bag man lunged at him, plucking at Rafael's arm with his yellowed fingernails. "I need to get back to the crossroads," he said. "I must have taken a wrong turn there."

"What the fuck are you talking about? What crossroads?"

"Look around you. They are everywhere. They are the places where you meet a stranger asking directions. Or maybe one who will point you on the right path."

The old man was crazy, but Rafael wasn't about to have a bum's blood on his conscience, so bracing himself against the smell, he grabbed the old man's hand. Tried not to drop it in disgust when he felt the knobby growths oozing everywhere. "Come on," he said. "This way."

And suddenly the bum's eyes were as red as the ruby chips in the medal his *abuela* had scrimped for months to buy for Rafael's First Communion, the medal that was now beginning to burn his skin where it hung around his neck.

He ignored the burning, ignored the feeling that the old man was peering into his soul, and instead tried to heave the bum up the stairs and out of there. But suddenly the balance was all wrong, like he was tossing nothing but a giant sack of balloons, and Rafael fell, then floated before he pitched over his own feet on the uneven steps and sprawled face-first onto the street. The gas can clattered out of his hands and bounced across the pavement, where a tall, dark shadow rose out of nowhere to scoop it up.

Shit. It was the priest that ran the place. The bastard that his *abuela* still scrubbed floors for and thought it a fucking privilege.

Rafael scrambled to his feet, but the priest didn't seem to notice. His eyes lingered somewhere behind Rafael, as if he had caught a whiff of the stinking bag man. Rafael didn't bother to turn to look. He knew the bag man would be gone. That he was never there. Just another fucking vision, like the fiddler warned them.

"What the fuck are you doin' with that?" Rafael snarled, lunging for the can.

"I could, and probably should ask you the same," the priest said. "Gang initiation?"

"None of your business."

"Unfortunately, someone burning down a church on my watch very much is." The priest met Rafael's eye, with about the same look that the old priests used to give him at school—back in the day when Rafael had gone to school—and asked, "Why did the Lazaritos want you to burn the church?"

"Not the church. Just the Outreach Center."

The priest raised an eyebrow. "Is that meant to be some kind of mitigating argument?"

"What the fuck does that mean?"

"Allow me to rephrase. Why did they want you to burn the Outreach Center?"

And Rafael gave up. Fuck the Lazaritos. He was dead to them already. "They said we had a leak. An informer."

"Did they say who?"

"No."

And the priest got that look that priests got just before they explained how genuinely stupid you were to get caught with your hand in the poor box. "Any chance, they were setting you up to be that informer?"

Miguel setting him up? The Lazaritos? But they were family. And family took care of you.

Just like family gave you second chances?

A siren began to howl in the distance, and the priest frowned. "I think you need to come with me."

"Why? You want to fuck me or exorcise me? Or maybe fuck me, then exorcise me?"

For a moment, the priest looked shocked. And then genuinely pissed. Scary-assed pissed, more scary than the Lazaritos, like his *abuela* before she started turning pictures to the wall. But all he said was, "If you need more incentive than not getting yourself arrested, shall I point out I have a gas can with your fingerprints all over it?" Then he spun and took off without waiting for an answer. Rafael only hesitated a moment before racing after him. After all, what choice did he have? If he got arrested, there'd be a shiv in his back courtesy of the Lazaritos before he ever saw a judge. Maybe it was time to throw himself straight into the arms of Holy Mother fucking Church. Maybe he'd become a priest. Hell, that was what his *abuela* had been praying for all along.

"Why do you think I would need to exorcise you?" the priest asked, when Rafael caught up with him. And fuck it, the bastard sounded interested. "Do you believe you're possessed?"

"What's it to you?"

"Well, like burning churches, it's rather my department. If nothing else, I could perhaps make sure it is an … accurate diagnosis." The priest never varied his pace. "Let's start with the five sense organs. Have you experienced a foul taste in your mouth? Feel like your eyes are being pulled inside? Rashes? An eerie sense of being touched?"

Yeah, if there was any eerie touching, one guess where that would be coming from. "No," Rafael said.

"What about the motor organs? Fidgeting and restlessness? Tics? Animal sounds?"

"No."

"Well, then, as candidates for exorcism go, I've got to say you honestly don't sound very promising," the priest told him. "So what exactly gave you the impression you might have been demonically possessed?"

Rafael glanced back down the block toward the church, where two cops were now climbing out of a patrol car, shining their flashlights over the front of the church. And at the Outreach Center steps, where a non-existent bum had just saved his ass. "Sometimes … I see shit. Hear shit."

The priest got an odd look on his face. "Well, sometimes, people seeing or hearing … things ... is my department," he said. "But in this case, I think there's someone else you need to talk to."

∞

Rafael had some serious second thoughts when he saw the house where the priest was taking him. The place looked like it already had a dozen or so kids buried under the floorboards. Well, that wasn't any worse than what the Lazaritos were likely to do to him, and Rafael still had a couple of knives tucked in his clothes, just like Miguel had taught him. Brother to brother.

Even creepier was the way no one answered the door. They were just buzzed inside and left to find their own way to a study where a man lay on a recliner like a corpse on a slab.

"I don't suppose there's any chance you're an erring husband sneaking back into the wrong house, is there?" he asked without opening his eyes.

"I'm sorry, Lukas, but we've got to talk," the priest said. "It's a matter of some urgency."

"Seems to be my week for it," Lukas sighed. He levered himself upright in his recliner, then stopped when he saw Rafael. "And you are?"

Rafael glanced at Father Gregory, who nodded meaningfully. Well, shit, Rafael didn't see how it was going to help, but Father Gregory said it was the only way to get answers. "I'm the guy that shot your son," Rafael said.

That got the doctor's attention; he did a regular spit-take. And then he turned to the priest. "This is your doing?"

"I prefer to think I'm just facilitating."

"Facilitating what?"

"Rafael is here to ask your forgiveness for shooting your son. Isn't that right, Rafael?"

"I didn't mean to shoot him," Rafael said. "Just scare him a little. The gun just went off."

Lukas wasn't even listening. "Are you insane?" he hissed at the priest. "You expect me to offer this ... thug some absolution...?"

"Hardly," Father Gregory said. "Absolution's my department. Forgiveness on the other hand—"

What the fuck? These two were talking like Rafael wasn't even there. "I don't need your fucking forgiveness," he said. "I need answers. The priest here says you can tell me what's going on with me. What happened to me. What happened to your fucking son."

The doctor didn't even seem to hear him. "Am I seriously to believe that you are asking me to investigate my own son's case?" he asked the priest. "Under the circumstances, mine can hardly qualify as a disinterested opinion."

"Fuck investigating, fuck disinterested. There's something wrong with me," Rafael snarled. "Me and all the rest of the Lazaritos. I'm seeing things. Hearing things. Priest says you can tell me what's going on."

At least this time, the doctor bothered to look at him. "I don't think I could give you an answer to that when I was sober. And, frankly, I'm not right now."

Rafael's fists balled. "Then maybe I should fucking well sober you up."

"Threatening Dr. Croswell doesn't exactly suggest you're sincere in your desire for reconciliation," the priest cut in. He eyeballed Rafael in a way that would have made his *abuela* flinch, before nodding toward the bottle at the doctor's elbow. "I admit our friend here seems to be a bit young, under a strict interpretation of the statutes, but perhaps we could all sit down and join in a drink like civilized men?"

"Help yourself," Lukas sighed, waving his hand at the table behind him. "The paper cups on the left should be sterile. The ones on the right might once have held a Borgia—the saint, not the pope—but still they may leave a bit of an unpleasant aftertaste."

Which was another one of those little private conversations the doctor and the priest seemed to be sharing, but whatever, Rafael sure could use a drink. Or five. But one sharp gaze from the priest kept him from grabbing the bottle and swigging from the neck like he was dying to. Instead, he took the paper cup the priest handed him, and sipped as decorously as if he was at a tea party. Not that he'd ever been to a tea party …

So," the doctor said, leaning back in his chair. "What seems to be the problem here?"

"I'm fucking seeing shit—"

"Hallucinations," Father Gregory cut Rafael off. "Maybe collective ones. Could there be a pharmaceutical explanation for that?"

"Obviously," the doctor snorted. "They're called hallucinogens. And yes, they can be collective. It's a little before my time, obviously, but I believe your office has an entire file devoted to apparitions in the middle ages that were eventually chalked up to ergot poisoning and the power of suggestion."

Fuck apparitions. Leave that to Rafael's *abuela* and her endless novenas to Our Lady of Fatima. How about they talk about drugs and hallucinations? Did they think Rafael was too young, too dumb not to have heard the stories about the government and LSD? The stories about a place called Tuskegee. Or Alcatraz. And how the government didn't waste time on lab rats when there were convicts and hookers to experiment on.

"Those same kind of drugs able to heal you when you get shot?" Rafael asked.

The doctor raised an eyebrow. "Theoretically speaking?"

"The hell with theoretically! Answer the fucking question. Can you change someone so they can't die? Or bring them back from the dead? And make them see shit in the process?"

"Leaving out the rather obvious reference to Mary Shelley, theoretically, I suppose it's possible."

"How?"

"Well, galvanization has been pretty much disproved since then. Gene splicing, DNA manipulation are all the rage these days, so I supposed you could start with that."

"What the fuck does that mean?"

For a moment, Lukas just sat there, thinking—just like some kind of professor out of some horror flick, right before he explained how Godzilla had mutated.

"All right. Let me see if I can put this into terms you understand," the doctor said. "Approximately fifty percent of human DNA has no known biological function."

"Junk DNA," Father Gregory said, taking a sip of whiskey.

"More correctly, non-coding DNA, but at least you know what I'm talking about." Lukas agreed. "Nature abhors a vacuum, and scientists abhor riddles, and so there's always someone sure that it must do something and determined to find out what that something is. In scientific parlance, to express those genes. And theoretically speaking, it's possible that one of them holds the key to some kind of ... regeneration."

He paused on that last word, reached for his glass, then stopped himself. "As a matter of fact, that's really what's going on with cancer cells. But there's the problem, you see? Tweak the wrong gene and you might do something to a person that makes cancer look like a blessing."

Fuck. What was the bastard saying? Someone gave him cancer? Christ, it was just like crazy Uncle Luis—the one who never was right after Vietnam—

was always saying. You come from the barrio, you've got only three uses to the white man: clearing a mine field, cleaning their houses, or being one of their lab rats. All thing considered, you were best off clearing their mine fields.

"You saying I'm infected with crazy DNA?" Rafael's eyes widened with dawning realization. "How do you know all this? You the one who did this to us?"

"Someone may have infected you with something," the doctor snapped. "I did not."

And Rafael believed him. Which meant he was no better off than when he had been talking to an invisible bag man on the church steps. But *someone* wasn't enough to set things right with the Lazaritos.

Then the priest leaned toward Lukas and spoke, in the sort of carefully gentle voice that Rafael had learned long ago meant a holy man was about to tear you a new asshole and rip you limb from limb, just like one of those martyrs his *abuela* had pictures of hanging all over the living room walls.

"Well, at the risk of sounding—shall we say—inquisitorial, maybe now would be a good time to ask, just for the record, do we have your word on that?"

The doctor's face went flat. "If you are really accusing me of what I think you're accusing me of, what good would my assurance be?"

"Absolutely no use whatsoever," the priest agreed. "But it does give me a chance to state for the record that I honestly do believe you had nothing to do with what's happened to Rafael and his friends."

"You believe in angels, too," Lukas snorted. "Is there a point here?"

The priest's voice got even quieter. "As I said, I believe you had nothing to do with what happened to Rafael and his friends. But would I be wrong in supposing that you do know how such a thing could be done? And even, perhaps, who might have the resources to do such a thing? Theoretically speaking, of course."

A long pause. Then the doctor reached for his drink. "Theoretically speaking, the way you alter people's DNA is inserting it with a virus," he said. "A vector virus, it's called. And just like any virus, it could be contagious—"

"That mean you can stop it? Cure it?" Rafael asked, embarrassed by how quickly he could begin to hope. Hope that maybe he wouldn't go crazy.

Hope that maybe he could find something to trade with the Lazaritos for his life.

But what if the answer was no? What if the thing was incurable? Like the virus that took his mother in the end.

"Not exactly the same thing. And the answer to either is a qualified maybe. Anti-virals can prevent the virus from reproducing. Virucides would actually kill them," Lukas said. His eyes stayed on Rafael, and maybe he was thinking about people like Rafael's mother, because all of a sudden something changed in his face. "Come by my clinic in the morning. Maybe I can find something that can help you."

He swallowed off his whiskey, a clear dismissal. But the priest didn't even pretend to take the hint. "Something like Rafael's own DNA—or, more accurately—the DNA that might have been modified?" he asked instead.

The doctor glanced at him sharply. "I'm sorry. I thought your degree was in theology, not medicine."

"You're quite correct," the priest said. He paused only briefly before he moved in for the kill. "Just as you're quite correct that the Office of the Promoter of the Faith rather prides itself on its record keeping. And, believe me, your report on Michael Grinnell is up to their lofty standards. Especially your speculations about the miraculous healing power of his DNA."

The doctor sucked in his breath with a hiss. "I thought you said you believed me when you said I don't have anything to do with this."

"That was when we were talking about the current situation. What's going on now," the priest said. "But what about then? Once upon a time. You never did address the question of who might have the resources to disseminate such a virus."

The doctor didn't answer. Just reached for the whiskey bottle and poured. And drank. And poured again.

"Once upon a time," he finally said, "there was a manuscript. An old alchemical manuscript that was supposed to have belonged to Father Enoch."

Old alchemical manuscript? Rafael tensed. "You talking about that Book of Stones?" He'd heard plenty about that old book around the *bodega*.

"Different title. Same tired point." Lukas's voice seemed to come from far, far away. "Geber called it Takwin. This book called it … the Awakener. And instead of magic crystals, it was an angel who was supposed to blow the breath of life back into humankind and relight the spark of the divine within them."

"A not-uncommon neo-Platonist trope," Father Gregory observed.

"Except for the minor detail that, in this version of the story, the Awakener is Lucifer," Lukas said.

There was a long pause. And then the priest raised an eyebrow. "I'll have to reread my Milton."

And it was all Rafael could do not pull out a knife and cut them both. Fuck Milton, whoever the hell he was. Fuck their old alchemical manuscripts. Fuck their little jokes like they were sipping brandy at some oak-paneled old-man's club. Rafael wanted answers. Rafael needed answers. His goddamned life depended on getting answers. "So what the fuck does some angel story have to do with someone fucking with my DNA?" he demanded.

Both the priest and the doctor glared at him, like some old professors on the public TV his *abuela* was always trying to get him to watch—just as long as it didn't interfere with her telenovelas.

"I guessed—maybe I should say I theorized—that maybe Michael's junk DNA had been … activated," the doctor said to the priest, deliberately ignoring Rafael. "And, before you ask, I have no idea how or by whom. But assuming it had been activated, maybe this story showed how his junk DNA had the power to awaken … things … in other DNA."

"That's quite some theory," the priest said.

"It wouldn't be the first time good science was couched in allegorical terms."

"So your report said," Father Gregory agreed, then frowned. "But it still doesn't explain what led you to this insight."

"I would have thought that much was obvious," Lukas said with bitter smile. "Michael Grinnell showed me how to read it."

"How to read your own report?" the priest asked.

"How to read and interpret the data. He was even kind enough to warn me to listen closely, because I was going to need it one day."

And Rafael's entire body went cold—cold and lethal—just like when he heard the wrong footfall behind him in an alley. "And why was he so sure you'd need it?"

The doctor's face tightened. "That's irrelevant."

"I don't think so," Rafael said. Because it didn't take a lot for Rafael to see the answer to his own question. Didn't take a lot to remember the gun going off between him and the skinny white kid. And then the white kid's blood splashing everywhere. On him.

Infecting him?

It made a kind of sick sense. Dr. Frankenstein tinkering away in his lab with "awakened" DNA. The kid whose gunshot wound healed by itself. Rafael's voice was tight when he finally spoke. "If you don't want to tell me, maybe I should ask your son."

For a moment, Rafael genuinely believed that Lukas was about to spring to his feet and lunge for his throat. But then the doctor sank back in the recliner and pressed his fingers to his temples as if in pain. "That's it," he said. "We're done here. If you want to come by my clinic tomorrow, I will see what I can do for you. I am a doctor, whatever else I might be. But I am done talking to you now."

Rafael believed him, but he wasn't satisfied. He wanted the whole story. Before he could wonder whether he could bring himself to beat the rest of the truth out of a cripple, a shadow swelled on the threshold of the study, and the doctor went white.

"Oh, come on, Dad," Jonas Croswell snarled. "Why don't you just go ahead and answer the fucking question?"

Chapter Twenty-four

"Language," the old man said.

Language? Seriously? Why didn't he just go ahead and insist Jonas say 'pretty please'?

"I think," Jonas repeated, "you should answer the fucking question."

At least someone said that. It sounded like his voice, but right now he wasn't real sure about anything he was seeing or hearing because the implications were …

Were impossible. Hell, it was one thing to joke about your old man being a mad scientist, a miserable asshole who'd rather hang out with a bunch of miracle-working body parts than you. But it was another thing altogether to even consider the possibility that you yourself had once been one of his little dead friends. That the old man had somehow cobbled you together out of a bunch of relics, right there on the slab—a saint's finger here, a consecrated communion wafer there, all mixed together with a bit of magic DNA that could bring you back to life.

"Eavesdropping?" Lukas spat. "Don't you have anything better to do with your time? Some schoolwork, perhaps? It is a school night, is it not? Refresh my memory, or do we not have a specific agreement about school nights?"

At least that was what the man who had snapped bolt upright in the recliner had said. But even though he spoke with familiar clipped fury, this white-faced stranger was not Jonas's fearless father. This man was afraid. And not of the drug-dealing asshole who had gotten them into this mess in the first place, and who looked like he was about to take a swing at someone.

"Back off," Jonas hissed at the kid. "Stay away from my father."

He would have gone straight for the asshole's throat, and the hell with the fact that the guy had killed Jonas once already. But his father cut him off with a weary sigh. "Please, Jonas. Let's try not to get blood all over the lab. Especially not yours."

The last words caused the freak to freeze, and then step back, both hands raised. "He's right. I don't want to fight."

"Why the fuck not?"

"Language..." Jonas thought he heard his father say distantly. But at the same moment, the priest rose between them, like some cross between the Exorcist and a third grade hall monitor, and pushed a stool over toward Jonas. "It might be better if we all sat back down."

"Better?" Lukas spat. "Perhaps my Bible studies are lacking, but I don't recall that Our Savior's miracles included putting the toothpaste back in the tube."

Father Gregory raised an eyebrow. "Given the circumstances, I'm not going to embarrass us both by invoking God's working in mysterious ways. But examine your heart, Lukas. Isn't it a lot easier facing this moment now than continuing to let it eat away at you like it has for the last sixteen years?"

Sixteen years? In other words ever since Jonas had been born? Or was the right word, created? *Awakened*? "So who'd you use to make me?" Jonas asked. "Which parts belong to what? Who's the saint with the eyeballs?"

"St. Lucy," his father said mechanically.

"And the tits?"

"St. Agatha."

"And which one is supposed to bless your throat?"

"St. Blaise."

"How'd you collect them? Must have taken a while. Did I lay around on the slab for years waiting because you couldn't find all the parts? What one was the last one? The dick? Is there a patron saint of dicks?"

"Technically no, although Abelard comes to mind," Father Gregory cut in and then turned back to the old man. "Lukas, as understandably difficult as you might find this, I think we would all benefit from some clarification here."

The old man's mouth twisted. "You mean, confession?"

"I don't care what you want to call it. I think we all need an answer to a simple question. Did you somehow replicate Michael Grinell's DNA in your son?"

"You mean, did I express the Lucifer sequence?" The old man waved off the priest's spluttered objection. "Spare me the comment about names. That was their name for it, not mine. The Pentagon always had it hands down over the Church when it came to catchy names."

"The Pentagon?"

"Almost as soon as I had even hypothesized that there might be some kind of scientific basis to Michael's cure, I was approached by certain people who suggested it would be in our country's interest to—for want of a better term—breed people like Michael Grinnell. For many reasons, I objected. Vociferously."

He paused and grimmaced as if reliving a bad memory, then waved at the wheelchair neatly folded behind the recliner. "I was about to go public with my objections when ... circumstances intervened. It was several years before I could return to the task, and when I did, I had, shall we say, considerably more motivation."

If the priest understood what the old man was saying, he gave no sign. "And that was when you finally succeeded in expressing some kind of regeneration sequence out of Michael's DNA?" he asked. "And somehow implanting it in your son?"

"I have no idea what I actually did, although, yes, that was the general purpose of the attempt."

"Why?" The priest looked like he knew the answer, but wanted to hear it spoken aloud.

For a moment, the old Lukas was back, drawing a long breath, as if he were dealing with a particularly incompetent student. And Jonas found himself rooting for the old man to launch into the priest, to rip him a new one, just like old times.

Instead the old man looked away. "I was desperate," he said, keeping his gaze carefully averted. "Desperate enough to even consider making the attempt, despite everything I'd seen of Michael—"

"What attempt?" Jonas asked.

"Desperate enough to believe that some junk DNA might be capable of creating a miracle. Or annihilating both mind and body," his father went on as if he hadn't heard him. "And at the time, either option seemed preferable to my actual circumstances."

"What circumstances?" the gangbanger demanded.

"What circumstances do you think?" The old man's voice cracked and for a moment, he fell silent. Then he sketched a weary gesture at the wheelchair that sat folded behind him. "Are you all so obtuse that I need to spell the rest of it out?"

Well, yes, he kind of did. Because Jonas could make no sense of what he was hearing. The old man desperate? The old man looking for a miracle? And what the hell was this shit about annihilation? Was that why he spent so much time with dead people? Because he wanted to be one?

"I was desperate," Lukas repeated softly. "And desperate men do desperate things."

Desperate things like … having a kid? Was that what Jonas was? A goddamned desperation play—and one that failed at that? Small wonder the old man couldn't stand the sight of him.

"Jonas," the priest said, "he doesn't mean—"

"What the hell do you know?" Jonas snarled, whirling on the only target he could find through the tears that suddenly blurred his vision. "Get the hell out of here. Now."

Something shifted in the priest's face—something that in another man might have been sympathy or pity—and he got to his feet. "Perhaps it would be best for us to go," he said to the gangbanger.

"No," the asshole said. "Not until he tells us what he's going to do about this."

"Do about what?" Lukas snapped. "An experiment I couldn't get right sixteen years ago?"

"An experiment that's fucking inside me now. Don't you get it? Some kind of shit's growing inside me and making me see and hear fucking angels."

Lukas's eyes widened in alarm. "I have nothing to do with that."

"You just told us all you fucking well invented it."

"I invented nothing!" Lukas snapped. "I admit I tried to use … to express—"

"Yeah, well, maybe we should ask the demon spawn here to give us a blood sample," Rafael snarled. "Just to make sure. Know what I mean?"

"Involve my son in this anymore deeply that he already is," Lukas said, his voice flat with menace, "and I promise you that I will find a way to make you regret that choice for what few days will remain of your life."

Shit, even Jonas believed him.

"Fuck off, man," the creep said. "You started this. You caused this, and now you owe us a cure."

"Enough!" Father Gregory cut them both off, in his shut-the-fuck-up-now voice, and everyone did. "This is neither the time nor the place. We will leave now. Dr. Croswell needs time now. Time to talk with his son. And then time to see the best way to handle this. And right now, we need to give him that time. I have every confidence that, if we do, he will find a way to set things right."

Lukas favored him with a grim smile. "Theoretically, I suppose anything's possible."

With a nod, the priest turned for the door, pushing the gangbanger in front of him. And then he stopped. "If it matters," he said, "I wish it hadn't happened like this."

"And it goes without saying you're not alone in that," Lukas replied. "Now, would you please leave me alone with my son?"

The quiet click of the latch that signaled the priest and the creep were both gone, and that Jonas was well and truly alone with his father, was the scariest noise Jonas had ever heard in his life. Even scarier was hearing his own voice break the silence. "How do you know it failed? Did you ever try?"

His father snapped out of whatever trance he had fallen into. "Try what exactly?"

"To find out if ..." Jonas broke off, groping for words that could express the impossible. "I could fix you," he finally muttered.

"You mean, did I try to isolate and express the Lucifer sequence in you and then use it to cure me?"

"You're the expert. You tell me," Jonas snapped. "Or were you saving that for an eighteenth birthday present?"

Lukas's shoulders slumped and he let out a long sigh. He seemed to have aged since Jonas walked into the room. "All right. You have a right to know, I admit that. But listen carefully, because we are not going to have this conversation ever again. Is that clear?"

"Perfectly, sir."

"The answer is no," Lukas said, ignoring the sarcasm. "No, I never did. And no, I never will."

"Why not? You think I'm that worthless? You hate me that much?"

Sheer exasperation flashed across Lukas's face. And then abruptly, the fight went out of him. He rubbed his hands across his face roughly, as if he wanted to erase himself, then looked up at Jonas. "I don't hate you." His voice was barelyl audible. "I hate myself."

"Because you got ..." Once more Jonas found himself groping for words. "Hurt?"

Lukas glared at him incredulously. "Because every time I look at you," he enunciated slowly, "I have to look myself in the eye and admit that for all intents and purposes, I bred a human being for spare parts. And difficult as you may find it to believe, even I have a problem with that."

No. Jonas shook his head, beginning to feel dizzy. Punch drunk. Because what Jonas found difficult to believe was that the old man had a problem with anything. Playing Dr. Frankenstein Jonas could believe. Having a problem playing Dr. Frankenstein ... that Jonas couldn't fathom. He couldn't believe Lukas Croswell acknowledged having any problems at all. Might as well believe someone had stolen away his father, and replaced him with ... St. Jude's middle finger.

"And what if I want to?" Jonas asked.

His father's face froze. "Want to ... what precisely?"

"I dunno. You're the mad scientist. You tell me. Let you take whatever samples you want? Let you test them? Recombine my DNA?" Jonas's lip twisted. "Hell, you've gone to the effort to breed me. You might as well at least give it a shot."

His father recoiled, and so did Jonas. He hadn't meant it that way ... well, maybe had. Fact of the matter was, there was some kind of demon driving him now, urging him to prod ... probe ... to goad his father's old wounds out of sheer incredulity that they even existed.

"Because there would be no point," Lukas said flatly. "The sequencing didn't work."

"How can you be so sure if you never tried?" Jonas kept pressing. "Because a fuck-up like me couldn't possibly have some kind of miracle gene?"

"Because I'm still not sure it's even possible to express that gene, but I can tell you that if someone actually did, the results would be unholy." Lukas paused briefly, apparently trying to control himself, but to no avail. Wearily, he gestured toward the cell phone sitting there on the desk. "You haven't read those records, and if I have anything to say as your father, you never will. God! Ezra Grinnell has barely been dead a year. They must have been working behind his back all along. Building on my research, my report on Michael, trying to ... it's not just the Lazaritos at the Outreach Center. It's dozens of shelters in dozens of states. All of them different, and yet, all of them the same. One guy sees saints who cure him. The next one leaps off the church bell tower, convinced he has wings and is going to fly. Another noses into the garbage and urinates on fire hydrants, convinced that he's some kind of werewolf. Whatever they've created, whatever they're distributing, it's completely unstable. For every miracle cure, there's one who'll self-immolate. Or head out with a submachine gun to the nearest high school. None of it follows any pattern. Just as whatever caused Michael's DNA to awaken followed no pattern. Michael couldn't control it and didn't understand it. The only real way to put it is, it sows chaos."

The old man broke off, his eyes as unfocused as if he was back in that same chaos. "And now, every day," he wound up distantly, "every goddamned day, I have to live with the fact that I even contemplated putting a child—no, putting *my* child—through that same hell just to help myself. And the fact that it didn't work is, in my mind, the closest thing I'll ever have to proof that there is a heaven, and it is a merciful one."

And suddenly Jonas found himself as jittery and disoriented and uncertain as when everyone was telling him he'd just come back from the dead. Because on the one hand, for the first time in his life, he was seeing—really seeing—his father, not the comic book evil bastard the old man thought he needed to be. Just a real, flesh and blood man, someone who had made some dumb choices, the same kind of dumb choices Jonas himself might have made.

He looked around the room as if hoping to find answers hiding somewhere. "But if it didn't work, how can you explain what happened to me when I was ... shot?"

Lukas looked up at his son. "I can't."

Jonas swallowed hard and took a step toward his father. "Then maybe I should try."

The old man eyed him narrowly. "What does that mean?"

"What if I told you I saw … something? My vision ... what if I told you an angel—no some kind of old priest—came for me? Picked me up like he was going to carry me off to heaven, then changed his mind and … kissed me back to life."

The old man's silence was thunderous, even by his own standards. Then he enunciated slowly, "Much as it would be lovely to believe in some kind of miraculous intervention, logic dictates that your experience was also some kind of hallucination. Fortunately, it seems to be a beneficial one."

"Maybe," Jonas said. "But you can't know for sure. Not unless you reverse-engineer it."

"Christ, haven't you listened to a word I've said?" Lukas groaned in frustration. "I never engineered anything in the first place. Michael showed me everything. I've got nothing on my own."

"You've got my DNA."

Lukas froze. And then he sank back into his recliner. "And what good would that do me?" he asked. "You're not a mutation. You're not a cure. You're just a very stupid mistake on my part. And one I will regret for the rest of my life."

Jonas stumbled back, his father's words a punch in the gut. *Stupid mistake.* Just like that, the *real* old man was back. The one Jonas didn't need to feel sorry for, but could simply hate instead.

"Hey, don't hold back, Dad," he snarled, leaping to his feet. "Tell me how you really feel. Anything else to add, or does stupid mistake pretty much cover things?"

Lukas shook his head tiredly. "You know that's not what I meant."

Did he? Did he really? "No," Jonas said. "It's exactly what you meant. So I guess it's up to me to find out what you did so I can understand what I am. And maybe, just maybe, when I do, I'll come back and try to fix you. That is, if you can bring yourself to accept any help from a stupid mistake."

"Jonas! Stop!"

A lifetime's conditioning almost stopped Jonas in his tracks—but only almost. Because Jonas was done—done with listening to his father, just as he was done listening to anyone. From now on, Jonas was only listening to himself.

"Catch me if you can," he snarled, as he snatched Trey's cell phone off of his father's desk and plunged out of the room and out of the fucking house.

Chapter Twenty-five

Something was very wrong with Lukas Croswell. You didn't have to be looking the man in the eye to see that. His voice cracked along the phone lines in the same autocratic syllables, but there was as much force in them as the clicking of typewriter keys. "I apologize for disturbing you," he said to Clare. "But I'm wondering if you would be in any position to get a message to Michael for me."

She glanced at Sean, who was already reaching for his chess set as if nothing had just happened between them. If something actually had happened between them. Had it? Or had she merely imagined it? Willed it, maybe even?

"His name's Sean," she said.

"Sean, then, if you prefer." Even the impatience in Lukas's voice seemed perfunctory. "The point being, is there any chance you could get him a message? Quickly, if at all possible?"

"I don't know," Clare said, her eyes still on Sean. "Maybe you could tell me exactly what message you want me to relay?"

Lukas hesitated, then said, "I need to ask him … about the last time we talked. He said things … predicted them. I'd like to know if … those predictions still hold?"

And all thoughts of what may or may not have happened between her and Sean vanished as Clare tried to process what she had just heard. "Dr. Croswell," she said, "is something wrong?"

A long pause. A deep breath. "My son … has gone missing."

"And you think Sean had something to do with it?"

"I'd hardly call him if that were the case, now would I?" There might be a little more of the old snap in Lukas's voice, but it was fleeting at best. By all accounts he seemed as bewildered as Clare. "I ... was hoping Mi—Sean might have some insight into ... I don't know. Can you reach him? Please. I ... I need help."

The words died off, as Sean pushed aside the chess set with a sigh. "I'm guessing this is for me," he said.

"Dr. Crosswell?" He listened, eyes closed, fingers pinching the bridge of his nose. "Nossir," he said, when the voice on the other end finished. "I honestly take no particular pleasure in this at all. Maybe when I was a teen-ager, I liked to gloat. But I like to think I've grown out of it by now."

Another torrent of words, and Sean just shook his head. "Oh, for God's sake, not you, too. Why won't anyone believe me when I tell them that it's not a Magic 8 ball?"

An angry burst cut him off. "I'm sorry," Sean said. "Obviously, I'm well aware the niceties of a miracle investigation are not your main priority right now. But they are—how would you put it?—germane to the matter at hand."

The next volley of words was enough to send Clare rocking back on her heels, even though she was halfway across the room. "I *am* trying to help," Sean sighed. "But I can't do that if you won't listen to me. What I'm trying to tell you, is that I don't see things. Or events. I see people. More accurately, I see *into* people. What's inside them. What they know, even though they don't know it." He shut his eyes, then said, "Would you please just listen to me? You want to know about the last time we talked. I'm trying to tell you. And what I'm trying to get through your thick head is, maybe I'm the one who showed you how to read that old manuscript, but you're the one who actually read it. Do you see what I'm trying to say? You were the one that figured it out. I just ... helped you see what you saw. Just like right now, if anyone knows what your son is going to do, it's you. So I need you to think about it. Then tell me."

A splutter, followed by a long silence, then a few, grudging syllables. Sean thought for a moment, then raised an eyebrow. "Actually, I've never owned a cell phone, let alone hacked or stolen one. And I can't say as I know what a burner computer is either. But if I'm not mistaken there is a computer in the Outreach Center that matches the description ... wait, wait, Lukas! Don't! You asked me to help, now let me do it."

A moment's pause, and then Sean said, "Because, with all due respect, I think the kid might be a lot more willing to talk to me than you right now."

Another rush of words. "No, you're right," Sean agreed. "I don't owe you a damned thing. But I will find your son and bring him home. And nossir, that's not a prediction. It's a promise."

Sean moved to end the call, then stared at the phone, apparently flummoxed at how to do that. With a smile, Clare took the phone from him. As their hands touched, he stiffened, and then his attention shifted reflexively toward the chess set.

"We'd better get moving," Sean said. "Although I honestly can't see that it's as urgent as Lukas seems to feel it is. I mean, how much trouble can a sixteen year old really get into?"

Clare raised an eyebrow. "Present company excepted?"

"Point taken." He studied her, his expression inscrutable. "So I guess the honeymoon is over. Although I'm sure there would be plenty who would rather just say that you had one hell of a narrow escape there."

She blushed. Had it really been a narrow escape? Had she really been on the verge of going to bed with him? And if so, what had she been thinking?

∞

"What was all that about cell phones and burner laptops?" she asked. "What does Lukas think Jonas is going to do?"

"Something about uploading hacked information to the internet," Sean said. "Which doesn't really sound all that likely if you ask me. Honestly, how could a kid his age even know how to do that?"

Clare laughed out loud. "Clearly, you've never taught a research methods class. All you can do is pray that they're hacking into the Pentagon instead of your Facebook account."

"Brave new world," he conceded. "I admit, I'm better with peat fires and hauling water in wooden buckets."

Clare found herself wondering wistfully what it might have been like for the two of them in the Gaelteach. Could it have been real? Or was that just a fantasy every bit as stupid as Cosplay Lolita?

"Then let's hope that the Outreach Center still has dial-up internet," she told him. "That should slow him down."

Sean was already in motion, pocketing the chess set and double-checking the straps on his fiddle case with swift efficiency. She slipped into the bathroom to get dressed and then eyed him as she tossed her few things back into her purse, wondering whether she was finally seeing him for what he really was. I like to run, he had told her. But this was more than liking. This was reflex. He was a creature moving on sheer instinct now. The only real question was, where was that instinct driving him to run? To save Jonas or away from her?

Sean glanced around the room, double-checking that everything had been gathered, before scrawling a brief thank you on the telephone pad, and tossing one of the twenties he had won at chess on it for the chambermaid. Of all the things not to forget, Clare thought, as she snapped shut her bag.

He grinned at Clare. "I tipped the room service waiter double that, but that was on the Englishman's tab."

Slinging his fiddle case over his shoulder, he took off, simply assuming she would follow. Only when they were out on the street, did he stop and turn to her.

"Clare," he said, "if it matters, I'm very sorry it's ending like this."

And that was it. A valediction for a honeymoon. But was he really sorry? Or was he grateful to have been saved by—if not the bell—a ringtone from a cell phone?

"Who says it's ending?" she asked. "We've still got plenty of money left over from the chess games. Save Jonas. Save the world. Then head to Danny's for a celebratory drink afterwards."

One look at his face, and she knew that wasn't in the cards. "All right," she said, "why don't you just go ahead and say it?"

He reached for her then stopped. "Because I know you're going to kick up a fuss."

"And what makes you think that?" she demanded, oblivious to the irritated pedestrians that swirled around them. "The red hair?"

"If you'd prefer to chalk it up to some kind of angelic super-power, be my guest." He looked down the street, avoiding her eyes, her hair. "The real point is, I hate to think my last memory of you is having pissed you off."

"About?"

"I don't want you along when I talk to Jonas. What I want you to do is take a cab home. And when you get there, lock the door. And don't answer it to anyone until you take a cab back to All Saints tomorrow, where you will meet with the lawyer. You should be relatively safe. Process servers prefer regular hours. And I have a feeling the Lazaritos will be … otherwise occupied."

She stared at him. "You've got to be kidding me."

"Not in the least."

"But … why?"

His face hardened. "Because right now, you are turning into a complication that I could genuinely do without."

"A complication?" she spat. "That's quite the sweet nothing to murmur in a girl's ear."

A passing businessman bumped into them; a woman loaded with shopping bags flashed them an exasperated look. What must they see? A pair of lovers quarrelling on the street—airing their dirty linen in public, her mother would have put it.

Sean seemed to have the same thought—or who knew, maybe he was reading her mind, calculating more possibilities. Whatever the case, they moved in unspoken accord to the relative shelter of the steps of St. Bartholomew's Church before he said, "Apologies for being direct, but, please, Clare. What I've got to say to the kid, I've got to say alone. I'm sorry, but you would only be in the way. So please, don't fight with me over this. Let me help Lukas now."

She paused, remembering how close she had been to falling in bed with this man. And then remembering the carefully controlled despair in Lukas Croswell's voice. "Fine," she said. "I'll go quietly, if you'll answer one question. What did you mean when you talked about your last memory of me? Am I going to see you again? Or is the entire lawyer business in lieu of sending flowers?"

A flush stained Sean's cheeks, and she knew what his instinctive answer had been. What his instinctive answer would always be. He blew out an exasperated breath. "The lawyer business is about me wanting—no, me needing—to know you don't think you owe me. For me to know that when—if—you decide you want me, there are no lawyers, no process servers, no drug dealers in the equation. I need you to let the lawyer handle things. Get Trey Carey off your back. The Lazaritos, too. So you know your life is your own." He hesitated before adding with careful indifference, "Then, if, in defiance of all logic, you still want me, you know where I live."

She stared at him. "You know, a woman could get tired of these tests of loyalty. If you weren't aware, you're beginning to make Cupid and Psyche look like a picnic."

Sean's face set. "Choose me as I am or don't choose me at all," he said. "And I'd be the first to say you're making the logical choice if you take the second option."

And, without waiting for her to say another word, he took off down the church's broad front steps and disappeared into the mass of pedestrians.

Chapter Twenty-six

There was something to be said for being a stupid mistake. If nothing else, you at least knew where you stood. Or so Jonas kept trying to tell himself as he worked the stolen cell phone with shaking fingers. The world might suck, but at least now he had—how would the old man put it?—clarity.

But what was he supposed to do with all this newfound insight? Start a Facebook page? Join the Dark Web? Post directly to Wikileaks? The thought was enough to make Jonas's palms sweat and his stomach clench. Because, fuck Snowden, fuck Chelsea Manning, it was one thing to slink through cyberspace, poaching a record or two, but was he really willing to spend the rest of his life in an airport bar in Moscow?

"It won't be you," someone said. "It will be your father."

The phone slid onto the desk from Jonas's slick hands, as a shadow rose out of nowhere. Jonas swallowed hard as he recognized the fiddler everyone kept talking about, the twin miracle boy Jonas wasn't supposed to know existed. Although if they were supposed to be twins, Jonas couldn't help but wish they had been identical. The guy was wearing a long coat and dark glasses that were so seriously cool Jonas wondered why he'd ever believed that a box of sticky black hair dye would make him look like a vampire.

"I can take care of myself. Don't need the old man."

"Well, actually, no, you can't. And, yes, you do. But that's beside the point here." Without being invited, the fiddler pulled over a chair and settled next to Jonas. "The point right now is, he needs you. And he might as well have taken out a billboard ad to broadcast that fact. Not exactly a strategist, your father. But you don't need to be a chess master to see that makes you one hell of a liability."

"I suppose that beats 'stupid mistake.'"

The fiddler considered the point. "Not sure exactly what that means beyond you're pissed off at your father," he finally said. "And all things considered, that's probably pretty understandable. He pissed me off pretty good back in the day. But are you really sure you hate him enough to let him fall into their clutches?"

"Their?"

"Trey. His friends. The military-industrial-prison complex. Pick your bogeyman."

"Hey, I'm the one surfing the Dark Web. He doesn't even know enough to change his passwords. So why're we all of a sudden worried about him?"

The fiddler snorted. "Because, at the risk of permanently damaging your self-esteem, your father's a lot more important to them than you are. You and me, we're nothing but tissue samples. And given what your father says is on that phone, it's beginning to look like we're a dime a dozen. But there's nothing they wouldn't do to find a way to make Lukas play along, because he's the one who still has the knowledge tucked away in here." Sean tapped his temple, then paused and held Jonas's gaze. "So if you go through with that hack, you're handing your father to them on a silver platter. He will be forced to choose between violating every value he has ever cared about or protecting his son. And you and I both know which one he will choose. So, at the risk of repeating myself, do you really hate your father that much?"

Hell, yes. I mean, no. I mean, what the fuck kind of question is that? "I need to know who I am," Jonas said, ashamed to feel the tears beginning to well in his eyes. "What *I* am."

"What you are is a kid figuring out that his father's as screwed up as you are. Like all the rest of us."

"That's not an answer, man. That's fucking Oprah. And he's not my father. He's just some scientist who bred me for spare parts."

The fiddler's face abruptly creased with humor. "Just between us, I'd say you're getting a little carried away with the spare parts thing. Now, if that's just to twist the knife in your old man's gut, why not? You have every right. Any son does. But if that's what you think is really going on, you're wrong. Don't be crazy."

"Why should I be the only one?"

The fiddler laughed out loud, as he pulled a pressed handkerchief out of his pocket and wiped both the computer and phone for prints. "Set a precedent. Lead by example and all that," he said. "So what do you say we get out of here and not leave your father twisting in the wind any more than he has to?"

But the old man wasn't twisting when they got to the van parked on the corner. He was slumped over the steering wheel so motionless that Jonas swallowed a lump of fear that his old man had done something desperate for the second time in his life.

"Told you, you didn't hate him that bad," the fiddler said kindly, before he slid open the side door of the van and motioned for Jonas to climb in.

"God in heaven, what now...?" Lukas snapped up straight at the intrusion, then stopped, his face frozen with shock. And then ... was it relief? "Jonas?"

"Sir?" From the back seat, Jonas took a step forward, crouched awkwardly against the van roof. The old man's eyes were red-rimmed, and Jonas's eyes were prickling, too. And all he really wanted to do was throw himself into his father's arms, but something seemed to freeze him, or maybe it was more like a pane of glass was still standing between him and the old man, just daring someone to shatter it as the two of them just stared at each other, both of them trying to figure out what came next.

"I left the phone in the Outreach Center next to the computer. Wiped them both clean of prints, of course." The fiddler climbed into the passenger seat as if he were smoothing an awkward moment at a party. "Seemed simplest to let Sister St. John handle matters. I'm sure she'll figure something out. Formidable woman. Wouldn't be surprised if she's a card-carrying member of the Assassini."

Lukas nodded. "Thank you," he said. "For that. As well as..." He sketched a wave toward Jonas.

The fiddler raised a shoulder. "Unfortunately," he said, unslinging his fiddle case and snapping it open, "I was a little less certain what to do with these. Found them thrown in with my own files. As you may or may not know. Names, dates, dosages. It's all there."

Lukas stiffened. "I thought you just said you were leaving the records to Sister St. John to handle."

"I said I was leaving the phone," the fiddler said. "Not the records."

"A bit of a fine distinction, don't you think?"

"Not really," the fiddler said. "These records belong to the shelter, not Grinnell. Which means even if you knew nothing about what was going on—which, for the record, I do believe is the case—they remain your responsibility."

Lukas stared at at the fiddler. "What on earth is that supposed to mean?"

"It means that, by all accounts, I've screwed things up a hundred ways to hell—so to speak. It's going to take a better man than me to figure out the right thing to do with these … Lazaritos."

Casting a sharp glance at Jonas, Lukas paled. "And if I refuse, you'll take it out on my son. Now that you know exactly how far I will go for him."

An odd expression flickered across the fiddler's face, and then was gone. "That's pretty ruthless even by my standards. Which of course doesn't mean—" he mused, before he shrugged. "Would you do it if I put it in those terms?"

"Are you really capable of doing that?" Lukas demanded.

"I dunno. You're the expert, remember. What do you think?"

Lukas studied the fiddler's face, searching for the truth. "So this is payback."

"High-functioning sociopath. Manipulative monster. Complete lack of a moral compass and all that." For a moment the two of them eyed each other like a pair of gunfighters returning for one last duel. And then the fiddler gave in with a tired shake of his head. "Oh, for God's sake, Lukas, think it through logically. If I'd wanted to use your son as a bargaining chip, I would have done it before I got him out of there, not afterwards. I know I told your kid you were no strategist—"

"No high-functioning sociopath either."

The fiddler's body stiffened, and he looked out the window. "You know, that phrase is really beginning to get a little old. Especially when I just saved your kid's ass."

Lukas shut his eyes, a trace of the old irritation surfacing. "*Quid pro quo,* then?"

"If it's easier for you to look at it that way." Folding his arms, the fiddler turned to Lukas. "The fact of the matter is, I need your help. Just as you needed mine. I'm no evil genius, Lukas, no matter how many reports you want to write. I can't make head nor tail out of those files, any more than I could have told you what that shit about the awakener really meant. I need you to take a long look at them, and decide what needs to be done about these guys."

"They're not 'these guys.' Those bastards shot my son!"

The fiddler's voice grew cold. "That's just an excuse, and you know it."

And maybe the old man did, and maybe he didn't. But Jonas knew one thing for sure. The old man wasn't *mad* at the Lazaritos. He was afraid. Afraid to face them. Afraid to face what he had done. Just as he was afraid to face what his son may or may not be. And just as, most of all, he was afraid to face himself. Suddenly, Jonas found himself fighting down the seriously awkward urge to just grab the old man and give him a hug.

Instead, he said, "Come on, Dad. You can do it. All you've got to do is stop thinking of them as those guys. Think of them as—I don't know—desiccated fecal samples. Or some other piece of dried-up shit from your lab."

Startled humor flashed across the old man's face. But before Jonas could decide how that might have stacked up to a hug, the fiddler cut in. "Or maybe you could think of them as lab rats?"

The humor evaporated from Lukas's face. "Is there a point here?"

"More a question than a point. What happens to lab rats when the experiment goes wrong?"

Lukas's expression went flat. "They get euthanized," he said mechanically, then shut his eyes. "God in heaven, even you can't be suggesting I kill them..."

"Even I thank you for that, Lukas." The fiddler's mouth twisted with angry humor. "And while your answer is, in fact, the one I anticipated, it might surprise you to know that I raised the issue more in the spirit of my doing something to actually rectify the situation rather than as any kind of policy proposal."

Without waiting for the old man's response, the fiddler matched his words with actions, opening the door, ready to evacuate a sinking ship. Jonas swallowed a surge of panic at being left alone with the old man. He supposed they had to talk. But how? About what? When that pane of glass that stood between them shattered, jagged shards of everything that was still between them threatened to fly everywhere.

Jonas could feel his father's eyes on him, as if the old man feared that pane of glass, too. And then the old man looked away.

"Michael, wait."

Just as the fiddler was going to hop out, he turned back. Lukas hesitated, and Jonas realized that for the second time in his life, he was seeing his father grope for words.

"I apologize. My estimation of both your character and your abilities are apparently flawed. Because once upon a time, you told me that having a son was a decision I'd regret all my life. And you couldn't have been more wrong. On the contrary, having a son is the best thing that ever happened to me."

Even though the old man kept his eyes carefully trained on the fiddler, Jonas knew his father was talking to him. *Trying* to talk to him, at least. Venturing a single, tentative tap on the glass that stood between them.

The fiddler raised an eyebrow. "Not mutually exclusive propositions," he pointed out. He studied each father and son . "Work it out between the two of you," he said, "whatever choice you make. Get it straight between you, or they'll just keep using you against each other. You can't force someone with a fork if he can't be pulled in two directions."

Yeah. Cute. But this wasn't a fucking chess board, Jonas wanted to scream. This was his old man who had bred him in some laboratory. The old man who Jonas had never done anything but disappoint every goddamned day of his life. And now he was supposed to believe that this was the old man who didn't give a shit about anything except Jonas? The old man whose eyes had been red-rimmed—red-rimmed as if he had been fucking crying—when he looked up to see him. The old man who actually seemed happy to see Jonas for once in his life—so happy that Jonas was pretty certain he had wanted to grab him and kiss him. It was like a nightmare in which he had to memorize Newton's equations for an exam and suddenly he let go of an apple and it floated straight up in the air. How in hell was he supposed to work that out?

The fiddler turned to Jonas before hopping out of the van. He wore a faint smile, almost as if he had heard Jonas's angry protests. "Me, I broke my Da's nose," he said. "It seemed to sort things out between us. Just a suggestion, that's all. Don't know if it's really right for you. Probably isn't. Most of the time, it's pretty much a matter of personal style."

And then he slid out the door and was gone.

∞

They sat in frozen silence, as the fiddler's footsteps died away. And then Jonas heard himself say, "I don't want to break your nose."

"If it's all the same to you, I'd just as soon not have my nose broken," Lukas conceded. He thought for a moment, then asked, "Any idea what you do want? Shall we venture another lame bonding experience?"

"Please, sir. No more doughnuts," Jonas said hastily.

Lukas chuckled grimly. "Couldn't even get that right, huh?"

The obvious self-pity in the old man's voice was enough to make Jonas swallow hard. Lukas Croswell feeling sorry for himself? Lukas Croswell, who could calmly spoon up ramen with one hand while examining the disemboweled intestines of St. Elmo with the other?

"Listen to me, Dad." The single syllable felt as unfamiliar as this new version of his father. "You need to tell me the truth. I need to hear it, and I need to hear it from you." Jonas paused briefly, steeling himself for an angry tirade, before he added, "And frankly, I think you need to say it out loud. Once you do, I don't think it's going to seem all that horrible anymore."

His father shot him a sharp look. "This is beginning to feel like we've moved past lame bonding straight to intervention."

"At least I haven't started by flushing your scotch down the toilet."

The old man flinched, then said, "I suppose I deserved that."

Maybe. But it didn't make Jonas feel any better at having said it.

"Look, you may not like the fiddler, but he's right about one thing. They can only use us against each other if we're trying to hide things from one another. So why don't you just tell me?"

"Tell you what exactly?"

"How you did it," Jonas pressed. "How bad is it really? What are you so scared of me finding out? Did you breed me in a test tube?"

"Honestly, Jonas. Do you sneak watch the SyFy Channel?"

"Sometimes," Jonas allowed. "But that doesn't answer the question."

The old man conceded the point with a sigh. "I paid a woman. A surrogate. It was all completely professional. Clinical. Dignified."

"You call that dignified, sir? Seriously?"

Lukas's face softened with unwilling humor. "I admit the dignity of the situation was compromised when I first had to face the possibility that there might be a law against boiling formula on a Bunsen burner. And speaking of shit, dried up or otherwise …"

Was that the old man smiling at the memory? Actually smiling, rather than baring his teeth as if he was anticipating the taste of the kill? It was about the same as watching the polar ice cap crack. It also made what Jonas had to say next that much harder.

"I'm sorry," he said. "I … I know it may only be twisting the knife—at least that's what the fiddler told me—but I still need to know. I've still got to hear it from you."

Lukas sobered immediately. "Hear what exactly?"

Jonas ducked his head, feeling his ears flaming. "Was there ever a question of … spare parts?"

From the way Lukas flinched, it might have been kinder if Jonas had just broken his nose. "I would have taken samples," he enunciated. "Tissue samples. From your mouth. With a swab. Maybe drawn some blood. Nothing more."

"No actual … harvesting?"

His father muttered something indecipherable about the SyFy channel. "No," he said heavily. "No harvesting. But, ethically, there's no difference between the two."

Jonas stared at him. "If you ask me, there's one hell of a difference."

The old man raised an eyebrow. "Then I guess I owe a debt of gratitude to the SyFy channel."

He sat for another moment, his green eyes distant—causing Jonas to worry that maybe he was going to burst into tears again.

"Then why not just take a swab?" he asked. "If nothing else, it would make up for the dried-up shit."

The old man froze. "I can't, Jonas," he said. "Please try to understand that I … just can't."

"Then what's the point? Why did the fiddler bring me back? What did he mean when he said you needed me?"

"Not that, I'm certain. Because if he did, he couldn't have been more wrong in his life. And he's a lot of things, but he's not very often wrong." Inscrutable emotion twisted Lukas's face. "Jonas, please. Point taken about the doughnuts, but … I don't need your DNA. I … need … you. I need some kind of lame bonding experience. Maybe we could watch a baseball game together?"

Jonas stared at him incredulously. "Do you even know what a baseball looks like?"

"I know what Babe Ruth's DNA looks like," Lukas said, a touch defensively.

"Seriously?" Jonas asked. "Why? Someone think he was a saint, too?"

"More like the other side. Someone was looking for scientific corroboration of the Curse of the Bambino."

"Did you find any?"

"There were … interesting anomalies."

Jonas swallowed hard. "As interesting as mine?"

"I think you're far overestimating your place in the gene pool."

And damnit, the old man was smiling. But before Jonas could get his head around that, they were interrupted by a resounding crash as the huge front doors of the church swung open and feet began to pound from every direction.

Lukas peered through the windshield. "What the hell?"

Chapter Twenty-seven

Sean didn't know how long it took before he was aware of the rustling beside him. It wasn't his father. He knew that much without looking. But it wasn't real either. Wearily, he turned to confront the old man in the porkpie hat. "Now isn't exactly a convenient time for a chess game," he said. "Especially if you're worried about the welfare of your sons."

But instead of the *orisha*, it was a priest, in a long, old-fashioned cassock that shimmered along next to him.

"You're new," Sean said without enthusiasm.

"Not really."

"Then let me guess. We were we just playing chess?"

"Yes," the priest said. "And no."

"As is so often the case."

"Perhaps the best way to phrase it would be that my brother and I are aspects of the same, and yet as vastly different as only sons of the same father can be."

"If you say so," Sean said. "So why are you here? Your brother too busy to make sure I'm going to make good on my father's debt?"

"I'm here to tell you there is no debt," the priest said. "Owed by your father, or owed by you."

"In other words, you're a figment of my imagination." Sean never broke stride. "In case you're wondering, that one doesn't have me falling to the ground in shock, either. I'm a lot of things. But one thing I'm not is gullible enough to let a ghost drive me into saving those assholes from extinction."

"I never had any doubt of it."

Sean shot the priest a sharp glance. "Then why exactly are you here?"

The priest cocked his head. "You really don't remember me, do you?"

"Nope."

"Then am I to assume you don't remember the first words you ever spoke, either?"

"The world remembers them. I asked my mother to fix me a drink. A screwdriver."

The priest laughed. In fact, he seemed to shimmer with laughter. "No," he said. "The first words you spoke were a week before that. They were preparing the church for a Mass of Thanksgiving for the founding of this church—the very service in which you most memorably fell ill. Do you remember any of this?"

Sean shrugged. "Does it matter if I do?"

But he was remembering, so much so that the priest's next words were little more than a voice-over narrating the filmstrip that was unscrolling in his head. "In those days, there was no Outreach Center. On cold nights, the homeless slept on the vents of the church basement for warmth. And that year, the homeless were camped out in droves. Not exactly the sort of people you want as greeters for your anniversary service. Your father was making arrangements to have them removed, when you said—"

Sean stopped and stared at the apparition, as the words rose to his lips out of nowhere. "And when St. Lazarus's wanderings brought him to Africa, he was hailed as the *orisha Babalu Aye*—Lord of the Earth, the Son of the Lord, the Wrath of the Supreme God. At once the Leper Saint and the great healer, his sores are a reminder of the double nature of all things. So it is always wise to care for the beggar saint, especially when you are at a crossroads. For you never know when you might meet Papa Legba himself. And the god of the crossroads can be a trickster, but he will always return an act of compassion with kindness."

And then he grinned incredulously. "So what's the great cosmic lesson to be learned here? My poor bastard of a father built the Outreach Center because his autistic son started babbling about lepers and tricksters?"

The priest smiled in the irritating way that priests always did, regardless of whether they were ghosts, avatars, or figments of your imagination. "Oh, I wouldn't say that."

Of course not. "Then why are you here?"

The shimmering seemed to redouble, just as the priest's voice suddenly seemed to echo from every direction. "To open your eyes to the fact that even the god of the crossroads only points the way. He cannot stop you from choosing your own path. From exercising your own free will. And willfully blind or not, the path you have always chosen to follow—then, just as now—is the path of compassion. And that, and that alone, is the only real mystery you need to understand, in order to understand your miraculous cure."

∞

Sean had to assume that, as cosmic pep talks went, it was meant to be touching. But frankly it felt like nothing so much as Gandalf bolstering Frodo before he threw himself into the flames of Mordor. Thing was, Sean had been thinking more in terms of preventing a break-in at a botanica and then heading back to Danny's for a well-deserved lager. All that shimmering and booming and talk of miracles sounded a lot more like his priestly friend believed he was contemplating the ultimate self-sacrifice. Which he really sincerely hoped he wasn't. And if his pet apparitions knew otherwise, he'd find a heads up a hell of a lot more useful than a pep talk.

Yeah, well. Time to hold that thought for a minute, because Sean was finally across the street from the church. And there at the far end, crouched by the back entrance of the botanica were the Lazaritos. Christ. It was an insult to call it predictable or inevitable. It was more like stupidity raised to the level of an art form.

But that was the thing. Sean didn't like art any more than he liked stupidity. Or cosmic pep talks. He liked the order of a chessboard, the mathematical relations that underlay even the wildest reels, the calm inevitability of seeing your life mapped out in front of you like a series of moves. Moves, not choices.

But what other choice did he really have? Hoisting the strap of his fiddle case on his shoulder, he shoved his hands into the pockets of his overcoat and got on with it.

"Excuse me!" he called.

Suddenly the closest punk shrieked, his eyes rolling back in his head. Sean sighed. It was not what you'd call an auspicious start.

"Calm down," he said. "I'm just here to talk."

The punk with the crowbar swung it up with both hands. "Jose's a pussy," he hissed. "I ain't afraid of you."

"Good, because little as I might like it, I'm on your side here," Sean said. "And I'm pretty certain that I'm about the only one around here who is."

"Shows what you know," the Lazarito said.

"Oh, I know about your friends." Sean jerked his head toward the half-jimmied lock. "They the ones that told you this was a good idea?"

Another punk licked his lips. "He be watching us. I tol' you."

"What the fuck you playing at?" the Lazarito demanded. "You think you're gonna hypnotize us again? Fuck with our heads?"

That would only be a redundancy, even if Sean could. Christ, why was he wasting his time? There would be those who would say letting them blow themselves to Kingdom Come was nothing but Darwin at work.

Chief among them, Trey Carey. And that was the problem here.

"No mojo this time. Just logic. Gasoline," Sean said, gesturing down at the cans they were carrying. "I'm assuming they told you to torch the place?"

"You want to fight, bro? You want I should take a swing at you?"

"I want," Sean said, "for you to take a deep breath, and then tell me exactly what you smell."

The Lazarito thought for a moment. Sean sighed. That wasn't likely to contribute to the situation. But then he hefted the crowbar from hand to hand as he took a cautious sniff.

"I smell gas," he said, and the crowbar wavered. "What the fu…?"

"It means, if you open that door, I won't have to mess with your head, because it will be a mess already." Sean looked at the gasoline cans. "That's nothing but window dressing. You'll never even get a chance to use it. One spark, and this botanica will blow sky high. And it will provide evidence of your criminal intent once they decide to piece things—along with what remains of you—back together."

"Shit!"

Two or three of the punks were starting to listen, but the main man stayed stubborn. Sean guessed that was why he was the main man.

"Why should I believe you ain't messing with our heads again?" he snarled. "You made us see things, why shouldn't you be able to make us smell things, as well?"

Well now, that was at least creative. Stupid. And wrong. But creative.

"Face it, you guys are nothing but pawns in another man's game. The Man's game. And pawns are always expendable. Especially when they're also the evidence in the case."

Sean breathed a sigh of relief as he saw the last point hit home. "That's what they told you, isn't it?" he pressed. "That you're destroying evidence. They just didn't happen to mention that you're the evidence you're destroying. Have to admit, that takes more of a sense of irony than I would have given them credit for."

"Who the fuck's they?"

"What the fuck's irony?"

"He's reading our minds, man."

"It's the fiddle, man ..."

"I tol' you. We got no business burning down a botanica. The saints will protect their own. Ol' Luisa always said so."

The main man might be hanging tough, but the others were clearly terrified. Which was nothing short of annoying. Terrified people were hell to deal with. Someday, maybe someone in the Middle East might figure that out.

"What the fuck does that mean?" the Lazarito asked.

"It means you've outlived your usefulness to your friends. And now they want you gone."

Which was at least a concept a gangster could understand. "But we done nothing—"

"Since when does that matter?" Sean said. "Honestly, how old are you?"

"Old enough," the leader said, but his heart wasn't in it. His face fell. "Shit."

"In a word."

"What we supposed to do?"

Sean nodded toward the Church of St. Lazarus across the street. "You could head in there and claim your right of sanctuary."

"You fucking kidding? That nun?"

Was about the only thing standing between them and a death that frankly no one would mourn. But as Sean tried to come up with a way to phrase that somewhat more … diplomatically, a small skinny Lazarito stiffened, then fell to his knees, his eyes focusing everywhere and nowhere at once.

"Our Lady Oyá! The owner of the marketplace, who keeps the gates of the cemetery. She wields lightning and rides the winds into battle, often fighting with her machetes side-by-side with Chango. She raises armies of the dead and stole Chango's secret of throwing lightning …"

The leader's hand clenched on the crowbar. "I tol' you—"

"No!" the skinny kid cried. "She says we have to listen to him. Says she will protect us, that if we go to the church, she be waiting for us there."

You didn't need Sean's powers to see it was all over but the shouting. "She tends to go by Sister Saint John these days," he said, thinking wearily that if he hadn't just earned himself a glass of Martin's best whiskey, he didn't know when he had. "I'm guessing it's simplest if you just go ahead and ask for her by name."

Chapter Twenty-eight

As Sean hurried away from the clamor that was already beginning at the church, another priest fell into step with him. But this one was wearing functional dark clericals rather than a cassock, and he easily matched Sean's long, loose stride.

"Sanctuary," Father Gregory mused. "At times like this, one can understand the temptation simply to cut through at sword point, as Thomas á Becket's murderers did."

"That your way of saying it was all for nothing? You're going to hand the assholes over to Trey anyway?"

"Render unto Caesar the things that are Caesar's. And to God the things that are God's. However, in one's dark moments, one can be given to wonder why God's things can never be a Nobel laureate for the faculty or a computer magnate with a bad conscience for the Board of Trustees." Father Gregory shook his head. "We all have our Gethsemanes."

"You made this my problem. I'm just returning the favor," Sean said. "So, if there isn't anything else, the church is back the other way. Your supplicants are waiting."

"The church will keep." Father Gregory flashed Sean a small smile. "If nothing else, I'd be the last to deny Sister St. John her moment in the sun. I want to talk to you."

"Why? My part in this is done."

"Perhaps I should recall to you the parable of the Lost Sheep. Matthew 18. Luke 15. As well as the non-canonical Gospel of Thomas. The good shepherd leaves his flock of ninety-nine sheep, in order to rescue the one that is lost."

"Especially when that one could control a fortune?"

The priest frowned at him. "You seem to be rather focused on that issue, if you don't mind me saying so."

"What I mind is people trying to buy their way into heaven. And you enabling them."

"I think that's a bit reductionist."

"Why else did my father need to splash his name all over everything? I seem to recall a text about when you give alms."

"Do not let your left hand know what your right hand is doing. Matthew 6:3," Father Gregory said. "Sound theology, of course, but Holy Mother Church is also in the business of accepting human imperfection. And if in some cases, that means splashing the occasional name, well, so be it."

"That so?" Sean stopped walking and turned on the priest. "That mean you'd accept my imperfection by putting my name on an endowed chair? In medieval studies? And that you'd offer it to Clare Malley in order to pay her back for the inconvenience and embarrassment?"

"Simony," Father Gregory said.

Sean paused. "Honestly, I've never been entirely certain what that word means."

"It's the act of selling church offices," Father Gregory said, "named for Simon Magus, who offered to pay Peter and John if they would give him the power of imparting the Holy Spirit to anyone he touched. Acts 8."

"I'm talking about her job. Not a church office."

"A veritably Jesuitical objection," Father Gregory conceded. "Nonetheless, Dante put simony in the eighth circle of Hell. The sinners are buried head first in the bedrock, with flames applied to their feet. Eternal suffocation and immolation."

"So what if I'm willing to be damned for her?"

"Perhaps I'm not willing to … enable you with that."

Sean stared at him. "You seem awfully concerned about my soul. Why, if it's not about the money?"

Father Gregory started to answer, then changed his mind. "Supposing we strike a bargain? It's a time-honored tradition when it comes to issues of damnation, after all. I'll answer that question honestly, if you answer one question honestly for me first."

Sean's mouth twisted. And he was supposed to be the master manipulator? Father Gregory was beginning to strike him as at least as good a chess player as the crazy *orisha* in the park. The only difference was the *orisha* tried to blind him with forks, false choices. Father Gregory's game was more about goading you inexorably down the straight and narrow.

He spread his hands. "Fine. Go ahead. Hit me with your best shot."

"Why are you so unable to forgive your family?" the priest asked. "You just risked your life to help those Lazaritos, despite the fact they are drug dealers and criminals. Why can't you show similar compassion for your own family's failing?"

"Well, technically, that's two questions. And do you really need to ask the second, given your calling?" Sean said. "A priest of all people should know that compassion's easy. It's really no different than a bunch of chess moves. See the right thing. Do the right thing. Pay it forward, if you can tolerate that expression. But caring, now that's an entirely different thing altogether. Caring sucks. And I don't see why you should blame me from running away from it, when, the way I see it, the priesthood's the biggest retreat on that issue out there."

If he was hoping to shock the priest, push him away, he should have known better. "As a matter of general principle, those are exactly the kinds of candidates for the priesthood that the Church is most eager to weed out," Father Gregory said. "Although priests are as subject to human imperfections as the next man."

And then he just stood there, waiting for Sean to answer his question, as if they were sitting on opposite sides of the grille in a confessional. Even worse, Sean knew that was exactly what was going to happen. Predictable, if not downright inevitable.

He folded his arms. Leaned back against a wall. "My father was, in his way, the best father I could hope to have had," he said. "Loved me unconditionally. Never gave up on me. Moved heaven and hell—as we've seen—to find a cure for me. On the other hand, he was a lousy husband. Slept around. Flaunted it. I don't think he ever actually hit my mother, but he humiliated her every chance he got."

"And you feel guilty because you couldn't protect her?"

Sean just laughed. "I feel guilty because I didn't blame him. She was stupid and needy. And political correctness be damned, she was asking for it. Grinnell money would have bought her an annulment in a heartbeat. And my father would have been glad to be shed of her. But where would she have been without him? She would have had to do something with her life besides suffer. She liked being a martyr; it was her thing. As a matter of fact, I'm sure she never forgave me for being cured. One less cross she had to bear." Sean shook his head. "I've been told I never could abide a fool. I couldn't abide her."

"In the whole of our lives, the family we are given is arguably the one place we have no free will."

"Nice words." Sean swallowed hard. "But does that justify me letting her die?"

Father Gregory paused, then said, "If from that I am to infer that you somehow saw her suicide coming and felt you could have prevented it, I'm sure you've already been told that you can't stop a suicide if someone is determined to do it."

"My mother had no idea what the word determined meant," Sean snorted. "She was always threatening, just to get attention. She liked making a scene. By all accounts, it's an ability my sister has inherited."

"Just for the record, I would not underestimate your sister," Father Gregory said. "Genetics isn't destiny, even in your case. But let's not muddy the issue. Please go on."

"I don't know how many times I saw it coming. Warned my father. Called the cops. Then one day, I just got tired of the drama..."

As if invoked by the word, the noise at the church redoubled. Sirens began to wail from every direction, and a police car raced by, followed by shouts and pounding feet from every direction.

Sean jerked his head toward the excitement. "Speaking of which, my father would have said I inherited my mother's taste for making a scene just as much as Marie did. I could have just hired them a lawyer."

"It would help matters considerably," Father Gregory conceded. "We could make it from an anonymous donor, if you would prefer."

"So this *is* about the money," Sean snorted.

"What do you think?"

Sean stared at him. "I think you still haven't answered my question. Why the concern, if not for the money?"

"Because it's my job," Father Gregory said with a laugh. "But you knew that already. Frankly, as infernal pacts go, you just struck a pretty lousy one."

Shutting his eyes, Sean thought for a moment, then conceded defeat. In fact, he was beginning to think about a long vacation from chess. "Fine. Go ahead. Tell Hays to put it on Grinnell's bill."

"Compassion? Or caring?"

"Neither," Sean said with a faint grin. "I just want to see the look on Trey's face when he has to sign the check."

ꝏ

Crouched around the altar of the church, the Lazaritos didn't look like much. On the other hand, the figure striding down the aisle toward the cops who stood uncertainly behind Jonas and his father was one serious badass.

"You will lay down your weapons or you will step outside the church," Sister St. John's voice rang out.

The cops just stood there.

"Ma'am, please be reasonable," one finally said. A couple of others nodded. The rest looked like they had been caught smoking in the schoolyard.

Sister St. John smiled. It was not a nice smile. It was the kind of smile Jonas could imagine her smiling as she stalked the aisles of a fifth grade class, wooden ruler in hand. She pointed to her forehead. "Do you see reasonable tattooed up here?"

One of the cops actually moved to look. Sister St. John froze him with a glare. "It was a rhetorical question."

"Yes, ma'am. But ma'am these guys are armed and dangerous."

"I have no idea how dangerous they may or may not be. But what I do know is that their arms, such as they are, are piled outside on the church steps. And they are here to surrender. Just as I am willing to surrender myself in order to ensure their safe conduct out of here."

"Ma'am, we don't want to arrest you."

"What you want has nothing to do with it. If you arrest them, you are arresting me," Sister St. John said. And stalked back to the punks, and linked her arms with two of them. With a nod, she instructed the others to grab someone's arm as well. Which Jonas figured might have had some dignity if they were marching down the Mall in Washington, but given the narrow aisle they had to squeeze down together, looked about as lame as the time Jonas had been forced to play a sheep in the parish school's Christmas pageant. And the cops didn't look much better. One or two of them—the ones that had once served as altar boys, Jonas figured—had holstered their weapons. Most of the others were holding them about as sheepishly as Jonas had brandished a sword in the class production of *Pirates of Penzance* in the lame arty school that had come after the parochial school. Only one was still holding his pistol in a two-handed grip, keeping it trained on the knot of gangsters and nun as they tried to make their way to the door. Frankly, he looked like an ass.

But before the untidy human chain could take more than a few steps, a shadow rose behind Jonas and his father, and a priest stepped through the heavy church doors, as tall and dark as if he had just arrived in Georgetown to confront Linda Blair spinning her head and puking pea soup. He stood there for a moment, taking in the situation, then nodded. "Ah, Sister St. John. Offering ourselves up as a sacrifice again, are we?"

"These boys have claimed the right of sanctuary."

"So I have been informed."

"Who by?" one of the punks snapped. "Who squealed?"

"Rafael. I tol' you he was a fuck-up."

"What do you say we leave your young apprentice out of this for the moment," Father Gregory said. "You have more than enough problems of your own."

He cast a long look at the tangle of gangbangers and the nun, like they were an altar boy that had farted during mass. "Are these our... for want of a better term, turbulent priests?" he asked Sister St. John.

"What the fuck does that mean?"

"He called us turbos. He think we're cars?"

"No, he didn't. He called us priests. He thinks we're gay."

"Not gay. Perverts."

"Yo, man, I'm not gay. Not a pervert neither."

Father Gregory favored the gangbangers with a stare that would have incinerated even Jonas's father. "Those were the words with which many would argue Henry II ordered Thomas á Becket's murder. 'Will no one rid me of this turbulent priest?' A request that four stupid brutes of knights were more than happy to fulfill. Although one can hardly say they were rewarded for their loyalty." Father Gregory's eyes came to rest on the leader of the gangsters. "Which seems to be the inevitable result in these situations. Stupid brutes like the knights find themselves excommunicated, if not worse, while the real villains walk scot-free."

"You calling me stupid, man?"

"Yes, frankly, I am." Father Gregory said with a sigh. "Unfortunately, that seems to be who Christ bids us succor. The stupid. The venal. The weak. The angry. The unfulfilled. Honestly, sometimes, it's enough to make a man lose his faith."

"Then maybe it takes a woman to show a man the right path," Sister St. John said.

For a moment, Father Gregory simply looked pained. Then he said, "I am afraid you misunderstand. If I were not determined to follow the right path, I could be back in my study at All Saints, enjoying an early evening drink. And I will not insult your intelligence by refusing to admit that is precisely what I would prefer to be doing." He gestured wearily toward their linked arms. "All I am proposing is that the right path could be somewhat … less theatrical. An anonymous benefactor has generously offered the Lazaritos top flight legal representation."

"Nossir," the biggest guy, the leader, with a big, ugly gold medal around his neck said. "No lawyers. Fucking public defenders just want to help the prosecutors make their numbers…"

Father Gregory shot him the kind of look that went a long way beyond farting altar boy—all the way to if the altar boy had suddenly doubled over, puking up his guts, as well as the communion wine he had sneaked in to get drunk on last night. And then he nodded toward the gaudy medal that hung around the punk's neck. And suddenly he looked like he was about to whip out a crucifix and tell someone very demonic and badassed that it was the power of Christ that compelled them.

"I blessed that medal for you on your first communion," he said. "At your *abuela's*—shall we say firm?—insistence. She said that you would need that medal's protection some day. Now, pace St. Christopher, who does ride shotgun in the All Saints van, I'm highly unsure of the protective powers of miraculous medals. But what I am certain of, beyond all question of miracles or turbulent priests or sanctuary, is the protective power of first rate legal counsel. So I am here to suggest—no, insist, for your *abuela's* sake, if not your own—that you take the cosmic second chance that someone, in his caring compassion, seems to have handed you."

∞

The aftermath was simple, disappointing even. The drug dealers climbed into the van like it was some kind of church bus, and everyone else just went home. Jonas eyed his father speculatively as he wheeled his way toward their SUV. The old man looked whipped, like he had gone ten rounds. Maybe tired enough that he would let Jonas drive. But before Jonas could point out what an appropriate lame bonding experience that could prove to be, there was a squeak of sneakers on the pavement behind them, and suddenly the old nun was standing between Lukas and his car.

"So that's it," she said to Lukas. "Happy ending for all? Justice is served?"

Lukas raised a shoulder. "I'm not much one to debate the justice of the universe. I think it might be better to say I'm glad this is over."

"Yes," she spat. "It's over. Over for you. You have your son back. The bad guys are under arrest."

Lukas raised an eyebrow. "Are you saying you want a bunch of drug dealers back in the Outreach Center?"

"They may be drug dealers, but they're someone's sons, too. They have names." And Jonas was startled to see that the old nun's eyes were full of tears. "Manuel. The leader, the one with the medal. Big guy—and all of nineteen. He was raised by his grandmother. His Abuela Inez. He fell in with the gangs because she didn't have time to supervise him—mostly because she worked twelve-hour days cleaning hotel rooms. And still always found time to volunteer to clean the church before Sunday Mass. Juan—he's the one with the stupid-looking pigtails that make him look like Heidi. His mother says regular novenas that he will finally see the light and cut them off. Jose's sixteen years old with an addict mother and an eight-month-old baby to support. He's trying to stand up and be the man of the house. And Rafael—"

"Shot my son," Lukas said, his voice carefully even.

"And needs to accept the consequences of his actions," the nun agreed. "Although I would point out that no one objected to you deciding on the consequences for your own son."

The old man's face hardened. "That sounds suspiciously close to blackmail."

"What it is, is simply the truth. Your son got into something dangerous in that medicine chest. Something intended for those kids. Something that someone gave them—used to set them up, to manipulate them."

"And that somehow exonerates them from what they have done?"

"That's up to the courts to decide. I honestly have no answer." Sister St. John swallowed hard, then went on, her voice low and furious. "But what I do know is that no one's hauling whoever supplied them with those drugs into court. And it doesn't look likely that anyone ever will. I don't know how justice will be served on those boys, but it will be served. But who is going to call to account the people who used them as lab rats—experimented on them along with setting them up, and, if I believe what they told me today, were prepared to euthanize them to cover things up?"

Lukas stiffened and paled. "We've worked together in this place for years. Are you seriously accusing me of being the one behind this?"

And if Jonas had believed for even one minute that old man was even capable of emotion, he would have said the old man sounded hurt.

"If not you, who?" the nun spat. And spinning on her sneakered heel, she hurried off toward the All Saints van. Lukas stared after her for a moment, and then wordlessly, slid into the driver's seat, folding the wheelchair behind him, before Jonas even had time to think that he had just been screwed out of his chance again.

"She's wrong," Jonas stammered, as he climbed into the passenger seat. "You didn't do anything. You gotta make her see that."

"Unfortunately," the old man said, "that wasn't at all what she meant."

"Then what ...?"

But the old man had already pulled out his cell phone and dialed.

"Hello, Marie?" he said with distant courtesy. "I'm terribly sorry to disturb you, but I'm afraid I have a tremendous favor I need to ask of you."

Chapter Twenty-nine

Jonas listened to his father's end of the conversation with slowly dawning horror. No. Fuck, no. The old man couldn't be planning…

"No," he said, when the old man finished the call. "NFW. No fucking way. I'm not going to let you do this."

"What do you propose as an alternative?" Lukas asked. "Ask Sister St. John to stage a protest march on my behalf? Frankly, she didn't sound very disposed toward doing that."

"But she's wrong. She's got it all backward."

"She's right about one thing. If not me, who?"

"But you didn't do this."

"Nonetheless, it is the relevant question."

"And what about the assholes who are really behind this? What about Grinnell? Are you just going to let them walk?"

"I'm going to need their help, if I'm going to help anyone," Lukas said matter-of-factly. "One crazy scientist launching some conspiracy theory about cloning some kind of super-DNA by experimenting on indigent populations, and the government can just laugh me off. But if I come forward with some kind of mistake at the clinic, a drug with pernicious side effects, the people in charge will be happy to throw me under the bus and play the hero getting the cure to whoever's affected."

Jonas's eyes widened. "What do you mean, throw you under the bus?"

Lukas shrugged. "I guess it depends how vindictive they—and the American public—feel. Which, when it comes to mad scientists, is usually is almost as vindictive as they feel about Congress. I suppose there's a chance they could go after my medical license or press criminal charges—although

I'm hoping the people in charge will see the wisdom in just accepting my resignation and letting matters die down quietly."

"And nothing happens to them?"

"Not that I can think of."

"That's not fair," Jonas protested.

"Life often isn't," Lukas told him.

Maybe. But why did it have to be this … fucking unfair? Shit, the old man was as much a victim here as any drug dealer whose DNA might have gotten poisoned—more of a victim if you asked Jonas. Hell, all they did was see ghosts. But the old man … hell, the old man couldn't walk.

"No," Jonas said. "I won't let you do this. You're no fucking saint. So why should you suffer for humanity?"

"Language," Lukas said reflexively, but he grinned despite himself. "You're right. I do make a lousy martyr. But I don't see any of the various relics I have lying around stepping up to offer themselves in my place."

Jonas shook his head. "It's not a joke. This sucks."

"On the contrary, it's the lousiest damned joke in the universe." Lukas turned on the ignition, his green eyes suddenly all business. "And I'm sure the people whose names are in those records the fiddler gave me would be the first to agree. So let's get started, shall we?"

We. Like … what? They were some kind of team? Or was that just the old man's customary we, which really mean I—an order for Jonas to shut up and keep his nose out of things that weren't his business. But this was Jonas's business. Hell, this was all Jonas's fault.

He folded his arms. "Fine. Go ahead and do it your way. But I want to come along. I want to be there when you do this."

"No."

"You said 'we.'"

"I misspoke."

Jonas drew a deep breath. "Well, then maybe I'd better speak more clearly, too. If you don't let me come along, the minute you leave without me, I am going to head straight down to the police station and tell them how I got into some magic DNA drugs hidden at the clinic, and I think those gangbangers did too."

Lukas's fingers gripped the arms of his wheelchair. "You will not…"

"Then don't make me. Dad—" The single syllable was beginning to feel more natural each time he used it. "Please. The fiddler said the only way they can hurt us is if we let them come between us. So we need to stand together on this, okay?"

He ducked his head, hoping his ears wouldn't betray him by flaming red, as they usually did. "If you want, I can even handle the computer end of things for you."

∞

The executive conference room at All Saints looked like it had stepped out of a comic book council where some secret Templar society was meeting to decide the fate of mankind. Wood paneling. Stained glass windows that stretch from floor to ceiling. Soft, plush rugs and a polished oak conference table with tall, carved chairs that looked like thrones. In other words, the old man looked like a natural when he took his place at the head of the table. Dr. Xavier himself.

Trey Carey strode into the room, ostentatiously immersed in his tablet, underscoring his point that he was a very busy man with little time for histrionics, but he glanced up at Jonas sitting next to his father with a frown. "Is this entirely prudent?"

"Seeing as the alternative is Jonas heading down to the police station to provide some rather striking exculpatory testimony on behalf of the Lazaritos, I think it's the better choice." Taking a deep breath, Lukas glanced at the other two people at the table, Father Gregory and Marie, in turn, considering them as if they were a particularly doltish group of students. "And that is why, in spite of her many sterling qualities, I did not invite Sister St. John to this little conference. I'm assuming that all of us have a vested interest in handling this matter quietly."

"What matter?" Trey asked. "What exculpatory evidence?"

Lukas pulled out the manila folder the fiddler had given them, and tossed it into the middle of the conference table. Jonas swallowed a mean surge of pleasure when he saw that Trey recognized it.

"The records in that file contain evidence that the Lazaritos had someone inside at Grinnell. Someone feeding them drugs."

"They're the bad guys, Lukas. How many times do I have to remind you?" Trey spread his hands, all self-consciously reasonable now. "Okay. Sometimes my office plays hard ball. I admit that. Sometimes we even play fast and loose with the rules."

"And sometimes, apparently, you entrap them."

Trey shook his head. "Entrap is just a word people like to throw around as if it's some kind of moral concept—"

"But morals are, if you will, my department," Father Gregory cut in. "What we're talking about here is ethics. A code of behavior, rather than any absolute notion of right or wrong."

"Yeah, well, I guess that's why you're the theology professor, not me," Trey said. "All I know is that we've invested over a year in this operation."

"And how long have you invested in the *other* operation?" Lukas asked.

Trey's face set. "I'm not sure what operation you're talking about."

"The illicit medical testing you've been conducting, not only on the Lazaritos, but apparently, also on other victims at dozens of other free medical clinics across the country."

"That's one hell of an accusation to make," Trey said. "You have any evidence to back it up?"

"Sister St. John found a phone in the Outreach Center. Your phone."

"You mean, the phone your son stole." Trey turned on Jonas, his eyes bright with venom. "Listen to me, kid. I've cut you a lot of slack for your father's sake. But you have no idea what you've gotten into stealing that phone. Christ, have you heard of the NSA? Because I've not only heard of them, I have them on speed dial. And I sincerely suggest that whatever classified information you've uploaded, you get rid of it now, even if it means unplugging the entire internet. Ask your father what we do to whistleblowers. We take you down. For real. And for good. You're not going to spend the rest of your life in an airport lounge. We're not those pussies in charge of this country. Trust me, if I shut down those little cunts with Napster..."

"Fuck," Jonas said, "you're the asshole that shut down Napster?"

"Language," Lukas sighed.

"He didn't steal the phone!" Marie snapped. "I gave it to him."

"Honestly, Marie, I have no time for your drunken displays on top of everything else."

"I'm not drunk. I'm telling you, I stole the phone. I was trying to catch you sexting, but apparently you're not even imaginative enough to do that."

"Overshared," Lukas said. "As I believe my son would say."

"Sexting?" Father Gregory asked.

"By all accounts, exactly what it sounds like," Lukas informed him. "Unfortunately."

"I stole your goddamned phone," Marie said. "Although seeing you pay the phone bill with my goddamned money, I don't see how you can call it stealing."

"Just watch me. Grand larceny. Theft of official secrets. A felony, not a misdemeanor. You want to spend your time in jail rather than rehab, I can make it happen."

"And that would not qualify as handling this issue quietly," Lukas cut in. "Which I believe is in all of our interest to do."

"What issue?" Trey demanded. "That I launched an undercover sting operation to bring down a drug network that has been terrorizing this neighborhood?"

"That you've used that sting operation to conduct clinical studies on the Lazaritos along with dozens of other indigent populations without the trouble of obtaining their informed consent. Win/win. You bring the bad guys down, and manage to conduct a healthy dose of illicit medical experimentation in the name of God alone knows what. Some kind of wonder drug that's supposed to unleash the hidden capacities of the human brain, as best I can gather." Lukas looked at the others in the room, and then back at Trey. "I'd prefer to save us all the embarrassment of even mentioning the notion of some kind of DNA with miraculous healing powers."

Trey lurched forward, hands balled into fists. And then just as quickly stopped. "If there was such a thing," he said, "I think you of all people would have an interest in making it work."

The old man flushed, and Jonas knew he had never come so close to hitting someone in his life. Hell, the fiddler said he had broken his father's nose; right now, Jonas would have gladly pummeled Trey's face into a pulp—even if it meant he got grounded for life.

"It's a matter of company, if not public, record that once upon a time, I did have a significant interest in making this work," Lukas said with preternatural calm. "Which is why when I say this thing needs to be nipped in the bud, you can take it as an informed opinion."

"And how am I expected to do that? You want me to plead them?"

"I'm not a lawyer, and I have no idea what the ethical legal action might be." The old man glanced at Jonas. "And the truth of the matter is, I'm not a disinterested party when it comes to that issue. I don't know that the drug can explain or excuse these people's actions from either a medical or a legal point of view. But what I do know is, it has to be stopped. Grinnell needs to make a public announcement. A product recall, if you will, of a tainted drug, with unpredictable and dangerous side effects."

"Unpredictable? Dangerous? That's your idea of handling things quietly? Sounds to me like you're trying to incite widespread consumer panic."

"It's called the internet. And those words are already out there." Lukas shook his head. "Although my son did not upload your files, you can't stop information from getting out in this day and age. All you can do is try to control how it does."

Trey shook his head. Casting a wary look around the table, he came to a decision. "Okay, look," he said, "supposing, just supposing there were such a project—"

"You mean, taking this as a theoretical construct?" Lukas interrupted with a wry smile.

"Yes, speaking theoretically," Trey sighed. "Do you seriously think anyone's going to believe that story?"

"No," Lukas said frankly. "And that's why we need another one."

"Such as?"

"Well, I thought about working a spin on the rogue bacteria and claiming I had unwittingly unleashed a new strain of the Bubonic plague, but I figured that would be almost as showy as some Lazarite DNA with miraculous healing powers. So I figured we could go with the old standard, faulty inoculations. No one pays attention to inoculations, unless it's September, and you're rushing to get your kids ready for school. So we announce side effects of an experimental drug that was administered without informed consent. We can call it a mix-up in the paperwork, or blame it on me. And we establish a compensation fund. As well as free medical treatment. For life, if need be." Lukas glanced at Marie. "That's why I needed to talk to you.

I'll need some help from the company on the last two. Otherwise, I'll take complete responsibility."

"But … it's not your fault!"

"So I wanted to believe," Lukas said. "My bad."

There was a long pause. And then Marie said, "If we have evidence that Grinnell has been actively involved in testing some kind of dangerous drug for the government, they both need to be held accountable."

"You don't know much about the government and accountability," Lukas told her. "I'm afraid you're going to have to be content with me."

"Well, we'll make them accountable! Trey's a prosecutor. Why can't he investigate that instead of the drug runners?"

"Investigate what?" Lukas sighed. "That the government is indulging in yet another illicit experiment in breeding super-soldiers? That a race of miraculously resurrected humans are being roused to launch a war on heaven? I doubt you could interest even my son in that."

Well, actually, if that really was the case, Jonas was kind of interested. And so was Marie.

She turned to Trey. "Why not? You know what's at stake and you're thinking of running for office next year. That kind of prosecution would be a lot bigger campaign boost than just some drug dealers. And … if you need a sweetener, I'll stay married. Campaign right there by your side. Stone sober."

An unfathomable expression crossed Lukas's face. "A gracious offer, but I don't think we need to resort to sacrificing virgins on top of everything else."

"I was never—"

"Stipulated," Lukas said hastily. "I misspoke. The point is, there's no point in fueling further internet rumors. What we need to do is find out how many of these people are out there, and do what we can to help them. *If* we can find some way to help them."

"And how are you going to do that when you don't even have a lab?" Trey cut in. "Lukas, I'm talking to you as a friend. Think this decision through."

"You're not my friend," Lukas said. "And I have thought it through. Not only that, I've already done it. I've emailed my resignation to Father Gregory. Cc'd the AMA, the American Academy of Scientists, and whatever other organizations I pay dues to, along with a score of websites. There's no turning back now."

Trey drew a deep, angry breath. "And what will that get you beyond destroying your own career?"

"My career was over a long time ago."

Trey just stared at him. "And so you're going to ruin other scientists' careers? Scientists who are doing real work, important work? Is that what this is all about, Lukas, some pathetic attempt to drag the rest of the world down to your own level?"

Lukas swallowed hard. And once more, Jonas was certain that he wanted—hell, he needed—to slug the asshole tormenting his father. "This is about justice for the poor bastards you treated as lab rats."

"You mean, the poor bastards that shot your son."

Lukas tensed. "Agreed," he said tightly. "Which is why you need to believe I would not be pursuing this issue if I could see a moral—or ethical—alternative."

Trey stared at him for a long time. And then his face twisted in disgust. "Always knew you were going to try to be a hero in the end. In fact, I'm surprised you lasted this long. You never had any spine."

"Once upon a time I did."

"And that's really what this is all about, isn't it? Payback. Against anyone and everyone who had the nerve to walk when you couldn't?"

And before Jonas could finally give in to the urge to slug this guy for real, Father Gregory cut in sharply, "May I remind you that Jesuit spirituality encourages self-reflection, not self-projection."

"What the hell is that supposed to mean?"

"That that comment was offensive to everyone in this room."

"You're taking his side in this then?"

"It isn't about sides. It's about solving a problem. And so far, Lukas is the only one here who is suggesting a solution. Unless you have a counterproposal?"

"Oh, hell, yes, I have a counterproposal," Trey hissed at Lukas, his voice soft and reptilian. "I propose that if that's really how you want to play it, I will throw the book at you. If you really want to fall on your sword for this, I'll make sure it's a jagged one. I will make sure you go to jail. Hard time. Federal prison, if I can manage it. No chance of parole. Your son can bring you cookies monthly. If you pay off the guards, maybe they won't even crumble them, looking for contraband."

Marie slammed her fist on the table. "Why? To prove you're a vindictive prick? Someone who hates losing so bad that you can't see it when someone's handing you a gift on a silver platter?"

"Or to rephrase things somewhat more politically, Lukas is offering you an easy answer to a damned sticky situation," Father Gregory added. "So I fail to see the problem here. Perhaps you could enlighten us as to what exactly you're trying to accomplish. Why not do things his way? Why not set up the compensation fund? The free medical treatment? It sounds to me as if it would make Grinnell look like a hero. So why not just do it? Do you have a problem looking like the corporate good guys?"

Trey raised an eyebrow. "Our customary way of doing that is by making contributions to worthy institutions. Substantial contributions that I'm certain will be sharply reduced if Grinnell finds itself embroiled in multiple compensation issues."

The priest let out an exasperated sigh as if he were dealing with a noisome child. "It seems to me that I've been explaining the issue of simony so often as of late that I might well offer a course on it."

Trey just stared at him. "I suppose that translates into everyone here is determined to be a hero. Fine. I'll have someone craft a statement." Trey favored Lukas with one long, last glare. "Enjoy your moment in the sun," he hissed. "I sincerely hope you decide it's worth it."

Chapter Thirty

Was it really Clare's fault that she had fallen in love with Indiana Jones at first sight? No, that she had wanted to be Indiana Jones. That she had aspired to the life of a dashing professor, her quarries the real location of Arthur's grave and the secrets of the world's standing stones from Orkney to Stonehenge to Brittany. Her mother had always dismissed such aspirations with a knowing smile, just as she had grudgingly approved Clare's getting a PhD as Something You Did For Yourself—the academic equivalent of a year spent abroad on a Kiwanis scholarship before you came home to teach at the local high school and provide your parents with grandkids they could spoil.

And it didn't matter that the reality of being a medievalist had been a far cry from Indiana Jones. That the past week had been closer to her fantasies of the professorial life than six years of post-colonial investigations of Crusader romances, nuanced rereadings of populist heresies, and feminist reinterpretations of convent life. That the only genuinely interesting piece of research she seemed to have read in her graduate career was an investigation of the dirt on medieval prayer books, which proved beyond a doubt that St. Sebastian was the most well-thumbed page in any medieval psalter—although it seemed impossible to determine whether that was because he was a plague saint or because medieval ladies had a guilty taste for his rippling torso. From the look of things, her mother was going to get her way after all. Clare would slink back to community life, after her little adventure playing at being a professor. And that, frankly, broke Clare's heart.

Fighting down the angry tears took so much effort, she barely heard the swift tap on the door, or Father Gregory's polite request to come in, until he was sitting in her visitor's chair that she had hastily cleared of a stack of student papers. It was scarcely comparable to the cathedral-like president's office, and yet he seemed to bring a whiff of its magisterial grace with him, as if he had censed the room with it.

Or a whiff of the Inquisition, as he studied her, his fingers steepled. Clare swallowed hard. What was he going to do? Fire her outright? Why should he? she reassured herself. She'd be gone in another year anyway—just an unfortunate blip on All Saints' serene radar—just like the miracle she was supposed to investigate … quietly. Much less scandal that way.

Father Gregory drew a breath, as if to pronounce a blessing—or a sentence. "I'm afraid I had to cancel our scheduled chat with the lawyer. Both he and I have had rather busy mornings, given the rather dramatic turn of events yesterday and today. But I feel very comfortable saying that, as far as you're concerned, the matter is closed."

Closed? All of it over? The miracles, the chess games, the fiddle music, the room at the Waldorf, all vanishing like a bad dream rapidly dissipating in the morning light, leaving nothing more terrifying looming on her horizon than the stultifying nineteenth-century iterations of the Lazarites?

"And Sean …?"

"I sincerely hope is meditating on the horrors of the eighth circle of hell, specifically eternal suffocation and immolation."

"Simony?" Clare asked, startled. "No. He just tried to hire me a lawyer."

"Actually, he was willing to fund a chair in medieval studies, provided I selected the right applicant."

Clare stared at him, stunned. And then she said the first thing that came to mind. "A professorship isn't a church office, even in a Catholic school. So it's not really simony is it?"

"Indeed."

Clare shut her eyes. Why quibble about definitions? If Sean had actually tried to bribe Father Gregory on her behalf, that was going to make the Cosplay Lolita a tempest in a teapot. "Look, Sean is a complicated man. Arguably even a difficult one. But surely you can see that he wasn't asking you—"

"As a matter of fact, yes, he very much was," Father Gregory said, cutting her off with a wave of his hand. "But it doesn't matter. You're quite correct about the issue of simony. Decisions about professorships are in the hands of a tenure committee, not the clergy. And that decision is based on your teaching and publication record. Not on promise of funding from an interested party. Or for that matter, on any court records that never should have been unsealed. If I am making myself clear?"

Clare just stared at him numbly. Her career, not a shambles then? How was she supposed to believe that? How was she supposed to believe he had forgotten that scene with Trey Carey? Erased the words "Cosplay Lolita" from his mind?

She drew a deep breath. "Thank you," she said. "I mean, thank you for taking the time to tell me personally. I … I know you're a busy man."

"Not too busy to ask my assistant to write a letter for your permanent files, expressing the president's gratitude for the invaluable contribution your research skills made to the investigation of the Cause of Father Enoch."

And that, apparently, was all he was here to say. She stared at him, stunned, as he pushed himself to his feet and started for the door. That was it, then? This was over with? He was … letting her off? Even giving her a letter of recommendation?

She shook her head. They were not equals, no matter how much he couched their conversations in the rhetoric of civilized debate. And she knew he was a busy man. Knew that she had presumed enough on their relationship already—if that's what you wanted to call nearly getting in a fistfight with the college's biggest donor. She should lay low, do her best to fly under his radar, and hope he forgot all about her for the next two years. But she found herself confronted with a burning question, and honestly, there was no one else she could think to ask.

In short, she knew she was about to initiate the patented Clare Malley self-destruct sequence—even if it meant she was going to crash and burn right back to the bosom of her sainted family.

"Is it so very wrong?" she asked.

Father Gregory turned, raising an eyebrow. "Is what wrong?"

"Wanting to believe in miracles? Wanting to reign in hell rather than serve in heaven? Being on the Devil's side and damned well knowing it?"

Father Gregory cocked his head as he considered the issue. "I suppose that would all depend on what you mean by the Devil's side," he concluded.

"To want something for yourself? To want to be special? To want something more than just a home and children? Because frankly I hate children."

A small smile crossed Father Gregory's face. "It is one of the distinct privileges of my position to be able to leave them to the nuns," he allowed. He paused for another moment. "But beyond that, I don't think you have to be a neo-Platonist to answer 'Not in the least bit wrong' to any of your questions. C.S. Lewis would call it *sehnsucht*, although, personally, I find the German locutions somewhat cumbersome. But I believe that any competent theologian—as well as the German ones for that matter—would agree that reaching for something beyond ourselves is what religion is all about."

"Even if you risk getting called a Cosplay Lolita?"

He studied her for a moment. "Even if you risk getting called a hubris-driven angelophany-junkie," he said.

It took her a moment to even parse his meaning—and her eyes widened. "Really?"

But the door had clicked shut and Father Gregory was gone.

∞

Sean had no idea how long he had been walking. All night, apparently. And most of the morning as well. Neither did he have any real idea where he had been walking. No *orishas* pointing the way at the crossroads this time. No priests to urge him down the straight and narrow, either. He was just wandering—more bewildered than he had ever been in his life. If, in fact, he had ever been bewildered in his life. Which he pretty much believed he had never been. Went with territory and all that. Another new feeling, then. This was rapidly turning in to a habit.

But eventually his aimless footsteps found the path back to Danny's—the way home, he supposed. As if he had ever had a home. So what did it mean that this was the first time he had ever regretted that?

What did it matter? Where else was he going to go? Shoving his hands in his pockets, he started toward the bar. And a familiar presence fell into step alongside him.

"Truth be told, I wasn't sure I'd see you again," he said.

"I won't be back after this," his father's ghost confirmed. "Time for me to move on."

"I thought so," Sean said, then added, "So what was all this? Some kind of expiation? Repentance? Redemption?"

"The words just tend to get in the way, really," the ghost said with a shake of his head that sent a single droplet of blood flying. "Might be better to say I just needed to finish things the right way. Things I started all wrong years ago. I did try ..."

"When you finally tracked me down to Danny's?"

"I had the cops waiting just outside the bar," the ghost admitted. "I was determined to make you come home even if they had to arrest you."

"For what? Killing my mother?"

"You know better than that."

"Maybe." Sean conceded. "So what happened?"

"I stopped to listen to the music," the ghost said.

Sean nodded. "*Niel Gow's Lament*, if I recall correctly."

"It was only supposed to be for a moment, but ... I had never heard you play. Well, I'd heard, but I hadn't listened. And once I did—"

"I know." Sean said. "You came regularly. Thursdays. Stood my drinks. Most people said I played best on Thursdays."

"Drove poor Marie crazy, but it was the happiest time of my life." The ghost's face shadowed. "You need to come home. She needs you to take care of her."

"I've got it on pretty good authority that she is more than capable of taking care of herself."

"You're right, of course." The ghost sighed. "Guess I was a lousy father to her as well."

"You were our father. That's all that really matters."

"Thank you for that," the ghost said. He paused, then added, "But now I'm holding you up. There's someone waiting for you at the bar."

Someone? As in Clare? Sean couldn't bring himself to hope.

The ghost smiled. "I never had the good fortune to love a woman, but I had the great good luck to love my son. You have a chance for something better. So, go take it, before it slips away."

"Truth be told, I'm still not even sure I know what love is."

The ghost laughed. "Our proof that the universe is inherently kind."

"Ben Franklin said that was beer." Sean said, but already his father was beginning to shimmer into nothingness.

"Go ahead and get things right with her," his voice drifted back on the breeze. "But, when you're through, remember there's still one more thing that needs attending to."

"I know," Sean said, but he was no longer talking to anyone but himself.

∞

To judge from the relief that flooded Martin and the regulars' faces as Sean strolled into Danny's, Clare had been sitting in his booth for some time, looking like nothing so much as some wronged wife waiting for her lout of a husband to creep back up the stairs.

"I tried to stand her a drink, but she was having none of it," Martin said, as the other men continued to study her with rapt attention. He passed Sean a bottle of whiskey and a pair of glasses. "Here's hoping for your sake, this will work better. By the way, what's wrong with pink wine? I thought the ladies liked their drinks sweet."

Clare shot him a baleful look, as if she had heard him from all the way across the room. "You need that me and the lads give you your privacy?" Martin asked.

Sean grinned. "She scare you that badly?"

"She's a formidable woman," Martin said. "Don't let the sweet face fool you. They're always the worst. Toss you right over those helpless looking shoulders and drag you home from the pub when you've stayed past closing."

"Personal experience?"

"I still light a candle for the good woman's soul every week. Although I'm pretty certain it's not necessary. She'll be tolerating St. Peter's nonsense no more than she did mine."

"It's the red hair," Sean called back to him as he headed across the room. "It'll be the ruin of us all."

"Martin's best regards, and it's an insult to refuse a bartender," he said to Clare, as he slid into the booth and poured two glasses with careful ceremony. "Besides, I have a feeling I'm going to need this. *Slainte*."

The whiskey burned down his throat in a satisfying rush, but Clare made no move to reach for her own glass. "We have unfinished business," she said.

Sean nodded toward the gouts of briny steam that rose from the table on the other side of the room. "Didn't think you were here for the cuisine."

"An endowed chair just for me? Seriously?"

Christ. What happened to the seal of the confessional? Was it simply not applicable in cases of infernal bargains? Or did priestly vows include meddling along with celibacy, poverty, and obedience these days? "It was just words. Blarney."

"It was another test."

All right. She was not going to make this easy. Blame it on the red hair, he guessed, but if that's how she was determined to play things…

"Actually," he said, "it was just … me. And you need to take a long, hard look at what that really means."

"Why don't you tell me what you think it means instead?"

Frankly, Sean needed more whiskey to answer that question. Or maybe he was just stalling as he reached for the bottle and poured with a hand that was so shaky he knew he'd never play tonight. Maybe he was just hiding from the fact that he didn't want to play tonight. What he wanted to do was answer the question.

"It means I'm a guy who'd do anything to keep you. Lie. Cheat. Steal. Go back to being Michael Grinnell if that's what it takes."

"It's not a question of what it takes," she said.

"But it always will be to me." He couldn't help himself. He took another gulp of whiskey. "Don't you see, that's how I think? It's how I'm wired. Life is just a chessboard. So you really need to ask yourself if you want to spend your time with a man who's constantly trying to stay three moves ahead of you, just to keep you from leaving. A guy who will whisk you off to the Waldorf or the Gaelteach or whatever it takes to keep you from discovering the pathetic truth that I am really just a bore who can play the fiddle."

And suddenly, for some reason, she was smiling, and it killed him that he couldn't figure out what that meant—even if at the same time, he couldn't help thinking it was sexy as hell. Not the smiling. The not knowing.

"I think that you are substantially overestimating your ability to manipulate me. Or anyone else for that matter," she said.

"Then let's put it a little more simply. You can do a lot better than me,

Clare Malley. Even with a billion dollars in my pocket."

"And if I don't care?"

"You will, eventually. And that's an official prediction."

"More like a self-fulfilling one," she said. She shook her head. "You remember what I said about Cupid and Psyche? Well, I meant it. I'm sick of the testing. We're going to finish this here one way or the other."

Reaching for the whiskey, she raised it briefly before she swallowed it off in a single gulp. "So here's how I see the situation. It doesn't really matter whether you're a fiddler who lives over a bar, or Father Enoch's first miracle, or even a billionaire master manipulator who wants to snatch me off to the Waldorf. Any reasonable person will tell me you're bad news. But the thing is, I'm not reasonable. I want to be with you—at least for now, and the hell with the future. The hell with the consequences. We'll figure that out when it comes. What I need to know now is whether you feel the same way. Whether you'll admit to yourself you feel the same way. So I want you to take off those damned glasses, look me in the eye, and say you never want to see me again, or I want to finish what we started back there in the Waldorf. No more tests, no more blarney. Just an answer. Which way is it going to be?"

He could sense, rather than see, the shoulders stiffening at the bar behind him, and he was mortified to think they might be laughing. Mortified to know that he was blushing. Another new emotion, he supposed. Frankly, he liked the other ones better.

It was reflex to reach for the whiskey. It cost every fiber of his being to reach for his glasses instead. "I think we should be taking this discussion upstairs."

"Why?"

He glanced over at the drinkers at the bar, who had suddenly immersed themselves in their glasses with studied disinterest. "Partly because we've entertained the lads enough for one night," he said. "But mostly because that's where my bed is."

Chapter Thirty-one

Lounging on Sean's bed, watching him get ready to play that night, Clare never felt so at home in her life. Her mother—and probably even her father, if his attention could have been drawn to the matter at hand—would have murmured something about Lydia and Captain Wickham, and any daytime talk show host would have certainly raised an eyebrow. But the past few hours felt like a more perfect idyll than the Waldorf ever could have been, from the swift, economical movements with which Sean polished and tuned his fiddle, right down to the rattle of the train on the tracks overhead and the smell of cabbage that wafted up from the bar downstairs.

"Is it me, or does tonight's meal actually smell appealing?" she asked.

"It's you," Sean said with a quick grin. He finished adjusting a string, then asked, "Are you starving or can you hold out until I take my first break? I usually call out for food then. Always get enough for Martin to share as well, although he pretends not to notice. Just happens to drop by my booth to chat when the food shows up. It's like those people who claim they've given up smoking because they only bum other people's cigarettes."

So there was something about him that needed improving. She glanced over at the tiny stove and sink, wondering how hard it might prove to chop vegetables and toss pasta. Somehow the thought of domesticating him was absurdly appealing. "What's the local specialty? Fish and chips with malt vinegar?"

"Arguably the only thing in this neighborhood that's more frightening than Martin's steam table is the deep fryer in the local chip shop," Sean told her. "They say it hasn't been cleaned since the Provos used it to kill an informer back in the seventies. How are you with Pad Thai?"

"Pad Thai?" She pushed herself up onto one elbow. "You know, for a man I bumped into at a homeless shelter, you're really one of the most civilized people I've ever met."

"Plenty of good food to be had in homeless shelters," he said. "Four star restaurants are dropping things off all the time. It's all just a matter of knowing the right time and place."

And right now, Clare could think of no better mantra by which to live her life. But her easy contentment died the moment they stepped through the bar's front entrance, and Martin looked up with a sharp, warning glance. Slowly, he inclined his head toward the unlikely sight of a coiffed and manicured blonde sitting in Sean's booth, staring disbelievingly at a glass of Martin's vile pink wine.

"Aw, hell," Sean sighed.

"She asked directly for you," Martin said apologetically. "Said she's your sister."

"You did right," Sean assured him. He reached for the pint Martin had already poured for him and handed it to Clare. "I don't know about you, but I have no intention of facing her without benefit of alcohol," he told her. "And the lager really is a hell of a lot better than the wine."

Martin poured another and handed it to Sean, who punctuated his words by taking a healthy gulp of his own, before he worked his way over to the booth where Marie Carey sat. He jerked his head toward the glass of wine. "So much for rumors of your newfound commitment to your sobriety."

"This swill would make anyone a teetotaler."

"Martin prizes temperance. I think that's why most of his liquor's so lousy." Sean gestured for Clare to precede him, then slid into the booth. "To what do I owe the pleasure?"

Instead of answering, Marie Carey glared at Clare, and Clare was startled to see her eyes were red rimmed and that there were hastily repaired smudges in her makeup. "So," Marie said. "There really is a woman."

"This is Clare," Sean agreed. "Clare, this is my sister, Marie, who seems to have lost track of her manners."

"I believe Father Gregory may have mentioned you in passing," Clare said inanely. She might as well not have bothered.

"Screw manners. I'm here to make a scene," Marie hissed at her brother.

"Strip myself naked and sing karaoke while you fiddle, if I have to. Whatever it takes for however long it takes. I'm not leaving here without you."

Raising an eyebrow, Sean took a long, considering draught. "Gotta say I didn't see that one coming."

Marie laid her arms on the table, oblivious to the damp spots on the wood. "So tell me, Michael, what will it take? Go ahead. Name your price. If half the family fortune isn't enough, you can have the whole goddamned thing."

He set his glass down hard. "My name is Sean," he said. "And I don't want your money. Never have. Never will."

"No, of course you don't need anything as mundane as a billion-dollar corporation," she snarled. "Well, how about your girlfriend? Have you thought about what she might need? Or want? Or do you really think a woman like that is really going to be happy spending the rest of her life living with you over a bar?"

Clare's eyes widened in fury. But before she could manage anything but an angry gasp, Sean laughed.

"In other words, she strikes you as the kind of woman who deserves more than I could ever possibly offer her. And to tell you the truth, I quite agree. As a matter of fact, that's exactly what I've been telling her all along. But taking my side in an argument isn't probably the best way to endear yourself to her on first acquaintance."

"Go ahead," Marie said. "Shoot off your nasty mouth as much as you want. I'm not leaving until I get what I want."

Clare felt an unwanted surge of sympathy for the woman. She might be—well, honestly, Clare was at a little bit of a loss for words to describe Sean's sister. Gobsmacked, actually. But her brother clearly still remembered how to push her buttons. And didn't seem ashamed to be caught doing it.

"But you see that's the thing I'm still not quite following," Sean said. "What exactly is it that you do want here? To lay our father's ghost to rest? Closure?"

"That boat sailed a long time ago." Shaking her head, Marie took a long look around the smoke-filled bar. "He never stopped looking for you, you know. Never gave up hope you'd come back and take what was rightfully yours." Her voice cracked and tears threatened to smudge her makeup once more, as she added, "Even after you tried to kill him."

Sean stiffened. "I broke his nose!" he protested. "One punch. Marquis of Queensbury rules. Now, if you want to talk about our sainted mother, everyone agrees I drove her to an early grave."

"Spare me the details. All I know is that, after you left, he didn't care about anything. Except you. Used to drift out at night, come back stinking of alcohol. Looking for you."

"Well, he was looking in the right places." With a sigh, Sean gave up and turned to Clare. "Apologies for the family drama. It's why I generally avoid the holidays."

"Drama?" Marie snorted. "You haven't seen drama. I might not have been born with the genius IQ, but if I have one real talent, it's drama. If the naked karaoke doesn't work, I'll keep trying until I find something that does. And I will. One way or another, I will find a way to embarrass you into coming with me. Trust me, I'm very inventive."

Sean leaned back. "Honestly, I can't say I much like your odds. I'm the sociopath, remember? Completely incapable of feelings—of embarrassment or anything else—"

"Oh, bullcrap!" Clare snapped. "You just use that as an excuse. You're more than capable of human connection—in fact, you're pretty darned impressive at it when you want to be."

His sister smiled, not a nice smile, and Sean went bright red and took a hasty drink. "Overshared," she said. "Seriously. But it's a start."

And Clare realized that she had seriously underestimated the woman sitting across the table from her. Sean was apparently rapidly arriving at the same conclusion. "Okay, okay," he said. "I'll give you round one. But as a consolation prize, could you do me the basic courtesy of explaining exactly what you're trying to accomplish here? Or is this purely recreational on your part?"

All of a sudden, the fight just seemed to go out of Marie. "It's Lukas Croswell," she sighed. "The jackals running Grinnell are going to throw him to the wolves. The one damned decent person in this whole mess, and he's going to get screwed."

Her voice caught, and she curled her shaking hands into angry fists. "Which is why I need you to come back and take control of the company. Hell, my life's the same no matter what. I get a trust fund administered by an asshole. Doesn't really matter which one. But it matters to Lukas. And that's why I'm here, and that's why I will sit here and put up with your shit until you come back from the dead and do right by him."

"I see." Sean nodded slowly. "So he decided to go public with the records, after all?"

"Seeing as you were the one who gave them to him, I assume you knew that all along. Which is why you need to step up and take responsibility."

"As I'm getting increasingly tired of explaining, it's not a Magic 8 ball. I had no idea what he was going to do. If you'd asked me to lay odds, I would've said he was going to burn the damned records and move with his son to California."

"Then you clearly don't understand a thing about the man." Marie swallowed hard. "Honestly, Michael. Even you should be able to see that this isn't a matter of odds. This is a matter of a man's life. Arguably the first man who has ever been genuinely decent to me—"

"Oh, God in heaven, Marie. Please tell me you don't have a thing for him. You'd be better off getting drunk on Martin's wine."

"I have a thing for someone who actually stood up for me when everyone else was just using me." Marie met her brother's eyes pointedly. "Or making a joke about it."

Once again, Sean flushed. And this time, he looked beyond embarrassed; this time, he looked genuinely ashamed.

"You're right," he said, rolling the words in his mouth uncomfortably before letting them fall. "I'm sorry." As he spoke, he reached to touch her hand, but she snatched it away, knocking her wine glass hard enough to make it slosh.

"Do not touch me!"

"Why not?"

"What do you think?"

"I honestly don't know or I wouldn't have asked."

She drew a long breath. "I may need your help. But I don't want you doing it again."

"Doing what?"

"Spying on me. Peering inside to see what makes me tick. Just like you used to."

"Oh," he said flatly. "I see. Well, if it matters, I don't need to touch a person to do it. Still, I'm sorry about that, too."

"Sorry? Do you really think that covers it?"

"Probably not. But there's not much more I can say." Grabbing a napkin, he began dabbing at where the wine had spilled onto the table. "Does it help if I add that was then, and this is now?"

"You're still you. I'm still me." She leaned toward him. "Call yourself whatever you want, you're still the same monster."

Irritation flashed across Sean's face, followed by unwilling humor. "At the risk of sounding petty, I don't particularly appreciate the name calling, no matter how applicable it might actually prove. Especially from someone who came to me for help."

"I don't want your help. I want you to help Lukas! We can't let him take the entire responsibility for this himself. He needs what a billion dollar corporation can do. He needs the spin doctors. Along with the corporate lawyers we pay so handsomely." She shook her head, her voice pleading. "Instead, the vindictive prick I'm married to is going to prosecute him. Prosecute him for saving the company's ass. So is it too much to ask you to take the reins of this legacy you've spit on for the sake of someone else, if not for yourself?"

For a moment, Sean just stared at his sister as if she were speaking a foreign language. Then, abruptly, his face lit with pure mischief.

"So why didn't you just tell me that in the first place?" he asked. "Screw the family fortune. I'd never say no to the chance to stick it to your asshole of a husband." Slinging his fiddle case over one shoulder, he swung himself out of the booth. "So what do you say, ladies? Want to go see how an amateur vindictive prick enjoys competing in the professional division?"

Clare and Marie eyed each other warily before they slid out after him, keeping a careful distance between them like a pair of cats. Clearly, sharing the holidays was still not a given.

Sean paused briefly at the bar before he reached for the door. "Sorry, Martin. Gotta see a man about a horse and all that. I promise I'll make up for the music on the weekend. But right now, I believe a guy left something for me—about a year ago?"

Wiping his hands on a dishtowel, Martin pulled a heavy envelope from beneath the bar. It was addressed simply to "My son, Sean." And the embossed return address in the corner was a legal firm.

Sean grinned as his sister's face slackened in disbelief. "He wasn't looking for me," he told her. "He found me a long time ago."

"He was coming here? All those nights, that's where he was?"

"Thursday nights, regular as clockwork."

"You and Father, elbow to elbow at the bar, sharing stories?"

"Mostly, I was playing, and he was drinking," Sean said. "We never spoke. But somewhere along the line, it seems like enough got said."

Chapter Thirty-two

The light flickering in the depths of the botanica was all the proof anyone could need. Pale and guilty, it could only be a flashlight.

But Clare never noticed the flashlight. Clare was staring raptly at the clutter in the shop's window. She had never actually been in a botanica, had only eyed the candles and beads and polychrome statues from the sidewalk like a teenaged boy sidling past a pornography store. Her mother would have been appalled; her father would examine the items in the window with the bewildered incomprehension of a man trying to understand sex toys. And as for Father Gregory—well, even if a hubris-driven angelophany junkie did lurk behind the college president's serene façade, she was fairly certain this display would defy even his Jesuitical logic. Beyond the bullet-proof glass, the Infant of Prague ascended in cheerful, plump clouds, the Virgin mourned in all her incarnations from Black Madonnas to Mater Dolorosas, and pietas and crucifixes all dripped gore.

"How did you know Trey would be here?" Marie asked her brother, as the three of them clustered in the shelter of a nearby doorway.

"I suppose I could tell you that St. Lazarus was back there at the crossroads, pointing the way, but honestly, all you need to do is think it through. Trey tried to set up the Lazaritos for torching this place. Why arson in particular, unless he really wanted this place burned down? And why would he want that? The most likely explanation was that he really did want some evidence destroyed along with the Lazaritos. And probably still does. Unfortunately, his hired thugs are a little out of commission right now—as well as probably feeling more than a little pissed off. People setting you up to die in a gas explosion tends to have that effect on you. But since the gangsters never died and the explosion never occurred, it stands to reason that the evidence is still here." Sean shrugged at his sister, offering her a faint grin. "Nothing but common sense. No Magic 8 ball required."

"But why not just leave it alone? No one can touch him right now."

"Partly because he's a vindictive prick. But mostly because he's running scared."

"I'm not sure Trey knows the meaning of the word scared."

"Oh, he's scared all right. Scared to death that someone is going to actually listen to those kids. He wasn't worried when it was just a bunch of gangbangers and a radical nun howling that they've been set up. No one was going to listen to them. But people tend to listen to lawyers. And if a respected doctor is willing to stand up and be counted as well …"

"Lukas."

"Makes me twitch when you say it in that tone of voice, but yes, Lukas." Sean's eyes slid speculatively to the light bobbling inside the building. "He's scared shitless. And that's making him stupid. So stupid, he can't see that what he's doing is the worst possible choice he could make. And to tell you the truth, I'm half-tempted to just let him go ahead and find out for himself. So we'd better get moving, and save the man from himself, before I change my mind."

Without waiting for anyone to second the idea, he pushed open the shop door.

Trey whirled at the sound, and his flashlight glanced off the enormous statue of St. Lazarus that stood on the shelf above him, filling almost the entire shop with the shadow of the crooked saint on his crutches, dogs licking his sores.

Then Trey snorted in disgust. "Get out," he snarled. "Go home. This doesn't concern you."

"Well, actually, it does," Sean said. He nodded toward the case full of vials and needles that lay open behind Trey. "I've been told Lukas Croswell is scheduled to give a press conference tomorrow. Would I be correct in assuming it has something to do with that?"

"I don't have time for this. Get out of here before I decide to shoot you just for the fun of it."

"Well, now, I doubt you're going to do that," Sean said. "Mostly, because

I doubt you have a gun. Bringing a weapon along in the commission of a felony will buy you five extra years at the very least. Now, the Lazaritos might be too stupid to think of things like that, but you're a prosecutor. Or has the need to crucify Lukas Croswell really made you that stupid?"

"I'm not stupid."

"Then you're not armed." Sean settled against the wall, folding his arms as he completed the syllogism. "And that's a good thing. Because shooting me would be a very stupid thing to do. Just like your plans to remove the evidence are really very stupid. But relax, Trey. We're your friends. We're here to save you from yourself."

"You're not my friends."

"No. I guess we're not," Sean allowed. "But we are here to save you from making a very bad mistake."

"Why?"

"Because nothing's going to change the fact that there's been a change of agenda for tomorrow's press conference. Lukas is about to find himself upstaged by Grinnell's lawyers making the happy announcement that I have been found alive, if somewhat down at the heels, with a copy of my father's will in hand—a will that leaves me controlling interest in Grinnell. Of course, it may take years before I'm able to step up and assume that control. In the meantime, the estate's conservatorship will be replaced by a transition team headed by Lukas Croswell and Father Dominic Gregory, whose first major task will be to investigate compensating the victims of a badly mismanaged vaccine. Samples of which might be found in the case you're holding." Sean waved a hand to cut off Trey's protest. "There's no question that much will happen. The only question is, what you're going to do about it. Now, sure, you can stall and fight and contest the will and tie things up in court for years. Just like you can stall and fight and try to hide the evidence that you were using those kids. But both of those would be very stupid things to do. Because both of those are very bad strategies. Fights that sooner or later you won't win. And when you lose, you will find yourself without my sister's money. Without a job. Without a Golden Parachute. And without a license to practice law. And why should you do that when you have a much better option?"

"Which is?"

"You can be the one to announce my joyous resurrection. Take your place on the transition team, and expedite the probate before you step down to pursue other interests and quietly divorce my sister."

"You're bluffing," Trey snorted.

"No, I'm not. I play chess, not poker, remember? And there's no bluffing in chess." Sean shook his head. "No, what I'm doing is offering you a fork. A forced choice. You've got two moves in front of you, one that will utterly annihilate you, and one that will let you live to fight another day. Now, I know which one a smart man would pick, but what I really don't know is whether you're a smart man."

Trey stared at him a moment, before pushing the case away. "This isn't over," he warned.

"No," Sean agreed. "Not even close. This is just one little skirmish in a hundred years' war. Because the fact of the matter is, you're going to fuck up again. You're going to lie or cheat or screw someone else sooner or later. You can't help it. You're hardwired. It's in your genes. Just like it's hardwired in my genes that I'm going to come after you when you do. In fact, I could see it becoming a sort of lifelong hobby. Oh, sure, they're telling me I'm a changed man. Love of a good woman and all that. And maybe even, it's true. But the simple fact remains, I've always had a nasty reputation for playing with my food."

Clare felt the blur of motion before she glimpsed it in her peripheral vision, and an arm snaked around her neck, pulling her jaw up hard, so she could feel the unmistakable pinprick of a hypodermic needle under her chin.

"Looks like you just blew round one," Trey's voice sounded somewhere distantly behind her. "Now, get away from the door and no one gets hurt. Maybe."

"You do not want to do that. How stupid can you be?" Sean's bantering tone vanished abruptly, and his face darkened with concern. "Look out!"

"Oh, come on. That game may work with a bunch of gangbangers—"

"Trey. Move. Now," Sean spat, just as his sister snarled, "Come on, Trey! What kind of husband are you? Wouldn't you rather hold me close instead?"

She lunged for Trey, but one of her heels caught and sent her crashing into the shelves instead. Beads, herbs, and candles tumbled to the floor—and the enormous statue of St. Lazarus dropped straight onto Trey, driving him face first into the open case of drugs. Suddenly free of Trey's grip, Clare lurched backward—and was caught by another pair of arms that pulled her tight.

"That was very stupid," Sean hissed at Trey, his face white with fury. "And you are about to find out exactly how stupid—"

"I … I don't think that's going to be necessary," Marie cut him off in a very small voice.

And they all fell back, watching almost reverently as Trey pushed himself away from the case of drugs, struggling to stand upright while staring at his blood-soaked sleeves. Broken vials seemed to have punctured him everywhere. Slowly, he raised his hands to his face, feeling for a hypodermic that had plunged through his cheek. Pulling it out, he stared down at it dumbly, as he ran his tongue across his wet lips, tasting the drugs. Then he spread his arms in silent anguish, rolling his eyes to the heavens like a latter-day St. Sebastian.

"Okay, okay," Sean said. "I think we'd better call you an ambulance."

But Trey spun with a cry, kicking aside the fallen statue of St. Lazarus before plunging out the door and disappearing into the night.

Chapter Thirty-three

Clare knew nothing about press conferences, but the group gathered around the temporary podium in front of the steps of the Church of St. Lazarus didn't seem like much of a turn-out. Stringers for the local papers, mostly. Reporters for All Saints student newspaper, a representative from the alumni office. A couple of science writers, on the off-chance that a wonder drug was about to be announced. She had to wonder if it was Father Gregory's way of keeping a lid on things in the name of dignity and discretion. And, surprisingly, she found herself wondering whether that was really such a bad thing.

She had no real idea what her role in all this was meant to be—or if she was even meant to have one—but Sean headed unhesitatingly down to the Outreach Center, where they found Lukas Croswell in the kitchen, in a fury all the more towering for the ruff of paper towels that sprouted from his collar, making him look like he had stepped out of a Holbein portrait. He was locked in a standoff with a sweet young thing in platform shoes and a tube skirt in front of a folding table furnished with jars, pots, trays, and a brightly-lit mirror.

"Come on," she cajoled, as she leaned over him, brandishing a brush. "Just a touch to liven you up."

"I do not wear makeup," Lukas told her. "Women wear makeup."

"It's not makeup. It's bronzer. And maybe a little concealer for those circles beneath your eyes. You look like you were up all night drinking."

"I was up all night drinking."

"Well, then. No point in facing our public like a pasty raccoon. Am I right, Jonas?"

Jonas made no response. He seemed incapable of answering, lost in slack-jawed admiration of the view from behind.

"First off, the first person plural locution is no more tolerable in you than in a doctor when he asks how we are feeling today," Lukas said. "And secondly, I am moved to point out that that description is more than a little insulting."

"But it is accurate," Sean said. The faint trace of a smile played across his features as he studied Lukas's face. "On the other hand, your nose seems okay."

"A little shiny," the sweet young thing opined.

"Not exactly what I meant," Sean said. "But that doesn't matter. Neither does Dr. Croswell's pasty skin, because, Dr. Croswell is no longer going to face his public."

Lukas went rigid, his knuckles whitening as he gripped the arms of his chair. "Damnit, you can't call this off. I will not have this thing covered up any longer, if I have to strip myself naked and hand out flyers in Times Square."

"Dad!" Jonas said, startled out of his rapt contemplation. "Really?"

"No," Lukas said. "I was speaking rhetorically. Obviously."

"Thank God," Sean said. "Because there is a far easier way."

Lukas subsided only fractionally. "And that is?"

Sean reached beneath his coat and pulled out an envelope. "Just came from the lawyers. Seems my father's will turned up."

Lukas stared up at Sean. "What a fortunate coincidence."

"Even more fortunately—at least for you —I'm about to turn up as well. Trey and I came to an understanding last night, but then … well, he was supposed to handle the announcement, but right now, no one can find him. So I guess it's going to be Marie and me."

The sweet young thing turned on him, bronzer brush at the ready, an appraising gleam in her eye.

"No," Sean said.

Lukas shut his eyes as any further discussion was cut off by a burst of sound from outdoors. "Please don't tell me Sister St. John has decided to grace us with her presence."

"Even worse," Sean said. "If I had to bet on it, I'd say Trey has shown up after all."

∞

The bored stringers on the local papers still talked about the day Trey Carey preached the Leper Armageddon. Those who had actually been there parlayed it into rounds of free drinks for life. The tabloids pounced on it with the fervor they usually reserved for reality TV stars' pregnancies and drug-raddled child actors' perp walks. The internet swarmed with cell phone footage and conspiracy theories, and the Twitterverse sprang to life with the weird poetry of what all agreed was Trey Carey's last press conference.

No one actually saw him arrive. If they had, they would have taken him as just another homeless wretch, blinking in bewilderment at the reporters gathered at the church's front steps, as he tried to figure out whether the Center was closed and there would be no free lunch today. Somewhere on his halting forward progress, though, he must have recalled who he was and why he was here, for suddenly he strode to the microphone with his customary air of command—and apparently oblivious to his torn shirt, bloody face, and matted hair.

Then the reporters noticed. And if they whipped out their cameras in anticipation of far more of a story than they had been promised, you could argue there was at least a whiff of concern in their shouted questions.

"What happened?"

"Were you mugged?"

"An assassination attempt?"

"Terrorism?"

Carey paused, as if trying to figure out the answer to the question. "It was the lepers," he said finally. "It was the lepers that did it. What do you want from me?"

A staffer stepped forward anxiously, but Carey waved her off—sending himself reeling into the podium in an eerie, intricate ballet. Grasping its edges, he righted himself. Then paused, staring out at something only he could see. "Goddamn it!" he breathed. "Why are you staring at me? It's the lepers you need to stop! They're everywhere. They're in among you."

"Get a doctor. Now," one staffer hissed to the other, before she asked Carey, "Sir, did you hit your head?"

"No one hit me. They don't have to." Running his hands across his blood-crusted face, Carey then held them out, trembling. "All they have to do is touch you. Just one touch. Like the Iron Fist Death Gung. One touch, that's all it takes. And then you're one of them, too."

One or two reporters lowered their cameras in stunned silence, and the nearest staffer groped frantically for her cell phone, while the other called out, "Excuse me, is anyone a doctor here?"

"One touch, and you're covered in sores," Carey plowed on. "Sores that you feel, but sores no one can see. That's how they move among us without being seen."

He stabbed a bloody finger to make his point, only to crash straight into a tangle of cables and electrical cords, sinking to his knees as he fought them off as fiercely as if they were a nest of vipers. "There's only one way to know a leper for sure," he yelled. "They have no balls! Because the balls are the first to go. Drop right off the minute they touch you and bounce away before you can catch them. Like a big pink Spaldeen. Big pink Spaldeens bouncing everywhere."

And for one brief, shining moment, the world witnessed the unlikely spectacle of reporters at war with themselves. Some of them shuffled and murmured and tried to turn their cameras away in the name of decency, while others elbowed their way into the middle of the cell phones that were flashing everywhere, hungrily sucking up images.

"They take your balls because they know you will march to save them. Straight into Armageddon if you have to! For that's what it will be. They will march on heaven itself to seize their lost penises. They will march on heaven waving them as their banners. For the prick is mightier than the sword. Even the flaming prick that guards Eden. He said his name is Uriel."

Staggering back to his feet, Carey flung himself at a grizzled reporter, arms held wide. "You know me, Frank. You've covered my office for years. You have to tell them the truth. You have to tell them what's going on. About the secret army. The secret army with no balls! You've got to tell them!"

The reporter stepped hastily out of reach. "Honestly, I think you may have a concussion."

"Damnit! Haven't you listened to a thing I said? The bastard got to me. The Leper Saint kissed me and made me one of his. But instead of my lips falling off, my balls fell off." Carey's face crumpled as he sank to his knees and held out his hands in supplication. "Feel my balls, Frank. For old time's sake. Please just feel my balls."

Sean folded his arms, as he surveyed the scene in front of him. "Well, if nothing else," he said, "that's sure to be Exhibit A in any argument for Marie's *decree nisi*. But I'm not sure I'm seeing the upside here."

And Clare had to agree. No matter how hard she tried to remind herself that the bastard had been willing to do it to her. Had done it to a bunch of kids whose major crime had been to see no other way out of their lives. "He doesn't deserve this," she said.

"No one deserves this," Sean agreed. "But if I was forced to pick a candidate—"

She glanced at him sharply. Because that was really the question, wasn't it? And that was always going to be the question. Had he picked a candidate? Had Sean forced this? Could he have forced it? And if he could, would he have given in to one final chance to play with his food?

From the look on Sean's face, he was asking himself the same thing. And that, she realized, was the only answer they needed. Not how much Sean could see or would see, but that they both understood the same question without saying a word.

She took his hand. "You tried to stop him," she said. "You told him to move. I heard you. He was the one who wouldn't listen. Maybe it's going too far to say he brought this on himself. But if you did anything to him, it's just like you were telling Lukas. You only released what was already there."

Sean didn't answer. Just squeezed her hand. Hard.

"Please!" a staffer shouted, bending over Trey's crumpled body. "We need a doctor, here."

Rubber squeaked briskly on the ramp that led up from the Outreach Center, as Lukas Croswell emerged, wiping his hands down with the paper towels he had torn from around his neck.

"I'm a doctor," he said. "Now, what exactly seems to be our problem?"

Chapter Thirty-four

Jonas had never seen his father in action. Or maybe he had just never watched. It didn't matter. The point was, the old man was cool—as cool as Rambo cauterizing his own gunshot wound with gunpowder. Transforming the panicked staffers into ER nurses with about three barked orders, Lukas had Trey Carey stabilized like some illustration out of a First Aid manual—feet elevated, wrapped in a heavy blanket from the shelter. And then he just sat with Trey, monitoring his pulse and vitals, until the ambulance arrived. Not so much as a sign that the bastard had threatened to ruin the old man's life.

But as soon as the ambulance doors banged shut, and its siren wailed to life, Lukas just seemed to collapse. "Dad?" Jonas said uncertainly, but the old man gave no sign he'd even heard him, instead wheeling straight through the growing crowd, back into the church.

"Dad!" Jonas said again, and went after him.

He didn't need to hurry to keep up. He knew instinctively where Lukas was going. Back to the storeroom—no, the archive—to return the records the fiddler had given him to the medicine cabinet Jonas had broken into what seemed like a lifetime ago.

"Look, just because you had an idea doesn't make you responsible for what other people decided to do with it," Jonas said. "You follow that logic, and Albert Einstein is responsible for the atomic bomb."

Lukas looked up, and for a moment, he didn't seem to even recognize Jonas. And then his eyes kindled with weary humor. "You know, you're pretty good with the casuistry for a kid who got himself thrown out of a Jesuit school."

"Casuistry, sir?"

And at least part of Jonas's blank-faced puzzlement at the word was real, but what he was really having trouble getting his head around was the way the old man just looked—bewildered. And he wasn't even trying to hide it.

"I need to stop this thing, Jonas," he said. "And I don't even know how to start. Hell, I don't even know whether I should destroy these right now, or whether doing that eliminates my only chance to find a cure."

"Well it seems to me that destroying them now prevents finding a cure. But nothing's stopping you from destroying them later if you don't do it now."

Lukas's face lit with startled respect. "That's not casuistry. It's logic," he said.

And suddenly there they were in another one of those seriously awkward moments, where the old man seemed to be working up the nerve to do something like ruffle Jonas's hair or even hug him, and Jonas couldn't decide which possibility scared him worse. Then high heels clattered down the stairs, and someone tapped on the door.

"We need to talk," Marie Carey said.

Lukas looked up at her. "About what I can only assume is your soon-to-be-ex-husband's memorable excursus on leprosy and the apocalypse?"

"It's connected," the priest, Father Gregory, said, manifesting behind Marie. "We need to make this right, but not by doing something wrong."

Lukas studied him with about as much distaste as he had the medicine bottles. "It's a little late for absolution, don't you think?" he asked.

"Actually, I would say it is the exact right time." Father Gregory held up his fingers, ticking off the points. "Confession? Today might have been abortive, but I'd argue your meeting with Trey would qualify. Penance? Seems to me you've been doing that for nearly twenty years—"

"Please spare me the cheap psychology, especially in front of my son. No point in tainting young minds."

"Then maybe we should try a different tack. Atonement, for example."

Lukas flinched. "You just saw for yourself what this thing can do. Tell me, how do you suggest atoning for that?"

"You're the genius, you figure it out," Marie said.

Father Gregory coughed gently before Lukas could turn on her in a fury.

"What Mrs. Carey means is that Grinnell suddenly finds itself in dire need of a new set of directors. A new, *ethical* set of directors. Which might mesh nicely with your attempts to find a cure for this plague. Indeed I would argue that it meshes completely with your ethical obligation to cure this plague."

"We're going to need a transition team to take over the conservatorship while the estate is settled. Father Gregory's going to be on it, but we want you to head it," Marie chimed in. And suddenly she got that look that women tended to get around the old man, and Jonas tensed against the memory of that last, final scene with the yoga instructor. Or the sheer terror on the face of the Jehovah's Witnesses when one touch of the old man's magic was enough to seriously drive them to renounce their faith. But the old man just flashed Marie an exasperated smile, in a way that hinted there might be some significant changes coming in the Croswell family home life. Which Jonas didn't really object to—although he personally would have taken the hot makeup babe. He just hoped Marie could cook, although he didn't really think it was likely.

"Thank you, Marie, but nothing's changed, Trey's … little performance notwithstanding," Lukas said. "I still have to fix this. I still need to make things right."

"No one's contesting the ends," Father Gregory said. "Just the means. Specifically, the one where you fall on your sword for absolutely no good reason I can see."

"Over a bunch of gangbangers who shot your son," Marie said.

The old man shut his eyes. "I would sincerely appreciate it, if you would leave my son out of this—"

"Grinnell will take corporate responsibility," Father Gregory cut in. "We can leave the sacrificial lambs to their more customary context."

The priest permitted himself a small smile to show he was joking, but the old man just shook his head. "It's too late," he said. "*Alia jacta est*. It's over. Done. The die has been cast. As I've said before, you can't put the toothpaste back in the tube. I've already sent my resignation letters out."

And Jonas felt his ears get very, very hot. As hot as they had gone when his father had found the cache of pills behind Jonas's bed. Along with the stack of *Playboys* he had shoplifted. So hot that he imagined that if you looked at them, they would have been bright red.

"Perhaps, sir," he said, "before you make up your mind, you ought to check your emails. See if they really went through, sir, if you know what I mean?"

And was it really his imagination that his father's eyes seemed to go straight to his ears? And stay there. "And why should I do that?" Lukas inquired.

"Fucking campus e-mail, sir."

"Language," Lukas sighed, but his heart wasn't in it.

"Yessir. Darned campus e-mail, sir. Never works, sir. Been down for days." Jonas turned to Father Gregory with his best innocent expression—the one that never worked when it came to the old man. "You recall getting an e-mail from my father yesterday?"

To judge from the look the priest shot him, the innocent expression wasn't working with him either, but Father Gregory still obligingly pulled out his cell phone and checked it. "Can't say I see anything here. Lukas, you'd better check yours."

His father's gaze stayed on Jonas, never blinking, as he pulled out his cell phone to check his messages. He evinced no reaction as he scrolled along the screen, then shut off the phone and pocketed it. "Darned campus e-mail indeed," he said. And maybe the ghost of a grin flashed across his face before his jaw set, and the old Lukas was back. "But that doesn't change the fact I need to pay for what I've done."

"What do you want to do? Join a Carthusian monastery?" Marie snapped.

Lukas glared at her as balefully as if she had whipped out a pork chop and scalloped potato casserole from behind her back. "They do have the virtue of silence…"

Father Gregory cut him off with another gentle cough. "There's a fine line between self-flagellation and self-indulgence, as too many of my colleagues have a regrettable habit of forgetting. Might it not take more courage to take responsibility instead?"

Lukas stiffened. "By getting off scot free when I've managed to ruin God alone knows how many lives?"

"If it helps," Father Gregory said, sketching a quick gesture, "*te absolvo.*"

∞

His father slid behind the wheel of the van, folding the wheelchair behind him with such quick, practiced gestures, that Jonas almost missed his chance. "Sir," he said hastily, "frankly, you look a bit tired. Would you like me to drive instead?"

His father frowned. "Do you have a driver's license I'm unaware of?" he asked, sounding genuinely puzzled.

"I have a learner's permit," Jonas said hopefully.

His father's gaze darkened with suspicion. "Legitimately obtained?"

"More or less."

"I see." Shutting his eyes, his father drew a deep breath, but somehow Jonas was certain that the old man was trying to control his laughter rather than his temper this time. It was almost as odd a sensation as seeing him smile.

"Then what do you say that tomorrow we head down to the DMV and take steps to get you a completely legitimate learner's permit?" Lukas asked. "As well as finding you a vehicle to practice in that does not require special permits? And in the meantime, I'll do my best to muster the strength to navigate the five minute drive home. Does that sound fair?"

Oh, well. It was worth a try. "More than fair, sir."

His father nodded, but he made no move to start the car. Instead he just studied his son with the kind of look that made Jonas worry the old man might be about to ruffle his hair. Which, given the sticky nature of the dye Jonas affected, could have proved beyond awkward.

"So just for the record, how lame was Father Gregory's password?" the old man asked. "Lamer than mine?"

Jonas took his time considering his answer. "I'm not sure it would be appropriate for you to know that, sir," he said. "But I will tell you he has a taste for cat videos. In fact, I think he feeds them out in the alley behind his office."

His father nodded. And then, abruptly, his face grew serious. "As long as we're on the topic of appropriate behavior, I suppose that now that we have gotten past the uncomfortable father/son chat about where babies come from, I owe you one about computer ethics," he said. "Preferably before you get yourself into some kind of serious trouble. But somehow now just doesn't seem to be the moment."

"Nossir?" Jonas said.

"No," Lukas said. And smiled. A full-out, awkward as shit, embarrassing, hair-ruffling smile. "I don't know if I can ever be the father you deserve," he said. "But I can't tell you how glad I am for the second chance to try. And I am going to try. I want to try. A hell of a lot more than I want any part in running Grinnell. Or any absolution, when it comes down to that."

And much as Jonas had longed—hell, had dreamed—of such a moment actually happening, now that it was here, he could think of only one thing to say. "Please, sir. No more doughnuts."

"No doughnuts," Lukas allowed. And then his eyes went to Jonas's hair, as if he were really about to ruffle it. And he frowned. "But, if it wouldn't be too much to ask, would you at least consider the possibility of allowing me to introduce you to my barber? As a personal favor?"

And this, Jonas realized, was another, more important chance than the driving. A chance he might never get again in his life. "If you'll do me a personal favor in return," he countered.

Lukas inclined his head. "As long as it's legal. Completely legal."

Jonas took a deep breath. "I want you to test my magic DNA," he said in a rush. "And see if it would ... you know ... work."

"You have no..." Then, just as quickly, Lukas broke off, his face softened, and the truly unthinkable happened: he laid his hand on his son's arm. "Instead, how about we agree that we will have this conversation again, when you're twenty-one and old enough to give me your informed consent?"

Another unthinkable. The old man compromising. Negotiating. Well, two could play at that game.

"Eighteen," Jonas said.

Acknowledgments

Thanks to Susan Brown for an incisive intervention on an early version of this manuscript. And thanks to the family I have found at Amphorae Publishing Group—especially to Donna J. Essner and Kristina Blank Makansi, whose belief in my work is surpassed only by their ability to make it better than I thought it could ever be. Thanks, too, to my actual family—especially my nephews, Erik (Toby Tobidous), Kevin, and Luke Obey, who, along with my fabulous sister-in-law, Ann Baird, are gradually schooling me in the gentle art of re-tweeting. And, as always, thanks to George, who really does help with the research.

About the Author

Erica Obey earned a PhD in comparative literature and published a book and articles on Arthuriana and nineteenth-century women folklorists, before she decided she would rather be writing the stories herself. She also holds degrees in creative writing and economics from C.C.N.Y. and Yale University. Her first mystery novel, *Back to the Garden*, was published by Five Star Mysteries in 2013. She currently teaches courses on mystery fiction and Arthurian romance at Fordham University. Along with their macaw, Fasolt, and a rotating assortment of cats, she and her husband divide their time between Upper Manhattan and Woodstock, NY, where you can find her gardening or exploring hiking trails for new story ideas. Please visit her on the web at www.EricaObey.com.

CPSIA information can be obtained at www.ICGtesting.com
Printed in the USA
LVOW07s1106270916

506363LV00002B/2/P